AMERICAN GODDESS

A myth made in Scotland

L. M. Affrossman

SPARSILE BOOKS LTD

Acknowledgements

To Margaret Morrison-Macleod and all
those who like to tread a different path.

To my sister, Wendy, for always getting my jokes.

Thank you to Jim Campell and Alex Winpenny for their
tireless efforts to make the vague musings of
my imagination into a finished novel.

Thank you also to Madeleine Jewett, Stephen Cashmore
and Lizette Balsdon who proofed the novel
with patience more usually ascribed to saints.

Many thanks to Erika Foster for reading the
book from an American perspective.

And finally to all the readers (too many to name)
who read earlier versions of the novel and
offered suggestions and insights that
added new depth to the final version.

Contents

PROLOGUE

Over cobbled streets, a dead woman was hobbling on broken feet. Her shift was smeared in tar. Her shaven head glistened with a nimbus of bright raindrops, which fell in a continuous shower from the steel plates of Edinburgh's forbidding sky.

She was limping to her death partly because she was a Catholic in a time of fearful and paranoid Protestantism, but also because she was wise in the old ways. And the keepers of the Law —who had already renounced and forgotten these ways, thousands of years before their own prophet shrivelled upon his tree of death— feared her wisdom and all those of her cunning breed. She was one of the few, very few, who still remembered the *auld wisdome,* and for her audacity she was persecuted as the God of men persecuted all women who sought to *know* and not merely to *be.*

They *wirried* her at the stake, melting the flesh from her bones, and still afraid of her, they let the rattling cage of her skeleton blacken and char until nothing was left but ashes. And even these they swept up with especial care and had them strewn upon unconsecrated ground.

That evening, as the black winds crept in from the North Sea, a breeze lifted and stirred the ashes, and blew them away so that they formed a fine dust that travelled through the air above the roofs of Christian homes and settled on the window panes of righteous men.

The next morning, the wives and maidservants of these men were forced to wipe away the *foule grit,* never thinking, as they wrung out their greying washcloths, that they were washing away the remnants of one of their own sex, nor that, with her passing, so went the final recognition that women had once been the keepers of an ancient and hidden knowledge.

Part I

THE FALL

As both Hughes and Graves were quick to point out, the Elizabethan concept of 'the witch' is inextricably bound up with the idea of the Great Goddess. And even a few years later, at the height of the persecution by James VI, it was clear that the very least of these women carried a trace memory of the Goddess of New Beginnings, maintaining a thread going back down the millennia to a system of belief far stranger than any conjured by the vivid imaginations of Jacobean paranoia.

Based on McBride B., 1988,

Surviving in the shadow of the Great Goddess

Journal of Cross-Cultural Studies, 0.696, Q1

CHAPTER 1

LUCK IS REAL. LUCK IS not something that can be courted or crafted or forced into obedience, but you can, if you are careful, sense that it is there. For those who know how to look, it reveals itself as a presence that hangs timorously in the air, changing the quality of the light, an echoless echo, an unfelt touch. It dangles, a golden apple just out of reach. But it's there for the taking. The trick is to know when to grasp.

All this Peter Kelso knew and believed, without particular awareness in his belief, only knowing that, when he awoke in his sleep-rumpled bed, his wife still lost in slumber at his side, a canting autumn sun had found its way through the chinks in the drapes and was filling the room with wands of yellow light. And he felt lucky.

He was humming a song to himself in the shower when he heard a groan from the doorway, and a moment later Ellisha stumbled in, hair escaping from its silk wrap, a hand smearing down one side of her face.

'Whthatimefuhfcksk?'

Peter stopped the shower and thumped himself in the chest with a fist. 'My people have been long in the land, but do not speak the Black Woman's tongue.'

'Try sign language then.' She flipped him the bird before staggering over to the sink, grasping the enamel edge and swaying slightly, as though she had stepped off the night's ocean and hadn't yet found her land legs.

He grabbed a towel and wrapped it around his waist. 'You still sound like an American even when you give the finger, you know.'

She had begun flossing her teeth and didn't turn around. He made out something that sounded like, *You can't take St Louis out of the girl*—or it might equally have been a sudden, if obscure, request to take the ratatouille out of the grill.

About to remark that, as a man of words, he expected the standards of communication in his home to be beyond reproach, he took a step closer then stopped. Ellisha wasn't flossing her teeth anymore. The floss, which was still grasped between her fingers, emerged from her mouth like a delicate strand of fate, but she was motionless, a freeze-frame of herself, staring down at a tiny sceptre of plastic lying between the taps.

The sight of it made his heart squeeze tight. 'Ellie—' he began.

'I wasn't going to use it.'

'You know you can't.'

'I wasn't.'

'Even if the reading was positive, it might just be the injections making your hormones spike. It doesn't mean—'

'I know that! You think I don't know that?' She swept the test off the sink into the mouth of an obese wicker frog that served as a wastebasket. 'I just—I don't know.' Her shoulders hunched. 'I liked having it here. It made things real. Like I was—like I could—'

'Ellie.' He pulled her around to face him. In the artificial light of the bathroom, her eyes looked black, but he knew them to be a startling clear green, like the moss agates he had collected as a child on holidays to Fife. 'Everything's going to be fine.'

'You don't know that.'

'But I do.' He drew her against him and began a slow two-step around the en suite's narrow confines.

'Peter!'

Without warning, he dipped her, lightly bumping her head against the cistern.

'Ow.' She pulled away, rubbing her ear.

'I'm sorry. Are you all right?'

'Freak. What's got into you?'

'I'm feeling lucky.'

There was an appalled silence. Then they were laughing so hard that Ellisha began to hiccup and toothpaste came down her nose. She wiped it on a towel then pushed her fingers into her stomach. 'I feel like I want to vomit.'

They stopped laughing, and it hung in the air between them, unspoken. *Morning sickness.* Was it possible?

Ellisha was the first to recover. 'Don't you have a job to go to?'

'I could blow it off. Come with you.'

'We have an extension to pay for, remember? And last year's vacation. And next year's. We're the lucky ones who have jobs, remember? I thought you Scots were canny about money.'

'We can live on your salary.'

'Mice couldn't live on my salary.'

He sighed. 'I'd better get going.'

'Good job it's your lucky day.'

The feeling of good fortune was stronger outside. He felt it as he made his way to the city centre, ignoring the gap-tooth hollows of shuttered shops that spoiled the city's grin, reminding everyone that the pandemic had left its scars. But luck was still on his heels as he crossed Princes Street, where scurrying leaves crunched under his feet and the low pulse of the sun charred buildings black with shadows and burned their edges, like haloes.

A rowan tree just beyond the Playfair steps caught the light as he passed under it, and burst into flames. Oddly moved, he stopped, drawn by the way the colour stood out, preternaturally vivid against the sky, as though lit from an unseen source. As an experiment, he removed his Aviators and dropped them in his pocket. At once, the colour faded; the magic fled.

Looking for God?

Peter stopped. The voice had spoken out of nowhere, the voice of a lost soul or possibly a penitent demon. Suddenly and eerily, he was aware that there was no-one else about. He forgot the aviators in his pocket and lifted his hand to shade his eyes, trying to peer through the shadows. *Where is everyone?*

'Hello?'

There was no reply and he felt faintly foolish, like a Victorian gentleman explorer calling out, '*Show yourself if ye be a man!*'

Then came a low whickering laugh and he turned sharply. Nearby, a man loitered in the shuttered doorway of a shop. It was a bleak narrow entrance, tucked between two brightly-lit storefronts yet belonging to neither. Peter couldn't recall ever having seen it before. But that was no surprise. Edinburgh was filled with these tiny forgotten passages that sprang up out of nowhere one day, and vanished into the mist next time you went looking for them.

The man's face was hard to make out, but Peter could see that he was above average height, a solid, standing stone of a man with long unkempt hair and eyes that caught the sun in yellow glints. Feral eyes, wolf eyes.

Peter became aware that they were looking at each other without speaking. He didn't move forward—the need to keep out of infection's reach still too engrained in his habits—but he cleared his throat in a way that sounded very nearly like a friendly laugh. 'Did you— I thought you said something.'

The man did not answer but crossed over to Peter's side of the road so that the shadows fell from him, and Peter now saw that the coat he wore was tied with a fraying piece of string. And he had no sooner noticed this, when a tang of urine and leaf-mould filled his nostrils, and instinctively he recoiled. A *jaikey*, a tramp, a hobo or whatever the destitute and the homeless were called these days. And something threatening about him too, an undefined quality. Not just his size.

When the man made a sudden thrusting motion in the direction of his chest, he leapt back. But realising that he was only proffering a copy of the *Big Issue*, he grinned guiltily for having shown his distaste. Who knew in the current climate how a man fell on hard times? There but for the grace of God and so on. Besides, this was his lucky day.

He delved into his trouser pocket and pulled out a couple of pound coins, keeping eye contact with the tramp to demonstrate their shared humanity, before pushing the coins into one of the man's grimy paws and taking the paper from the other. Still smiling, he asked, 'Earlier, you wanted to know if I was looking for God?'

The man shrugged, and his eyes drifted over Peter's head. A poor man, Peter thought. But not a meek one, no. Men walked out of the wilderness or the desert with eyes like those.

Some of his unease came back. He was aware, as most people are who earn their crust through words, that his strengths were situated more on his tongue than in his fists. And if this gaunt monolith was not too eaten away with drink to use his bulk… Yet the sun still pulsed above the castle mound, and he remembered that this was a day for taking risks. He persisted. 'You asked if I was looking for God.'

The man was leaning on the railings, looking down towards the roofs of the art galleries, with their strange resemblance to the temples of Athena. He did not turn around. 'Aye. If you're looking, Scotland's the place to find Her.'

CHAPTER 2

AS PETER MADE HIS WAY along the George IV Bridge, luck still scintillated in the air, but his encounter with the tramp had spooked him. The powerful shoulders, the burning eyes. The smell of leaf-mould and rot. Auld Nick stepping out of legend to strike a poisoned bargain. Not that two pounds for a copy of the *Big Issue* seemed much of a bargain. *Something about him.*

Peter glanced sharply over his shoulder. Then, giving in to a super-stitious reflex he hadn't known he possessed, unfolded the paper, half certain it contained some sort of cryptic message. Instead, he found a wad of chewed gum, a tooth mark, clearly visible on its rubbery sur-face, and the cold realisation welled up inside him that the jaikey had not been a *Big Issue* seller, but a conman, a chancer, a *snig,* who had doubtless fished this crumpled copy out of a bin and foisted it on the first fool to cross his path. Well, it had certainly been his lucky day.

It was after nine when he arrived at the agency, having discreetly rid himself of the paper in a roadside bin, labelled *Glass and Plastic Only.* He hurried across the Georgian hallway and up the stairs to the first floor, passing the ghosts of men in greatcoats and powdered wigs. For-gotten men, whose memory lingered only in the worn depressions at the centre of the steps and the constantly falling particles of stone dust. But Peter was not sensitive to such things, and he ran through them with the carelessness of a man who has no idea that his life is about to change forever.

He blew a kiss at the receptionist when she mockingly pointed at the clock, then stopped to share a few laughs with the concept boys before entering the general office. Susan, who sat opposite him at the long, worm-eaten desk they shared, was staring disconsolately at her laptop. She was younger than Peter by ten years, with close-cropped hair and enormous glasses which gave her a permanent look of startled wisdom. He nodded at the computer. 'Trouble?'

'We had six hundred emails last night. I came in early to deal with them. And now there are over three hundred more. I tell you, if they did biblical plagues today, God would just fill Pharaoh's inbox with spam!'

'Delete anything that came in before Monday.'

'Are you crazy? I like working here.'

'Do you?'

She squinted at him through the dimness. 'No.' Then, pushing her glasses up her nose. 'Why are you late?'

'I met the Devil on the way to work today.'

'No you didn't.'

'How would you know?'

'Because he's been sitting in his office all morning. And he wants to see you.'

Peter glanced at the panelled door at the far end of the room. 'He said that?'

'Poked his forked tongue around the door and asked for the "new boy".'

'I've been here eighteen months.'

'I've been here six years and he still calls me "Um …er".'

He drummed a little paradiddle on the desk with his forefingers. 'I'd better go see what he wants.'

'You're not worried?'

'I'm feeling lucky.'

His eyes were on JD's door. It was so firmly closed that not even a chink of light escaped at the edges. It looked ominous, but he squared his shoulders and let the feeling of luck suffuse his pores. *Keep cool. This time tomorrow, I'll be sitting in my own office.*

He had taken an unconscious step in the direction of the office when Susan called after him. 'I forgot to say, Ellie called.'

'Did she leave a message?'

'Nope.'

He retraced his steps, grabbed the receiver from the phone and quickly dialled. She answered after three rings.

'Hi.'

'Ellie, it's me.'

'Peter. How funny, I was just thinking about you.' She said it with genuine wonder in her voice as though forces, other than the usual, must be involved for one person to call just when the other happens to be thinking about them.

'Ellie. Is this concerning— I mean, is it about— Have you heard?'

She laughed in the open unabashed way only Americans can laugh. 'No. No, nothing. We won't hear anything until this afternoon.' She laughed again. 'Hey, I'm supposed to be the jittery one.'

'Susan said you'd rung. Why didn't you call me on my mobile?'

'Because you left it charging beside the bed this morning.'

'What?' He felt in his jacket. 'Is that why you called? To tell me I forgot my phone.'

'No. The roofer's been round. He says he's found another problem.'

'Another?' Peter pulled a face.

'Yes. And don't pull faces.'

He stared at the receiver.

'A wife doesn't need to be psychic to recognise when her man is pouting. It's something to do with the wet rot.'

'I thought we had dry rot.'

'We did until it drowned in the wet stuff.'

'How much does he think it'll cost to repair?'

'Eight.'

'Hundred?'

'Thousand.'

'You're kidding.' Peter made frantic calculations in his head. 'What happens if we say no?'

'He leaves us with half a roof. What should I tell him?'

Peter bit down on his lip, glanced towards JD's door. 'Tell him to go ahead. I told you. I'm feeling lucky today.'

There was a beat before she said, 'You won't do anything crazy?'

'It'll be fine.'

'You're sure?'

'I made a deal wi the De'il this morning.'

JD's office felt cold, despite the fact that the floor vents were blasting out heat. It was a phenomenon that affected only this corner of the building, and gave rise to rumours that JD was able to suck the energy out of a room, even from the National Grid.

JD was reading an open file on his desk and did not look up, merely grunting in response to Peter's cheery *You wanted to see me?* After a moment or two's awkward silence, he lifted a hand to wave it at the empty seat before him. Peter took it, aware that it was several inches lower than JD's, and sat there, trying not to shiver. *Look relaxed. That's the key.*

Not wanting to focus on JD's formless bulk, he became attracted instead by his sweating forehead. It glistened softly in the electric light. JD went on reading, and Peter fought with the muscles of his face, which were beginning to stiffen, congealing his congenial expression into self-parody. He cleared his throat to loosen himself up, and the sound came out recklessly, scattering the silence. JD lifted his head which seemed to sit, without benefit of a neck, directly on his shoulders. There were veins, the colour of averagely good Merlot, criss-crossing his nose.

'I hear you've been busy.'

Peter's smile returned. 'You've heard right.'

'You jumped Sikora inside the Dome last night.'

'I ran into him. I was in there having a drink.'

JD's eyes bugged. It made Peter think of a species of yellow-skinned toad he'd seen once in a documentary about South American swamps. He watched as JD took out a handkerchief and mopped his brow. 'Fucking hot in here.'

'God, yes.' Peter mimed loosening the collar of his shirt.

'Sikora says you were talking about velvet and silk.' A glance at the file. Words had been written down. 'Tinkling crystal. Brandy. Cigars.'

'I was priming him.'

He was about to say more but, behind him, the door opened and one of the concept boys popped his head around the door.

He coloured when he spotted Peter. 'Sorry, boss. I was looking for Emma.'

'No idea. Did you ask Maggie?'

'She says she's out on a shoot.'

'So it's a fairly safe fucking bet that she's out on a shoot.'

'I thought you might know when she'll be back.'

JD's brows shot up in search of his hairline, and the youth withdrew his head in a turtle-like motion. 'I'll ask Maggie.'

JD's eyes found Peter's. 'Do their mobiles fry their brains?'

Peter gave a conspiratorial *youth of today* shake of his head, though he was fairly certain that JD was at least twenty years his senior.

JD sat back, tapping his thumbs together. 'Priming, you say.'

A test. Wants to know what I'm made of. Dangling me. He clenched his teeth into a smile to prevent them chattering. 'It's a psychological technique. Jung, Freud, that sort of thing.'

'I know what psychology is.'

'Of course. Well, it's just an extension of what we do here. Clients come in wanting us to create a campaign that will persuade people of a need they never knew they had, whiter teeth, luxury holidays, a new car. And how do we do it? We show them images of happiness and beauty and extravagance. We make them want more without knowing they want more.'

JD's thumbs tapped together. 'What's this to do with Sikora?'

Peter, suddenly aware that he was leaning forward with the eagerness of a schoolboy, sat upright. *Body language. Reflect it back. Make us equals.* Casually, he leaned back, let his hands fall onto his lap, tapped one thumb on the other. 'Sikora's our client—'

'Our biggest client.'

'Our biggest one, yes. Exactly. All that buying potential. But aren't we missing a trick when it comes to selling to him? When I ran into him last night—*all the research, learning Sikora's habits, gauging the best time to strike*— I deliberately fed him all the primers I could think of, images of sophistication, gorgeous vistas, candlelight, Chopin playing in the background, just a hint of sex. I bought the best brandy. We smoked cigars in my club.'

'Your club?'

'Yes.' An impulse buy. Eye-wateringly expensive, but it would pay for itself when he was made partner. Forgetting himself, he leaned forward again. 'I'm telling you, JD, this works. Sikora was excited. He saw himself suddenly. Not just as the owner of a chain of cheap hotels, but as an entrepreneur, an artist, a man wanting more.' He paused to draw breath, hoping JD would evince some degree of approval, but nothing in JD's face moved. Talk to him in his own language. Draw him in. 'You've got Sikora by the balls now.' He made a lewd gesture and winked, though it cost him. Made him feel like a cheap comedian winking at his audience and drawling, *Am I rrrrright, folks?*

JD's thumbs stopped tapping. 'So, now you know all about how the business runs.'

'I wouldn't claim that,' Peter said hastily. 'But I've got ideas about expansion. Ways to make a difference.'

JD barked a laugh. 'You have confidence, I'll say that much. We lack that. As a nation I mean. Especially after the world went tits up. Lot of people lost their edge.'

'A lot lost more than that.'

JD's eyes narrowed. 'You can go pretty far with confidence. And you've got that hungry look. You want to get on, make it big.'

Peter gave a modest smile. He began to say something about luck, and having the knack of recognising it, when JD asked, 'How long have you been here? A month?"

'Eighteen.' He held up his hands. 'I know what you're thinking. The new guy. But I've got a lot of ideas. I'm ambitious—'

'Ambitious enough to take everything you've learned here and set up on your own.'

Peter blinked. 'No, It's not like that.'

JD shifted position, leaning forward, fist under chin. 'Sounds exactly like that.'

'I know how it looks, but—'

'You've tried before,' JD said. He lifted a file from the desk and ran his thumb along the edge. 'Jazz Creative? That was you, wasn't it? Went bust six months before you came here.'

'The pandemic hit a lot of businesses.'

JD opened the file and peered inside. 'Seems you had other ventures that failed without needing the pandemic's help.'

Peter swallowed. 'I was young. Learning. I made mistakes.'

'And now you thought you'd set up again with Sikora's help.'

'You've got it wrong!' There was a mechanical smile on Peter's face, while a secret part of himself was screaming to keep calm. *Remember, you've got responsibilities. You're going to be a father by the end of the day. Think of Ellisha.* Inside his head the tilted green eyes were pleading with him. *Not this time. Promised. No more risks.*

But a snarl was forming deep inside him, and the snarl had formed around the spiked lump of knowledge that the man before him was blind. He kept going, trying to flatter JD, talking of 'we men of vision' and an opportunity not to be missed. But something flat had crept into his voice. An emptiness, like one of those moments deep in the night, when he awoke clammy and gasping, certain he had been falling into some yawning chasm that had opened beneath him.

He lost his sense of himself, was aware only that words were being exchanged, meaningless, empty words that later he wouldn't be able to recall. And there were arguments, which circled around and back on themselves, but ultimately led to the same point until he found himself standing at the door.

With his fingers clasped around the handle, the snarl made him glance over his shoulder and spit, 'Sikora's going to call. You know that, don't you?'

'He already called.'

Peter's fingers tightened. 'What did he say?'

'Wanted to cancel his contract. Decided we're not sophisticated enough for his needs. He's going with Saatchi.'

A wave of heat hit Peter as soon as JD's door closed at his back. Susan was waiting, strangely frozen beside his desk. And next to her was Wee Tam, the security guard, ironically named for proportions so monstrous that he had to duck to fit through ordinary doorways. Peter felt he should say something, but the words would not form. He took a reflexive step towards his desk, but Tam blocked his way. 'Nae need. It'll a' be sent on.'

Peter shook his head slowly. 'I don't understand.' Though he understood. He understood perfectly. Tam moved towards him.

'Ah huv tae see you out the door. Just procedure, aye?'

'Surely that isn't necessary,' Susan burst out. She flashed Peter a *what-the-hell-is-happening?* look, and the anguish in her voice broke through his daze.

'Susan. It's okay. Really. All of it. Just a misunderstanding. I'll sort it out. I promise.'

Tam had opened the door and gestured for Peter to follow. He obeyed, keeping up a charade that Tam was there at his request, a problem with a client, a secure package requiring delivery. But silence followed him through the office, conversations breaking off as he passed, and when he winked at the receptionist, she looked away and pretended to take a call.

Outside on the pavement, he took several steps then checked himself. He turned to look up at the front door of the building he had just vacated. At his back the roar of traffic felt alien and unrelated to him, and he was assailed by the strange disorienting sensation that accompanies dreams where the dreamer soars, feather-light along the horizon's edge, only to awaken under the immense weight of gravity, earthbound, a lump of clay clinging to the debris of a distant star.

The day was still golden. The sun, higher now, sent rays of light ricocheting from panes of tall glass and car windscreens. They caught in the irises of his pale northern eyes making them water and, numbly, he reached into his pocket for his aviators. His fingers closed around the shape of their gone-ness, and he remembered, with sudden clarity, the tramp distracting him with a pilfered copy of the *Big Issue*. Then he started to laugh, and he went on laughing, painfully, helplessly, until his legs felt weak and his eyes leaked burning tears.

CHAPTER 3

IT WAS DARK BY THE time he turned into the curving Georgian street where his house was situated. His first instinct had been to go straight home, to lay his head on Ellisha's lap and lick his wounds. But as he walked back down the Playfair steps, he was gripped by such an immense anger that he was afraid of his own violence.

So, my CV has a few exaggerations. Well, maybe more than a few, but everyone's CV contains a little fiction. Dear God, if Christopher Hitchins is to be believed, even Mother Theresa's resumé has a few whoppers.

One or two people were throwing curious stares in his direction, and he realised that he had spoken aloud, muttering to himself like a madman. And, unable to control the froth of rage bubbling over his lips, he jammed his hands into his pockets and walked, head down, until he came to a local drinking den known as the *Liquid Lunch*. He stayed there, hunched in a corner, drinking pints, with no idea of the time—his watch was also missing, doubtless pilfered at the same time as his aviators—until some instinct, coupled with the sidelong looks of the barman, took him on a meandering course homewards.

An immense sense of his failure seized him as he entered the top of his street. He crossed the cobbles unsteadily through alternating pools of darkness and light, the lampposts along the edge of the private gardens looming like branchless trees and, behind them, the trees branching like rows of fantastical lampposts. A steady mizzle of rain had begun to grow heavier, the drops beating a tattoo on his bare head.

'Ellie?' He called her name as soon as he was inside the door. The hallway was in darkness and he snapped on the light, looking about the corners, as though she might be hiding there. 'Ellie?'

He went from room to room, blundering about the intricate bird's nest of their home, tripping over the familiar objects that Ellisha had collected as they travelled the length and breadth of the country, hopes fixed firmly on the next opportunity, the one that would fix everything, while Ellisha picked up little bits of debris from their lives and drew them together in a strange wild mixture of imagination and domesticity.

Don't think of it so much as interior design, and more me putting the inside of my head, outside my head.

How batshit crazy is it inside your head?

Imagination can't be put in boxes.

Numpty

Asshole.

In the light of this latest failure, everything took on a strange, poignant significance. He paused to examine the odd, sometimes faintly disturbing curios—a little jade god hidden away on a dusty shelf, a row of bird skulls arranged around an antique perfume bottle, an ammonite dug up in Compton Bay, fairy lights strung across bare oak branches brought back from Birnam Wood, the drowned brown limbs of winter roses in a cut-glass jug—objects that hid in the shadows and revealed themselves slowly, like the elements of a familiar yet troubling dream. It was the dark fairy-tale of his childhood, peopled with *glaistigs* and *shellycoats* before the cold light of the internet caught everyone in its beam and drew the enchantment out of the world.

At the bottom of the stairs he flicked a switch, and the birdcage lamps illuminated his way up the long curve of the staircase. 'It's me. I'm home.' His voice echoed against the slant of the ceiling, where Ellisha had stencilled a quote by T. E. Lawrence to the effect that the dreamers of the day are dangerous because they are the ones who might act upon their dreams.

The bedrooms too were empty, and a sobering tightness gripped his heart as he made his way up to the attic. 'Ellie!' There was an edge to his voice as he threw open the attic door. 'Are you in here?'

The attic was a vast, cavernous space covering the top floor. It was floored,

though the rafters were bare. When it was sunny you could see a permanent shower of dust motes falling gently from the ceiling. Here and there were items covered in white sheets and a huge fold-out table on which were spread plans for renovation. A little light filtered in from outside through the Velux window, and framed against its oblique outline was Ellisha, her back to him, her forehead against the glass. The dimness turned her skin from its usual dark brown to a velvety black.

'Ellie?' He moved towards her, needing her to turn round and look at him, to smile at him in that way that said, *You're home.* An excruciating need opened up in him to rest his head on those breasts that had something of the full moon about them, a heavy fecund look that drew magnetically. He could see the plump swell of her buttocks beneath the fabric of her dress, and his hands ached to touch the little round tumulus of her belly, which seemed to contain a mystery he never quite managed to unlock.

But she didn't turn, and he came up behind her suddenly worried she was having one of her headaches, those blinding lightning strikes that left her curled in the dark like a small terrified animal, and him outside helpless and excluded. 'Ellie?' He put his hand gently on her shoulder, and only then did he discover that it was trembling slightly because she was crying. And now he forgot the things that had been dragging behind him all day because he understood what was wrong. He turned her around and rested her head against his shoulder. 'We can try again.'

'Not one,' she said, her words half lost against his jacket. 'Six of them. And not one viable. It's no good, Pete. We might as well admit it. I'm a dried-up old stick.'

He held her away from him. 'Don't say that. You're beautiful. And you'll make a wonderful mother. I'm not ready to give up. Are you?'

She looked up at him, biting her lip. 'That was our last chance. The NHS won't fund any more.'

'Then we'll go privately.'

'It'll be thousands.' She looked about. 'And we've just taken on this mortgage. And the plans for the renovations—'

He put his finger on her lips. 'We'll do it. I promise.'

She was looking into his face, as though she was trying to read something there. He thought she was about to give him a watery smile or a friendly punch in the chest. Instead, she frowned. 'Pete, have you been drinking?'

He laughed, and pushed her away. 'It was nothing. Just a celebration. I had a meeting with JD, and he loves my ideas.'

'Really?'

'Couldn't get enough of them.'

'Oh, Peter. That's wonderful.' He saw her bravely push aside her troubles to be happy for him. 'I tried to call you at the office, but Susan said you'd gone out.'

A cold thrust of reality stabbed between his shoulders but he kept smiling, pulled her to him. She tried to push him away, nose wrinkling. 'Seriously, you are wasted.' He didn't answer, but turned her so that she could see what he could see, the two of them reflected in the window, ghosts in the glass, hovering, unreal, ready to slip back into the Void.

'Ellisha.' He whispered her name, feeling himself stiffening, and there was enchantment in the sensation. Sounds faded away: the hum of distant traffic, the beat of the rain, even the slow groan of the house as it settled under their feet. Ellisha seemed to feel it too, because she tensed, as though listening, as though there was an ancient music, they could both hear, and their bodies recognised the dance.

He saw a shiver slither down her spine, and he bent down and whispered urgently in her ear, 'I feel cold. Let me feel your warmth.'

She turned towards him, her face still a concentrated blank. But when he put his arms around her, she made no objection, and so he lifted her into the air, his hands under the swell of her buttocks.

She looked at him for a moment, as though she saw, not his face but another face he did not know he possessed, a bolder, prouder face created from the infinite possibilities of himself in her eyes. And then, in a flash, the elegance of the music was gone and there was only a wild thrashing beat that tore clothes and pressed their fingertips together, and sent them on a mad chase across each other, over breasts and bellies and buttocks, frantically seeking those soft dark places where the terrible isolation of aloneness is alone no more.

And when he slipped inside her, there was a sense of thrusting into the moist giving earth, into a cave that blossomed with sighs and small sounds, which increased as he thrust deeper in. And he was drawn as though along a black underground sea by the tidal crash of his breaths until there was a gathering then a salty rush and the gentle release of blackness.

CHAPTER 4

'WAKETHFKUFUFU'SSAKE.'

He opened one eye painfully to find Ellisha crouched over him, a dust sheet pulled around her, toga-style; she was pulling on his arm.

On creaking elbows, he pushed himself up. 'Are you speaking English or some sort of code?'

'We're late, you moron.'

'Late?'

'For work? Or did you win the lottery last night and forget to tell me?'

Her comment caught him sharply in the solar plexus and suddenly he was wide awake. *Tell her. Tell her everything now.* But she was already out of the door, leaving the stencil of footprints on the dusty floor.

'Ellie? Ellisha?'

He found her in the bathroom, tugging at her hair. 'Forgot to wrap it last night. Now I look like roadkill.'

'You look beautiful.' The compliment was sincere, but something flat in his voice made her pause and glance over her shoulder.

'What's up?'

Tell her! He took a step closer.

'Ellie, look I—'

'Ew. Peter.' She backed away. 'Take a shower. You smell like something crawled in here and died.' Her voice became nasal behind the refuge of her hand. 'Something that smelled really bad before it died.'

'Fine. I'll take a shower. Nag.'

'Hobo.'

He opened his mouth again, but she had already turned back to the mirror and now she was humming a little tune. And it was so good to see her trying to be happy again that he couldn't bear the thought of spoiling it. *Later. Tell her tonight. A day won't make any difference.*

⚭

But he didn't tell her that night because she came home angry and stressed.

'I mean she asked for me. I heard her at reception asking for the 'black archivist'.' She was banging pots in the kitchen, and Peter had to shout to make himself heard.

'Who asked for you?'

'Babs McBride. Professor McBride. Are you even listening? She asked me to bring across Goodison's paper on the Great Goddess.'

'The great what?'

Ellisha banged a frying pan down on the hob then turned to him with a look of exasperation. 'The idea is that God was once a woman.'

He laughed. 'You mean God had a missus?'

'No, not at all. I mean that the first great god, who was worshipped above all others was, in fact, a great goddess.'

'That's pretty out there.'

Ellisha made a vicious rip in a packet of pasta. 'Plenty of evidence for it. Read Marija Gimbutas or Eleanor Gadon. In prehistoric times procreation was a mystery. Women seemed in control of life.'

'I didn't know you were so interested.'

'Really?' She stopped in the middle of emptying the pasta into a pot. 'Why do people always find that odd? I'm an archivist. I spend my time in dusty rooms surrounded by strange old books and manuscripts. Yet whenever I talk about anything outside Seinfeld or baseball, people think it's weird.'

'You're American. Everything about you is weird.'

He expected her to laugh, but she said in a small, sad voice, 'Books talk to you. Books don't hold their secrets. Not like people.'

An electric shock jolted his heart. *She knows.* He swallowed. But she had spun ahead of him.

'So I thought I would ask her.'

'Ask who?'

'Professor McBride. Babs. I thought I'd ask her about the Goddess.'

'And did you?'

'Sure. I asked her if she thought that the world would be a better place if women were in charge.' She thrust a jar of passata at him. 'I need you to open that.'

'What did she say?'

'Bit my head off. Said, "The religion of the goddess isn't some hippy gathering where peace and love reign." Pass me that knife.' She began sawing at a beef tomato with surprising hostility. 'Apparently, the Eternal Mother has a vicious side. Men used to cut off their balls in Her honour.' She lifted a spoon and began to stir the pasta, and a disturbing image of smoking cauldrons and whispered incantations flashed up in Peter's brain. *In thunder, lightning, or in rain?* As he thought this, the cap came loose in his hands with a satisfying plunk, and he handed it back.

'Guess men have their uses after all.'

'Jerk.'

'Weirdo.'

Days passed. In the mornings he roused himself, showering and shaving with all the urgency of his usual routine, bantering with Ellisha as though nothing was wrong, and talking of elaborate projects he was undertaking, projects that became real in his mind as he talked about them, as though he had slipped back into childhood and the barriers between desire and existence had become blurred. He became quite inventive, and found himself describing intricate battles with J. D. Battles, which he always won through his superior powers of persuasion and wit.

To all this, Ellisha listened wide-eyed, and the more trustingly she accepted his accounts, the more desperate and disgusted he felt inside. And, unable to disentangle himself from the tightening knots of his own lies, he would hurry from the house, often without breakfast, with the air of a man compelled by pressing business, which could not wait. *Fix things. Just a chance to get on top. All I need.*

His sense of purpose would follow him down the streets in the direction of JD's offices. But, once he was sure that Ellisha was lost somewhere in the maze of Edinburgh University, a kind of mental inertia would overtake him. He would seek out cafes—dingy little places where his face wasn't known—and drink cup after cup of bitter coffee, while he talked to faceless men and women on the end of his phone.

He never met them. They remained discarnate voices, who listened attentively to his every word, who grew eager and excited as he spoke, and were moved to make great promises. But when the phone calls ended, the promises dissolved wraith-like into the ether, and when Scotland's pallid sun rose the next day, he would have to start all over again.

Then there were the letters. Ominous brown envelopes gathering on the floor beneath the letter box, like dead foliage. His mortgage was late; payment on his car was late; the utility bills were waiting. Where had all the money gone?

After six weeks, he decided to go it alone. Why not? He had more vision in his little finger than JD and all his bloated ilk put together. Confidence was all you needed and he had that in spades.

The bank manager, a thoughtful, silent man, with a high domed head, listened to Peter's ideas and shook his head. 'I'm afraid I couldn't consider you for a loan. Your credit history is patchy and you have nothing to offer as collateral.'

'I thought the house...'

'You have re-mortgaged your home twice in the last year.'

'We're doing some renovations. And there's been a problem with the roof, you see. But when it's finished the house will be worth more than when we started.'

'I am interested in what it is worth now. And it may be many years before you recoup your investment.' The manager opened a file and ran a finger down some figures. 'And you've taken out a number of loans in the past that have not, as yet, been cleared.

'We're working on it.'

'You have been paying the minimum balance. And there is the matter of the credit cards.'

Give him something. Show him I'm serious. 'I—I recognise that we'll have to tighten our belts a little. But I'm confident that I can pull this off.' *A chance. All I really need. A pinch of Lady Luck.*

The manager cleared his throat, and Peter said, rather desperately, 'My ideas are good.'

'I have no doubt. But you are thirty-nine on your next birthday,. You have a number of failed ventures under your belt already, and I seem to remember you telling me that you and your wife are trying for a baby. I cannot, in good conscience, offer you a loan at this time.'

'I see,' Peter said coldly. 'Then perhaps I'll try elsewhere.'

'That, of course, is your prerogative, Mr Kelso. But, if you will take some friendly advice, don't quit your job just yet. Stability may not be exciting, but families thrive on it.'

'Peter? Peter, wait up!'

The voice roused him from the grey nothingness he had been walking through. He gave an involuntary jerk and was astonished to find himself in the meadows behind the university library with no earthly idea of how he got there. The last thing he remembered was the scrape of the chair as he got to his feet in the bank manager's office. And now it was a shock to be outside. Cold light filtering down from a grey, unlovely sky, an iron day with no magic in it. The unexpected sharpness of the air made him draw in breath.

Suddenly Ellisha was at his side, a chaplet of raindrops caught in her hair. She was panting a little, her breath coming out in cotton-balls of puffed air. 'Jerk. Why didn't you stop?'

'I didn't hear you.'

'What are you doing out here anyway?'

His heart knocked against his ribs. 'Oh, I—' He played for time. *What to say? Out for lunch. What if it isn't lunchtime? How long was I in the bank?* The sky told him nothing and his watch was gone. She was still looking at him.

'So much happening. Needed to come out and clear my head for a bit.'

A frown had appeared on her forehead. Doesn't believe me. Tell her. Just come out with it. 'Ellie—'

'Did you remember to refill the bird feeder?'

'What?' He blinked. 'No. I was in a hurry.'

'What about all the starving wildlife in our garden?'

'There is no starving wildlife in our garden. You feed them ten times a day.'

'Well, what about all the mildly peckish wildlife in our garden?'

'You're probably the reason for the spike in Type Two diabetes in chaffinches.'

'They come to me. I'm like Snow White.'

'Aren't you a little warm-toned for the role?'

'Nazi!'

'Narcissist!'

He was warmed by the glow of her voice, felt the need to go on hearing it. 'Never mind what I'm doing here. What are you doing out here? I thought you worked in dusty old rooms, poring over ancient manuscripts.'

'Sure. If I was an archivist from the Dark Ages.' She waved a hand breezily towards the university buildings. 'Babs wants someone to pick up papers for the archive. Apparently, she asked for me personally.'

'Professor McBride? The rabid feminist?'

'She isn't. Well, she's rabid all right. But feminist? I'm not so sure.' Her face lit up. 'Come with me. You can meet her. Have you got time?'

'Well—'

'Oh, come on. You work too hard. Let JD earn his living for once. If he complains you can fire him.' She took his arm and tugged it. 'You'll love her. It's rumoured that she dated Jacques Derrida in the seventies and he described the affair as making love to a gorse bush.'

'Sounds delightful.'

'Ah, but she has one of the most brilliant minds the university has on campus; that's why they can't fire her no matter who she offends or how outrageously she behaves.'

Without actually agreeing to meet the gorse bush who was not exactly a feminist, Peter found himself following Ellisha down Middle Meadow Walk. She had let go his arm to swish through the frost-brittle leaves, laughing like a child at the disturbance her feet made. 'Listen, Peter. Winter's whispering. What do you think he's saying?'

'Arrrrgh! Gerroff me!'

'Ass.'

'Airhead.'

36

He took her hand. Everything felt strangely dream-like, insubstantial and paper thin, with the dark ink of reality bleeding in from the sides.

CHAPTER 5

THEY STEPPED OUT OF THE Meadows on to Teviot Place, and were just turning left when a familiar figure stepped out from behind one of the unicorn-topped gate piers. Peter recoiled a little. 'You.' The tramp was exactly how he remembered him, a slab of a man in an overcoat tied with string, yet somehow bigger and now sporting a pair of Calvin Klein Aviators that were slightly too small for him. The tramp adjusted the glasses and said, 'I know you.'

'Well, that's hardly—' But the tramp paid Peter no attention. He was looking at Ellisha.

Ellisha smiled. 'I don't think so.'

'Ah do, strange maid. Ah've seen you before.'

'I get that a lot. Just got one of those faces I guess.' She looked over her shoulder at Peter and mouthed, *Poor thing.*

'Ah read fortunes,' the tramp said. 'Ah've goat the Two Sights.'

Peter reached out and tugged Ellisha's sleeve. 'Let's go.'

But she didn't budge. She was looking up at the tramp's face. 'Could you read mine?'

'Aye.'

'How much?'

'Ten.'

'A tenner?' Peter couldn't believe what he was hearing. 'Are you mad? Forget it. Come on, Ellisha, he's a fraud.'

She ignored him. 'How does this work?'

'Ye kin ask me three questions.'

'Okay.'

'But ye huv tae pay me first.'

'Right. Peter, give him the money. I left my purse back in the office.'

'Ellie, I'm not going to—'

Suddenly her face was close against his, her eyes enormous, pleading. 'Please. I want to try.'

And he saw what he hadn't seen before. *Blind idiot. Too wrapped up in my own problems. Hurting. All those smiles and jokes, but inside empty, eaten out by pain, the need, the need, the need for a child.*

He opened his wallet reluctantly, trying to remind himself that plenty of decent people had fallen on hard times. *Giving money. Act of confidence, sign of belief in myself.* 'I've really only got—'

She snatched the note out. It was a twenty, his last. He had tried to take out fifty that morning but the machine had refused, flashing up a message that read, *Insufficient funds* in letters backlit with a hellish green glow. He'd made a joke about it to the queue forming at his back, implying he had used the wrong card, while fumbling his way through a second attempt. That time he managed to extract his twenty, which left exactly sixty-four pence in the account. Not enough to buy a first-class stamp. All the money he had in the world.

'Ah huvnae ony change,' the tramp said.

'Take it.' She held out the note crumpled in her fist, and Peter saw that the fist was trembling.

'El—' The words died on his lips. He looked furiously at the tramp. *Go on then, take it. But give her hope, you bastard. It's the last thing I can buy her.*

The tramp took off the Aviators and, to Peter's astonishment, thrust them towards him. 'Haud these for a bit.' Revealed, his eyes still had their yellow, wolfish tint. He stared at the note suspiciously, as though he expected her to jerk it away the moment he reached for it.

'Take it.'

Almost reluctantly he accepted it, squirrelling it away in a pocket, before saying, 'Ask then.'

'Am I pregnant?'

A pause. 'No.'

Peter struggled to hold in a snort. Hardly the stuff of miracles. A pregnant woman wouldn't need to ask. The tramp glanced in his direction. 'Ah kin tell you're no for believing. It maks things harder.'

Ellisha looked round. 'Don't spoil it, Peter.'

He grimaced a smile and took an unwilling step backwards. 'Go on.'

Ellisha started to say something then broke off. She looked down at the ground then back up. 'Will I be … a mother?'

'Place your hauns in mine.'

Ellisha obliged, and Peter watched those slim brown hands encased in the big calloused white ones, and fought an urge to drag her away. They waited. The tramp seemed to be concentrating. After a few moments, he rolled his head back. He appeared to be listening. And growing impatient, Peter began to fidget and grumbled a little under his breath until Ellisha looked over her shoulder, frowning. As she did so, the tramp lowered his head and moaned softly. 'Ah see it.'

She was all attention. 'Yes.'

The tramp's eyes fluttered and he looked down at Ellisha. *He's good*, Peter thought sourly. *I'll give him that.*

'What do you see?'

For an instant the tramp did not answer, and Peter was wondering if they were going to witness a repeat of the eye-rolling performance, when, all at once, he drew in a sharp breath and a froth of words streamed from his lips.

'Here is the man, alone in the garden.
There, at the centre the tree. The woman,
Coila, mother tae a grey, dreich land
Bright Étaín, daughter tae a fiery star
Whose slender limbs stretch across chasms o' time
Whose mouth is a dark green space dispossessed
Whose breasts, ripe-hanging golden apples, call

40

Across the rim o' the world's beginning
For her love's deliverance. An' his death.'

Peter took a step forward. 'What is that? A poem?'

The tramp blinked then said in his normal voice. 'Ah just gie the message. Sometimes it sounds like poetry. Other times no sae much.'

'But, am I going to be a mother?'

'Ah'm sorry. But you've had your three questions.'

'No, I haven't. I only asked two.'

'He asked if it was a poem.'

'That doesn't count.'

'Ah dinna mak the rules.'

'Of course you make the rules,' Peter cried angrily. 'You make it all up.'

Something dangerous appeared in the eyes of the tramp. His hands clenched into fists.

'Easy now. Easy.' Arms spread, Ellisha placed herself between them, talking gently, as though to a wild horse. 'It's okay. Don't look at him. Look at me. I have a question. I want to ask you something. Not about me. Something personal.'

There was a pause. The tramp's eyes flicked from Peter to Ellisha.

'You don't have to answer, but may I ask?'

An almost imperceptible nod.

'I want to know why? Why are you living like this?'

'Ellie!' Peter hissed.

'I know what my husband is thinking. But he's wrong. I have a feeling about you.' She waved a hand at the universe. 'You're meant for better things.'

The tramp did not reply, and, after a moment, Ellisha shrugged. 'Okay. I guess it's time to leave you be.' She began walking in the direction of the university, and as Peter was left facing the great standing stone of a man, he wondered what to say. But it was the tramp who spoke first.

'Ye kin gie me back ma glasses now.'

He caught up with her as she disappeared through a deep stone arch into one of the university quadrangles. 'Ellie.'

She turned and slipped her arm through his. 'I'm sorry.'

'It's okay.'

'I'll pay you back.'

'Don't be daft.'

'No, really.'

'It's fine.'

She squeezed his arm. 'Those were your Aviators he was wearing, weren't they?'

Hastily changing the subject, Peter said, 'I thought Professor McBride taught Religious History.'

'She does.'

'Isn't this the Medical faculty?'

'No fooling you, Hawkeye. I was taking a catalogue of the documents that are kept in the artist's flat this morning, and I need to give the keys back.'

They entered the Museum of Anatomy through a neoclassical door, flanked by the giant skeletons of two elephants. And everywhere that strange decoupage of the Victorian mind, oil paintings and Greek statuary next to waxworks of open torsos, models of the human head and the bones of a child.

Uneasily he asked, 'Do you come here often?'

She was peering into a cabinet of Tibetan religious relics fashioned from human skull caps. A quick, shrewd glance over her shoulder. 'What's wrong? A little death got you spooked?'

Before he could answer, she spotted a plump young woman over by one of the glass cases. She was making sketches of a dissected foot, and looked up when Ellisha called over to her. 'Is George in?'

She hooked a thumb over her shoulder. 'In the skull room, I think.'

'What's he doing there?'

'Looking at skulls probably.'

Ellisha glanced at Peter. 'Only the brightest and the best work here.'

'Shall we go?' He took a step towards the door at the far end of the room, but she pulled a face. 'They don't like members of the public back there.'

'Afraid I'll faint?'

'Don't. They'll have you filleted and displayed in a glass case before you hit the ground.'

'I won't.'

'Seriously, don't.'

A school party came in. Boys and girls in grey uniforms, trailing behind a teacher who was walking backwards, a forefinger to her lips. In the rear were several mothers and pre-schoolers. As they passed one of the mothers, a tall woman, attractive but unkempt in the way mothers of small children often are was saying to her companion, 'I mean if you pay that amount you expect the psychic to be something special. But he was terribly vague. Then again, I can't believe that it would cost so much if there wasn't something in it.'

She stopped suddenly and pointed at Ellisha. 'Do I know you?'

Ellisha smiled and shook her head and the woman moved on.

'What is it about you?' Peter whispered.

'I don't know.'

He watched her try to make a toddler, in an over-sized red duffle-coat, smile. The child regarded her with an inscrutable long-lashed look, which slowly melted into a gappy grin. Ellisha started to say something, but the child's mother called her name, and the toddler turned and trotted off without waiting to hear.

Ellisha stared after her, a haunted unhappy look in her eyes which made Peter feel an unbearable pain and the need to say something reassuring and hopeful, but she made an impatient movement with her shoulders. 'Are you okay to wait for a minute?'

He made a play of considering whether he had time. 'Sure. For a minute.'

She was longer than he expected, and after a while the silence of the place began to press in on him. He took a step in the direction of the school party, meaning to listen to whatever the lecture was about, but one of the mothers stared at him suspiciously and he backed away feeling unreasonably guilty.

Left with the exhibits, he wandered aimlessly between the cases. But they added to his unease. A display of mammalian skulls, the death mask of a murderer, a papier mâché model of an eyeball looking back at him. He gazed at the eyeball for some time, imagining Ellisha beside him, whispering, *don't blink first,* then he moved on to view a glass case containing the lacquered remains of a man.

There was something haunting in the sight of a body that was haunted no more by a living presence, and the extraordinary ordinariness of death made him lean closer, searching for a spark of something human. But all he saw was his own reflection caught in the glass, his living face ghosted over the ruined one. Beside him, someone said, 'What do you think he did?'

Peter started and found the dishevelled-looking mother at his side. The toddler was hanging on to her skirts. It stared at him expressionlessly, then coughed.

'I—I'm sorry?'

Up close he noted that she had a round, mournful face which was turned towards the case. 'Why do you think he ended up spending eternity in here? He doesn't even have a name.'

'I don't know.' Peter gave an embarrassed laugh, uncertain whether she was serious or not. 'Maybe he annoyed his boss or his wife.'

'I reckon it was his bank manager.'

'What?'

She was patting the child's back—it was still coughing—and did not answer. A little afraid, Peter pressed, 'Why the bank manager?'

'Because they're basically evil.' She smiled up at him in a mournful way. 'I should know. I'm married to one.' The child was still coughing and she frowned. 'What's the matter? What have you got in your mouth?'

Peter saw Ellisha exit the Skull Room and waved to her. As he did so, the woman said, 'Spit it out. Just spit it out!' She was down on her knees shaking the child by the shoulders.

'Is something wrong?'

The child's expression was eerie. She seemed to be looking at something that wasn't in the room. Then, without warning, her face flushed full of blood like a thermometer with the mercury rising too fast. *Choking*, Peter thought wildly. *She's choking.*

'Let me through. I'm a first aider.' One of the teachers, a slight woman with a determined face, was pushing her way towards them. She looked at Peter accusingly. 'Did you give her a sweet?'

'No. Of course not.'

His answer was ignored as she dropped to her knees beside the mother and began slapping the child's back. 'Come on now. Come on.' But the child was still struggling. No longer coughing, it was making a dry rattling sound, a savage inhuman sound, wind passing through the empty sockets of a bird skull. *The sound of something leaving.* In time with this thought the child's eyes grew wide and rolled back into her head. Two soft poached eggs replaced her gaze. Peter watched in frozen horror; hands clasped to his mouth as the child began to die. Behind him, someone was calling for an ambulance, but the universe felt strangely empty and he knew with absolute certainty that it would not make it in time.

'You're not doing it hard enough. Here. Let me.' Miraculously Ellisha was at his side as though she had materialised rather than simply walked across the floor. She grabbed the child and hit her on the back. An eye-popping look of shock. But nothing else. No bite of poison apple vomited on to the floor, no gasping neonatal breath. The child's mother began to rock back and forth, moaning over and over, 'My wee girl. My wee, wee girl.'

Ellisha glanced up at him, eyes dark with fear. *It's not working.* And for a moment he thought she would admit defeat. But her hand rose, like the only moving part in a jammed mechanism, and she brought it down so hard he thought, *My God. She's killed her.*

But the child began to sob.

'Look!' The teacher was pointing at a small diamond-shaped object about the size of a grape lying on the floor. A toggle from the child's duffel coat. Movement came back to the room. Everyone began talking at once. The mother grabbed her child from Ellisha's arms and started to weep, and several women gathered around to comfort her. In the excitement of it all, Peter turned to Ellisha. She was standing apart, looking down at her hands as though she did not recognise what they had done.

CHAPTER 6

IN A KIND OF DAZE, Peter and Ellisha crossed the quadrangle that led to the Department of Religious History. Students passed in little huddles of twos and threes paying them no notice, and beyond the archway the hum of traffic was unbroken. Peter stole a look at Ellisha. The muscles of her face had pulled tight and her eyes had a look of silent horror about them. But they were still the same tilted eyes that opened beside him each morning and the face was still Ellisha's face. She had not changed, and yet she had.

Not until they entered an impressive building, which for some reason, reminded Peter of buildings he had glimpsed from the Grand Canal in Venice, did he ask, 'How did you know what to do?'

'I didn't.' Ellisha's expression was caught in the shadows. 'I moved without thinking. I don't know. Like I was possessed.' She shook her head. 'No, not exactly possessed. I just *knew*. I don't know how to explain it.'

Professor McBride had an office in the basement. 'She said it was the deepest pit they could cast her into,' Ellisha explained, as they descended an uncarpeted staircase. They walked along a corridor lined with plaster replicas of antiquities, and stopped opposite a frieze of a headless centaur rearing up on its hind legs. Peter watched as Ellisha knocked on the door then opened it a crack.

'Dr McBride— Oh! I didn't realise you had a tutorial today.'

'No, no. Come in. Come in.' A gravelly voice more commanding than welcoming.

They squeezed into the room. It was plain as a convent cell, the low ceiling chequered in white fibreglass panels, walls whitewashed but almost invisible behind dozens of floating shelves which supported well-thumbed books with faded spines and a number of small artefacts, including a tiny stone goddess with pendulous breasts and no hair. In a small space there was a corkboard covered in black-and-white photos. Many of them featured a young woman in miniskirts with long blond hair, arm in arm with older men, often wearing sports jackets and smoking pipes. He thought he recognised Sartre.

In the centre of the room, two students—a blond, vague girl and an owl-eyed boy in round glasses—were sitting, like Hansel and Gretel, at a narrow wooden table, their eyes fixed with a kind of understated terror at a witch-like figure hunched behind the desk.

Dr Barbara McBride was dressed with the kind of shabbiness that academics deliberately affect as a badge of defiance. Her long grey hair was disarranged and, although it was barely ten o clock in the morning, she was clearly drunk.

'Hi,' Ellisha said softly. 'You wanted me to collect—'

'I know you. Why do I know you?'

'We met when I brought over the Goodison paper.'

'No. That's not it. Alisha isn't it?'

'Ellisha.'

'Ell-ish-a?' Something predatory glittered in the cowled eyes. She rounded on her students. 'Do you recognise the name?'

Somehow she had conveyed that it would be terrible not to answer, and the boy said uncertainly. 'I don't—I mean, I'm not sure. But could it be related to Elisha, the prophet in the Bible?'

'Interesting.'

The boy brightened.

'But wrong. Not to worry. What's a couple of thousand miles and a few centuries, eh? Elisha, Aleisha, Alisha are all variants of a Hebrew word via Greek meaning *noble* or possibly even *God is powerful*. Ellisha is quite a different name. Sanskrit in origin. It translates as *illusion* or *one who creates illusion*.' She turned to Ellisha. 'Do you know why your parents called you that?

'No.'

'Must have had a reason, though. You should never ignore names. They have more power than you imagine.'

Ellisha shrugged, then her lips curled in a little demi-lune smile. 'Maybe they wanted a hippy?'

'Did you ever ask them?'

The smile vanished. 'Mom and Dad died when I was quite young. In a car crash.'

Peter, astonished by the audacity of the interrogation, interrupted in a friendly manner, 'I'm Peter, Ellisha's hus—'

'Hmmmmph.' Babs ignored his outstretched hand. 'Peter? Means stone. Stone man. Man of stone. But also a verb, to peter out, to fade, to disappear.' She waved a claw at the room. 'Well, don't just stand there. Take a seat. We'll be done in a minute.'

This was easier said than done. Ellisha perched on a set of library steps, while Peter rested his back uncomfortably on the wall above the radiator. Babs waved a hand at the two students.

'And while we're on the subject of names, let me introduce these two. Zach and Deborah. For some reason their parents chose to name them after Old Testament prophets. Presumably with ironical intent, as they are both entirely lacking in vision.'

Both students went pink at this description, and embarrassed, Peter could only manage an uncomfortable nod in their direction.

Her attention turned back to Zach and Deborah. 'Where was I?'

'The infallibility of the deity,' Zach suggested.

Babs threw him a venomous look. 'Indeed. What an infallible thing the deity of men has become. He's been sucking up power for thousands of years, first the power of women then the power of all the other gods. Gods once had weaknesses, you know. They were capricious and angry and jealous. But the God of Abraham lives in a very strange, exalted place. He takes credit for all the good in the world.

And when things go wrong, earthquakes, tsunamis, the death of a child, his cronies throw up their hands and say his ways are too damn mysterious to interpret.'

'Or that it's our fault because we displeased him.' This again from the boy.

'Good point. What does God have to do to get a bad press?'

'Yes, but isn't— I mean …Well I think religion is a comfort,' Deborah said nervously. 'I mean as a Christian I think that's the point of religion. To give comfort.'

'Yes. Yes. That's always the argument *for* religion,' Babs answered. She was lighting a tipped cigarillo despite the sign that clearly read *No Smoking* above her desk. 'But for every bit of comfort, how much is there in the way of guilt and fear and sheer inertia to change things? What about Galileo or the American reporter on his knees awaiting a beheading or the poor devils dragged up Castle Hill to be burnt as witches? How much comfort would it be to feel the flames licking about your feet?' Babs banged her fist down on the table, startling everyone and sending an apple-shaped penholder rolling from the desk. Ellisha bent to pick it up.

'Dr McBride,' she said in a soothing voice. 'Perhaps I should make some tea.'

'No need. Brought my own.' After some fumbling about under the desk, she produced a thermos and poured herself a generous measure of a liquid clearly unrelated to tea. She took a gulp then a long drag from the cigarillo. An ectoplasmic cloud of smoke escaped from her mouth. There was something compelling about her sheer hauteur, an insouciance that bordered on the negligent. *How on earth does she manage not to set off the smoke detector?*

He realised that she had caught him looking. Her gaze wandered up towards the nicotine stain around the detector then back to his with a conspiratorial twinkle. For an instant he felt she was trying to tell him something. But she shrugged and turned back to her students.

In a calmer voice she continued, 'Our young friend here, Zachariah, doubtless with fewer hairs on his pubes than he has on his chin'—Zach turned scarlet—'has struck at the heart of the problem. Why are those men and women, with their faith in God their father, so afraid to die? What could be lovelier than to return to the arms of one's own maker?'

'Perhaps their faith isn't strong enough?' Deborah suggested timidly.

'Yet this is what they BELIEVE! They fight wars over it, sacrifice their children, lie, murder, rape in its name. A few ghastly ones even go round forgiving everyone. But always, when the darkness nears, they rage against the dying of the light.' She held up a hand and waved off a protest from Zach. 'Yes, yes. There are always a few exceptions, the saints, the martyrs, the suicide bombers. But a drop of deadly nightshade in an ocean does not change the ocean.

'So how do we explain this?' She paused and looked round the table. The students avoided her eye.

Babs opened her desk drawer, produced an ashtray and stubbed out the remains of the cigarillo. It was a gesture of disgust and everyone knew it.

'We explain it,' Babs said in her stinging nettle voice, 'by showing that the godhead is incomplete. We're missing something.'

Biting her lip, Deborah ventured, 'Is it the Goddess? The feminine side of religion?'

Babs drank heartily from her cup then, smacking her lips together, set it down. 'Perhaps. The world has been too long under the influence of men. But the Goddess isn't some sort of sticking plaster to mend mankind's woes.' She glanced sharply at Ellisha as she said this, revealing that she had recognised her from the start. And, with one of those unanticipated veers of consciousness, she demanded suddenly, 'And what do you believe, hmm, daughter of a Sanskrit dream? Do you imagine, somewhere deep within you, resides the glassy essence of a soul? A measure of the divine suffice to make the angels weep?'

'I—' Ellisha ran her tongue over her bottom lip. 'I don't know.' Clearly, she would have liked to have left it there, but Bab's headlamp eyes left no scope for concealment. A little expulsion of air, a squirm of her shoulders. 'I wouldn't say I believe in *nothing*. But you're right. I don't have a strong sense of belonging to any particular faith. I've never found anything that I could really hold on to.'

'Apart from your rock? Your stone man.'

'Apart from Peter, yes.' She darted him a quick, loving look that moved him and made him feel despicable at the same time. Babs was pouring herself more 'tea'. 'But you've never felt touched by the unseen hand? No thrill of religious experience? The *magnum sacramentum* hasn't tingled in your veins?'

Ellisha wrinkled her nose. 'I don't—'

He could feel her gaze, knew she was appealing to him. *What do you think, should I tell?* But he couldn't look her in the eye, and he had no sense that this was a turning point or that Babs' words were weighted. After a moment, he saw her shrug then square her shoulders. 'When I was thirteen I was struck by lightning.'

Babs put her flask down. 'What do you recall?'

'Not much. It was a beautiful July day. No wind. Clear blue sky.'

'Is that possible?' Deborah asked.

'Oh, it is.' Babs had hunched forward, chin clasped between her bony fingers. 'Lightning can travel over twenty miles from where the storm is. And you would have no clue it was coming.'

'I didn't,' Ellisha said, with a laugh. 'I think I remember a crackling sound. Then I couldn't see anything but white light for a few seconds.

I guess I passed out. Because I don't remember anything else until I woke up at home, with the doctor examining me.'

'But you made a full recovery?' Babs was studying Ellisha as though she was a striking artefact unexpectedly revealed by blowing sands.

'Mostly. You're never really okay after a lightning strike. I get headaches and sometimes I see things in my peripheral vision, shadows, flashes, that sort of thing. On the upside, I have an amazing Lichtenberg figure on my back.'

'A kind of scar?' Zach asked.

'Yup. The capillaries got fried under the skin. Sometimes they fade. But mine is still here all these years later. I guess it's part of me now.'

'When you were thirteen,' Babs repeated ruminatively. 'You're certain?'

'Day after my birthday. You don't tend to forget a present like that.' Her brow crinkled. 'Why, is it significant?'

'It depends. Had you started your menses?'

'Now, wait a minute!' Peter jumped to his feet. Things were getting out beyond a joke. But Ellisha put out a restraining hand. She seemed fascinated. A mongoose caught in the thrall of a python. *Or perhaps*, he thought uneasily, *a pythoness.*

'I'd started the week before. It was kind of a big deal because I was first out of my friends.'

'I see. I see. A moment of transition. A rite of passage. *Mutatis Mutandis* if you will. Plenty of resonances in the mythic scheme of things. Lightning is divine. It purifies. Herakles, Asclepius, Semele were all struck by holy fire before they were deemed worthy of heroic status. The Incas laid out child sacrifices on mountain peaks to be struck by lightning because they thought it made them divine. All are mortal before the touch of the celestial.' She took a long meditative sip from her cup. 'The gods singled you out.'

Ellisha laughed. 'I don't believe in the gods.'

'Immaterial if they happen to believe in you. But, of course, I use the term figuratively. Gods is just a word for opening up the dark places in consciousness. Mythology, that's the key to everything. *Ignis Dei*.' She rounded, without warning, on her students. '*Ignis Dei*. No idea what that means, eh?'

Her smugness was irritating. Feeling side-lined, Peter racked his brains for a pithy putdown. But his schoolboy Latin wasn't up to the task. *Dei,* something to do with God. But *Ignis*? Ignorant? Ignoble? Ignominious? Nothing quite fit.

'*The spark of God* maybe?'

Ellisha had spoken softly, so softly that Peter wasn't sure she had spoken at all, but Zach slapped his hand on the desk. 'Of course. I was thinking fire. But *ignis* in the sense of ignite.'

Babs sat upright, the reanimated corpse in a horror movie. She glanced narrowly at Ellisha, her face a peculiar mixture of anger and fear. 'Who told you? You didn't get that on your own.'

Ellisha laughed gracefully. 'Why is it no-one believes that Americans can know Latin?'

For a tense instant, things might have gone either way, but then Babs recovered herself. She turned back to her students, swerving off in a new direction. 'Religion has had millennia to create a satisfying system of belief. Yet the best the great theological minds of the world have come up with so far is *God loves us*, which is, of course, in patent contradiction to everything the universe is telling us. So, what's missing? What do we really need?'

'More sex,' Zach suggested.

'A man's answer.'

He came back with, 'No more discrimination. If we all learned to see each other as equals there might finally be peace in the world.'

'Terrible idea,' Babs snorted. 'The purpose of religion is to make people feel special, unique, chosen by God. Without discrimination there is nothing to separate the elect from the herd. Humans will forgive their fellows all sorts of sins; theft, war, destruction. But not the sin of equality. It stifles us. Petrifies us. Not in the sense of filling us with fear, but the old use of the word. Same root as stone-man here. *Petra*, Latin for rock or crag. Literally to turn to stone, to be inert, paralysed.'

'We need a better story.' Suddenly all eyes were on Peter, and he looked at Babs defiantly.

'Ah, our stone-man has it.'

'What do you mean, Peter?' Ellisha asked.

What did he mean? For an instant intuition had flashed inside his head, brilliant, blinding. But now it was gone. He stumbled over his tongue, trying to mould the heavy clods of words into a recognisable shape. 'A religion needs to tell a story, to … to appeal to some forgotten longing buried deep down in the subconscious.' It was hopeless. He was using clay to depict light, but Babs was pleased.

'That's it, Stone-man.' She gave a rasping, smoker's laugh. 'Humanity loves a story. Give men philosophy and they'll learn to think. Give them a compelling mythology and they'll change the course of the stars. Forget sex. Narrative's the real generative force guiding mankind. It wasn't a foetus the Angel of the Lord deposited in Mary's womb. It was a legend. *Fons sapientiae, verbum Dei*, as they say.' She rolled an eye towards Peter. 'Get your wife to translate that one.' She began to cough, a deep, dragging sound, like the sound of the tide draining over gravel. The coughing went on and on. She banged on her chest with her fist several times to no obvious effect. Ellisha jumped to her feet. 'I'll get water.'

Babs swatted a hand at the air to indicate that it wasn't necessary, but Ellisha had already gone. Peter watched, half in horror, half in fascination until the spasm wore itself out and Babs relaxed.

'Fine now. Just something caught at the back of my throat.'

Peter nodded. From the corner of his eye, he noted that the students were trying surreptitiously to clear away their things. Babs noticed it too. 'Yes, yes. Run along, children. You are in grave danger of having a thought enter your heads.' She was pouring herself another drink from the flask. Suddenly she slammed the cup down, sending a little tsunami of liquid across the desk. 'Don't think I don't know what they ask you. What's the old witch up to, eh? What's she cooking up behind closed doors? Ignis Dei. That's what they want to know. Ignis Dei! The Woman's Secret. But the old witch won't tell.'

The students gave a last frightened glance at their mentor then fled the room. Babs looked into the dregs of her cup then said in a softer voice. 'Old witch, one of their kinder nicknames for me.'

Alone, an unpleasant silence fell. Babs lit another cigarillo and sat smoking it morosely. Peter walked across the room and sat down on one of the wooden seats, wondering what was keeping Ellisha. His gaze took in the black-and-white photographs pinned to the corkboard. And with a jolt he understood that the woman in the miniskirts was Babs. She had been attractive in a raw-boned sort of way, and he wondered if he should offer a compliment. Babs' eyes were on the door. 'Silly bitch.'

'Ellisha?' he asked coldly.

'Deborah. She's grown up defending a religion that stripped her of her power as a mother and a creator, and still she defends it. *Ye shall overthrow their altars, and break their pillars, and burn their groves with fire.*' She looked at him expectantly until he said without conviction, 'Judges?'

'Deuteronomy 12:3. Fascinating thing, the religions of Abraham. They pour filth over the fairer sex until they're so blind with self-loathing they can't open their mouths but to proclaim the righteousness of their tormentors.' Then she added cryptically. 'You need to watch out for her.'

'Deborah?'

'Ellisha.'

'Why?'

She sucked in her lower lip and looked at him consideringly. 'How would you describe her?'

He smelt a trap. There was something of the Sphinx in Babs' expression. But he could think of no plausible reason not to answer. 'I suppose I would say—' he began, then stopped. Babs' eyes were like hot coals. 'Bright,' he answered with a sense of defiance. 'I would say she is extremely bright, burning almost. And beautiful. Spirited. Fanciful—'

'Fey?' interrupted Babs. 'Touched by the angels? Psychically charged?'

'You are mocking me.'

'No, not at all. More things in heaven and earth, Horatio.' Her gaze rose upwards, stalling at the smoke detector which seemed to hold a kind of fascination for her. 'There's a vibration about her. You feel it too, the thrum of the incorporeal, the glimpse of a Presence, God's feminine side, the *Shekhinah*.'

'Ellisha is an innocent,' he said coldly. 'She sees the good in everything.'

The basalt eyes came back to him. 'Ah, but innocence like that makes her look like a seer.' She held his gaze for an uncomfortable period then shrugged. 'Ah well, ignore me. Nothing to my arguments but sophistry and illusion, as dear old Hume would have it. Did you know he was better known as a historian than a philosopher during his lifetime? Perhaps I should take his advice and commit my words to the flames. No smoke without fire, eh, Stone man?' She blew out a smoke ring and let it ascend lazily towards the smoke detector.

'You're lucky the battery's dead,' he said irritably.

'Took it out myself.'

Despite everything he laughed. It wasn't hard to imagine Babs swaying on top of the desk, pliers in hand, cigarillo dangling from the cracked corner of her mouth.

'Hey, look at you two.' Ellisha was coming back into the room with a steaming mug. 'Laughing away like old friends.' Then to Babs. 'I heard your cough stop so I decided to make some tea. I keep herbs in my bag in case I run out when I'm at work.' As she passed Peter she said, 'Peppermint and ginger.' Then she whispered under her breath, 'For hangovers.'

'I'm drunk, not deaf,' Babs said. But the mug was accepted from Ellisha's hand and she took a sip.

'God's womb!' Babs pulled a face. 'What did you put in here?'

'Feverwort. It tastes a little bitter, but it helps. They called it *Christ's ladder* in olden times.'

'Tastes more like the contents of Christ's bladder.' Babs put the tea down and shuddered.

'Babs, you should really—'

'I'll get to it. Don't start nagging me, like a scolding wife.' Babs sunk her chin into the chalice of her hands. 'It's bad enough that they're going to sack me.'

'They're not going to sack you.'

'Robert Graves had it right, you know. Rosy-cheeked lecturer, wise old professor and then useless old deadbeat. The White Deity, the Great Goddess. She's always a triple whore.' She flashed Ellisha a pitiful look. 'Should have behaved myself, flattered them, the great deans and dons. O Immortal Fathers I lay my womanhood down at your feet. Before you I am prostrated, prosecuted, prostituted, prosodic.'

'It would be enough if you didn't insult them to their faces.'

'They won't sack me,' Babs suddenly contradicted herself. 'They know I'm on to something.'

'You mean Ignis Dei?'

'Oh no you don't, girlie.' Babs was shaking her head in the exaggerated pendulum swings of an unbalanced grandfather clock.

'Babs!' Ellisha said in a hurt voice.

Babs was unrepentant. 'It's how it works here. They ask questions. It seems innocent. No. No.' She tapped the side of her nose. 'Ignis Dei. It goes with me to the grave.'

Ellisha straightened up. She shot Peter a look then pointed to a couple of boxes in front of Babs' desk. 'Are these the papers you wanted me to collect?'

Babs nodded.

'Great. We'll take them then get out of your way.'

Something in the calmness of her voice penetrated the exoskeleton of disappointment and alcohol that was surrounding Babs' frail human part, and without warning she crumpled, like antique furniture crumbling to motes when the dust-sheet is pulled off. She lowered her forehead to one hand and rocked it against the heel of her palm.

Ellisha glanced at Peter with a *time to go* look, and they quietly took their leave.

CHAPTER 7

IT WAS A SHOCK TO come back outside and find it was growing dark and that the streetlights had come on. Peter must have muttered something to this effect because Ellisha stopped and hefted her box higher on her hip.

'Ten days to Christmas, and you're surprised it's getting dark by three thirty?'

'Ten days?' He couldn't hide his shock. How did that happen? A moment ago, it had been autumn. But now he thought about it, all those blind hours holed up in one dingy little café after another, the fading light more like a symptom of his mental darkness than the turning season. But Christmas? Tinsel and fairy lights, the Christmas market, carol singing on George Street. He had walked through it all like a ghost, feet not quite touching the earth.

Ellisha was looking at him. 'You haven't forgotten, have you?'

'No. No, of course not.'

'Because I'm expecting a lot of presents. Big ones.'

'Isn't Christmas the season of giving?'

'Yup. And I'm giving you plenty of notice.'

'Ingrate.'

'Scrooge.'

The boxes were heavy, and their progress slow. Ellisha kept glancing at him, as though on the point of saying something, until, frustrated, he cried, 'What?'

'I think she's found something.'

'Who? Babs?'

'Mmmm.'

'Well, she was certainly mysterious enough. All that leering about Ignis Dei. Why? What do you think she's found?'

'God, maybe.'

He looked at her in surprise, but Ellisha was staring into the distance. He thought of the flask beneath Bab's desk. 'It's not unusual for people who drink heavily to find God.'

'Except. It isn't God, not exactly. I've been reading her papers in the library. And she never comes right out and says it, but there are hints. I'm pretty certain that she's found a third way.'

'Third way?'

'Between God and the pain of nothingness.

'Isn't that just Humanism?'

Her face had a tight pinched look, and she hugged the box of papers to her more tightly. 'No. Not humanism or ethical atheism or anything like that. It's more. I think it's a narrative of some sort. That's why she was so excited when you talked about the importance of having a story. Whoever found this story would have something very powerful. Something worth living for.' She threw him an intense, searching look. 'Maybe even worth dying for.'

Carefully, he asked, 'Have you asked Babs?'

'I've tried. But that's the trouble with Babs, the minute you try to pin her down she starts talking in riddles and allegories. And she's got so much knowledge that she could tell you her darkest secrets to your face and you wouldn't even know. Even blasted she can be slippery. She's like the enchantress in a Mediaeval legend holding out the *San Graal* and watching your fingers slip through when you reach out to take it.'

Still puzzled by the turn of the conversation, he pressed, 'You really believe there's something to this Ignis Dei malarky? It's probably all nonsense.'

'It isn't. It can't be.'

'How can you know?'

They had stopped, and she lifted her face to him. The flat disc of cadmium light from a lamppost behind her head made her look like a Mackintosh angel. But there was something in her eyes he had never seen before, something empty and despairing.

'It just can't.'

By the time they reached the archives, the strangeness had gone out of Ellisha and she was back to her old self. She saw Peter's face and laughed. 'Lovely, isn't it?'

He let his gaze cross a structure of such surpassing ugliness it made him wince. 'Here?'

'Yeah.'

They paused on front steps, looking down at the boxes. 'I can help you take them in.'

'It's fine. I've kept you way longer than I meant.' She frowned. 'I mean, don't you have to get back?'

The urge to stay was so strong in him that he had to grit his teeth with the effort of pretending otherwise. 'I do,' he said. 'Can't keep everyone waiting.' He looked back the way they had come, but still his feet did not move. 'What a day!'

'Well, I won't say it hasn't been fun. But I can live without any more surprises for a while.'

As she disappeared through the doors, he blew her a kiss, but her back was to him and she didn't turn around.

He spent the rest of the afternoon in the frantic pursuit of Christmas presents, fighting his way through crowds, which seemed to him like the happy inhabitants of hell, with their vacant, satisfied expressions and the meandering slowness of their gait, and all the time, his brain running in smaller and smaller circles. *No good trying to take money out with my bank card. Risk putting more on the credit card? A few*

items. Nothing much. Perfume. A scarf. Call me a miser. Make a joke out of it. Let her have Christmas, though. I can do that. Come clean on Boxing Day.

He realised the girl behind the checkout was looking at him.

'I'm sorry, sir. Your card's been declined.'

'Oh.' A hot flush creeping behind his ears.

'I can try again.'

'Sure.'

'It's probably the machine. Sometimes it acts up.' Her tone was so reassuring he was certain she didn't believe him. It was hot inside the shop. He could feel himself begin to sweat. But his hand, half way to loosening his collar, froze. *Guilty. Give myself away.*

'I'm sorry.' The girl's voice was a stage whisper. 'I'm afraid it's been declined again. Do you have another card?'

He fumbled in his wallet. 'Try this one.'

A queue had formed behind him, eyes boring into his back, impatient, assessing him. His scalp prickled.

'I'm sorry.'

Forcing an exasperated laugh, he turned towards the queue. 'Not my day.' They stared at him, stony-faced. His throat was tight, something blocking his windpipe. The girl held out the useless card and he took it and shoved it back in his wallet. 'I guess I'll have to go elsewhere.'

'I'm sorry. Have a nice day.'

It was all he could do to prevent himself from breaking into a run.

He began walking blindly the length and breadth of Edinburgh, through grey streets, past expressionless people who all seemed to be rushing in the other direction. In his fist were his last few coins clasped so tightly they felt meaningless. And the more he walked, the more he was assailed by a strange double feeling that everyone was looking at him and that he was utterly insignificant and unnoticed.

When he finally reached Arthur's Seat, he climbed the grassy volcanic slopes using his phone as a torch then stood looking down at the city, which was nothing but a clutter of senseless shapes peopled by ants under the black dome of the sky. The sight of it made him unbearably lonely. He had wanted to be a good man, a man who made a difference, and he had failed. All that he was—all that he would ever be—was a particle of universal dust, a random speck with the great misfortune to one day wake up and look around itself.

He thought of Ellisha and how, ten years ago, their meeting so arbitrary felt fatefully ordained. Him running down the Playfair steps as she ran up. Both dreaming. A collision inevitable.

—*Asshole!*

—*Excuse me?*

—*Nearly sent me flying. Don't you look where you're going?*

—*It's not me that's the hurdie here.*

—*What did you call me?*

—*An asshole.*

Laughing. Those sonorous American cadences ringing like a church bell.

—*I like your style.*

—*Come for a coffee.*

—*Slick. What makes you think I've got time?*

—*Well, I've got all the time in the world. We can share.*

And all through it, his eyes filling with the wonder of her. Raindrops caught in the spirals of her hair. Her olive-coloured eyes and her skin, dark like wild cherry bark, standing out against the grey Edinburgh backdrop so vividly, she seemed not quite real.

Contradiction and possibility; she might have been Eve stepping out of The Garden possessing the promise of everyone. And, as she stood on the steps before him, hesitating, he thought, *Promise her. Promise her anything, as long as I can have her.*

And now? Now there was nothing left. No more dreams. Not even promises. Useless. A failure. He stared into the void until the darkness pressed against his skin, until he no longer felt like a man, but a tiny creature standing inside an ancient mouth ready to be swallowed.

Just a few steps.

He moved inside himself, but his body did not respond. *Forget it all. Everything solved.* How often did it happen that way? News reports he had read out loud to Ellisha over breakfast. *Seemed fine at dinner. Laughing. Making jokes. No-one had any reason to think he wanted to kill himself.*

Just a few wee steps.

A fierce wind had begun at his back, and he swayed a little, felt his balance beginning to slip. *How long will it take? By the laws of the universe there's no difference between a pebble falling and a man.* To prove it to himself, he kicked a stone lying at his feet, but somehow the stone became part of him and suddenly he was rushing forward headlong, scattering coins like the beneficences of a king, his hands desperately grabbing fistfuls of air, the whole world turning on its axis and nothing but blackness stretching up to swallow him.

He skidded to a halt and heard the pebble falling over the edge. Salisbury crag. It fell for a long time, and he listened to it striking sparks against a hundred and fifty feet of volcanic rock waiting below to snap his bones. Panting. His chest rising and falling, pumping the bellows of his lungs to suck in life and more life. A note singing in his ears.

The note became more insistent, and mechanically, without thought or will, he reached into his pocket for his phone.

'Hello?'

'Peter. It's Susan.'

He was so far away he couldn't place her. Owl glasses and a startled look of wisdom. 'Susan, yes. Of course. Susan.'

'Are you okay?'

'I'm fine.'

'Am I interrupting something?'

His eyes slid towards the void. 'No, nothing.'

'Good. I just wanted to apologise.'

'What for?'

'Your things. I know it's been weeks. But Wee Tam's going to drop them off at your house on his way home.'

'No!'

'I'm sorry.'

'Tell him, no. I don't want any of it.'

He heard her draw in breath, pictured the owl eyes growing rounder. 'I'm sorry. But he's already left. I'm not sure if I can contact him.'

By the time he reached his front door, his limbs would scarcely obey him. He had run and run, his thoughts burning with the muscles and tendons of his legs. *Got to stop it. Finding out. Not like this.* Hope rose in him to see the house was in darkness. Not home yet. A chance. In his pocket his phone vibrated and he fumbled it out of his pocket, not registering the name. 'Ellisha?'

'Susan.'

His heart jumped.

'I got hold of Tam.'

'Thank you.' He barely had breath to say it.

'You're sure you don't want your things? There's a really nice pen here. I think it's Cartier.'

'Keep it.' He was fumbling his key in the lock.

'Really?'

'Really.'

'Wow. You must be doing okay for yourself.'

'You know me. Always the lucky breaks.'

Susan rang off, and the door, yielding to his weight, opened suddenly and he staggered forwards, knocking over a coat stand and sending coats and jackets flying through the air like phantoms.

'Ellisha? Are you home?' He threw open the door to the sitting room and came to a cold dead stop. A single lamp was burning, but it was enough to illuminate Ellisha, who sat in the centre of the Persian rug, and placed around her, like mushrooms in a fairy ring, were all the brown envelopes he had hidden in his bedside drawer.

CHAPTER 8

LIGHT PRECEDING THOUGHT DREW CONSCIOUSNESS towards a new awakening, a new day and the mercy of a few blind moments of forgetfulness, until memory's blow falling like an axe jerked him into a sitting position. He was breathing heavily as though, all through the night, a malignant succubus had been crouching on his chest and he was suddenly released. Through the curtains the thin light of morning burned his pupils and he closed his eyes and lay down again immediately. *Oh, the evils of drink.* Stay like this, cocooned in the red-tinged darkness, just a little longer. But gradually his eyelids rose in slow penitence to the day.

He lay for a moment, unsettled, nothing familiar. His bed strangely narrow and the ceiling in the wrong place, and it came on him gradually that this was the sitting room and he was lying on the couch. He had pulled a crocheted throw over himself, but there was a deep chill in the room. The boiler had been broken for more than a week and there was no money to repair it. The curtains were badly closed so they sagged and pouted, leaving gapes through which a continuous shower of sleet could be seen, and beyond all this came a soft canticle of cursing from the kitchen as Ellisha tried to make their one gas-canister heater work.

He lay not moving, his body pulsing hot then cold. There was a dryness under his tongue, his limbs heavy and aching, as though he were ill. He needed a drink. No. Not wanted, needed.

Somehow, without conscious awareness, the shift had happened. A drink at dinner had become an entire bottle. Then another to relax him and another to help him sleep; to help him through the rejections; to calm his nerves; to stop the shaking. Now he needed one just to get out of bed. *Just a small one. Just to get going.*

The need drew him from the relief map of the throw to an unwelcome encounter with himself in the mirror above the fireplace. He met a stranger: dishevelled, unshaven, mouth melted downwards with disappointment.

By the time he had made it out into the hallway the phone had rung and he could hear Ellisha answering it. Even though she was whispering, the alien pitch of her voice carried through the walls.

'Hi? … No, no. My fault. Things have been … you know … difficult.'

Silence.

'No. Pretty much the same… hardly leaves the house.' Bright false laughter. 'No, in this weather, I wouldn't blame him either. … Worried though. Just lost interest in everything … No. He won't see one. … Today? I didn't— It's just I can't just leave him.'

Peter entered the downstairs bathroom. The showerhead dripped into the bath, an insistent reminder that he should wash. When was the last time he'd taken a bath? But the bathroom was cold and there was no hot water. Later. He would do it later. He could still hear Ellisha. 'I see…Yes, yes. I understand.'

He went back down the hall and into the dining room. As gently as he could he eased open the door of the drinks cabinet. And suddenly, the wasted muscles of his abdomen contracted. The cabinet was empty. An Arctic coldness swept over him that set off a furious trembling throughout his body. 'Ellisha. ELLISHA!'

He heard her say. 'Uh oh. Got to go.' Then the click of the phone. But it wasn't enough. 'Ellisha! Where the hell are you?'

'What is it? What's wrong?' She was standing in the doorway and her eyes slid towards the open cabinet and her face closed.

'Where is it?'

Without answering, she turned and left the room. He followed, yelling in a random senseless way because he couldn't bear how she looked at him now, as though he was some unsavoury stranger that, in other circumstances, she would have crossed the street to avoid.

It was worse than the looks he'd had to endure when the next round of IVF had to be dropped and when the plans for the attic were stopped half way through and the roofers left with the job unfinished and when the letters from the bank became filled with strange legal-ese from which the words *overdue* and *court-order* and *bailiffs* jumped out. And every day his failures became written deeper in the lines on her face and the dark circles under her eyes until looking at Ellisha became more painful than looking in the mirror.

He followed her into the kitchen now and he watched as she reached into the bin and pulled out a bottle of *Woods Old Navy Rum*. Last night it had been almost a third full. Now it was empty. Ellisha banged the empty bottle down on the counter next to a book, the cover of which he noted irrelevantly was of a bloated naked woman with pendulous breasts and no hair. The author was Professor B McBride.

'There. Is this what you lost?' Her voice was filled with fury and helplessness.

'What did you do? What did you DO?'

'I poured it down the sink.' She was yelling now too.

Down the sink. Of course, she had poured it down the sink. But hearing her say the words sent needles through his brain and he raised his fists to his temples. 'Why? Why? Why? Why?'

'What was I supposed to do?' She was beginning to cry. 'You lie in that bed all day. You barely speak to me—'

He shook his head. There was a pounding inside his skull. Her handbag was hanging from a hook and he grabbed it down roughly and poured its contents on to the table.

'Peter. What are you doing?'

'Looking for your purse. You need to go out and get another bottle.'

'I can't.'

He ignored her, fingers mauling the innards of the bag. She said it again more quietly. 'I can't.'

He froze still looking down at the counter. 'What are you talking about?'

'There isn't any cash. I had to make a payment on the electricity or they were going to cut us off and I had to buy food. One of us still wants to eat. And I don't get paid till the end of the week.'

He swung round. 'Ask for an advance.'

She made a noise in her throat somewhere between a growl and a scream. 'It's a university. Not a strip joint. And, in case you haven't noticed, I've been here with you, unable to go out, nursing your sorry ass, mopping up your vomit and begging you not to kill yourself.'

'Don't do me any favours. Get back to your shitty little job if that's what you want.'

'I can't go back to my shitty job. They just cut my hours. To help me out, they said. Not at all that they've been looking for ways to trim the budget for months. So, lucky me, I get to stay at home watching you lying face down in a puddle of your own self-pity day after day and…'

There was more but he didn't hear it. He started walking away and suddenly he was face down on the bed. The room was cold and the sheets needed changing, but darkness was all he wanted. He squeezed his eyes tight shut.

When he opened them again, Ellisha was in the room. She wasn't looking at him, instead pulling items out the dresser and flinging them into a bag. With difficulty, he pushed himself up. 'Where are you going?'

'To stay with a friend for a few days. To think things through.'

'Who?' he asked weakly.

'You don't know him.'

Him?

She zipped the bag shut and stood, framed by the bedroom door, looking down at him.

'You have to choose, Peter.'

He took some small hope from the fact that the bag was not large.

'It's me or the void. You made me choose once.'

Memories crowding inside his head: her limp body, his panic, the almost empty bottle of pills. His pills. Too many nights, his mind racing, unable to sleep.

He looked up at her helplessly, but she shook her head then turned and walked out of the house. The sound of the door slamming a second time was the loneliest sound he had ever heard.

The house, which had seemed so safe, so much the comforting cocoon into which he had willingly crawled, became desolate without Ellisha, a body devoid of its living spark. He paced from room to room, even up to the attic, where the buckets were lined up under the dripping roof. But the walls began to move closer and the ceilings sank, until, feeling like he was suffocating, he hauled some clothes from the wash-basket and, after dressing, dragged himself outside.

He walked without direction or purpose, aware of the dirty sodden banners of sky flapping above him, making no attempt to avoid the slushy puddles that slopped freezing water inside his shoes when he stepped in them. Some small part of himself was aware of feeling cold yet also of feeling nothing at all. Cold, warmth, pain, rage, love, they seemed distant pinpricks that lit the life of another man, a man he had ceased to be.

On the Royal Mile, he became fascinated with his appearance reflected in the glass entrance of the Radisson. Coat flapping open, shirt wrongly buttoned, his unshaven face, the eyes dull and hopeless within their web of lines and shadows. He looked like the tramp, worse than the tramp. He, at least, had shown some dignity.

Tears stung at the back of his eyes. *Come to this … in a year. A lousy year. How?* But an unacknowledged part of himself whispered, *Chancer, blowing promises in people's faces, like sand. Then cutting and running. One step ahead of disaster. Faster and faster. Until—*

He walked on, but inside his head was a darkness that made him see the cracks in the paving stones as thin dark veins spreading across the city, and he looked at them curiously, like a doctor who spots the first corrupting signs of disease in an oblivious patient. It gave him a strange, doom-ridden sense of satisfaction, and he kept going, following the cracks, as though they were leading him somewhere, head down, immersed until something hard hit his shoulder and he recoiled.

'I'm sorry, I—' The habit he had developed of avoiding the eyes of others made him slow to realise that he knew the object of his collision.

Grey hair. Eyes that could cut diamonds.

'Professor McBride?'

'Babs.' She was rubbing her elbow. He started to explain who he was, but she cut him off. 'Yes. Yes. Husband to the Strange Maid. Our very own Stone Man.'

Faint recognition tugged at the back of his mind. 'I've heard Elisha called that before.'

Her eyes narrowed. 'Then whoever said it, spoke wisely.'

'I'm not sure about that. It was an old wino we met in the street.'

Something changed in Babs' face, and remembering her excessive tendencies, he feared he had given offence. 'Look, I'm sorry,' he began, but she cut him off.

'Don't be so quick to judge those who dull the pain with spirits. They're usually poets, or prophets, which is much the same thing. *Ver-*

itas can be found *in vino* if you bother to look. And, sometimes, you have to drink yourself out of your five senses to find your sixth.'

He felt a stab of irritation. 'I guess.' He made a move to pass her. 'Sorry, I'm in a bit of a hurry.'

'Yes, I can see that.' Her eyes were crawling over him, cataloguing the stains on his shirt, the five-day stubble. After a moment she asked, 'What is it you do?'

'Do?'

'Your profession. Your occupation. Your *raison d'etre*.'

It was a goad, he knew. Coldly he said, 'I'm between jobs right now.'

'But you did something before.'

'I gave people dreams.'

She stared at him shrewdly. 'Madman or ad-man?'

'Ad-man.'

He expected some caustic remark, but her eyes narrowed, pondering his response. 'Interesting. That needs a good deal of feel for the subconscious. At the end of the nineteenth century, you would probably have been one of the great psychoanalysts.'

Not knowing how to answer this he made noises about having to get going. But she said suddenly, 'Come with me.'

'Where?'

'I'm going to an AA meeting.'

He bristled. 'I'm not an alcoholic.'

'No?' She eyed him. 'Well, I am. So you can accompany me.'

The meeting was held in a bleak little church dedicated to Saint Brigid. The sheer grubbiness of the place—bleak fluorescent lighting, plastic folding chairs, A4 posters announcing the meeting times of the Ladies' Guild or the Boys Brigade or a collection fund for a departing church warden—made Peter's last shreds of dignity rear up in protest.

'I really can't—'

To his surprise, Babs nodded. 'Of course.' Then she added venomously, 'Ellisha can do better.'

He paused. 'Look, I'm not an alcoholic.'

'No-one ever is.'

The room had that peculiar quality of being cold yet stuffy. He hunkered down and tried not to be noticed. First came the welcome, followed by a grey-looking man with hunched shoulders and a drooping moustache had the floor. His story was predictable: difficult childhood, broken relationships, isolation, degradation, disintegration. When everyone clapped at the end, Peter joined in.

The chairperson called for another volunteer, and he stiffened, afraid Babs would try to push him forward. But Babs had her eyes closed, a personal incantation against her own demons he supposed. His gaze wandered. Two rows down a woman in a knitted cardigan was crying softly to herself.

At the break Peter stood in line, helping himself from one of the leaning towers of Styrofoam cups and pouring execrable liquid from a dented urn marked *coffee*. Babs appeared beside him and offered him a plate of biscuits.

'You should have one,' she said. 'They take away the taste of the coffee.'

He took a bite then said, 'What do I have to do to take away the taste of the biscuit?'

Just then a man in a tweed jacket that had seen better days came up to speak to Babs. He was clearly her sponsor and, not wanting to intrude, Peter wandered a little distance to a table covered in books and pamphlets. They did not appeal to him, but he flicked idly through the titles: *Increased spirituality through the twelve steps/A Higher Power/ Seeking and doing HIS will/Transcending the Lower Self.* He opened a book at random and read:

It becomes obvious that doubters, who argue that they feel nothing spiritual, and use the AA group as a substitute for a Higher Power, will soon transcend and learn to call God by name...

A tap on his shoulder. Babs was back. 'It's starting up again.'

'Right ... yes.' Peter blinked. He could see the woman in the pink cardigan. She was smiling now and vigorously shaking the hand of one of the speakers. She looked renewed, as though she had experienced a religious revelation. Somewhere at the back of his mind, a thought began to smoulder. Something trying to come together. What was it? He could feel the shape of it worrying at the edges of his brain. Back in his seat, he gave Babs a sidelong glance. She was staring ahead with the fixed expression people adopt when they want to pretend they don't know they are being watched. *She wants me here. Wants me to witness this. Why?*

He was so preoccupied with these thoughts that it came as a surprise when the meeting ended and Babs got to her feet. 'Thank God that's over.' She was brushing the biscuit crumbs from her skirt. 'Time for a drink.'

'But?'

'Got to come. My talisman against the senate. Can't throw the old girl out on her ear if she can show she's trying. *Poenitentiam agite* and all that.'

Instinct formed a protest in his throat, but an immense weariness drew his shoulders up then dropped them in a shrug. 'Sure. Why not?'

They walked through the dimming streets, footsteps echoing on the cobblestones. Babs seemed to be lost in thought, but suddenly she asked, 'So, what did you make of it all?'

'The meeting? Well, it was ... interesting.'

'Nonsense. It was dull as ditch-water and you know it. But it reminded you of something.'

'It felt— I don't know—religious, I suppose.'

'Your parents were devout types.'

He glanced at her in surprise.

'Don't look so shocked. The children of believers always carry the mark.'

He made a gesture of defeat. 'My father was the local minister.'

'Not Edinburgh. Not here.'

'In Findbrae.'

'Never heard of it.'

'Go to Aviemore.'

'Yes?'

'Then keep going.'

'Ah.'

He waited for her to make further geographical enquiries, but she stopped and leaned against a lamppost.

'Is something wrong?'

'We're here.' She pointed at a small public garden surrounded by railings.'

'I thought we were going to a bar.'

'Need a smoke. Can't do it indoors anymore. Fine if we pollute Mother Nature though. Shall we go in?'

It was fractional, but she spotted his hesitation. 'Unless you're afraid.'

'Of course not.'

She eyed him shrewdly. 'No? I would be.' Her fingers wrapped around the latch on the wrought-iron gate. 'I could be leading you anywhere, Tir na nOg, Orbis Alia, the Wood Beyond the World.'

He turned his collar up and took a step towards her. 'I'll take my chances.'

They entered a little universe of dying greenery. Near the centre was a stone bench where they sat down, Peter hunching inside his coat and Babs rummaging in the pockets of her voluminous jacket.

'What did he teach you?'

'I'm sorry?'

'You said your father was a minister. What did he teach you?'

'To trust in God.'

'That was foolish.'

'You don't believe in God?'

'I don't believe in trusting Him.'

He watched as Babs pulled out a silver flask from inside her coat and offered it to him. 'Drink?'

'Thanks.' He took a sip, taking his time over it. A single malt, a good one. The hint of warm aromas rising from the neck made his bones ache.

Babs was looking at a bit of moon sticking through the tops of the trees. 'So, Stone Man, what are you after?'

'Sorry?'

'You want something from me. That's why you sought me out.'

He laughed uncertainly. 'We bumped into each other by accident.'

'There are no accidents. Ask Freud if you don't believe me.' She was lighting a cigarillo, puffing gently on the end to bring it to life. Between puffs, she added, 'Come on. Spit it out. The hours are numbered.

He stretched his legs, feeling the stiffness in the joints, then said brokenly, 'Ellisha's left me.' He was so shocked by this confession that it momentarily silenced him. Babs let a mouthful of smoke slowly escape between her teeth. 'Loss can be an epiphany as much as gain, Stone Man. You can't rise from the flames unless you've first been consumed.'

He nodded, and something in the strange stillness of the garden gave him the courage to say, 'I need something to get her back.'

'What might that be?'

'I need... a story.'

'Ah.' Babs took back the flask and drank thoughtfully. 'Fallen foul of the God of men, have we?'

'Doesn't do it for me. Never has. I was a grave disappointment to my father. He couldn't understand that I didn't need his stories, that I was in love with a story of my own. The story of who I was going to be.' He tried to sound casual, but his legs were beginning to shake. 'It sounds stupid to say it aloud.'

'Not in the least. You felt you had a destiny. And that, as old Larkin would tell you, never can be obsolete.'

'But Ellisha was part of that destiny. When I met her, it was as if she saw through me, that she was able to read the story inside me, and it excited her.' He gave a rueful smile. 'A story is nothing without a reader to love it, right?'

'So now you want a woman to save you?'

He looked into Babs' stygian eyes then shrugged. 'Yes. If that's what it takes. I don't know what's happened to me these last months. I've fallen so far from the kind of man I want to be that maybe I need a woman to save me.'

Babs gave a snort. 'Careful, Stone-man, the goddess has a nasty side. We like to remember her lamenting over her dead lover. Aphrodite mourning Adonis. Isis weeping tears of blood for Osiris.

'But remember, she may be the queen of flowing sorrows according to *Langhorne*, but she has always known that the king's blood will be sacrificed in her honour. All the legends tell us that the king, be he Dionysus, Jesus, Attis or old John Barleycorn, must die for the queen of heaven. And there are just as many myths that suggest she is complicit in his death. Still certain you want to know?'

Dumbly he nodded. 'If you'll tell me.'

She laughed unpleasantly. 'Not so fast, Stone Man. Do you think, because our livers are pickled, we share a bond? Romulus and Remus suckling on the teat of a bottle of Wolf Blas, is that it? My secret stays with me. Even when they cast me out, back into the light, a reluctant Proserpina. *Semper in tenebris.* Eurydice with her hands over her ears.'

He rose to his feet. 'I'm sorry, I should get going.'

'Now, now. Don't be so sensitive.' She lit another cigarillo, took a drag then blew out a deft smoke ring. For a moment, it hung between them in the stale air, like the last vestiges of an angel then vanished into the shadows. 'So passes the glory of the world.' She heaved a sigh and leaned back. 'What did you see?'

'Sorry?'

'When you looked over the edge.'

The gathering night was beginning to make shadows of their faces, but he knew he was revealed. *Does she know? Or is she guessing?* 'Nothing. I saw nothing.'

'And what did that Nothing say to you?'

'I really don't—'

'Don't play coy with me, Stone Man. You've looked into the Void and think you've seen something. If you hadn't, you'd be a heap of broken bones with that useless sponge inside your skull dribbling out of your ears.' She reached over and rapped her knuckles against his skull. 'Not that it's as precious as you imagine. Not the alpha and omega of existence, you know, despite the current trends to reduce us all to accumulations of curiously arranged atoms. Do you know that the brain was the only part of the body Egyptian embalmers were in the habit of throwing away? No fools our gypsy brethren. They knew the brain is a poor receptacle for the possibility of a soul.'

'I really don't know what you think I've seen.'

'No?' She looked at him sharply. 'Have it your own way.' Another prodigious sigh, which ended in a paroxysm of coughing. She shook off his clumsy attempts at help, but he heard her mutter, 'Perhaps it is too much. Too much for one person to carry.' She looked back up at the moon, and he wasn't quite sure whether she was addressing him or some lunar deity of her strange imagination. 'I'll give you something. I'll give you the beginning. You'll have to work out the rest for yourself.'

He barely trusted himself to nod.

'Do you believe in witches?'

Caught by surprise. Shaking his head before he had time to think. 'No.'

'You should. Because the story I'm going to tell you is true. It describes what happened when a king interviewed a witch here at the tolbooth in Edinburgh.'

He sat back down, shifting his weight slightly to find the patch he had warmed with his buttocks.

'Sitting comfortably?'

'No. Not—'

She cut him off. 'Good. Because this is not a comfortable story.'

Part II

THE GARDEN OF EARTHLY DELIGHTS

WESTERN SCHOLARSHIP BECAME AWARE OF The Great Goddess as early as the 19th century (cf. Eduard Gerhard and J.J. Bachofen). And the later work of Sir Arthur Evans at Knossos served to confirm that the primal creator in mankind's journey is in fact a creatrix.

But the Goddess of Beginnings is a strange one. She has no claim to invulnerability in the manner of Abraham's aloof deity. Think of endlessly weeping Eleos or of Diomedes wounding Aphrodite in battle or even of Egyptian Sekhmet clutching her pounding head, having foolishly allowed herself to be tricked into drinking dyed beer when she wanted blood. The Goddess knows she is not the alpha and omega of the universal narrative, but merely its prologue. She is a Mother watching her children grow to maturity, waiting for them to act.

Only much later, in the face of increasingly patriarchal systems, was she forced to humble herself. Consider the origins of Bharat Yoni (Great Clitoris) who was downgraded to the role of mere wife or of proto-Teutonic Nerthus' forced gender reassignment into the masculine Niord. The Abrahamic religions have spent millennia attempting to eradicate the Great Goddess from conscious memory. But she is far from gone, far from for-gotten…

Extract from McBride B., 2012,

New perspectives on the role of the Great Goddess,

British Journal of Religious Anthropology, 2012, 0.098, Q4

CHAPTER 9

IN HIS OWN EYES, HE was, without doubt, a fair monarch. Iacobus Rex, he would be the sixth James to rule Scotland and first to take the English throne. His lineage, typical of the day, was both proud and bloody. The body of his murdered father was not far away, in Holyrood. His mother lay, *sans tête,* in Westminster Abbey. But he did not think on this much. He did not mourn for his mother, having known her but little as a child, and having been influenced mainly by the counsel of men to consider her a dangerous and sentimental fool.

By his own reckoning James himself was no fool. What he lacked in physical prowess (and he knew himself lacking despite the buzzing cloud of courtly flattery that followed him everywhere) he made up for in knowledge. He was widely read, and had found the praise (and in this he was certain of its authenticity) of his tutors easy to obtain. By the age of thirteen he had read Lucretius and felt himself an authority on Virgil's Aeneid.

And he was proud of his nickname (begun by himself) as the Scots Solomon, unaware that across the water Henry IV of France endorsed this title, saying mockingly of James that he could certainly claim to be a son of David, by which all understood him to mean David Rizzio, the little Italian secretary to whom his mother had been so devoted.

But, as James climbed the stinking steps of the tollbooth, he thought only of himself as wise and fair. Wise enough to recognise witchcraft in the near sinking of his ship as he returned with his bride from Denmark. And fair in that he had taken the extraordinary step of insisting on interviewing one of the witches himself. Not for him the way of Spain, with their black-cowled Inquisition, nor of Germany, where it was rumoured that the torturers fed their victims henbane-laced potions to make them rave and froth, and confess to whatever devilries were whispered in their ears. James was a scholar, a seeker of truth in the most profound sense, and he would hear the evidence with his own ears.

The authorities were afraid. *Dinna gang there, Yer Grace. She's gleg-gabbit and no tae be trusted. She'll fill yer grace's lugs wi the De'il's cant. And wha here has the courage tae save yer grace agin sic saulless-ness?*

But James would not be deterred. He had nearly lost his life in the black waters of the North Sea, and if this was the work of cunning folk, he must know it for himself. But, for all that he insisted on going in alone, snapping at his guard to wait outside at the ready, his mouth was dry and loins were well *girdit* before he found the courage to open the door to the Iron Room.

What had he expected? A radiant darkness? The Devil's leering face suspended in thin air? Instead, he was assailed by the surpassing foulness of the atmosphere, which still pervaded the place despite the clumsy attempts to clean up in respect of his arrival. James lifted a silver pomander infused with nutmeg and deer musk to his nose to little effect while his eyes, timorous as a woman's, always seeming to be in the act of flitting away from something, rolled uneasily towards the room's sole occupant.

Her face was in shadow, her limbs drawn awkwardly back by iron chains to heavy metal bars in a manner that clearly prevented either movement or rest. Fleetingly he wondered if it was true that cold iron was a discomfort to the fey, that it prevented them transforming themselves into winged creatures, such as owls or bats, and taking flight.

In truth she did not look dangerous, her bald head hanging down, her modesty barely concealed through a stained shift of coarse weave. But looks were, of course, deceptive. He must remember her reputation. She had cured a man of elf-shot and had flown over North Berwick in a ship, shaped like a chimney, to meet with Auld Nick, and had stayed the night drinking wine with him. This was no ordinary woman.

He decided to make a feinting attack and began, 'Sae, Mistress, I have heard whit you and yer sisters would claim, and I am here this day tae call you all extreme lyars.'

Her head remained bowed, and James might have believed that she was insensible, except for a few inchoate groans, more like tremors escaping from some abysmal region below the earth than speech. But it came upon him slowly that he was being addressed. Against his own will he took a small step forward. 'Dae ye hearken me, Mistress Falsehood? Ye claim ye have had commune wi the De'il and monie magicks aside, but I believe no a word of it.'

Slowly—so slowly in fact that James would later believe that he had been trapped in a kind of *fey* time, where millennia may pass in the same manner that minutes pass by in the world of men—she lifted her head and brought her gaze up to meet his. It was hard to tell her age. Certainly no maid. But hag? The ravages of torture had bent and twisted her, robbed her of her hair, but her face, wiped clean of blood, had a certain fineness of lineament, a kind of vulnerable dignity, which James had heard manifested itself only in the very noblest countenances after extreme suffering. Such was said of William Wallace or the martyr Patrick Hamilton. It was too dark to see the colour of her eyes, but he fancied that they were a clear luminous green, like those of a mewing malkin.

'Ye heard me?' he said hoarsely

A soft moan. 'Wa-ter.'

James felt the hairs stand up on the back of his neck. He needed to go closer, and it was true that his doublet and breeches were well-stuffed against attack by stiletto, but what protection had he against enchantment? He swallowed hard then, with faltering steps, approached. There was a pitcher, left purposely in the prisoner's eyeline, and he lifted it and held it to her lips. She drank clumsily, choking and gasping, the water rattling in her chest, as though her torturers had seen fit to fill the cavity of her body with pebbles.

When it was done, she shook the drops from her lips and her gaze was clearer this time when she met James' eyes.

'I ... am no a leear.'

'I am telt that, unlike yer sisters, ye would confess tae naught.'

'I ... am no a leear. I have answered anely the truth.'

'That will, ah think, be my privilege tae find oot. But I am further telt that when you performed your cures, you muttered unco strange prayers, aften in leeds that the folks aboot ye didna ken.' He leaned a little closer. And, without knowing what led him to do so he said, *Domino non invocaverunt.* Why he should suspect that she would understand Latin he could not say. And, indeed, she was a long time in answering. She seemed to be experiencing some internal struggle, and more to herself than in reply, she murmured, *I anely speak the truth.* But then she seemed to come to a decision and answered him fluently in the Latin tongue, albeit oddly accented.

'Your Grace, to speak truly is ... my oath.'

'Yet you have chosen to lie to your inquisitors.'

Again, a long silence, then, 'I answered their questions ... truly.'

It was James' turn to be thoughtful. He must be careful not to allow himself to be sucked into deceitful ways. Yet, if he was to believe the premise that her answers were true then either she was innocent (his gorge rose against such a conclusion) or was it not ... could it not be that her interrogators had been asking the wrong kinds of questions? His uneasy eyes hardened in their expression then narrowed. 'I will ask you again: is it to Our Lord that you address yourself when you pray?'

A low rasp, painfully exhaled. James was not moved.

'Speak up. You answered well enough when you sought to perplex me.'

He watched as she shifted her head from side to side, as though trying to clear an obstruction from her throat. She coughed and looked plaintively towards the pitcher, but he made no move, and finally something seemed to give, and she answered weakly, but with perfect clarity, 'No. … Not to your Lord.'

The colour drained from James' face, and his Latin forgotten, he cried, 'It *is* the De'il then.'

'It is whit men would ca' the De'il.'

He tried to remember his scepticism. 'Ye wid hae me believe that, tae your mind, it is no the De'il that ye conjure but something else?'

Her head was sinking. 'Be-lievvvvvvvvve.'

James stared. He regretted her loss of hair, moved as he was to haul her head up by it. And the thought of touching her chin being repulsive to him, he cast about before hastily filling the pitcher and threw water in her face.

She came up spluttering and choking, like a hag pulled from the dooking stool. Her nobility was altogether gone, and her eyes looked wide and terrified. A trembling took hold of her, and for a moment he was afraid she had lost her wits and he would gain nothing more out of the encounter. Yet, if she banged her fists against the doors of insanity, they held tight against the onslaught, and slowly reason began to steady her features. He returned to his Latin.

'I stand here before you, God's anointed, and before either of us leave this foul dungeon, I will know what you know.'

Her eyes swivelled towards the door, and briefly there was such longing in them that he was certain that she would try to strike a bargain. Instead,

'Go! Go now. I say this as a friend to Your Grace, and one who never wished him ill. A wise man would choose to run, while he is still clad in the armour of his ignorance.'

Anger doused him, as though the contents of the pitcher had been thrown in his face. He might have put his hands around her neck then and saved the cost of a garrotting, but he mastered himself. Was it not said that, between the Crucifixion and the Resurrection, Christ himself had spent three days in Hell? Surely he, James, could match that act in as many hours.

He leaned as close to the foul creature's ear as he dared, and it was as well, because rage had made him hoarse. 'As the servant of the Lord, I command that you tell me all you know of the demon to whom your prayers and supplications are addressed.'

She had taken an oath to answer truly, and so she answered James with the truth. And while she did so, Death stood in the doorway in the shape of an owl, and there would be no escape but through him, and because of this she took her time and talked, James listening attentively as a lover.

And so they were, for several hours two souls in the stygian darkness, the hunched, *shilpit* king with the wise eyes and the broken twisted woman, who had kept her secrets far too long.

The terrible knocking from inside the cell awoke the guards from their dwam and set them springing back from the rattling frame, their dirks at the ready.

'Wha gangs there?'

'Let me oot! Let me oot!'

The guards exchanged glances, but did not move. It was the King's voice, but so high and affrighted that it was scarce recognisable, and besides the door was not locked. The same thought evidently struck the owner of the voice for there was a rattling and scraping and the door swung wide on its hinges, revealing the person of the King.

Through he came, wild-eyed, his body trembling from head to foot, and so apparently afflicted by his experience that the younger of the guards forgot protocol and cried, 'Whit is it that ails Yer Grace?'

But James ignored him. He grabbed the elder guard by the shirt collar and spat his command in the man's face. 'Burn her! Burn HER!'

CHAPTER 10

PETER WAS SITTING ON THE floor of the living room when he heard the key in the lock. Pausing in what he was doing, he waited. The footsteps walked towards the bedroom, hesitated then came back towards the living room. From the floor he watched as the door was slowly opened.

'Ellie?' The sight of her, standing in the doorframe, made his heart turn over. It had been more than a week since she had left, and he saw at once that she had lost weight and there was a pinched look about her face, the kind people get when they have been weeping steadily for days. 'Ellisha.' He was afraid to get up in case he frightened her away. She stiffened and looked back the way she had come.

'Oh, Peter.' Her hand was to her mouth, and he was suddenly painfully aware that he was unwashed and bearded, still in his dressing-gown, a mad desert prophet cross-legged in a wilderness of books and papers. He began scrambling to his feet, knocking over a carefully arranged stack of volumes he had dragged all the way back from the library.

Ellisha had taken a step back, and he held up one hand, trying to reassure her, while he made a vain attempt with the other to catch a fluttering cascade of papers falling from the counter. 'It's okay. I'm okay. This isn't—' He had been about to say, *This isn't what it looks like.* But it was exactly what it looked like, chaos. He tried again. 'I'm sober. I haven't touched a drop since you left.'

He took a step towards her and she stiffened, drawing herself in as though frightened. It broke his heart, but he was so eager to explain he couldn't stop himself. 'Ellisha, please. I love you. I hit rock bottom. I let you down. But I'm trying, trying to be a better man. I went to a meeting. An AA meeting with Babs McBride.'

She looked incredulous. 'Professor McBride goes to AA?'

'Only for the biscuits. But the idea started when I was at AA. I heard things that got me thinking. And I saw the power of belief in an entirely new context. I think she took me there on purpose. There were all these leaflets talking about spirituality. And a woman in a pink cardigan, who looked as though she had been reborn. Then we talked in the Wood Beyond the World.'

'The wood— What?'

'It's not important. What is important is that I've woken up. Before—I felt dead inside. But now I'm brimming with all these new thoughts. I've found something.' He saw her face close and hurried on. 'Not just a new idea. It's something I can believe in. Like there's a new voice inside my head.' He scrabbled about on top, then eventually under the coffee table and began pulling out leaflets. 'See, *Twelve steps to spiritual awakening*. Or *The spiritual thirst for wholeness*. And here's another.' He held it out. '*Life with a higher purpose*.'

She stared at the leaflets for a moment then looked back at him with a worried frown. 'Peter. Do you think God is talking to you?'

He laughed. 'No. Not God. Not exactly.' How to make her understand? 'All my life I've been looking for something.' Hunkering down on his knees before her, spreading out the fliers. 'Over and over, trying to reinvent myself. The successful businessman. The man who sold dreams. Always thinking I could lose myself in a bigger firm, a better client, a fancier watch, a more exotic holiday. But it didn't work. It was all hollow. Empty words provoking nothing but empty thoughts. I was running my life on an equation with a sum total of zero.'

A flicker in her eyes made him add quickly, 'Not you, of course. You are my reason to keep going. To find a way out of this—this mess I've got us into.' He reached his hands out then let them fall limply to his lap when she didn't respond. 'Ellie?' His heart was a struck note. He was so afraid of chasing her away he could not go on. She stood looking down at her shoes, her eyes widening from time to time with the swell of her thoughts, before saying, 'I lost my job today.'

'Ellisha, I'm sorry. What happened? I mean how—'

She let out a long weary sigh and her body slumped. 'I've been working as a waitress at a coffee shop since the university cut my hours to practically zero. I was so grateful to get that job. It wasn't easy. Unfortunately, the manager, Colin, wanted me to show him how grateful I was after hours, alone in his office.'

'I'll kill him.' Peter was on his feet. And, forgetting he was in nothing but his bathrobe, headed for the door until Ellisha's panicked voice called him back. 'Peter, no. Please don't make a fuss.'

He didn't stop until he felt her hand on his shoulder. 'The guy is seven feet tall in his socks. The only person getting killed if you go around there is you.'

He froze. Be rational. Show her you've changed. Turning slowly. 'There must be something we can do. He can't just throw you out on the street. These aren't Victorian times. There are laws.'

'It's my word against his. Do you think he's going to say he sacked me because I won't let him put his hand up my skirt or because I'm a lousy waitress?'

'You're a great waitress.'

'Is that supposed to make me feel better?' But she smiled a little and he felt his heart bursting. To prevent himself from succumbing to the urge to take her into his arms, he said, 'Stay. Please. I'm going to change things. I'm going to fix all of this. I promise.' She winced a little at this last, and he hurried on. 'All my life I've been looking for the one big idea. I truly, honestly believe I might have found it. I'm not there yet. I need to read a great deal. But I'm on to something. And maybe—' he tried to appeal to her sense of otherworldliness '—maybe all that's been happening is some kind of sign.'

She looked at him warily.

'You lost your job today. I found something to believe in. Maybe the universe is telling us that we're meant to be together in this.'

'Did the universe tell you how we're going to eat?'

'We'll work it out.'

She looked back, towards the door, and his spirits plummeted. He was afraid to breathe. *Her scent. So near. Touch. With my fingertips. No, don't. Frighten her away. She doesn't believe me. Why should she? Another half-baked dream. Ach, I'm no good. It won't work. Tell her to forget it. Forget me. Oh, for a drink, a drink, a drink.*

A rustling noise made him blink. Ellisha had shrugged off her coat and stood before him oddly vulnerable, almost a nakedness about her that made him fierce with tenderness. He didn't trust himself to speak.

'So, tell me about this idea.'

They moved through to the kitchen, where Ellisha insisted on cooking something for him. 'When did you eat last?'

'I think... I don't... I think...'

'That's what I thought.'

There wasn't much in the cupboards, but Ellisha managed to rustle up a strange affair with an egg and some pasta and a little leftover parmesan. He leaned against the doorway, partly because he was afraid of extinguishing the fragile truce between them, and partly because he hadn't washed in days and smelt worse than the parmesan. But gradually he crept closer, lured by the aroma of cooked food.

Over the years he had become a man for whom eating was an afterthought. His manic desire to get ahead so often blotting out all other desires. But now the smell of good food filled him with a warm sense of calm, a feeling of healing.

The kitchen was such a mess that they returned to the living room. Ellisha made a half-hearted attempt at clearing up while he sat on the sofa, trying, between mouthfuls, to explain his idea.

'I don't believe in God.'

'No kidding.' She picked up a greyish item of clothing and held it gingerly between thumb and forefinger. 'What is this?'

'Underpants. Never mind that. Do you believe in Him?'

She dropped the pants back on the floor. 'I did.'

'Not now?'

'I don't know. I've told you before, I don't believe in nothing.' Her voice grew smaller. 'It's more like… somehow, I lost Him.'

'Lost God?' He could barely contain his excitement.

'Yes.'

'What if I told you that there's a third way?'

'Third way?'

'A way between God and the Void. Don't you remember? You talked about Babs having found a third way. A way to escape the Void.'

'The Void? What do you mean?'

Pausing, fork hovering before his parted lips, the food suddenly tasteless. *This isn't going to be easy. Have to dig deeper. Time to look in the mirror. Show her own reflection staring back.* 'You know what I mean about the Void.'

Ellisha was bent over, picking up dirty dishes. She froze for a second then shot him a hurt, accusatory stare over her shoulder. 'We don't talk about that.'

'No, we don't talk about it.' Sitting by the hospital bed. Time suspended. Little lights blinking unfathomable code from strange machines. His eyes closing with exhaustion then snapping open again. Mother of all hangovers and he hadn't had a drop to drink. Laughter from the nursing station, whirr of trolley wheels. Echoes and sighs. The curtain swishing open, and the weary face of a medic. *Ellisha? Can you hear me? Ellisha?*

Fingers fluttering at the oxygen mask, charcoal stains around her mouth. *Ellie, it's okay. I'm here. Don't try to talk. You've been lucky. Found you in time. I know. The baby's gone. But we can try again. We've all the time in the world. Everything's going to be all right. I promise. I promise.*

Ellisha had bent closer into the shadows, her arms wrapped around herself as if in pain. But, as soon as he stopped speaking, she started picking dirty plates from the floor. She banged them together, a shamanist ritual against evil. He watched nervously. Too much, too soon. Should have waited. What now? Stay silent or keep pushing? Ellisha banged the plates down on the coffee table. He swallowed.

'I've seen the Void too, Ellie, the nothingness of everything.'

He saw her back stiffen, fingers tracing the moon's rim along one of the plates.

'What do you mean?'

'I mean—' He took a deep breath. This was harder to say than he had imagined. 'I tried to kill myself. Just before you found out about everything. Up on Salisbury crag. It was dark. I stood, looking out at nothing.' The memory of the wind started to blow in his ears and he shivered a little. 'I was going to do it.' A small unconscious gesture from Ellisha struck him in the heart. 'I'm sorry. I was being selfish. I thought—if I thought anything—that you would be better off without me.'

Ellisha was still looking down at the plate. 'What changed your mind?'

'I slipped and that brought me to my senses. But it isn't that simple. What I saw there—'

'Nothingness?'

'The Void. It changed me.' He took a risk. 'And I know it changed you.'

'And this made you decide that there was no God?'

'In a way. There was nothing in the nothingness, and yet there was something. I don't know how to explain it. I think it's all part of a story. I think if I had that story, there isn't anything I couldn't do.'

'Let me get this straight. You don't have this story?'

'No.'

'And you don't know what it's about?'

'I think I know some of it. It's to do with witches and God … or not exactly God, but extremely old beliefs.'

'I thought you said you didn't believe in God.'

'I don't. But I can sense there's something big in what Babs is saying. She's stared into the Void too. And it made her go looking. You said it yourself. She's found something.'

'But, even if you could get it, how is a story going to change anything?'

He stopped pacing and whirled around. 'The Jews conquered Israel with a story about one god above all others. Look what the Christians have done with the idea that a dead god can rise again. Communism. The Cold War. There's no such thing as 'just' a story. There are only good stories and better ones. Don't you see, Ellie, some stories change what washing powders housewives buy and some stories change the world.'

'And this is the story that will save you?'

Joyful, he gave a high pure laugh. 'This is the story that will save everyone.'

She was looking at him so strangely that the laughter died in his throat. There was an appalled silence in which a clock started to tick, and the radiator under the window groaned and settled itself. His mind screamed, *A joke. Tell her it was all just a joke. Go out tomorrow. Get a job. Any job. No more chasing rainbows. Forget all that. Live simply. An ordinary life. You and me. Our love. All I need.*

His lips parted, but she got there first.

'You asshole.'

There were tears in his eyes. 'Tease.'

She nudged a tower of books with a toe. 'So how do we start?'

CHAPTER 11

HE AWOKE THE NEXT MORNING in a state of panic. Ellisha's returning, a dream? Not the first time he had felt her weight on the mattress, warm breath in his ear, only to awaken alone and emptier than he had known was possible. But the daylight wasn't fickle. His fingers found her still furled in sleep inside the cornucopia of duvet she had twisted about herself during the night. He reached out to touch her shoulder, but hesitated to disturb such deep tranquillity, hand hovering before he curled his fingers and withdrew. He felt reborn. However, a cold hand of premonition squeezed his heart, and he thought, I must take care of her. Whatever happens I must always make sure no harm comes to her.

He was sneaking about the kitchen, wondering what he could surprise her with for breakfast, when he was interrupted by a crunch. Ellisha was in the doorway, her nakedness hidden by a moth-eaten piano shawl. She was eating an apple, wine-red, an apple out of a fairy tale, white bitten flesh turned towards him.

'What you making?'

'Pancakes.'

Her brow crinkled. 'What with?'

'Eggs.' He had found an egg that wasn't too out of date at the back of the fridge.'

'And?'

'And …' He was rummaging around in a cupboard. 'And flour.' He pulled a pack out and laid it triumphantly on the counter.

'That's cauliflower rice.'

'It is?' He read the packet disconsolately. 'When did we ever eat cauliflower rice?'

'Never. That's probably why it's still in the cupboard.' She took another bite of the apple.

'Where did you get that?'

'It was in my bag.'

'Is there another one?'

'No.'

He tried to hide his disappointment. It had been so long since he felt hungry that the return of his appetite was a sharp new pain. 'No?'

'Just a muffin, seven chocolate biscuits and a breath mint.' She looked at him defiantly. 'I may have been fired, but I wasn't going empty-handed.'

He looked at her, agog. 'I think I might want to marry you.'

'Too late. I'm taken.' She turned back the way she had come. Over her shoulder she called, 'Get ready. You can eat on the way.'

He felt a stab of surprise. 'You want to go now?'

'Sure. Why not?'

Why not indeed? His awakening into the grey light of day had made last night into a dream, a story he had made up to please her and, in his heart of hearts, hadn't really expected to be believed.

She was looking at him, frowning. 'Don't you want to come?'

'No. I do. I want to.'

'Let's get going then.' She threw the apple at him hitting him in the chest.

'Ow. What was that for?'

'We're about to go seeking forbidden knowledge. Kinda traditional, isn't it?'

They walked along South Bridge, turning on to South College Street, full of high spirits until Ellisha came to a sudden stop.

'It's gone.'

'What?' Looking about, he could see nothing different. But she was pointing a little further on, to where the road became a paved walkway.

'There. It was just there.'

He followed her to the edge of the pavement, where there were several cracked slabs surrounding a tree stump. Ellisha was staring down in dismay. 'Don't you remember? That beautiful old hawthorn that was here. They've cut it down.'

'Maybe it was dangerous.'

She threw him a look of contempt.

'They might plant a new one.'

'No, they won't. It was just an old tree to them.'

He took her hands. They were warm despite the chill. 'Did it mean so much to you?'

'Yes. No. I don't know how to explain it. When I see trees cut down, it actually physically hurts me.' She placed her hands on her abdomen. 'It's like some of the beauty of the world got taken away. Something more than beauty. I—I can't explain it.'

He bent down and kissed her forehead.

'You think I'm mad.'

'I think you're beautiful.'

She made a face and pulled away. 'It isn't mad, you know. They always say that man first learned to worship God in caves. But I don't believe it. I think the first place mankind felt "otherness" was in forests. I mean, think about it, every temple was built with great soaring pillars. And what are pillars but stone trees?'

'Frankly, I think the first place man found God was when the first woman let him touch these.' He made a playful grab at her breasts and she ducked away, laughing.

'If that were the case temples would look like igloos.'

'The Inuit are a highly spiritual people.'

They were still laughing when they reached Teviot Place. But something of the enormity of what they were attempting dawned on them as they crossed the quadrangle and the laughter died. Peter felt his heart begin to pound and Ellisha asked uneasily, 'What do you think she'll say?'

'She'll say *no*.'

'Then why—'

'She'll say, no, to begin with.'

'What makes you think she'll change her mind?'

'You.'

Ellisha stopped. 'Me? Why me?'

He reached out and tweaked a curl of her hair at her temple. 'I don't know. She's interested in you.'

'Did she say something?'

'Maybe.'

'What? Tell me!'

'No, I don't want to spoil the mystery.' He started walking.

'Jerk!'

'Jezebel.'

The descent to Babs' office was colder and darker than he remembered. But this time hope lit the way. The door reared up sooner than he was expecting, and he hesitated, almost shyly, before it. 'Do you want to do the honours?'

Ellisha's eyebrows rose. 'Only if you tell me what Babs said.'

'That's blackmail.'

'Then you knock.'

'Fine.'

But, as he lifted his fist, the door opened a crack. A young woman stood looking at them. She had rimless albino eyes and the sloppy dress of someone who wants to be taken seriously.

Peter smiled broadly. 'Hi.'

She looked at him uncertainly. 'Hi.'

'We're here to see Dr McBride.'

Something shifted in the girl's face. 'That's not possible.'

'Really?' He said it in a tone that suggested he was expected. 'And you are?'

'Kirsten. I'm one of Professor Calvert's PhD students.'

'Ah yes. He mentioned you to me.'

'He did?' She flushed.

'Really great work.' He tried to look past her. 'Is Dr McBride in?'

Ellisha leaned forwards. 'Is she lecturing? We can come back later.'

A glance from one face to another. 'You don't know?'

'Know? Know what?' But he did—he knew—even before she said it. And, while his brain was processing what his ears were mechanically recording, his mouth repeated, 'Dead.'

'When?' Ellisha asked.

'Last week.' Kirsten's eyes grew astonished with memory. 'I found her. Lying face down on the floor.'

Peter stiffened and avoided Ellisha's eye, but he knew they were both thinking the same thing. The drink. He felt he should say something, but Kirsten had turned confessional. 'I mean, I'm not even one of Dr McBride's students. But Professor Calvert asked me to remind her that there was going to be a bit of disruption this week.' She made a vague gesture at the ceiling. 'We're having a new fire safety system wired in today and Dr McBride hadn't taken the news too well. We all heard her yelling that fire was a gift from the gods and accusing Professor Calvert of trying to tear out her liver.' She pressed the back of her hand to her lips in an unsuccessful attempt to hide a smile. 'He came right back at her though. Told her she was doing a fine job on her own without his help. But I don't think he wanted another confrontation so that's why he sent me in to remind her.'

'And she was dead when you found her?'

'Oh? No.' Kirsten looked startled. 'Not when I found her. She was lying face down next to her desk. I wasn't sure if she'd had a fall or just collapsed there. Professor Calvert wanted to call an ambulance. But she wouldn't hear of it. Insisted she was fine. Things got really nasty. The whole department could hear her. She was yelling that he was a plagiarist and a hack trying to rob her grave before she was cold, and that he'd never get her secrets. And a whole lot of other incoherent stuff. Eventually he let her have her way. Her housekeeper found her body the next day. Heart attack. At least that's what I heard.'

Kirsten trailed off. She had begun to look past Peter and Ellisha with that unfocussed gaze that prefaces phrases like, *I really must be going,* and for a moment the world went black inside Peter's head. Without looking, he could feel Ellisha's eyes burning into him, wanting to know what he was going to do. *But Babs is dead,* his mind screamed. *Say something. A question. Keep her talking.* 'The funeral.'

She blinked. 'Sorry?'

'What are the arrangements for the funeral? We'd like to go, pay our respects.'

'It's private, I'm afraid.' She glanced down the corridor and lowered her voice. 'Not even Professor Calvert is going.'

He made his smile rueful. 'They didn't get on, did they?'

Kirsten gave a nervous laugh. 'Well, I don't want to talk ill about the dead. But Dr McBride wasn't exactly the most popular member of the faculty.'

He rolled his eyes. 'I guess she made a lot of enemies.'

'And then some. Between you and me, I don't think many of her colleagues are exactly heartbroken. Professor Calvert told me to clear out her office as quickly as possible. He has someone new starting on Monday.' With a restless glance over her shoulder, she added. 'I really need to get back.'

'Wait!' Peter put his hand out as the door started to shut. She looked at him curiously and he felt a flush so hot it chilled him. 'I think— I believe Professor McBride may have left something for me.'

She looked at him suspiciously. 'I don't know anything about that.'

'I'm sure she said something.' He was faltering, a poker player losing his nerve. 'I— You see—'

'We're from the archive,' Ellisha said extending a hand. 'I should have said that earlier. We've come to collect some of Dr McBride's papers.'

The girl looked down at Ellisha's hand, hesitating. 'I don't—'

Ellisha took a step forward. 'Think about it. You know me.'

The girl's gaze moved up and she broke into a smile. 'Of course. I thought you looked familiar.' She held the door wide. 'Come in.'

As soon as Kirsten's back was turned, he raised his eyebrows. Ellisha spread her hands, clearly as astonished by herself as he was. Their silent communication was interrupted when Kirsten turned round to ask if there were any particular papers they were looking for.

'Anything to do with Ignis Dei.'

'Ignis Dei? What's that?'

He pretended to examine a book on the desk. 'Just something she mentioned. I thought it would be an interesting addition to the archive.'

Kirsten began rummaging in a box sitting on one of the chairs. 'You knew her well then?'

'I don't think anyone knew her well,' he said cautiously. 'She was an extremely private person.'

'You can say that again. Is it true that she was involved with Jacques Derrida in the seventies?'

'I believe so.'

'I love the idea that he described the affair as making love to a gorse bush. Suits her, don't you think?' She pulled out the apple-shaped penholder and held it in her hand like Rosetti's Eve. 'I mean she was prickly, but no matter how bad a hangover you had, you always listened in her lectures.'

The sound of a phone ringing in another room startled them all. 'I have to get that,' Kirsten said. 'Excuse me.'

As soon as the door clicked shut, Peter turned to Ellisha and asked tensely, 'Anything?'

Ellisha was at the desk, meticulously going through the drawers. She looked up and shook her head. 'Try on that shelf over by the door.' He did so, lifting each book down then shaking it out. *There must be something. Some way of getting to the truth. It can't end here. Not like this.* From underneath the desk, Ellisha asked, 'What exactly are we looking for?'

'I'm not sure. Notes. An old pocketbook written in code. Something that looks hidden.'

Ellisha pulled a box on to the desk and started thumbing through the contents. Kirsten's voice could be heard talking on the phone in the next room. After a minute, Ellisha asked, 'How do you know that Babs didn't store it on her computer in an encrypted digital file?'

'She didn't like computers.'

'She told you that?'

'No, her fountain pen did.'

'Really?' Ellisha was looking at him in an anxious, *please-be-joking* way. He bounded over to the desk and held the pen up. 'It's a Montegrappa. The kind Hemingway used. Babs wasn't of the Digital Age. She spent her whole life inside the heads of some of the most ancient thinkers in history. She was closer to the scribe dipping his quill in lampblack than the PhD student tapping out a thesis on a laptop. She wouldn't have trusted her innermost thoughts to a computer.'

He grinned triumphantly, but Ellisha was looking at him in a way that made him frown and say, 'What?'

She bit her lip then sighed. 'Okay, say you're right. What makes you think she hid her research here? Maybe she took it home. Maybe she buried it. Maybe it was all in her head.'

'It's not in her head. She was too scared of people discovering it. And, if she kept it at home, we'll find her home address.'

'Her home address.'

'Sure. Why not? The university will have it.'

'Then what?'

'We blag our way in.'

'And what if no-one has a key?'

'Then… then we come back at night. Babs was a recluse. We wouldn't be disturbed, and a broken window would just look like an act of vandalism on an empty property, and—'

Ellisha had pushed the box aside and was staring at him strangely. He was suddenly aware how his voice had risen. 'Peter.' She said his name softly, as though speaking to someone mentally fragile. 'You're talking about breaking and entering. We can't do that. You know that, don't you?'

'But—'

She shook her head and, suddenly, the book in his hand felt heavy as lead. He dropped it on to a chair. 'I know.'

'She really got to you.'

He was thinking of the sharp knuckles rapping against his skull. *Not that it's as precious as you imagine. Not the alpha and omega of existence…* 'I guess. She was so much like an old force of Nature. Like the embodiment of the first law of thermodynamics. She ought to have been incapable of being created or destroyed.'

Ellisha came round the desk and took his hand. 'An old force of Nature that woke up one day and found itself teaching Religious History to a bunch of vacant-eyed students.'

106

She was trying to make him laugh, and he managed a weak smile. 'Let's go home.'

As Ellisha bent to pick up her bag, she said, 'It's funny that Derrida likened Babs to a gorse bush. Did you know that the Celts used gorse to remedy lost faith? There's something poetic in that.'

It brought an unexpected lump to his throat. The idea of Babs restoring lost belief was both comic and poignant, and emotion evoking presence brought her suddenly into the room in a sweetly sharp smell of alcohol and tobacco. He could almost hear that caustic voice laughing at him. *Come to rob Pharaoh's tomb, Stone Man?*

Suddenly, his eyes were wet and—as a native of a land where powerful emotion might be demonstrated with nothing more visible than a slight thinning of the lips—he tried to hide his reaction by turning his head away and blinking rapidly. He found himself looking at the ink blotter on Babs' desk. It was covered in stains and smears and the beginnings and endings of random thoughts. *...the waking grave of all my dreams* and *...they saw the De'il's face in the reeking lums that cast a smoky pall above the city...* Inscrutable as a cryptic crossword. *And yet...* He snatched up the blotter, feeling like Jean-François Champollion the moment the glyphs of the Rosetta stone morphed into meaning. 'Of course.'

Ellisha was at his side. 'What is it?'

'Look!'

'I don't—' she began then paused. 'Is that a footprint?'

'Babs was on the floor because she fell off the desk.'

Ellisha started to ask something then shook her head. 'What?'

'She told me. She'd done it before. To take the battery out of the detector.'

'So why would she be up there just before they wired a new one in?'

He didn't answer. He was looking up at the smoke detector, fitted as it was, in a ceiling panel, and fancied that the panel looked loose. Ellisha was watching him anxiously. 'Are you all right?' He ignored her, glancing sharply in the direction of the door. *Was there time?* Kirsten was still on the phone. He heard her give a young vigorous laugh, and suspected she was talking to a boyfriend. He looked back at the smoke detector. It was a risk. How would he explain himself if he were caught? But risk had been the driving force of his life, that need to find something bigger and better.

'Ellie, watch the door.'

She looked at him, startled. 'What? Why?'

Without answering, he pulled out Babs's chair and climbed up on the desk.

ɔ

The box was a large one. It was a miracle that Babs had managed to heft it up there in the first place. Struggling to carry it all the way home left him breathless, and there was a hollow shaft in his stomach at the thought of how close they had come to leaving without it. Ellisha had not offered to help, walking at his side, hands shoved deep in the pockets of her coat, her face closed and her thoughts unreadable.

Now, in the sitting room, they sat on either side of the box—still in their coats as the temperature inside was very little different to that without—and looked at it with the reverence reserved for amulets and faerie tokens: objects with a tendency to magically transform from too much contact with prosaic touch. Ellisha lifted a hand and massaged the back of her neck, as though something was pressing into her.

'I don't like this. It's stealing.'

'It isn't stealing. Babs wanted me to have this.'

'You barely knew her.'

'You know how she was. A minute with Babs was a lifetime with anyone else. And I don't believe there was anything random about her either. She took me into the Wood Beyond the World and told me that weird tale about King James for a reason.'

Ellisha was still rubbing her neck. 'What reason.'

'It was getting too much for her. The secret was too big. She wanted—no, she needed— someone to know. And she chose me. She wanted me to know.'

'You want her to want you to know.'

'It's more than that. I can't explain it. I'm right about this. I feel it somehow.'

'With your woman's intuition?'

'Sexist.'

'Sissy.'

They stared at each other, and Peter felt something desperate rear up inside him. In a voice that belonged to some part of his brain not quite controlled by will, he found himself saying urgently, 'I have to do this, Ellie. I need it. I want you with me. But, if you won't help me, I'll do it alone.'

She didn't make a sound. A gust of wind flung itself at the house and the window casements creaked.

'Ellie?'

'When you've finished with her papers, we give them back, right?'

'Of course.'

A small nod. 'Okay.'

'Okay?'

She was getting to her feet. 'I'll put some coffee on then we'll get started.'

They worked in silence, sitting on the floor of the living room, the papers spread out about them. Peter was tired from his walk and the neglect he had put his body through. In other circumstances he would have left it to another day but, afraid Ellisha might change her mind or have another attack of moral rectitude, he persevered. And, little by little, he was drawn in, and his coffee grew cold and untouched.

An hour passed. Then another. Peter had heard of the monumental efforts by linguists to decipher the Rosetta Stone, but it seemed a small affair in comparison with decrypting the tangled scrawlings of a mind that seemed increasingly deranged. He disentangled a note that read:

Agree with Propp, fairy tales all originating from a single source. But not locational. Not a place. A psychogenic source? Dare I say <u>spiritual</u> source? … But why only tales containing magic or witch-craft stemming from this foundation? Why not others? …

Propp is right again, "The tale at its core preserves traces of very ancient paganism, of ancient customs and rituals. The tale gradually undergoes a metamorphosis, and these transformations and metamorphoses of tales are also subject to certain laws…"

He sat up straight when he read that, then read it aloud. Ellisha put down the notebook she was reading and came to read it over his shoulder.

'Do you think it means something?'

'I don't know.'

He went on excitedly. But the text grew rambling. An attempt to trace parallel versions of fairy tales back to their prehistoric origins became increasingly obscure, then abruptly petered out.

Stifling a yawn—Ellisha's little brass carriage clock showed it was after midnight—he began thumbing through a notepad until his eye fell on a familiar theme.

Fear of death. Thanatophobia. Universal. Inescapable. Inexpli-cable in the presence of Faith… Yet cross-ref early afterlife mythos shows up… nothing??? In the harshest, most inhospitable eras of mankind why no promise of comfort, redemption etc.

The rest of the notepad was filled with references and terms too technical for Peter to follow.

'Found anything?'

He glanced up. 'No. You?'

Ellisha was rubbing her eyes. She sighed and lifted another notebook. 'Not yet.'

'You should go to bed.'

'Are you going?'

'I want to go on a bit longer.'

'Then I'm staying too.'

Some indefinable time later he opened his eyes. His head had slumped on to his chest, and he lifted it and gazed around furtively.

'Ellisha?'

She was sitting cross-legged in the centre of a crop ring of papers. Her face hidden in a deep well of shadow and he wasn't certain if she was awake.

'Ellie? Are you all right?'

A small twitch of her shoulders in acknowledgement. Stiffly, he started to get to his feet, but a draft sneaking through the gaps in the window frame made the curtains shiver. The tiny distraction drew his eyes. And when he looked back, he had the strange impression that something had happened in the split second of his absence. 'Ellisha? What is it?' He closed the distance between them and dropped to his knees. 'What's wrong?' He thought she would go on sitting in silence. But very slowly she lifted her head and looked at him with such a strange, faraway expression that he couldn't tell if she was aware that he was there. She smiled with infinite sadness and said calmly, 'There is no God.'

The air was gelid, smelling of old books. The curtains were still fluttering in the draft. Lumpy couches. Threadbare rug. Nothing had changed. Yet everything had changed. The world had shifted on its axis.

There is no God.

CHAPTER 12

'THERE IS NO GOD.'

How could this be the revelation he was looking for? Blinking, like a man suddenly unable to read the lines of a familiar passage, he took Ellisha's hands in his, found them icy. *I have no belief.* He said the words inside himself, almost as an article of faith. Was he not a member of a small race of hairless apes in an unremarkable corner of an equally unremarkable galaxy, or so he had believed?

But when Ellisha said those words, *There is no God*, it was somehow different. Instead of emptiness he felt something moving on the face of the Deep. Instead of the crushing loneliness of the mundane, he felt the birth of mystery.

She was shivering.

'Come to bed.'

'I can't.'

He stood up, and a moment later returned with blankets. Wrapping them around them both, he formed a warm cocoon, a nestling egg inside which they might speak. When she had stopped shivering he said, 'You found something?'

She nodded. Then, frowning, shook her head. 'Found? I'm not sure. In a way. But other things… they just came. I don't know from where. There were things I figured out— No.' She pulled a face. 'That's the wrong way to put it. Things I didn't know, that suddenly I understood.' Leaning forward, she began scrabbling in amongst Babs' effects. 'All these things… they should have been properly catalogued. But you know Babs, how secretive she was.' An A4 sheet pulled from a torn Manilla folder. 'This is original research and, if what you say about it being hidden is true, then it isn't published or archived. As far as I can tell no-one knows it even exists.'

She smoothed out the paper and held it towards him. Peter looked. It was a faded photocopy of a much older document. In amongst the smudges and the annotations in spidery red ink, he spotted a few words in Latin, but the cursive script might as well have been a random dance of bird's feet for all he could make out. He gave her a puzzled look.

'What is it?'

'Do you remember what she told you about James VI interviewing a witch?'

He nodded.

'The broadsheets claimed that she confessed to plotting his murder on the way back from Denmark. But this—' She brandished the A4 sheet triumphantly. 'This says differently. This is the original document.' She laid it on the floor and began running her finger across the lines. 'It's hard to read. Some of it is in Scots and other bits are in Latin.'

'Do you read Latin well enough to translate it?'

Pulling a face. 'I took a Classics course for a couple of semesters. So, no. But Babs has translated in the margins of this copy of the document here. See, there's a bit where the witch claims that it is not the Devil that she worships, but what Christian men might call the Devil. What she told you before is all true.'

He sat back on his heels, disappointed. 'Is that all?'

She reached out and squeezed his knee. 'The important thing to understand is that this backs up Babs' theories.'

'Which are?'

'That a much older form of religion was existing in the shadows, being handed down from mother to daughter, even while the church sought to stamp it out.'

Something stirred in Peter's memory. 'Memories of the Harvest King? Worship of the Great Mother?'

'More than that. Something much older.' Ellisha's forehead creased. 'It's not clear. But it's hinted at. She uses old Celtic words, *neo-bhith*, inexistence or non-existence. And here, where she describes the deity using *thoir am bith*.'

'Meaning?'

'It's hard to put clearly into words. But I think it has the sense of coming… or better, of bringing something into being.'

Peter gave a puzzled laugh. 'She worships something that's not there?'

To his surprise Ellisha lurched forwards and grabbed his hands. Her skin was still cold and she was holding him so tightly he could feel where her fingers would later leave bruises on his flesh. 'Don't you see? Don't you understand?'

Dumbly he shook his head. She let him go and he felt a pang of loss. She was biting her lip.

'I think I've gone mad.'

'Tell me.'

'There is no God because we haven't brought the Deity into existence yet.' When he made no comment, she asked tentatively, 'Peter, are you okay.'

Instead of answering he stood up abruptly and headed for the door.

'Peter, wait. Where are you going?'

'I need air.'

'Then I'm coming too.'

Out they went, through streets sticky with melted frost, because Ellisha's words were too big to be contained inside the house, and because it was better to be out in the cold dampness of the air than cooped up in the damp coldness of the house.

It was still early and the roads were eerie and empty. The flagstones magnified their footsteps and sent echoes spiralling up between the tall Georgian buildings on either side. Ellisha wore a knitted wool scarf and Peter's gloves were on her hands. Peter's hands were clasped behind him, and he hunched forward, his face drawn tight in concentration. His head was spinning, and no matter how often she explained he still had the same questions. 'You're saying that they knew there was no God?'

'Yes. I think so.'

'And it wasn't a kind of atheism?'

'No… I'm not sure. It's hard to explain. Belief in an afterlife isn't as universal as you think. That was Babs' whole point. There are hunter-gatherer tribes in Africa and South America who live as our ancestors did thousands of years ago, who simply believe we live then we die. And if you look at the classical world there are dozens of other examples.'

'Really?'

She gave him a sidelong glance. 'I thought you read Babs' book.'

'Tell me anyway.'

'Well, in the Mesopotamian epic, Gilgamesh fears returning to dust and being forgotten. And Homer describes the dead as shades living in Hades without will or personality. And in ancient Egypt there was a drab, dark place for the deceased, the opposite of the living world, which was similar to the *Sheol* of the Jews, which isn't Hell as some people think, but a kind of dreary pit where the dead gather near their kinfolk.'

A hot wave washed over Peter. He had knowledge of that pit. He had found it opening up when the last drops of liquid were drained from a bottle. The pit seemed a strange place to be fighting for.

'And this is the secret women were dying for as late as the reign of James VI?'

Ellisha gnawed the knuckles of her left hand. 'Not exactly. There's more to it. A divine force… a… a *numen* that acts as a guiding principle. But somehow God does not exist… yet.'

A truck heaved past, its groaning plated body releasing a dragon's breath of exhaust fumes and spray over them. Peter shook off the droplets and shivered. In a brisker voice than he had used before he asked, 'Can you be sure that this document is real? I mean Babs didn't publish it? Can you be certain it isn't archived somewhere?'

'No. I can't be sure. I'm not even certain I'm interpreting things correctly.' Her step faltered, and she turned to look up at him.

'I know the evidence is sketchy. I know I'm filling in gaps, taking huge leaps in the dark, but somehow I know I'm right about this.' She shook herself and looked up at him helplessly. 'But even supposing I am, I still don't see how any of this is going to help us.'

She doesn't see it. 'If I can only broadcast this idea to the world in the right way, you'll never have to want for anything again. This could make us rich beyond our wildest dreams.'

She pulled a face. 'Right now, my wildest dreams are about paying the electricity bill.' A shake of her head. 'And how are you going to promote this big idea? There's no money to get it off the ground.'

'I—I don't know. I still have my father's gold cufflinks. Perhaps I could raise enough to print leaflets.'

'Then what? We stop members of the public and ask: Have you heard the good news? There is no god.'

'You're making it sound ridiculous!'

'Because it is ridiculous. Do you even hear yourself, Peter? All this—this—crazy talk. You've just swapped one addiction for another.'

'You think it's mad?'

'Don't you think it's mad?'

A hot silence flared between them, then Ellisha sighed. 'I didn't mean that. I'm glad you've given up drinking. But don't you think a job would be a better way to help us become rich. Or solvent? I'd settle for solvent.'

He looked at her, appalled. 'That's really all you want?'

'Yeah. And, while you're at it, you can use your father's cufflinks to pay for the electricity.'

They walked on in tense silence for a bit then he said coaxingly, 'I know you feel it.'

For a moment she didn't speak, then, shrugging, spoke in a cold flat voice. 'Last night I sat alone in the dark for hours, referencing and cross-referencing, translating and analysing everything Babs had written. It was such a mess. I shouldn't have been able to make sense of it. No-one should.' A defiant glance. 'But I did. It all just came to me somehow. Like I understood. Like I was supposed to understand.'

They were by the West door of St Giles' cathedral. Saint Margaret and Mary Queen of Scots looked down on them. Suddenly she turned and scurried up the steps. He called after her.

'Ellie. Where are you going?'

But she was slipping inside.

He followed her, down the north aisle, beneath the eyes of green men hidden in the corbels of the vaulted ceiling. He felt them following his progress until he found her standing beside the angel font, a hand tracing the folded wings. Her gaze was directed towards the Burne-Jones window with its tryptic of goddess-like figures in white. He put his hands on her shoulders and said softly, 'There's a sense to it, even if we can't quite see it yet.'

'The story of an unmade god?'

Overhead there was the twitting of two starlings who had somehow made it into the nave and were circling in amongst the ceiling's vaulted arches. He tilted his head to look at them. And something in the gesture brought Ellisha around to face him. 'What is it?'

'I don't—' His eyes closed. Ellisha's voice, a long way off. Fingers fidgeting with the font's scalloped edge, and the rising of a shape, a form, as yet unlit, but solid, real. His mind fumbling the planes of its surface like a blind child knowing yet unable to grasp.

'Peter?'

A crash above their heads made them jump. One of the starlings had flown into the Byrne-Jones window. They rushed forward, reconstructing what their eyes had not been able to follow, and found its limp body lying on the cold slabs.

'Oh, poor thing.' Ellisha crouched down, reaching a hand out to tentatively nudge the little corpse.

'It must have been attracted to the light. Is it dead?'

Ellisha nodded grimly. 'Poor little broken soul.'

Gears shifted; levers released. 'What did you say?' Ellisha was getting to her feet, and didn't answer. He grasped her shoulders and whirled her around to face him.

'Peter! Don't! You're hurting me.'

'What did you say?'

'About the bird?'

'I don't know. That it was broken?'

'A broken soul. That's what you said, isn't it?'

She squirmed free of his grasp and crossed her arms over her chest, rubbing at her shoulders. 'Yes. I guess. I was remembering that mythologically birds are used to represent the carriers of souls.'

'But you said. Broken. A fractured soul. As though a soul isn't necessarily indivisible.'

'I don't—I was just babbling.'

'No. It's genius. The missing link in the narrative.' He was laughing now. 'I see it. I see the story.'

'Peter, you're not making any sense.'

'Ignis Dei. The Spark of God. It's the soul.' He began walking up and down excitedly. 'Babs understood. She knew she'd stumbled across something incredible. She was afraid to share it. But it was driving her mad, poisoning her, leaking out of the seams in hints and insults.

'And I thought—I don't know, that she was harbouring some secret, something I could turn into a commercial success, something I could use to turn my life around. You know the sort of thing, the covenant to the ark, Templars and conspiracies. A book, film rights. But this is bigger. Much bigger. We just have to handle it right.'

'I don't understand.'

'Neither do I. Not fully. But we're holding something incredibly precious, the key to Shangri La. The Holy Grail.'

Ellisha was laughing now, a thin nervous laugh to cover her fear. 'But probably it isn't even true. I was so tired and cold last night. By the time I'd pieced it together I was delusional.'

'But that's the beauty, don't you see? What religion ever began without madness? Think about it. A man claims to be the Son of God and persuades a bunch of nobodies to throw off their worldly goods to follow him. Everyone thinks he's a lunatic. But suddenly—' he clicked his fingers '—the world changes direction. And now everyone's trailing behind him.'

'Jesus?'

'Zoroaster. Or Mithras Or Mani, take your pick.' Leaning forward, an urgency in his face. 'Don't you see? It doesn't matter. The message is what counts. It catches fire.'

'So you want to spread the good news.'

'No. No, you don't understand. Belief evolving unchecked and uncontrolled. It's the Blind Watchman.'

She was shaking her head, but he wasn't finished. 'Think of the consequences of letting nature fashion the shape of faith. Every belief system you can think of starts with the best of intentions, but then mutates in order to survive. It becomes a parody of itself, every faction believing that they are purer than the other until they fall to fighting, like a snake biting its own tail.'

'You think you can produce something better?'

'Why not? Think of the state of the world. Everyone's reeling from job losses, financial collapses, loneliness, depression, hopelessness and fear. We've got something entirely new here. Something that could save the world.'

Her face was still shadowed with doubt, and he went on eagerly, 'Even supposing I'm wrong. I'm clutching at shadows, pulling meaning out of desperation and the garbled scribbles of an old drunk. Does it matter? We know so much more now. Psychology, science, technology. What if we could distill all the good things, avoid making the same mistakes? Would that be so terrible?'

She was biting her lip. 'You know it can't possibly work.' But she was relenting, taking that unconscious step towards him.

He swept her hands up in his. 'I can do this, Ellie. I feel like I'm meant to do it. It all makes sense. Like the pieces of a puzzle finally coming together inside my head.'

'You sound like you might just believe it.'

'I believe this is my chance to do something good. To save lives.' Impetuously, he swung her around startling a frightened peal of laughter from her.

'Peter, you dope. This is a holy place.'

He stopped and put his head close to hers. He was panting a little, not from the exertion, but with the new, unnamed thing that was opening in his heart. 'With you at my side,' he whispered hoarsely, 'I am going to make the whole world holy.'

CHAPTER 13

< THE THEISTS TOLD YOU THERE WAS A GOD: THEY WERE WRONG.

THE ATHEISTS TOLD YOU THERE WAS NO GOD: THEY WERE ALSO WRONG...>

IGNIS DEI, Church of the Unmade God:

VLOG file, released American Eastern Time 4:00am.

Peter watched Ellisha getting ready. It was important to him that everything be perfect, down to the last detail. He had approved when she slipped into a pale green sleeveless shift that fell to the floor. But, when she lifted a necklace, he shook his head, insisting that she forewent jewellery for a simple circlet of twisted ivy and plum-coloured hellebore that he placed on her curls in an arboreal halo.

'How do I look?'

He didn't know what to say. She looked weightless, ethereal; a goddess stepped from the greenwood. He swallowed. 'You look like Morgan le Fay.'

She frowned a little at that. 'I look like a Wiccan wannabe.'

'You look as though you're glowing.'

She quirked her mouth. 'Like a woman in love?'

He lifted her hands and pressed his lips against them. 'Like a woman who is loved.'

< THE PIT IS BLACK. THE PIT IS BOTTOMLESS. YOU HAVE LOOKED, BUT YOU HAVE NOT FOUND.

GOD IS NOT THERE.

THE HEART IS HOLLOW. THE HEART IS A WELL OF EMPTINESS. YOU HAVE SOUGHT, BUT YOU HAVE NOT FOUND.

GOD IS NOT THERE.

THE SOUL IS UNFORMED. THE VESSEL IS EMPTY. YOU HAVE PURSUED ETERNITY BUT ALL YOU HAVE CREATED IS DUST.

GOD IS NOT THERE…>

IGNIS DEI, Church of the Unmade God:

VLOG file, released American Eastern Time 4:00am.

They were silent on the journey to the top of Princes Street, sitting together in the back seat of an old Vauxhall. It belonged to a friend Ellisha had made during her brief stint at the coffee shop. 'Who is he?' Peter had asked in a tone of carefully crafted nonchalance.

'Oh, just some guy I worked with. He's very young. We got talking because he thought he knew me.'

He was indeed very young. He had long hair and the soulful eyes of Jesus, and, at another time, Peter might have found him funny. But now, with so much riding on the outcome of the day, watching his sad Jesus-eyes following Ellisha's every move made him irritable and nervy.

He was afraid that Ellisha would notice the band of pale skin on his wedding finger and ask where his ring was. And what was he supposed to say? Ten days ago, he had gone to a local pawnbroker and raised the money to pay for the venue. If everything worked according to plan he would be able to buy it back in a few weeks' time. There it was again… *if everything went to plan.* That same phrase playing on an endless loop inside his head.

After all, what have I got to lose? Only everything. Clinging to my marriage like a drowning man. If this fails. If Ellisha leaves— He could not finish the thought. *Everything will work. It has to.* As they went down the stairs, Jesus-eyes was still hanging off Ellisha's every word, and Peter half expected him to hand him the keys before announcing his intention to climb into the back seat next to his wife.

They rode through the streets in jittery silence. Now and again, Peter glanced towards Ellisha, but she was staring out of the window of the car, gnawing on the back of a knuckle. He had never seen her so nervous, and the closer they came to their destination the more she seemed to diminish.

He reached out and gently pulled her hand away from her mouth and cupped it gently in his own. 'It'll be okay.'

She looked at him as though he were mad. 'What if no-one comes?'

'They'll come.'

'Would you?'

'Yes. Of course.' But she had spotted his hesitation.

'It won't work.'

'It will. I promise.'

She turned away and went back to gnawing her knuckle.

And the closer they came, the more he began to share Ellisha's fears. Signs looming from street corners—*St Colme Street, Albyn Place, Queen Street*. Bold signs. Black typefaces. In every direction, the air categorised into neat compartments. Suddenly he knew himself back in the real world, and the light of day made all his grand plans grow transparent and absurd. A small boy waking up from a game of make-believe.

—

< AWAKE!

I AM HERE

DO NOT GIVE IN TO DESPAIR

REJOICE!

I WILL COME

YOU WILL NOT BE ALONE

FOR IN ETERNAL DARKNESS
THE SPARK IS THE GREATEST LIGHT>
    IGNIS DEI, Church of the Unmade God:
    TWEET, released American Eastern Time 4:00am.

Not too late to pull out. Put up my hands. Mea culpa. A joke. A game. A wonderful game. Weren't we just playing, sitting in the lounge, Babs' papers scattered around us like blossoms?'Okay, Peter, how do we start?'

Now there was a question. How are new belief systems born? The revelation surely. The divine spark, which in their case was a spark of the divine.

'We need a message. One that sounds as ancient as time.'

'But, isn't this a new revelation?'

His hands moving with the symphony of his thoughts. 'People are afraid of new ideas. But they're in awe of the old. Bury an idea in the sand then excavate it in a thousand years and they'll fight to get hold of it. There's a subconscious belief in humans that knowledge is somehow like wine, that it matures with age.'

She pulled a face. 'You really think the internet is the way to reveal this "revelation"?'

'We will need followers. Without a following this is nothing but an intellectual game. Our target audience are people like ourselves. Like you and me. People who have stared into the face of the Void and felt they can't take any more. We're looking for people teetering on metaphorical ledges. People who order books on spirituality or past lives or loss of faith, people who don't know how to overcome a bereavement. People who are looking. People who are lost.'

'But how will you get your message out there? The world we live in has largely turned its back on prophets.'

'But not on profits.' He spread his arms wide in mock benediction. 'The internet is the largest audience in the world. How many people were at the Sermon on the Mount? Hundreds? Thousands at a push. In cyberspace we can reach millions.'

'I wouldn't know where to begin.'

'You don't need to. Words are my calling. All you need be is your own beautiful self, Ellie. Just be my follower and leave the rest to me.'

< YOU HAVE LOOKED INTO MY FACE AND RECOGNISED ME. YOU HAVE LOOKED INTO YOURSELF AND FOUND ME. COME. IT IS TIME FOR THE NEXT STAGE. I WILL BE WAITING IN EDINBURGH, ANCIENT CITY OF THE NORTH, ON THE FIRST DAY OF THE SECOND MONTH. THE DAY OF GENERATION. CALL IT WHAT YOU WILL. LUPERCALIA, FESTA CANDELARUM, IMBOLC, OIMELC, CANDLEMAS, FÈILL BRÌGHDE, THE OLD CHRISTMAS, GROUNDHOG DAY. COME IN PERSON. COME IN SPIRIT. COME THROUGH VIRTUAL SPACE. BUT COME. COME! COME! ...>

IGNIS DEI, Church of the Unmade God:

VLOG file, released American Eastern Time 4:00am.

The car slowed to a stop and sat there, the droning insect hum of the engine ticking over.

'There's some sort of holdup.' Jesus-eyes had spoken.

Ellisha jerked and threw a frightened glance at Peter. 'We can't be late.'

Winding down the window Peter looked across a narrow slice of Edinburgh obscured by the jointed segments of a traffic queue, which disappeared around the corner out of sight. The wail of sirens reached his ears.

'Can you see anything?'

'No. An accident I think.'

She sat back in the seat, fretting. Then asked almost instantly, 'What should we do?'

A squinting glance at the street sign. *Elder Street* 'We can walk from here.'

Stiffly they emerged from the creaking leather seat and stood self-consciously on the pavement. Ellisha was wearing a long black coat with a high collar that hid most of her attire, but she was sparking agitation, and one or two passers-by turned their heads to look in her direction. Quickly he reached down and took her hand, which was clammy with sweat.

'It's all right. We can do this.'

'If no-one comes—'

'Then we'll have had a pleasant walk in the sunshine.'

'But it's so important to you.' He read the fear in her eyes. *What if this fails? Will you start drinking again?*

He squeezed her hand. 'We'll think of something.'

She was licking her lips as though her mouth was dry, and he thought of all the work she had put in over the last weeks, helping him to record his carefully crafted messages then upload them, slowly building a mystery to draw in the lonely, the hopeless, the dispossessed. But now under the stern winter sun the shadows threw the angles of the buildings into harsh relief and the virtual world seemed no more real than Lyonesse or Tir na nOg. He felt a sharp pang of premonition. No-one was coming.

'Ellisha?'

'Yes?'

He had been about to say, let's go home. *Let's forget about the whole silly project. We'll spend the last of our savings on a bottle of non-alcoholic wine and laugh about how we started believing our own story.*

And in the morning, I will look for a job and we will be a family, just us two. But she looked so grave and determined to see it through that he shook his head. 'Nothing. Just I love you.'

She glanced at him, biting her lip. 'You don't think anyone's coming.' She started to walk.

They turned on to Waterloo Place where he had booked a conference room with the capacity to seat a hundred. Feeling like a gambler on his last roll of dice—there was nothing left after pawning his wedding ring—he had handed over the crisp notes and feigned a smile of confidence at the girl taking his booking.

—We have a cheaper room, sir, that seats up to twenty-six.

The smile was rusty from lack of use.

—No. We need all the space we can get. Only wish you had a bigger room. Everywhere's booked up. You know how it is.

—Is it for a wedding, sir?

A wink.

—Can't say too much.

She was interested now. Eyes widening.

—Really?

He leaned across the counter towards her, lowering his voice.

—Something pretty big is going to go down here.

But now he looked ahead and saw a congestion of bodies blocking the way and his heart sank. They were never going to get through. Ellisha was obviously thinking the same thing. She shot him an anxious look and he forced a reassuring smile and mouthed. 'Don't worry.'

But the way forward did not look promising. As they drew closer, he could see police cars, yellow tape, a jostling crowd. They exchanged glances. Another incident?

'Should we turn back?'

'No.' Ellisha lifted her chin, and he saw, with a pang, that it trembled a little. 'We can't turn back. Not now.'

Anxiously they made their way ahead. The crowd was densely packed and it was difficult to reach the yellow tape 'What if they won't let us through?' Ellisha asked in a tight voice.

'We'll find a way.' But his voice was flat, unconvincing. To make up for it, he took hold of Ellisha's arm and forced a path up to the tape. He hailed a harassed-looking constable.

'Sir? Excuse me. We have to get through. We're—' he chose his words carefully '—chairing a meeting at the conference centre.'

The constable was young, his chin still pock-marked with acne. He shook his head. 'Can't let you in, sir.'

'What's going on?'

The constable gave an uneasy shrug. 'We're still trying to establish that. People have been pouring into the area since early morning.'

Suddenly everything went quiet inside Peter's head. 'What reason have they given?'

'As I said, sir, we're still trying to establish—' Peter leaned forward, fighting the urge to grip the man by the lapels. 'You have to let us through. It's urgent.' The constable took a step back, his face shuttered. 'If you'll stand back, sir.'

From behind there was a gasp. He whirled round and saw that Ellisha had removed her coat. It was lying in folds on the pavement, a shed skin, and she was standing there, unveiled, green in the Candlemas light: revealed.

CHAPTER 14

'IT'S HER!'

A woman's voice? A man's? Later Peter could not recall who called out first. Only that he and Ellisha were somehow on the other side of the tape walking stiffly and self-consciously through the crowd, which had fallen silent and awed, parting spontaneously to let them through.

And the strange dream-like quality of it all. The eerie corridors of silent human faces. The lack of sound, a susurration in itself, a subliminal whisper, branches stirring on a windless day. Turning to Ellisha and feeling the motion of his turning, and seeing her pale and expressionless, her movements the drifting movements of deep shock.

Where are we going?

But she had orchestrated her own publicity stunt, and now he could only follow, up through a wooded path. Calton Hill, rising before them, like a revelation. And understanding opening up inside him. A prophet must address the people from above. *I am set upon my High Places and my arms are trained for battle...* He, with his flair for the dramatic, should have known. Where, but on a mount, had Christ chosen to deliver his sermon? Even Moses had received all of the Law on the slopes of Mount Sinai. And this was Calton Hill. *Cragge Ingalt.* The old name. *The place of groves.* Sacred groves. Out of the shadow world of ancient worship. Had she known all along that this was where they should be headed? He felt strangely redundant, an architect watching someone else taking possession of his creation.

They were at the base of an unfinished temple of soaring, evenly spaced columns. A Scottish Parthenon of greying sandstone to commemorate the fallen. Of which war? Peter couldn't remember. He followed Ellisha around to the rear, while the crowd surged in the front and for an instant, standing in a scattering of empty bottles and ma-rooned plastic bags, they were hidden from sight.

'My God.' His voice sounded unnaturally loud and he lowered it at once to a whisper. 'There must be fifty thousand people out there. More. A hundred thousand maybe—' He broke off as he saw Ellisha was looking at him with a kind of horror. A sudden jerking movement brought her to his side. She was saying something, but her voice was so low that at first all he made out was a rasping noise.

'What is it? What's wrong?'

'I can't.' She grasped his hands as though she would not let go. 'I thought I could. But I can't.'

He felt his mouth go dry. 'What are you saying?'

'It's a lie. We've made all this up. We can't go out there and con thousands of people with a lie.'

Blind panic. She could be talked out of it. He had talked frightened people back to reason before. 'It's not a lie. We read Babs' research ourselves.'

'We heard what we wanted to hear and made up the rest.'

'Ellisha, listen to me. All stories are fictions. There is no single great truth; only the story we follow in our heads. Our story is one of hope. All those people, they've seen the world brought to its knees. They're here, today, from god-knows-how-far, because they want to hear our story.'

But she only shook her head. And looking down he found the face of a frightened child looking back at him. 'It's only a lifestyle choice, Ellie, a new way of looking at things. Think, if we can prevent just one person from throwing themselves into the Void then it'll be worth it, hmmm?' He tried to tweak a smile from her, and when she didn't respond, he went on a little desperately, 'We'll tell them eventually. Once we've proven it works, we'll 'fess up, write a book, go on talk shows. We can sell it as a great psychological experiment. It could set us up for life. Give us the money to—' reaching out to trace her empty belly '—to do anything we choose. Ellie, I need you. You don't have to say a thing. All you have to do is follow my lead.'

Her eyes filled with tears. 'I want to go home.'

But home was through a living wall of silent, hope-filled faces. They had made it this far over a thin crust of anticipation, but Peter could feel the immense tectonic power building below the surface. Desperation and despair had driven these people to this spot and they would not simply shrug their shoulders and go home if things were called off.

'Ellisha,' he spoke firmly. 'I have to go out there. Are you coming or not?'

But she stared at him wildly then buried her head in his chest. A muffled, *I can't,* was all he could get out of her.

He wrapped his arms around her, looking over her head at the leafless trees, and feeling helpless and powerless in the midst of vast indifference. *There is no God.* Gently, he put his hands on her shoulders and pushed her away.

'We cannot simply walk out of here. It would be an act of madness to try.' She stared at him vacantly, a sleepwalker's gaze, but did not argue. Relieved, he closed his eyes for a moment, and when he opened them again, looking up towards the turning vault of the sky, seeing the luminous-edged clouds spinning past, like pictures inside a Victorian zoetrope, a Cecil B DeMille sky, ready to be split asunder by the voice of God. Too real to be real. The eager faces waiting on the far side of the temple could see this sky too. It had all got out of hand. Time to end things. He took a deep breath. 'I believe if I talk to them reasonably I can persuade them to leave.'

As he stepped out between the pillars onto the tiered platform the wind caught in his hair and made his vision blur so that, for a moment, he could see nothing but a many-eyed mass seething before him. A jolt of childhood memory. Dared by the older boys to sneak into Auld Leckie the newsagent's back-shop, the place where adult men were seen slipping out, collars up, hat brims pulled down over eyes, brown paper packages held tightly to their chests.

In he had gone, a bony skelf that could slide unnoticed beneath the black curtain that covered the doorway. Then slowly straightening up, transfixed, walls of flesh, immobile yet somehow churning. Eyes, limbs, breasts, penises, buttocks, tangled, floating, unrelated. Grins of upside-down mouths poking their tongues out at him. Wanting to run, but his legs like jelly. Trembling, trapped, the flesh-pit slowly resolving, faces pulling out of chests, limbs unfurling. And the wild beating of his heart slowing down as something human came back into the picture.

It happened now. That slow dissolve from chaos to meaning, the emergence of human shapes in all their multifarious hues, and even, thrillingly, one or two camera crews. The tension was magnificently poised, and the eeriness of their focus made his courage fail a little. He threw an anxious glance over his shoulder. Ellisha was standing still, arms held stiffly at her sides, looking at the ground. He turned back. Then, as if it were necessary to draw their attention, slowly raised his arms.

'Friends!'

He saw the shape of the word spreading out across the crowd— turning heads, whispers behind hands—cracks spreading across ice. Everything hung on what he said next. *If they turn—* He could not finish that thought. His heart was a struck chord. Unprepared. All those hours spent writing proposals and outlines for an audience of less than two dozen. And now, raw and unrehearsed, he faced the largest audience of his life. A terrible loneliness constricted his throat. What power would guide him through this?

'Friends,' he began again. His voice sounded thinner this time. His lack of conviction raised a discontented murmur, feet shifting, hostile glances. Forcing himself to stand very still, he cast about for a way to reach them, but his head was filling with random thoughts. Babs' saturnine voice, *Careful, Stone-man, the goddess has a nasty side. Adonis and Tammuz and old John Barleycorn are all sacrificed to the Queen of Heaven...*

Movement down below made him blink. An angry-looking man was pushing his way through the crowd. *If he gets here, if he addresses them, it's over.* His mind jumped ahead of failure. *No blame. We tried. Let's go home. Let's love each other, and let that be enough.* The man was almost at the platform. Peter could see him clearly now, shaved hair, like a marine, face blotched purple with anger. Peter cleared his throat.

'You were not born believing the lie.'

Immediately, the angry man stopped. The shuffling and murmuring died away. Peter began again, louder this time. 'You were not born believing the lie. It had to be told to you. And you have been told it so often and so earnestly—perhaps you have even been threatened if you refused to believe it—that it has become a kind of truth to you, but in your heart you have always known that it was a lie.'

There was a tingling in his fingertips, and he realised that he had been clenching his hands into fists this whole time and had only just let them go.

'The lie attempts to destroy the secret you are carrying, the secret you have always known. You were born with this secret and have carried it all your life, even as a small child. And that secret is simply that there is no God.'

When he said this a little sigh rose up from the crowd. They were nervous. He was exposing their innermost thoughts. But it was too late to turn back, and he found he had no desire to. Words were coming thick and fast into his brain, and he felt their power flowing through him.

He was back in the game, persuading difficult clients that he was a wordsmith, a jargon wallah, a lexical juggler plucking his illusions from the air. It rose in him, hot and compelling, an irresistible alchemy that changed him even as it changed those who listened, raising his heartbeat and flushing his skin. He raised his voice.

'When you asked why you were here and what was your purpose—for no child is born with knowledge of God—you were fed the lie. When you asked about all the savagery and injustice and suffering in the world, you were told the lie again. And when you looked into the Void and found only the Void looking back, you were told that you had not understood the lie or been pure enough for the lie or willing to allow the lie into your heart.

'But why was the lie ever told?'

Several angry suggestions that he did not make out were shouted from the audience. But it was clear that he had them. The over-excited ones were shushed by the majority, and Peter went on, his voice growing in power as he made the pitch of his life.

'It was not told at the beginning. And that is the truth of it. The ancient of ancients knew that they lived, they died, they returned to dust. The hunter-gatherers of our century, the Hadza and the Pirahas, do not talk of the life to come. But only of the "here is" and the "now is". And that is some of the truth of it. But it is not the whole of it. There is a second secret.

'This is the knowledge of the "not yet" and "what is to be". It was women who first understood this revelation because they were, and are now, the creators of life. And so it was known as the woman's secret. They alone understood that God does not give life to us, but that we give life to God. They understood that we are not born with souls but with the potential to create them. And that each soul brought into existence is a tiny living cell in the unfurling mind of the deity.'

His throat was dry with shouting, but he continued, filled with the sense of being understood even as his own understanding lagged behind.

'The power of three has been emblazoned on mankind's heart since the earliest times. The Great Goddess and her three faces. The ash, the oak and thorn of the Druids. The three jewels of Buddhism. Even the Christians could not rid themselves of that ghostly third when they created their Holy Trinity. Unity, duality, triad. Woman, man, child. We feel it in our bones.

'That First Awakening was the spark which ignited the material universe and sent stars, like fireworks, shooting through space. And this awakening brought about the Second Awakening, which was consciousness, yawning and stretching itself into existence. The "it" becoming "I", the mirror that sees itself and is reflected over and over until it glimpses infinity; the universe trying to unlock its own secrets. And thus came the knowledge of the Third Awakening. The spark yet to come. And it was the women who first discovered this secret.

'And as women first knew the secret, they called Her Goddess and worshipped Her Sacred Possibility and the day when Divinity would come into the universe.'

He paused, lowering his head and breathing heavily, hands raised above his head to indicate that he wasn't finished. It was a trick he had seen his father use in the pulpit. *I can do this. I can be the prophet of a new age.* He lifted his chin and spoke confidently into the crowd.

'But the men were jealous of the secret. They did not want to await God. They tore down the temples and the sacred groves where the women worshipped. And the memory of their betrayal still lives in the aboriginal forests of Africa and Australia and South America, where they tell of a time when the women pretended to be spirits, and how, when their secret was found out, a great battle ensued between the sexes, which the men won.

'And the terrible Lie was hatched.'

People had begun to hold hands, row after row, as far as he could see. Some were openly weeping.

'The men would not wait for God. They claimed themselves guardians of the Truth, and that they would not create God, but were created by Him. They did not explain the suffering or the injustice or the savagery in the world, they did not explain the emptiness they felt because they lacked souls, but claimed that the world was a product of his Love. And when anyone questioned the nature of God's love, they killed them.

'In time, the dormant nature of the Deity was forgotten. Men and even women came to believe that they were shameful bits of matter polluted by original sin. They forgot they had the power to create divinity and knelt down before altars begging to be forgiven. They watched evil prevail and innocents die, and still they proclaimed His Love, His Existence.

'Eventually, even the women forgot the secret of "not yet" and "what will come" and remembered their goddess as a false deity. They bowed down before the Terrible Lie and made themselves its slaves. And if any woman protested, they scourged her and drove her from their community and handed her over to the men.

'But not all the women forgot. They knew that Death could not be conquered by getting down on one's knees. They knew that men and women came into the world empty and that souls must be fought for. These women lived and died and returned to dust. They were often persecuted and hunted down for their secret. They were burned and hanged and stoned, but they did not forget the true meaning of mankind.

'They did not forget that we are Ignis Dei, the spark that will ignite the Divine Fire. For centuries, for millennia these *en-souled* ones have hidden, knowing that the spark must not go out. They are hidden no longer …'

His words were interrupted by a spontaneous cheer that rose from the crowd. Peter's smile broadened and he grew a little taller until it occurred to him that the crowd was not looking at him.

He turned instinctively. And there she was, Ellisha framed between the central pillars, hair blown about and catching the light, like a fiery crown. Her dress rippling against the curves of her body. She held her arms out towards the crowd and he had never seen her so beautiful. Not beautiful as she was to him, nestling asleep in the crook of his shoulder or full of fire and fury—*Did you see, Peter? Did you see? They cut down the old hawthorn. Butchers!*—No, this was a different kind of beauty. Something unearthly, almost untouchable. It set her apart. Great Mare, Queen of Heaven, Lady of the May. She was luminous.

He held his breath, waiting to see what she would do, and slowly, so slowly he was not at first aware that she was moving, she turned her back on the crowd. He saw now that she had undone the back of her dress. And there it was for all to see. Her mark. The tree growing out of her back, graven image carved in flesh. He had wondered what words she would use. Now he saw that no words were necessary. A deep hum was coming from the crowd. Three notes rising and falling.

Ell-ish-ah!

Promise, climax, sigh.

Ell-ISH-aaaaaah!

All of creation was held in those syllables. The spark.

He looked at Ellisha. Had they done it?

But the mood of the crowd was changing, a desperation had entered their chanting and lone voices were crying out, 'Speak! Speak! Talk to us!'

'Ellisha,' he hissed. Her back was still turned, but her shoulders tensed. Her stage fright not a momentary thing then.

'Speak!'

The crowd was so close, less than five feet away. Some tacit agreement had held them back from mounting the platform, but if they surged forward there was nothing to stop them. No bodyguards or line of police. No secret tunnel or fire escape. He opened his mouth then closed it again. His rhetoric was spent. He could not be both the flame and the means to douse it. In the distance he could make out the uniforms of policemen. But signalling to them for help might cause irreparable damage to their cause. Or it might cause a stampede. And there were children in the crowd.

His eye was caught by a single man pushing his way forward. Not the angry marine of earlier, but well-dressed, his hair greying at the temples, an almost clerical quality about him, but also—Peter screwed up his eyes against the light—something familiar.

At the bottom of the platform the man paused, meeting Peter's gaze with a steady look of his own. There were yellow glints in his eyes, like a wolf's. Peter felt recognition slackening his face. *You?*

'Ah kin help.'

A dumb nod and the man was at his side. He faced the crowd, but then fell silent. Fearing he was overawed, Peter opened his mouth intending to intervene, but the man began speaking in a raw untrained voice that carried nonetheless.

'Those of ye, who hail frae these parts mibbe ken who ah am. Ma name is Duncan MacCaa. Ye'll huv passed me aften enough. I used tae stand in the Street and beg fur money. Ah won't tell ye ma story because it's no ony different tae yer ain. Ah liked drink and ah liked drugs. I lost everything ah had, ma job, ma wife. Ah lost God. Ah even lost maself.' He rubbed a hand down the back of his head, as though surprised to find the long greasy hair missing, then made a sudden stabbing motion of his arm through the air at Ellisha. 'But She came. And She didna walk past me or despise me or gie me mouldy coppers frae the bottom of her pocket. She spoke to me. Directly tae me. As She's spoken tae each and every one of ye.'

It was strange. Peter could hear the capital letter each time the man said *She*. He feels it too. Her presence.

'Ah'm no one fur speeches. But I tell ye this. She turned ma life around. She saw somethin in me and she asked me, *Why?* Why are ye living this way? No-one ever asked me that. An when ah couldna answer She told me that She had a feelin aboot me. An She gave me all her money.'

Remembering his twenty-pound note, Peter felt his brows rise a little, but this bear of a man clearly knew how to hold an audience and Peter wasn't about to distract him. Even Ellisha was slowly turning back, drawn by his words.

'That wus aboot a year back an as ye can see—' a sweeping gesture encompassing himself '—Ah've turned ma life around. Ah'm remade.' A pause followed by a frown. 'Ah dinna pretend tae ken how it ah works. But ah dae know that it's no wi words she changes ye.' A huskiness entered the big man's voice. 'Once ah'd met her ah couldna go back tae ma auld ways. Ah threw away the bottle in ma pocket an ah walked oot of ma auld life, an ah didna look back. Ah'm Her's now if She'll huv me. An ah'll live the life She wants for me.' He looked down at his hands then raised his chin aggressively. 'An ah'll tell ye this fur nuthin. Ye'll no hear Her by staunin there shouting, *Speak!* Ye'll only hear Her when ye start tae listen wi this!' A massive paw thrust against his heart.

Then, to Peter, perhaps the strangest thing in this day of strange things happened. A thing that was perhaps not strange by the standards of the world, but a very unScottish thing. In this land of grey skies and tight, unrevealing smiles, a great standing stone of a man got down on his knees and stayed there, head bowed, while, down below, the crowd went wild.

Peter's eyes darted towards Ellisha. Slowly she descended from between the pillars. She stopped in front of the kneeling man and laid her hands on his shoulders and held them there when those shoulders shuddered. Then she lifted her head and met the gaze of the crowd. A billowing shadow of silence rolled across them and they stood, awed by the sight of a great bear of a man laying his power at the feet of this woman with the figure of a tree growing out of her back.

Peter saw an old man in the second row lift his left arm and tilt the hand, fingers spread. And there was no need for explanation; it made perfect sense. The tree, its outline mimicked in flesh. Had he not laid his own arm across her back in the same way, spreading his fingers amongst those fierce branches? More hands were rising.

He looked at Ellisha, who shared a fleeting grin of triumph from the corner of her mouth before squaring her shoulders and setting her jaw, as though the crowd were some capricious mythological beast whose reins she found herself holding. He let his gaze follow hers across a vast forest of arms, barely able to absorb the incredible thing that was happening below.

Something was being born before their eyes, some new thing that, together, they had brought to life. It welled up inside him, a huge sense of belonging, and he saw himself suddenly, as if from above, a gaunt man dressed in black, standing on an outcrop, watching a wondrous new power rippling out across the world. And it was so heart-wrenchingly beautiful it made his throat tighten and tears leak from his eyes.

Only that morning he had prayed earnestly to a God he did not believe in. *Send me a hundred people to fill up that room for Ellisha's sake. Or seventy or even fifty. Just enough to trigger the publicity we need.* And later, during the car journey there, he had watched Ellisha gnawing on her knuckle, thinking, *Twenty. We could still pull it off with twenty.*

But they had come in their thousands and tens of thousands: despairing, hollow men and women, who had lost everything, had stood teetering on the edge of the Void, who had held glinting knives to their wrists or hung metaphorical nooses about their necks even as they walked through the days smiling reassuringly at friends and family. They had come, some from half way across the world—not for him, he saw with a pang—but because they had seen something familiar in Ellisha's face, and heard his message as Ellisha's message, which had called to them across time zones and cyberspace, drawing them to this digital goddess, who seemed to live beyond the North Wind and east of Westernesse.

And now they stood on Calton Hill where, long ago blue-eyed priests had drawn blades across the throats of struggling animals. The place where women, freed from shame or modesty, had daubed their naked bodies in green sap and jumped over Beltane flames in forgotten remembrance of the Gathering Spark. They stood in this place of blood and fire because they had toppled the new gods, and known only despair. And now they sacrificed their darkness and their skepticism, and opened up their veins to the savagery of the past and the magnificence of the future.

They were chanting again. And this time there was no stopping them with words. Camera flashes. A bobbing sea of microphones pushing forward. Overhead, the wump, wump of a helicopter; a TV crew was filming. They would be on the national news. Possibly even news channels across the globe. A success. Beyond imagining. Beyond their wildest dreams.

He turned triumphantly towards Ellisha. But she ignored him, looking out across the crowd, her eyes wide with fear. And there it was, like the moment a dream grows dark. There were more people pushing their way up the hill. Late-comers, stragglers, hangers-on, day-trippers, tourists, passers-by, all pouring on to Calton Hill, pushing forward to have a better look.

—Ellisha! Ellisha! Over here.

—Look up, Ellisha! Here!

—We love you, Ellisha!

—When's God coming? Do you have a date yet?

—Does Ignis Dei believe in the afterlife?

—We want to create our souls. Tell us what to do!

—Ellisha, look here! Just for a second. Turn around!

—How many souls must be created before God can come into being?

—Where are you going?

—Talk to us! We need you!

—Come on. Give us a smile.

'Go back,' he shouted. 'Give Ellisha space!' But his voice was lost in the roiling beast of the mob. They had surged around the back of the monument, and others were pulling themselves up the stepped edifice. The air turned gelatinous. The threat of the edge. Unconsciously he had been stepping backwards. He felt himself rocked with the pressure of advancing bodies and someone knocked against his shoulder, nearly sending him toppling.

'Please!' He could barely breathe. Press of bodies all around him. Movement. A sudden surge; he was almost lifted off his feet. Hands clutching him. The pocket of his jacket ripped.

'Ellisha? ELLISHA!' She was only a few paces away, but already barely visible, dragged forward by an unseen current, while he was held back by the swell of bodies. For an instant, she managed to turn her head, and he saw fear carved across her face. Briefly glimpsed. Then she was gone.

Reach her. Pushing forward with all his might. Unable to budge. A scream. A woman's? 'I am so sorry. I—'

Up ahead he could make out MacCaa, that lump of fallen meteor roughly hewn by wind and rain into the shape of a man, pinioned against one of the great sandstone pillars.

'Ellisha!' Peter's voice was swallowed up in the voice of the crowd, which now sounded like an unending scream. *What have we done?*

There was a roar of outrage. Unhindered by fears or niceties, MacCaa was pushing his brute frame through the press of bodies by the most direct route; he had knocked a photographer out of the way, breaking his camera.

'You'll pay for that. You'll pay! That's my bloody job, mate.'

MacCaa paid no attention. Acolyte. Defender of the faith, now he was Samson in reverse, there to defend the child of a godless God.

Helpless observer, Peter watched as MacCaa dived into the seething mass of bodies and plucked Ellisha from the jaws of the mob. She came up very still, her dress torn in several places. Through the gaps, the livid branches of her scar were visible.

A shockwave of silence spread through the crowd. They looked at the motionless body of their prophetess with puzzlement, as though it was an extraordinary thing to destroy the herald of a new age.

Head thrown back, arm trailing. There was an obscene emptiness about Ellisha's body, no more related to her essence than a haunch of venison reveals the shape of the leaping deer in the forest. Peter felt a high thin pulse beating at his temples. He observed everything with the numb detachment of a man who knows he is caught in a dream. MacCaa, his hands clumsy, blunt tools pawing at faerie flesh, looking down at Ellisha's limp body, as though he could not understand why she was not moving.

He heard—though he could not possibly have heard—a gasp. Ellisha sat up and threw her arms about MacCaa's neck. Then she turned her head, searching. He felt his heart press against his chest. *Find me. Please.* She paused, looking in his direction, though he could not tell if she was seeing him, and, for an instant, they were caught in a strange moment of unbeing, as though each were dreaming the other. And suddenly everything rushed back, as though the Void, that dark moon, had sucked meaning from the world, and now let it flood back in, the bright ache of the sky, the tidal roar of the crowd and, in the distance, the thin wail of sirens.

CHAPTER 15

A SMALL WINDOWLESS ROOM. HE had been sitting in it for what seemed like hours. No-one would tell him anything. From time to time a police officer poked his head around the door to check on him and he asked plaintively, *Is my wife here?* But he received no answer beyond a shrug.

He waited, hands on knees, uncomfortably aware of the sweat patches under his arms and the creases in his trousers, while his mind ran in circles chased by an impending sense of doom that his thoughts articulated as *Trouble. We're in big trouble!*

He continued to wait. High on the wall was a vent where plastic ribbons fluttered continuously with a click-click-clicking noise. He tried to figure out how time was passing by counting the clicks but kept losing track. *Should have asked for a lawyer.* Then again he wasn't all that sure if he was under arrest.

The door was unlocked, and two men appeared. The smaller of the two had a neatly trimmed beard and dark furious eyes. The second man, older, heavier, with a sweating bald head reminded Peter of the Scottish children's rhyme *Baldy Bane*. He took a laptop out, and what looked like recording equipment, from a bag. He then set a notepad and pen down on the desk before taking a seat and leaning heavily on his elbows. The smaller man took a seat beside him, at the same time introducing himself as DC MacAlpin. He had a calm, neutral voice, which carried such an undertone of threat that Peter instantly forgot to listen to Baldy Bane's name.

There was a silence. The plastic ribbons made their faint clicking noise as they blew against the vent. Baldy Bane made some adjustments to the equipment, before nodding to his partner.

'State your name.' This from MacAlpin.

'But you already know.'

MacAlpin tapped the recorder. 'For the record.'

'Ellisha? My wife. Is she safe? I've had no word.'

'Just answer the question, sir.'

'My name is Peter Kelso.'

'And you organized the rally for an organisation calling itself—' consulting his notes '—Ignis Dee?'

'Ignis DAY. I explained all this when they brought me here. Please, no-one will tell me anything.' *She can't be dead. Surely they would tell me if she was dead.*

MacAlpin looked at the recording device again and Peter sucked in his lower lip then sighed. 'I was involved in the organization.'

He expected to be asked details of his intent, but Kenneth MacAlpin looked down at his notes again. He appeared to read something twice. 'Ignis Dei is a religious organization?'

'I—' He hesitated.

'It isn't a religious organization?'

'Yes. No. Not exactly. We're a system of belief.'

Baldy Bane hadn't said a word. But he watched closely, writing things down from time to time. Peter tried to include him in his answers, but he returned only a blank flinty stare, which made Peter anxious. MacAlpin was speaking again.

'You were preaching on Calton Hill.'

'I was explaining. Ignis Dei is a new spiritual norm.' *So baselessly stupid-sounding when said aloud.* He looked anxiously at MacAlpin, trying to gauge his reaction.

'A spiritual norm with no God?'

Ah, so he had been paying attention. 'We claim that there is no God yet.'

MacAlpin and Baldy Bane exchanged looks, and Peter wasn't sure whether he had won the point. MacAlpin turned back with a shrug. 'A religion without God. That's a new one on me.'

Peter refrained from pointing out that Buddhism or Unitarian Universalism worked on similar principles. There was a small pause, then MacAlpin rapped his knuckles on the table, and Peter noted that he wore a thick gold band with an intaglio of a man in armour. 'You didn't think to inform us that you intended to host a rally on Calton Hill.'

Is it a duty to inform the authorities? He searched his scant knowledge of the law and found it wanting. 'We didn't allow for the numbers,' he began hesitantly. 'It was intended as a small gathering. We were taken aback by unexpected popularity.'

'Yet, you ran an aggressive social media campaign in the months prior to your launch, did you not?'

He wanted to shake his head, to explain that no-one could have predicted success on that scale. The gathering force, invisible, silent, drawing closer, a storm ready to break out of cloudless skies. In his mind's eye an image of Ellisha flashed up. Careening out of the bathroom dressed in the threadbare piano shawl, towel wrapped around her damp hair, a hectic look in her eye making Peter think she was about to speak in tongues. In her hands, a tablet was clutched against her chest.

—*We got Hisashi Nakamura!*

—*For dinner?*

—*Peter! You can't say things like that. Nakamura is the most influential vlogger out there.*

—*I know. I know. This is amazing. I mean I thought we'd made it when that "Divine Journeys" channel featured us. But this is huge. Nakamura's got thirty million followers. Do you know what this means?*

—*Of course.*

But they hadn't, not really.

He spread his hands. 'I—I suppose.'

'You suppose? Were you or weren't you a part of the media campaign?'

'I was.'

'You seem nervous, Peter.'

He looked hard at MacAlpin. It was easier to pretend Baldy Bane was not in the room. 'Is it unusual to feel discomforted by strange and aggressively put questions?'

MacAlpin let the point go. The intaglio on his little finger drummed against the desk. 'Do you understand the extent of the damage your followers inflicted? Calton Hill is a world heritage site, and there are reports of offences against the monument, the observatory and also to personal property in the area.'

'But they were peaceful. Ignis Dei is a peaceful organization!'

'What we saw was a full-scale riot. Have you any idea the cost of the police operation, let alone the damage? We're probably talking tens of thousands.'

'Aye. More like hundreds of thousands,' Baldy Bane said agreeably.

Peter's glance ricocheted between the two men in alarm. 'We didn't intend harm. We only wanted to reach people in need. To help them.'

'Peter, inciting a riot is a criminal offence.'

'It wasn't like that. Those people, they were just desperate, frightened individuals, who had felt hope for the first time. It went to their heads. I should have foreseen the impact—'

He caught sight of triumph glinting in MacAlpin's eyes. Has me now. Good as confessed. He fought for dignity, then in a voice that shook slightly, said, 'I think I need a lawyer.'

Instead of an answer there was a knock on the door. MacAlpin glanced at Baldy Bane then rose to his feet. He opened the door a crack. Twisting his neck round, Peter could see a heavily built man in a suit standing outside. They spoke in low whispers, only a few phrases intelligible. 'No … no, I don't think so … no, nothing…' Something in the tone made Peter feel inexplicably hopeful. He watched closely as MacAlpin shut the door and stood a moment, his shoulders a little slumped.

Just as he was beginning to think he wouldn't speak, MacAlpin turned to face him. 'Wait here!'

'Am I free to go?'

MacAlpin twisted the ring on his finger, his angry eyes fixed on Peter's face. 'Just wait here.' He jerked his head at Baldy Bane, who was already gathering together the laptop and recorder. A moment later they were gone.

His wait was not a short one. Or perhaps it was only that time had no meaning in a place where there was no interaction, no human recognition, not even a hostile one.

'Mr Kelso?'

The voice was English, confident and capable-sounding, the kind of plucky tones that made the listener think of World War II and Bletchley Park. Peter found himself looking at an unfamiliar woman. Fiftyish, statuesque with short white-blond hair. She was exotically out of place standing in an Edinburgh pokey, her clothes arranged about her in geometric folds like an Art Deco ornament.

She was looking at him with the kind of uncanny piercing expression rarely encountered in humans but universally found in garden robins, and he realised belatedly that she was holding out her hand and that he was supposed to take it.

'Perdita Bonneville, so nice to meet you at last.'

He shook hands, noting that her fingers rested only briefly before they were withdrawn.

'Are you my lawyer?'

She didn't smile. 'Follow me, please.' Turning, she left the room without waiting for his response.

He caught up with her at the desk, where the sergeant on duty returned his belongings. A little dazed, he thanked the man for keeping them safe, aware of the foolishness of his words even as he spoke them.

'Peter?'

The belt dropped from his hands onto the desk with a clattering sound. *Ellie!* The word was not spoken, but resounded inside his head as though a gong had been struck. She was standing behind him in the company of a female officer, the confusion on her face, he suspected, a mirror of his own.

At her side before he knew it. 'I thought—when you disappeared—No-one would tell me anything.'

'I know.' There was a brave smile on her face, but she was biting her lips. Her distress filled him with a tender rage. He wanted to yell and slam his fists on something. But the solid presence of the police sergeant and Perdita Bonneville inhibited him. Time for all that later.

A clearing of a throat drew his attention back to the room.

'We need to leave now.' Perdita was holding open the door. 'The press doesn't know you're here yet, but they can't be far off.'

Meek as children, they followed her from the police station on to the cobbled road, of which street? It was dark outside and he felt disoriented. *Grayfield Square? Could be. After all there were trees on the other side of the road. What time is it? After midnight surely? Well after by the look of the sky.* It hardly mattered. All he knew was that he was stunned with lack of sleep and not quite certain that he wasn't dreaming. Ellisha was clutching his hand very tightly, and he guessed that she, too, was focussing more on the gleam of the rain-washed cobbles than the sheer immensity of what they had done.

The hum of an engine. Perdita was leading them towards the silhouette of a waiting Bentley. Etheric plumes of vapour rising from the exhaust, blacked out windows; it did not belong in their small Scottish world.

Perdita had the passenger door open, and he could see the inside glowing, like some fiery pit of brimstone. Instinctively, he stopped, and felt the tug on his arm as Ellisha moved forward. 'Peter, what's wrong?'

'I don't—' How to put into words? 'What if this isn't as it seems?'

'It seems like someone rescuing us from a shitstorm.'

He tried to match her levity. 'You say that. But what if Auld Nick's waiting for us inside?'

'Seriously, Peter. The Devil?' When he didn't move Ellisha tugged his arm again, and gestured with her head back towards the police station. 'That's the devil we know. For now, we'll be better off with the one we don't.'

He had never ridden in a truly superb car before, and it was hard not to be impressed. Even through his exhaustion he noted how he sank into the leather seats and how there was plenty of room for his legs. Perdita joined them in the back of the car.

'I'm sorry you had to spend so long in there. Please believe me, we were doing everything in our power to expedite the situation.'

'And who is "we"?'

'At present I'm not at liberty to say. But I promise everything will be explained shortly.'

'We're not going home first?' Ellisha asked.

'I'm afraid that is impossible.' She reached into her bag and drew out an iPad. 'You may want to see how things are taking shape.'

Ellisha took it from her. 'Where should I look?'

'Everywhere.'

Ellisha obeyed. The screen flickered and suddenly there were aerial shots of Calton Hill. He felt his jaw slackening. The crowd looked like a massive squirming beast, featureless as a worm, moving with a relentless writhing motion towards the monument. The shot cut, and he saw Ellisha, the low February sun catching her hair. And something in her dignity, in the quiet way she held herself apart, even the way she held her arms out to the crowd, took his breath away.

Ellisha selected another video, and a tall woman, dishevelled in the way the mothers of small children often are, appeared. 'Is that—'

Ellisha peered at the screen. 'I think it is.'

The woman was obviously answering a question. She was nodding vigorously, her eyes swivelling uncertainly between the interviewer and the camera.

'… I mean we all saw it? Hannah was dead! She wasn't breathing. And I just lost it. I was screaming. Then—' a nervous glance at the camera '—she came. That woman came. Just appeared out of nowhere.'

'And then what?' The interviewer's disembodied voice.

'She—she took hold of her… and Hannah was alive. We all saw it.'

'And what happened afterwards.'

'Afterwards?' A confused look.

'To the woman?'

'She just… well, she just disappeared. I didn't see her again … until today.'

'When you saw the coverage on Calton Hill?'

'Yes. I knew it was her the minute I saw her.'

'How could you be sure?'

'It's not easy to explain. There's something about her. It's like you *know* her. Like you've always known her.' The words beginning to tremble.

The interviewer asked quickly, 'And Hannah shows no ill effect from her encounter?'

'No. She's a brilliant wee thing.'

'How do you explain it?'

Clearly too emotional to answer the woman just shook her head and spread her hands in the universal gesture of, *I can't. I can't.*

The camera swung round to focus on the interviewer, a young woman in a trench-coat, holding an umbrella up. 'Well, there you have it. Someone who has met the mysterious Ell-ish-ah up close and personal. And what an encounter. It seems the woman, who attracted thousands to Calton Hill today, is both known and unknown by everyone who meets her.'

Ellisha clasped a hand over her mouth. But the newscaster was still speaking. 'There are some who are saying today's phenomenon is the appearance of an ancient goddess, others who claim that it's an elaborate hoax. Who can say? Perhaps the world simply grew tired of being afraid. All we really know for sure is that she's tapped into some subconscious Zeitgeist, born of these deadly times, and that Edinburgh hasn't seen anything like it. As to what's coming next, we'll have to wait and see…'

Perdita leaned over and flicked the channel. A tall African American woman was being interviewed. Behind her was a jostling crowd, many of whom had their arms raised in the tree symbol. 'I dunno,' she was saying. 'I can't answer that. I only knew I had to come when I got the call. I can relate to her, the message she's sending out. God knows I've tried every religion there is. I've been all kinds of Christian. I've been Buddhist, Muslim. Hell, I even tried being Jewish once. Nothing felt right. You always feel like you're the bottom rung, that you're not really making a difference.' Behind her there were several nods of agreement.

'But this feels like the start of something new. Ellisha is giving the power of religion back to the people. She—' Her next words were drowned out by a cheer. The woman's eyes were shining. 'She gets you. It's like she knows you and you know her. What she says makes sense.

We want God we gotta earn Him. I hear her … in here.' A stab at her heart.'

Lowering the tablet, Ellisha turned to Perdita. 'Is this really happening? It's really happening. Is it?'

'It's happening.' Perdita's smile was amused. 'We're at the beginning of something extraordinary.'

Peter felt Ellisha's fingers tighten on his thigh. 'It's really happening.'

CHAPTER 16

THE LAST THING PETER EXPECTED was to fall asleep. The constant layering of strangeness upon strangeness made rest seem impossible. Every time he closed his eyes he saw a swirling montage of images: the crowd losing their heads, the heart-wrenching moment when Ellisha disappeared from sight, MacAlpin leaning across the desk, furious eyes blazing: *Inciting a riot is a criminal offence!* Over and over they played inside his head, amplified and distorted by the sound of blood pounding in his heart. Sleep seemed very far away. Yet, sleep he did, because the next thing he knew an unfamiliar voice called his name.

'Peter, are you awake? We've arrived.'

Groggily, he opened his eyes and found himself looking into Perdita's cool face. She looked immaculate, not a hair out of place, and it made him aware of his own sleep-crushed appearance. On his shoulder, Ellisha was slumped like a withered flower, head rolled against his chest at an awkward angle. He shook her gently. 'Wake up. We're here.'

She pulled herself upright like a sleepy child, and looked around, wiping her mouth with the back of a hand. 'Where's here?'

Perdita leaned forward and opened the door. Cool air rushed into the cabin. 'Why don't you see for yourself?'

It was not yet light outside, but the sky had grown pale and starless. They got out on stiff limbs and stood looking up at a sprawling Gothic mansion—turrets, stone mullions, iron finials, crestings—a house from a dark fairy-tale. He glanced back down the driveway and could not see its beginning. A vague sense of the car stopping then gates slowly opening played in his brain, but uncertainly, hovering somewhere between memory and dream.

From behind, he heard Perdita say, 'Extraordinary, isn't it?'

'Is this where you live?' Ellisha asked. She was shivering in the early morning chill, and he put his arm about her. Perdita laughed. It was a cold sound. 'No. This is one of my client's homes.' A buzzing sound. She lifted a phone to her ear. 'Yes? Of course. I'll bring them up.' Her smile glittered cold as the vanished stars. 'Mr Avery will see you now.'

They followed Perdita inside, across a wood-panelled entrance-way and up a curving staircase to a sitting room on the first floor. Perdita knocked, and there was a reply. American, Peter thought as they followed her in. But too soft for New York. West Coast, San Francisco, LA, somewhere like that.

The room was sumptuous: velvet couches, tasteful rugs, above the fireplace a nineteenth-century landscape. Naismith, he guessed and was impressed. Yet, at the same time, he saw nothing that was familiar or comforting. No scattered books or photographs on the mantelpiece. No scruffy house pet or comfortable old cushion. Even the flower arrangement on the table had a sculpted professional air. It made him ache for Ellisha's scattered jam jars and milk jugs filled with snowdrops and trailing strands of ivy.

Avery was standing by a cocktail cabinet pouring himself a drink when they entered. He was grey-haired, about seventy, casually dressed; plain shirt tucked into jeans, thick-rimmed glasses, a trifle old-fashioned. He might have been an accountant save for the deep tan of his skin, which cracked around his eyes like weathered leather as he looked up, smiling. 'Glad you could make it.' He strode across the room and took Ellisha by the hands. 'A pleasure to meet you.'

A little dazed, Ellisha whispered, 'Mr… uh?'

'Avery. Phil Avery. Call me Phil.' He frowned suddenly. 'You tore your dress?'

'In the crowd. They got over-excited.'

Avery was still holding her hands. 'We can't let that happen ever again.' He glanced at Perdita. 'Perdy, can you rustle up a shawl or something?'

'Of course.' The contempt in her voice made Peter look at the floor, but Avery didn't seem to notice. He was still looking at Ellisha. 'It's the funniest thing. But I feel like I know you. We've never met, right? I would have remembered us meeting. But I still feel like we have.'

'We hear that a lot,' Peter said.

Avery turned at once. 'Where are my manners. Peter isn't it? Can I call you Peter?'

A picture of Babs' sardonic smile flashed into Peter's head, and he was tempted to say that he had been called considerably worse than by his Christian name, but natural reserve made him nod politely. The understatement of this reaction seemed to tickle Avery. 'Great,' he announced, beaming. 'That's great. Like I said, call me Phil.'

'Thank you.' Above the flash of capped white teeth, Peter saw a hard, uncompromising intelligence hidden by the gleam of the smile. *Can we trust this man?* Avery was pointing to the cocktail cabinet. 'What's your poison?'

Ellisha accepted whisky and, after the briefest hesitation, Peter asked for orange juice. Avery poured two substantial measures and a not ungenerous amount for himself, then they sank gratefully down on the sofas and took the first few sips in silence. 'You like that?' Avery asked.

'It's a very fine malt,' Ellisha agreed. 'Very smooth.'

'It's a Craigellachie. Special edition. They make it just for me.'

'You enjoy our national drink then?' Peter said.

'Better than the non-alcoholic one. What's that dreadful orange soda you're all so mad about?'

Ellisha laughed. 'Irn Bru. I used to think it was some kind of joke they played on unsuspecting foreigners.'

Avery gave a chuckle, and just then Perdita returned, carrying a cream-coloured cashmere shawl. She handed it to Ellisha. 'That should do for now. We'll find you both clean clothes after we've had our meeting.'

'Meeting?'

'The English, always so formal,' Avery said, shaking his head. 'Don't make it sound like the boardroom. They don't even know who I am.'

'Ah.' Perdita swept her hand towards Phil. 'Mr Avery does not like the limelight, but he's one of the richest men on earth.'

'Time Magazine named me amongst the world's twelve most reclusive billionaires,' Avery added, flashing that almost fluorescent grin. 'Funny I never thought of it that way. To me, it was just a case of the product mattering more than the person.' He waved a hand towards the drink's cabinet. 'Pour yourself a drink, Perdy, while I tell these folks what I have in mind.'

Despite saying this, Avery took a minute, sitting back in his seat and contemplating the tawny liquid in his glass, before beginning. 'I won't deny it. I'm interested in you.'

Peter noticed that he addressed these words at Ellisha. But his gaze clearly made her uncomfortable, and she pulled the shawl tighter around her shoulders before asking, 'How long have you been watching us?'

Avery laughed and tapped the side of his nose. 'A while. Little bird whispered in my ear you might be the next big thing.'

'But you knew to come. I mean here, today, to Scotland. You knew Calton Hill would be big.'

'Now that,' Avery cried, pointing his finger like Uncle Sam, 'woulda been something. But I'm afraid I sent Perdy here along to be my eyes and ears. I was curious to see how things would turn out. Lucky for me I was in Berlin when she calls and says, "Get yourself over here.

They're causing quite a stir."' He turned to Perdita. 'Hey, did you show them the feedback?'

'I did.' Perdita had fetched herself a brandy in a balloon glass, and perched with it on the arm of a chair. 'The stats are impressive.'

'Have you seen how many hits your website has?' Avery asked.

'I'm afraid we haven't had the chance to review them,' Peter said quickly. 'I intend to go over them as soon as I get a chance.'

'Of course,' Avery nodded. 'How many hits do you think you have? Take a guess.'

'Ten thousand,' Ellisha ventured. Then, when Avery shook his head, 'A hundred thousand? Not—you can't mean—a million?'

'Try a hundred times that.'

They gawped at him, like wicked children who have set a spark in a tinder-dry forest then run away as the flames spread out beyond control.

A hundred million? It's not possible. A number like that, not real. Inconceivable. Like one of those improbable numbers in the Old Testament, Moses judging millions or the number of species that would have had to enter the ark. A number expressing a truth greater than its literal self. He shook his head. 'I can't believe it.'

Avery watched their appalled expressions with amusement. 'Believe it. I'll tell Perdy to fire it all up for you in a moment. It's very impressive. Although, I have to tell you, I'm a lucky guy, a lot of impressive things come my way. And I've reached a point in my life where I can pick and choose.' He leaned back, his head tilted. 'These days, I rarely pick anything out. But you, Ellisha Kelso, are something else. I can't figure you out.' He leaned forward suddenly, looking into Ellisha's face. 'Was that all pantomime out there? Or are you the real deal?'

Peter glanced sharply at Ellisha. How would she react? Did she even understand the shift in power that had taken place on Calton Hill? He cursed the lack of opportunity to talk alone. *Should have made an excuse. Come up with a plan.* Avery was waiting, and Peter held his breath.

She did not blink. She met Avery's gaze with absolute composure, expressionless, the face of a *Kumari Devi,* one of those girls hand-picked as living goddesses in Tibet, a girl whose smallest twitch or grimace could change a man's fate.

Avery sat back. 'Okay,' he said. 'Okay. You claim that there is no God in your universe?'

'That is correct.'

'Isn't that simply a reinvention of Buddhism?'

'Not at all. There is no divine principle for us. No underlying divine nature to be discovered.'

'Perhaps Scientology or Logical Positivism or New Age Goddess worship would be closer?'

Peter was impressed that a businessman would be familiar with these terms, but, then again, Avery had the air of a polymath. Ellisha gave a small shake of her head. 'We claim no expertise in those philosophies. I can only tell you that we offer something quite unique in the history of belief—' her lips morphed into wryness '—or you might even say in the history of unbelief.'

Avery took a sip of his whisky and nodded slowly. 'But can it really be a religion without God?'

'Can Confucianism? Can Taoism or the Jains?'

'Granted. But the systems you mention still offer the comfort of the eternal soul.'

'We offer people the act of their own creation. What greater comfort could there be than that?'

Avery swirled his drink inside the glass for a moment, considering before asking, 'How can we know what goodness is without God? Without some universal sanction?'

Peter guessed that, whatever Avery's beliefs may or may not be now, he came from a profoundly religious background. The kind his mother would have called a God-in-the-bones. And now he asked again, 'How can we know goodness or morality without God?'

Peter wondered whether to intervene, but Avery was staring so intently at Ellisha that he felt strangely distanced from them, as though watching characters interacting on a screen. He glanced at Perdita, but she was as cool and expressionless as a graveyard statue. Ellisha smiled at Avery, as if she answered questions of a profound philosophical nature as a matter of course.

'We know the same way we have always known. Even elementary school children know the difference between right and wrong. Do you imagine that you developed your sense of right and wrong from the Bible? The Ten Commandments? The Golden Rule? Was Jesus the first man to preach *do ut des*?

'The Jewish scholar, Hillel, was telling us to *Do unto others* a generation before the Christian Messiah, and the same idea emerged hundreds of years before that in Greece, China, India, Persia.' She took a sip of her whisky and tilted her head back. 'But, if you really need your morality from a divinity, go back a few millennia and the Egyptian goddess of truth, Ma'at, is there in the papyri preaching the same message. You see, we evolved to seek the good. And we do not need to be told what is good any more than we need to be told to feel love.'

Avery did not respond immediately. He sat back in his chair and steepled his hands, the tips of his forefingers against his lips. *He's trying to hide it*, Peter thought. *But we've struck a nerve.*

'Well,' Avery said. His voice was carefully controlled. 'You've given me a lot to think about.' He swung around suddenly. 'What do you think, Perdy?'

Perdita uncrossed her legs then flicked a bit of lint from her trousers before answering. 'Convincing enough. But tomorrow will be the real test.'

Peter glanced at Ellisha—did she follow any of this?—but she still had that stiff, Kumari Devi look about her and did not acknowledge him. Avery had turned back to study Ellisha, and Peter felt the need to take charge. He rose to his feet. 'Thank you for your hospitality, but it has been a long day, and I really think Ellisha and I must head back home.' He felt a tug on his arm.

'Don't be an ass, Peter. There is no going home.'

Stunned more than chagrined, he sat down again. Avery was looking comfortable once more and Ellisha took a breath. 'I—Phil, you should know, there was quite a lot of damage done. The police are holding us responsible—'

'That's all taken care of.'

Avery said it quite matter-of-factly, as another person might say, *It's my round* or *Let me pay the taxi*. And Peter realised, with a chill, that here was true power. Not the Bentley or the mysterious ride through the night or the residence with its turreted roof and antique-stuffed rooms. But this. The quiet assumption that things would be done his way.

Avery leaned forward. 'You've been very patient. Pete's right. This has been a big day. An incredible day. And here I am, bringing you all the way out here and not making a whole lot of sense. Believe me, I am fascinated by what you have to say. I'm very close to buying in.'

Ellisha frowned. 'Buying in?'

'What you've brought into the world is quite incredible. But you've said it yourselves, you don't have God providing for you. You're going to need backers.'

'You want a share in Ignis Dei?' Peter asked cautiously.

'Exactly. It isn't easy for a man in my position to find something that sets me apart. Bill Gates has his humanitarian programme. Elon Musk wants to reach the stars. Maybe I want a little bit of immortality. Maybe I like this idea of creating God. But I'm not quite there. Tomorrow, I'm going to ask something of you, and we'll take it from there.' He held out his hand to Ellisha, as if concluding a deal. Ellisha took it, and they locked eyes for a moment. Peter watched, seized by the feeling that they were communicating on some deep level that excluded him. But then he was shaking hands, both with Avery and Perdita, and their drinks were refreshed, and the atmosphere became almost party-like until Ellisha stifled a yawn, and Avery immediately put down his drink.

'Where are my manners? You're exhausted. I'll get someone to take you to your room, and we'll talk after you've had a chance to rest.' He bent forward and patted Ellisha's shoulder. 'Until tomorrow.'

A housekeeper took them to their room, and showed no sign of shock when Peter asked, 'Where are we?'

'This is Mr Avery's Scottish estate. You're not far from Langbank. Dumbarton rock is just over the water.'

'Does he live here?' Ellisha asked. This made the housekeeper smile.

'I've worked here ten years. And this is the first time I've met him.' She opened a door. 'Your rooms are in here. There are fresh clothes for both of you, and if you need anything at all, there's a phone by the bed. Just dial zero.'

After she had gone they stared at each other. 'Do you see this place?' Ellisha whispered. She pointed up at the high raftered roof. 'I used to think we were well off, but our entire house could fit inside the hallway here.'

They explored their 'room'—which was not a room at all, but a suite connected by several internal doors—holding hands like naughty children searching for Christmas presents, spurts of giggling escaping from time to time the pressure of their lips.

'It's incredible.' He was whispering.

She squeezed his hand. 'I know. Like a fairy-tale.'

There was a great crackling log fire, and he picked up a marble figurine from the mantel and felt its cool edges beneath his fingers. Turning it over, he saw the signature was Rodin and nearly dropped it in surprise. *What could it be like to have wealth like this? To set a priceless object down as though it was a common, everyday item, perhaps even to have forgotten you owned it.* Half chokingly, he said, 'This is beyond our wildest dreams.'

'Is it?' Ellisha had run over to the window and was tugging at the heavy curtain. 'It must be nearly dawn.'

He put the figurine down. 'Do you realise who Avery is, what he can do for us?'

She wasn't listening. 'Of course.'

'Okay, who is he? Go on, take a guess.'

'Our fairy godfather? Santa Claus? Jesus?'

'All of the above. With his backing, we'll be able to do whatever we want, make Ignis Dei into whatever we want.' He came up behind her, slightly annoyed by her indifference. 'What are you looking at?'

She pointed through the retreating dawn shadows. 'Look, isn't that a figure on horseback on the far side of that river?'

He laughed. 'Perhaps it's Merlin?'

'Here, in Scotland?'

'Certainly. There are very old legends that say Merlin was driven into the Caledonian Forests after the Battle of Adderdyd was lost. And other legends that say Arthur had a son called Merevie.' He pointed across the water. 'He was born in the Tower of the Red Hall on the south side of Dumbarton Rock, a strong and handsome lad, who might have become king.'

'Why didn't he?'

'Because he was known locally as "the fool of the forest" due to his preference for riding alone amongst the trees.'

She wiped away the mist from the diamonds of glass, as though trying to see more clearly. 'What happened to him?'

'There are different traditions, but some say he was gored to death by a boar.'

This made her eyes shine. 'He was the son of the goddess.'

'You think?'

'You're forgetting, I've spent a lot of time reading dusty old legends at the university. It's a common motif: Adonis, Diarmid, Osiris. They all take on the role of son or lover of the goddess then, later are killed by a boar, or some say it is really a sow, who is nothing more than an avatar of the goddess herself.'

An icy little echo from the past whispered inside his head using Babs' voice. *Don't forget, Stone-man, all the legends tell us that the King must die for the Queen of Heaven.* And he shivered. 'What makes her so keen to murder?'

'It's not murder. Not in the way we think it. It's sacrifice. Transition from one state to another. She sacrifices him to create something new. To become something new in herself. It's why male scholars so often dismiss goddesses as embodiments of the harvest or renewed fertility, all that watered-down nonsense. As though the resurrection of the year was like flipping over a page in a calendar, rather than what it truly represents.'

He lifted his eyebrows. 'Which is?'

'A weapon of mass creation.'

'Then the goddess will have no complaints about what we are about to do.'

'What's th—'

He was tearing Ellisha's dress down before she had time to finish the question, burying his face in her bared breasts as though he would eat her alive, as though he would swallow the moon.

But she stiffened. 'Peter. Do you think this could all be real?'

He came up for breath, gasping a little. 'What's that?' Her eyes were round and earnest. 'Out there, on Calton Hill, I felt something.'

'What?'

'When I heard you addressing the crowd. I don't know, it seemed so real.' She looked past him towards the crackling fire. 'Before, it all seemed like a story we were half making up. But when I saw all those people looking up… believing.' She searched his face. 'You felt it too?'

The intensity of the question took him by surprise.

'Didn't you?'

'Yes. Yes, of course.' All he could think about was the taste of those breasts.

'I knew it.' She threw her arms around him, and he pressed his lips into her flesh, wanting to catch everything about her, even her doubt, and hold it to himself.

Before he knew what he was doing he had her down on the floor, her dress a torn rag tossed on the carpet. He scooped her legs up, pushing them back towards her head, forming her into a crescent moon, virgin moon splayed ready for ripening. With one hand he loosened himself from his trousers and plunged into her, making her scream because men had pledged themselves to her today and he needed her to know that she belonged to him even as he lost himself inside her. The possessor in possessing, possessed. And, in the heat of the moment, quite failing to notice that forgetting that she was now using the language of belief.

CHAPTER 17

THEY AWOKE LAZILY, LATE INTO the morning, with sunlight burning gold behind the curtains. With his fingertips, he brushed Ellisha's face which was still damp and unfocussed with sleep. 'Did any of yesterday really happen?'

She blinked at him dreamily. 'You're not in Kansas anymore, McToto.' Then she sat up, wide-eyed. 'What time is it?'

A clock on the bedside table read eleven thirty. Ellisha clapped her hands to her mouth. 'Are we late? Did we miss it?'

'Miss what?'

'Whatever it is Phil wants us to do today?'

'Avery isn't the kind to wait about. He'll send for us when he's ready.' He reached out to stroke Ellisha's breast, but she was already climbing out of bed. 'Come on. I want a bath before they come for us.'

The bathroom was a nineteenth-century fantasy: roll-top bath, gold taps, deep green tiles, polished wooden floors. Ellisha's eyes lit up. 'Let's get in.'

'Both of us?'

'Pussy.'

'Witch.'

While the taps ran, lightness took hold of them, and they danced round each other like children, exclaiming about the ridiculousness of everything because somehow that was the only way to make it real.

'What have we done? What have we actually done?'

'You really didn't think we could fill a hundred seats?'

'I didn't think we could fill ten.'

'Your face when that cop said thousands had been filing into the area.'

'Yours when you thought you had to address them all.'

When the bath was ready they climbed in, Peter first then Ellisha sitting with her back to him between his legs. There was a small table beside them, supplied with an elegant array of toiletries. He reached for one, and began to soap Ellisha's hair. And, in doing so, the hard, cold stone that had lived inside his chest for months, making it hard to breathe, melted away. It was a moment of perfect happiness. And some buried part of him recognised it and tried to hold on to it even as it dissolved in distraction.

Ellisha had spotted a TV remote, and was waving it like a wand at a screen mounted on the wall opposite.

'I want to see if they're still talking about us on the news.'

A riffle of images, like the pages of a book. 'Wait!' He put a hand on her wrist. 'Go back.'

Reluctantly, she tuned into an early morning chat-show. A man was seated between two presenters. His dog-collar shone in the studio lights and the byword at the bottom of the screen (though Peter had no need to read it) clearly stated that this was the Reverend Hart. He had a plump pink face and sparse pale eyebrows that added to his rather supercilious expression.

Ellisha glanced over her shoulder. 'Someone you know?'

'He was the minister in Findbrae, where I grew up, took over after my father died.' He took her hand and stroked it without moving his eyes from the screen.

'But you don't like him?'

'My father and I couldn't agree about God. But I admired his convictions. He thought God made him a better person, and he tried to be one. But Reverend Hart is a different kettle of fish. The church is a career to him, and he'll say whatever he thinks will gain him advancement. I didn't stay long in Findbrae after my father's death, but I saw enough to know that, no, I don't like him.'

Reverend Hart was speaking. He had a soft malicious voice. 'Of course, people have been using terms such as The Sermon on the Mount. But I'm afraid it's all just nonsense.'

The female presenter leaned forward. 'So you don't think that we're looking at a new religious phenomenon?'

A dismissive quirk of the lips. 'I'm afraid it's all just rubbish theology. There is hardly a need to "create God" when we already have His revelation through the teachings of Christ.'

'And, while the "green goddess"—' Ellisha snorted at this '—remains a mystery, you believe you can shed some light on the acolyte?'

Peter's hand tightened on Ellisha's shoulder.

'Oh, I know him.' A decorous look down at the fat pink hands on his lap before cold eyes lifted to the camera. 'If I am not greatly mistaken that was Peter Kelso.'

'The son of the former minister.'

'Indeed yes. I can't imagine what his father would have thought.'

'About him losing his faith or finding another one?' This from the male presenter.

'That is really not for me to speculate.' Reverend Hart was shaking his head, a disappointed parent ready to forgive. 'If he is listening, I want him to know that he is in our prayers, and we hope he will find the wisdom to return to us.'

'You don't think that established religion has much to fear then?'

A priggish smile that pulled in his lips. 'Oh no, no, no. Not yet, no.'

The female presenter lifted a hand to her ear. 'I believe we have some footage from Reverend Kelso's church in the village of Findbrae.'

The scene dissolved and he felt a lump in his throat when he saw the granite church, seeming so small, that had been the centre of his father's life. A pang of self-doubt made him wonder, *Am I mad? Did that pink-faced Judas have a point?*

Ellisha reached for the remote and killed the screen. 'Don't listen to him. We're going to do great things with Ignis Dei.'

He looked down at her wonderingly. 'You really think so?'

She leaned back on his chest and looked up at him, a halo of soap bubbles ringing her face. 'Remember last night when I told you I felt something standing out there on Calton Hill?'

'Yes.'

'Well, I know what it was.'

He stroked her hair and a bubble escaped, floating up, a fugitive particle of the moon returning. 'What was it? What did you feel?'

'I felt holy.'

A short time later Perdita came to ask if they were ready to meet with Avery. They followed her, damp and self-conscious as children ready for their first day at school, dressed in clothing that had awaited them inside the huge Victorian armoire standing in the corner of the bedroom. Ellisha wore an ivory dress with lace inserts in the sleeves, while Peter had been provided with a dark suit of excellent cut that might have been made for him, except for a trifling shortness in the sleeves.

Avery was waiting for them in the library. He welcomed them warmly, insisting that they help themselves from a table spread with a mouth-watering array of pastries and croissants. At the smell of freshly-ground coffee reaching his nostrils, an awareness of hunger came crashing over Peter and he felt almost dizzy at the thought of food. Needing no second prompting, he helped himself to a generous plateful, and fell upon it almost before it was decorous to do so. In the middle of his first mouthful, he noticed that Ellisha's plate was empty.

'What's up?'

She wrinkled her nose. 'I don't know. Everything's moving so fast. My stomach can't keep up. It feels like it's fizzing. Besides.' She pinched the soft curve of her hip. 'I could stand to lose a pound or two.'

Avery waited until they were both seated, smiling like a benevolent father. Peter began to feel prickles of electricity lifting the hairs on the back of his neck. *We've placed ourselves in this man's hands. And we know nothing about him.*

As if he knew what he had been thinking, Avery coughed and said, 'I realise this all seems strange to you. I am not trying to be mysterious, but—'

His words were cut off by the sound of the door opening. Perdita came in, supporting on her arm a tiny woman with intense black eyes and a hint of something native American about her features. Avery made the introductions. 'This is Alessandra Fernández. My researchers have been out there, interviewing people who made the journey to Calton Hill to see Ellisha.' He flashed the woman a reassuring smile. 'We believe Alessandra has something very special to ask.'

They both got to their feet, but Ellisha hurried over and took the woman's hands. There was something tender in the moment, and Peter cursed himself for having left his phone upstairs. *A perfect moment. Should've captured it. Got it out on social media. Missed opportunity. Have to be quicker thinking in future.*

Alessandra looked up into Ellisha's face. 'I know you.'

He expected Ellisha to say, '*I get that a lot*' or '*You only think you do*'. But she only smiled gently, and said, 'I think you have something to tell me.'

'I—' Alessandra searched Ellisha's face, then dropped her gaze with the fright of one who feels they have overstepped boundaries. A second attempt. 'My daughter, Elena, I want to tell you about her.'

Ellisha nodded encouragingly and Alessandra went on, 'She was so beautiful. My only child...'

'Go on,' Avery said.

Alessandra looked down at the floor. 'She was beautiful and full of life. But she was headstrong and proud. Knew what she wanted always.' A tear leaked from Alessandra's eye, and she pulled a hanky from her pocket and dabbed at it. 'She wouldn't listen. I couldn't stop her.' She looked to Ellisha again, pleadingly. 'I am from El Salvador. 'They—the gangs; they are very dangerous in my country—they wanted my daughter to join them. They say she can be a drug mule. She likes the *Salvatrucha*, wants to go with him. And when I say, no, they ask for two thousand American dollars.' She broke off and stared into nothingness for a moment.

'Tell me,' Ellisha said softly.

'I do not have that kind of money. I am a hairdresser. My daughter is at school. Soon they call us up at all hours, saying they will burn my shop if I do not give them my daughter. They call my nieces and nephews and threaten them. They even leave a corpse in the street outside my house.'

Peter glanced at Avery in shock. For a moment everything felt unreal, as though they were all actors on a stage playing to some unseen audience. But Alessandra had begun to speak again. 'We have to go. I know that. I sell everything to get us out. And I am lucky. I get to America. I marry a good man, a wealthy man.

'But my daughter. She cannot settle. I give her everything. But she wants her *Salvatrucha*. She wants her roots, and to see her grandparents, her *abuela y abuelo*. She cannot be satisfied with life here. Last year, she ran away. We could not find her. My husband hired the detectives. We don't hear much. Then, just before her seventeenth birthday, they come... they come...' She broke off, looking down at the ground again, as though there was something shameful in admitting grief.

Avery finished for her. 'They told her she was dead. As far as we can tell, it was some kind of revenge killing. Her *Salvatrucha* got it into his head that she was cheating on him with another gang member. They took her out to some lonely spot and—' Avery struggled to get the words out '—they cut her head off, even while she was pleading her innocence.'

It felt cold in the room after that, as though words could alter physics. Peter realised that he was still holding a plate stacked with croissants, the butter slowly congealing inside their slit innards, and hastily put it down. The noise of the plate making contact with the table introduced a mundane note, shattering the spell that had fallen over them. Ellisha's shoulders jerked slightly, and she leaned towards Alessandra. 'There's something you want to ask me.'

Alessandra lifted her face with wide-eyed astonishment, as though she could not believe her next words would be true. 'They killed my daughter,' she went on brokenly. 'When I see the pictures of her corpse, I want that they should shoot me also. From the day I find my daughter has gone, it is as though my world has stopped. I am praying, praying all the time, but it is just the sound of my own voice talking to nothing. I want to die. My husband, he tries to help. He says God must have his reasons. But how can there be a loving God who would do that to my daughter? My daughter, who was good and pure.' She paused then looked up at Ellisha almost accusingly. 'I hear people are talking of Ignis Dei. I see it on the internet, but I don't know it. My husband shows me, on Calton Hill, what you are saying, and here, it makes sense.'

Ellisha's back was rigid. 'Ask me.'

The faintest of nods. 'I want … I need—' Alessandra's voice had fallen to a whisper, less than a whisper yet Peter could hear every word. 'I need to know … Is there hope I will see my daughter again?'

Peter felt himself tense. Here was the million-dollar question, the mystery Ignis Dei must answer if they were to have any credibility in the world, because giving up the old ideas would be hard, even for those who had watched their hopes disintegrating in the Void. Even as Alessandra accepted the principles of Ignis Dei, she was still clinging to the superstitions of her childhood, searching Ellisha's words for hints that the universe might, after all, be supremely concerned with the needs and desires of an individual. Peter felt every muscle in his back go rigid. *Avery's holding open the door to untold riches and support. But if we want to cross the threshold, we have to pass the test. Can Ignis Dei provide meaning?*

They waited for Ellisha's response. Perdita cleared her throat. A floorboard creaked. *Why doesn't she speak?* Peter could feel ley-lines of tension straining his neck. *A sign. Give me a sign.* But there was no sign. Ellisha went on looking at Alessandra with that strange blank expression that belonged to a Sybil or a Kumari Devi.

Alessandra's eyes filled with tears. 'Please, I need to know.'

The flayed ends of this woman's grief were raw and bleeding. The sight of them would have moved stone. Yet Ellisha did nothing. Peter felt panic rising. He was on the verge of whispering *Don't blow it* when he became aware that Perdita's cool eyes were on him. An imperceptible shake of the head. Or did he imagine it?

Alessandra said miserably, 'My daughter, her soul was not nothing. They, the *traquetos,* they saw my love for her, how it make her shine. They know she is a part of me, and they think if they kill her, they will kill me too. But her soul is part of my soul—' She broke off, looking to one side, as if a voice had spoken to her. Then, ever-so-slightly, she inclined her head and slowly lifted her gaze. 'Her soul is part of my soul,' she said again. 'When I make my soul, I will draw her back to me. This is what you are telling me?'

Ellisha gave the palest of nods. 'You belong together in the *Mysterium of Soul.*'

Peter glanced at her sharply. Where did that come from? The phrase was not familiar yet seemed to speak to Alessandra, because her chin lifted and her back became a little straighter. 'Thank you,' she whispered, taking a little bowing step back. 'Thank you.'

A great tension had lifted in the room. Peter felt his shoulders slump and watched as Ellisha drew in a deep breath and closed her eyes. He realised the others, even Avery, had followed suit. Yet he continued to watch her, as though he didn't know her, as though she had become a stranger to him, this woman who had such stillness about her she might have been Queen Mab presiding over dreams. And watching, the world fell away. For an instant, he felt a perfect sense of serenity, as though he was sinking into a deep forest pool filled with green lights. And a voice from inside his head whispered, *There's magic here.*

CHAPTER 18

AFTERWARDS, AVERY ASKED THEM TO wait, while he had a word with Alessandra and Perdita in private. He urged them to enjoy the breakfast buffet, but Peter found that his appetite had gone. He poured two large cups of the freshly-ground coffee instead. Then they sat before the crackling fire on a ridiculously large sofa talking in whispers.

'You knew'

'Knew what?'

'How to guide Alessandra. You knew what she needed.'

Ellisha stared at him. 'I didn't know anything.'

'But—'

'I had no idea what to say. How do you tell a mother she'll never see her daughter again?'

'Yet you comforted her. I felt—' now he was not sure '—something.'

'I guess.' Ellisha took a tentative sip of her coffee. 'It was like the night when we read Babs' papers, when I finally understood that God was not here *yet*. I felt mad, like I was just making it up, and, at the same time, somehow I wasn't.'

Outside the door, they could hear the faint murmur of voices. Ellisha glanced over. chewing her lower lip.

'I don't like this, Peter. What are we getting ourselves into?'

'I think it was a test.'

'Did we pass?'

'I don't know.'

Ellisha looked on the verge of arguing, but the sound of the door opening made her retreat into silence. Avery came in. He had an odd shuffling walk, hands in pockets, mildly frowning, that gave him the air of being locked away in some hidden location inside his head. But

Peter thought, *It's an act. He wants people to see him as an ordinary guy they'd pass by in the street, but he sees everything, calculates everything.*

Avery helped himself to a coffee then sat down on the couch opposite. He didn't say anything for a while, studying Ellisha quite openly and thoughtfully, before asking, 'So, where do you think you're taking this?'

'As far as we can,' Peter said, and Avery's shrewd eyes shifted.

'Tell me more.'

'You've seen what Ellisha can do. She can move people, change them.'

'And you? What are you? I'll be blunt. From here on, Perdita will be running the show and she's asking what you'll be bringing to it.'

And Peter heard the question beneath the question. *Do I need you?* It took the air from his lungs. With the muscles along his jaw tightening, he answered stiffly, 'I'm the first follower.'

He expected to have to explain, but Avery nodded. 'The one who spreads the word.'

'Who gives it recognition and shape.'

'And you'd be happy in that role? A man like you?'

He's fencing with me, Peter realised. *He wants me to fight back.* He met Avery's eyes, and despite the differences of age and status, it was clear that they had something alike in their natures. It gave him the confidence to say, 'American entrepreneur, Derek Sivers, acknowledged the First Follower's importance. And if I remember correctly, he described the leader as the flint, and the First Follower as the spark that makes the fire.'

A glint of amusement entered Avery's eyes. 'So you're a spark?'

'Ignis Dei,' Peter said. 'The Spark of God.'

Ellisha made an uncomfortable motion with her shoulders. She clearly didn't like the direction of the conversation. And afraid she would try to deny everything, he plunged on with the advantages of his vision. He spoke of the humanitarian aspects, the education programmes they could support, the water purification plants, the funding of blue-sky research. And the more he talked the more real it became in his head, his hands moving rapidly through the air conducting his thoughts. 'Ignis Dei speaks to something in people. And isn't that the Holy Grail? To expose an idea that people feel in their heart of hearts they've always secretly known?'

Avery was clearly listening. He leaned forward, tapping the steeple of his fingers against his lower lip. 'We've plenty of ideologies in the world that work for folks. What makes you think it's time for a new one?'

Peter was ready for him. 'When Lord Sacks accepted the Templeton prize, he was quoted as saying that each time there is a revolution in information technology there is a spiritual revolution. And no spiritual system has used the internet and social media as powerfully as Ignis Dei. Any way you look at it, Ignis Dei is an epiphany, a revelation, a meme that is spreading across the globe. We've pushed the envelope, and right now we're in the lead with the most incredible idea this century has seen. Maybe this millennium.'

A log on the fire crackled, then spat, catching Peter by surprise and breaking his flow. Avery reached for a brass poker and pushed the log back. He sat for a moment, looking into the flames. 'And you came up with this idea by yourselves?'

Peter felt Ellisha stiffen, but he went on confidently. 'We've done our homework. The idea of Ignis Dei is based on myths that began at the dawn of time, a continuum of realisation that is beginning to wake up inside the heads of millions of people across the world. And—' He hesitated, wondering how hard to push. 'We were privileged to have access to undisclosed research.'

Avery's eyes shifted to Ellisha. 'Through your work as an archivist?'

'Yes.' She said it faintly, and Peter knew they were thinking the same thing; how does Avery know that? But there was no time to ask, because Avery had sat back, arms folded across his chest in a manner that suggested he had heard enough.

Fighting the urge to take Ellisha's hand, like contestants in a game show, Peter forced himself to take a sip of coffee. It tasted bitter and he found it difficult to swallow. Avery was speaking. 'Alessandra tells me that what you and Ellisha have here is something wonderful. Something uniquely spiritual. And, I have to say, I trust Alessandra's intuition.'

'Thank you,' Peter started to say, but Avery wasn't finished.

'But something's still bothering me. I don't doubt you two are sincere. This is a phenomenal thing you're trying to do, trying to persuade people to earn their own souls. But it's one thing to click a thumbs-up on a computer screen and quite another to feel it here.' He patted his chest. 'What makes you certain you can make people really believe?'

'We aren't certain. We don't need to be,' Ellisha said.

Peter choked on his coffee. 'What my wife means—' he began hastily, but she withered him with a look.

'I can speak for myself.' She looked very frankly at Avery. 'I want to tell you a story. You're right. I'm an archivist. And, one day, I found the department head in a state because a very important client had reneged on a promise to donate his mother's papers.

'His mother was someone very famous, but reclusive. She lived alone with her son for the best part of forty years. He'd promised the papers to the archive, but at the last minute, he changed his mind. Said he didn't believe we could help him, and no-one was able to talk him round. I don't know why, but someone thought I might be able to persuade him.

'I didn't have a clue what to say. All the arguments as to why he could trust us had been made before, and made well. So I went to see him without any plan in my head. But, when I met him, I knew somehow that he just needed someone to tell him he was doing the right thing, to recognise that it took courage to give up his mother's work when it had been his whole life.

'He listened to me and didn't say much. But the next day he handed everything over to the head archivist. Not because he believed in us. But because I had believed in him. And that's why Ignis Dei will work. Because we'll believe in the people who follow us. We'll believe in their courage and their goodness and their ability to find the spark within themselves and turn it into something incredible.'

Peter listened in amazement. This was the most serious speech he had ever heard Ellisha make. No wisecracks, no punchline hitting him in the solar plexus, making him gasp out reflexive laughter. He began to wonder who this woman was, who had the shape of his wife and the mouth of an assured stranger. He looked at Avery, wondering how he had taken it.

Avery didn't say anything. He lifted his coffee and swirled it, peering down at the surface like an old fortune-teller, his foot tapping out a metronomic rhythm on the floor. There were calculations going on behind his eyes that Peter couldn't begin to fathom. It made the colours in the room grow too vivid.

Avery's foot stopped tapping. His gaze was diffuse, and when he spoke it was as if he were addressing some inner part of himself. 'I think we've got something here. I really do.'

What exactly is Ignis Dei? That was the question Avery posed. What exactly are we taking to the world? And they had seven glorious weeks to work it out, like a time allotted by a fairy tale, days melting ineluctably from light to dark, but always with the assurance of more light, while they took the hazy outline of Ignis Dei and fleshed out the detail.

'First move,' Perdita said. 'A team to establish Ellisha's social media presence.' She had lifted some notes she had jotted down and was studying them.

'But isn't social media our strength?'

A cool glance over the rims of a pair of Chanel glasses. 'Beginner's luck, I'm afraid. Have you even considered your strategic direction?'

Peter had to admit he had not.

'We need professionals to handle this. Gurus, who know how to work magic across the internet. Besides, you'll have your hands full.'

Peter opened his mouth to protest, but Ellisha nudged him. 'She's right. Leave it to them. I want you with me. I can't go out there on my own.'

'Do we want to go on tour?' Avery asked.

Perdita handed her notes to an assistant, who took them and hurried from the room. 'Certainly. But we want a few weeks to get the concept of the Prophetess bedded in.'

'We'll need lawyers, accountants—'

'Sound men, photographers. Cameras everywhere. We can't allow a single shot to be missed.'

'Press officers, security and publicists—'

'Money men, executives—'

'Hairdressers, stylists—'

'There's the matter of money,' Avery said.

Ellisha looked up. 'Money?'

Avery chuckled. 'You two are visionaries. You need to be. And the kind of rarefied space you occupy doesn't allow much for practical detail. But we need to have a way to tie people into Ignis Dei.'

Ellisha raised a brow. 'Like a contract? Isn't that how the Devil works?'

This made Avery smile. 'Don't be too hard on the Devil. He's an astute businessman. He understands that inputs affect outputs. You give something for free and people don't value it. They need to buy into it, literally. And the more they hand over the less easy it is for them to walk away.'

'I don't believe that,' Ellisha said. But Peter interrupted hastily, 'No, Phil's right. Christians have tithes, Muslims *Jasonat,* and Sikhs use *Dasvandh.* Investing gives them a sense of belonging. Besides, if Ignis Dei is going to change the world it's going to cost.'

'That's it in a nutshell,' Avery said. 'You have good instincts. I like that.' Turning to Ellisha, he added, 'Take my advice, don't disdain money. Your husband's planning big, and you'll need cash, plenty of it.'

Ellisha looked mulish, and he leaned forward and patted her knee in a paternalistic fashion. 'But each man to what he does best, eh? I don't pretend to be able to move a crowd with the power of my voice, and you don't want to think about the money. That's okay. Leave all that to me.'

⬤⬤

Later, alone and breathless in the canopied bed, Peter ran his hand along the ferny branches of Ellisha's scar. 'What about a summer solstice festival?'

'Or a winter one. People need that one more. Light in the darkness, you know the kind of thing. But I don't want it to end up being a pale imitation of Christmas. Even if Christmas is a pale imitation of Yule, which is a pale imitation of Saturnalia.'

'Or maybe we should be concentrating more on the everyday rituals.'

She looked up at him with a smile of genuine sweetness. 'We could reintroduce circumcision.'

'No.'

'Prevents cervical cancer.'

'NO!'

She shrugged. 'Sure. What were we talking about?'

'Holidays.'

'Yeah. How about St Clitoris' day?'

'And how would we celebrate that?' he asked, shocked and amused in equal measures.

She rolled over and opened herself up to him. 'All day long.'

Finding the image for the prophetess of a new age was not easy. 'This is paramount,' Peter had explained. 'Ellisha has to look the part. We were amateurish on Calton Hill, and we were lucky because we had the element of surprise. But, from now on, we can't put a foot wrong.' And Avery had listened to him and was genuinely interested in what he had to say, interrupting occasionally with a question then nodding to himself at the answer. Even Perdita seemed impressed by Peter's attention to detail, although 'I don't disagree,' appeared to be the epitome of her repertoire of praise.

Peter felt bolstered by the kind of faith he had found in no-one but Ellisha. The fact that Avery and Perdita believed in him, believed in his vision and his ability to make things happen satisfied a part of his nature that he rarely acknowledged, the sense that he did not exist except through the recognition of others, and there was a strong urge in him to repay the investment. But almost immediately things started to go wrong.

Though his vision for Ellisha was strong, somehow reality and concept refused to mesh. 'No.' He shook his head as Ellisha emerged from the dressing room for what seemed like the seventeenth time that day.

'No?'

He saw her exchange a glance with Perdita, while the head stylist, Stefano, dropped his head into his hands.

'Perhaps if you gave it more of a chance,' Ellisha said pleadingly. Peter agreed to let her walk up and down a little all the while shaking his head.

'She looks regal,' Stefano insisted. But Peter wasn't satisfied. 'Something's missing.'

'Maybe it's me,' Ellisha said. She looked tired. They had been at it since breakfast and there had been no breaks, not even for lunch. And now her hand was rubbing at her shoulder, the fingers creeping towards her scar, something he had noticed her do when a bad headache was coming on. 'Maybe I can't do this. I'm not a model. I'm a little, mixed-race woman with a big ass.'

'You're beautiful,' Peter said, and the stylists both agreed. Mariam, the junior stylist, a young woman whose frothy afro was like a burst of exuberance above the neutral black of her clothing, added, 'You have something.'

'What kind of something?'

'That's just it. It's indefinable. It's not your eyes or your mouth or how you move. It's just there, and we can all see it.'

She's right, Peter thought. She's every bit as beautiful in this brocade gown as she was in that chic little Chanel suit or that "goddess-in-the-green" attempt with all those diaphanous skirts and tinkling jewellery. But something still isn't right.

There was a knock on the door and a timid-looking girl came in to offer refreshments. She turned to Ellisha with a deferential smile, asking in an American accent, 'Can I bring you a glass of Green River?'

'I doubt it,' Ellisha said. 'You can't get it over here. Phil and I were just talking about it.'

'Mr Avery had some flown over for you last night.'

There was a silence. Ellisha's glance ricocheted between Peter and the girl. 'For me?'

'Mr Avery wants you to have everything you need.'

Ellisha stared, too stunned even to say thank you. The girl didn't move. She seemed to be waiting, and Peter was just beginning to wonder if he should step in, when she burst out, 'I want you to know I believe. And I'm doing the best I can to gather my soul.'

It was all he could do not to laugh out loud. Not because it was funny, but because it was shocking to hear such innocent faith and know Ellisha was the cause. Seemingly oblivious, the girl gave the burning tree salute—just as they had seen the crowd give on Calton Hill— and scurried from the room.

Once the door had shut, Ellisha's lips parted in astonishment. 'Wow!' She whirled around to face Perdita. 'Did you know? You must have known, right?'

Perdita's lips pursed into something akin to amusement. 'I didn't know. But it doesn't surprise me. Phil is a man who has known power for a long time. He wants you to be happy.' Then obscurely she added, 'And he wants you to see that extreme power is a kind of magic.' Her phone buzzed and, excusing herself, she left the room. Ellisha and Peter were left looking at each other.

'Power is magic,' Ellisha said softly.

'Next time tell him you can't start the day without diamonds.'

'Ass.'

'Ingrate.'

There was a mild clearing of the throat and Ellisha and Peter broke off, embarrassed. 'Stefano.' Ellisha turned. 'Where were we?'

'We were deciding if this look was the one.'

'I'm sorry,' Peter said. 'It's not right.'

Fire spread up Stefano's neck. It pulsed in his temples. 'That is an original Alexander McQueen.'

Ellisha looked pleadingly at Peter, but it was Mariam who put it into words.

'She looks as though she's playing a part.'

'It's fairy-tale Gothicism.'

'We need something timeless.' Mariam said. And Peter understood what she meant. 'Like—Like—' She lifted a book from the desk called *The Changing Shape of Female Beauty* and flicked to one of the illustrated sections. It showed several small statuettes of prehistoric Venuses. Stefano looked over her shoulder, his eyes widening with theatrical dismay. 'You want Ellisha to be short, fat and *naked?*'

'No. You don't get it.' Mariam walked away, thumbing through the pages and nodding to herself. 'These women were worshipped at the dawn of time. Over thirty millennia before the birth of Christ.' Mariam let a breath whistle over her lips. She turned another page. 'I get it. I totally get it.'

Ellisha looked at Peter with a *what-the-hell* expression, but he shook his head, as mystified as she was. It was too much for Stefano. Pushing back his seat, he rose to his feet and gathered up discarded accessories from about the room, throwing them into boxes with cries of, 'I guess we won't be needing Armani! We won't be needing LaCroix either!'

'Mariam?' Ellisha said gently. 'What's going on?'

Mariam looked up. 'Give me two hours alone with Ellisha, and I'll show you.'

Two hours later, Peter returned to the dressing room with Avery and Perdita. Mariam was waiting for them, a little rumpled, her skin shining with a faint sheen of sweat, as though she had been working feverishly. She had pushed the tables and the clothes rails to the corners of the room, and placed a single chair in the open space at the centre.

'Setting the scene,' Peter said. 'But you understand, it has to work no matter what.'

'I understand.'

Once they were settled, Mariam stood by the dressing room door. She looked like a nervous little girl, deep breaths, hands clasped in front of her. 'Ready?'

'Ready.'

She opened the door and spoke to Ellisha. 'You can come out now.'

There was a moment's delay, just a fraction, then Ellisha appeared. She walked without hesitation into the centre of the room and stood before them, her expression calm and unreadable.

'Well?' Mariam burst out. 'What do you think?'

What do I think? His eyes ran over the simple shift, the *terra rosa* colour of burning sand, her arms and throat bare of jewellery, the utter simplicity of a woman who did not need adornment. But it was her hair that held him. Seven raised plaits framing her face, reaching back along her scalp forming a crown, while the remainder of her hair flowed free to her shoulders in a halo of curls. He pressed the back of his knuckles against his mouth. Mariam was talking, 'You see, my grandmother was from Ethiopia. She showed me a picture of herself as a young girl, with this style of hair. She said it was a very ancient tradition, going back thousands of years, possibly even tens of thousands of years, to the time of the oldest gods. But the funny thing is, when she described them, she always used the word *kehmehra*, which has a sense of, to heap up or to gather in the old Ge'ez language. And, when I heard Ellisha talking about the idea of God-potential and the coming divine, I knew it made sense. And I've tried to recreate a look that reflects all that...' Her voice trailed off, and she looked pleadingly at Peter.

He was looking at Ellisha, her wild-cherry skin, the moss agate green of tilted eyes. Mariam was still regarding him anxiously, but he could feel a slow smile forming on his lips. 'It's perfect.'

At his side, Perdita put it better. 'No, better than perfect. Divine.'

Part III

PARADISE REGAINED

...THE IDEA THAT THE GODDESS is subject to the laws of human justice is a modern conceit. She, like all the Old Eternal Ones, is partial to the scent of blood.

Chaucer echoes this in his Knight's Tale, where best friends Arcite and Palamon, fall for the beautiful and royal Emilye. In this form she is the embodiment of the Queen of Heaven, and her lovers must fight to the death to win her. Both young men invoke divine aid from a patron deity, and it is notable that the true fight is less betwixt mortals and more between he who chooses Venus, i.e. the god of women, versus he who chooses Mars, i.e. the deity of men.

The underlying mytheme is laid bare and, before the day is done, the Great Goddess will be down on her knees weeping for her dying lover even as she turns her gaze towards her new paramour, who emerges as the rising king.

McBride Barbara, Gateways and Goddesses,

Bell & Ashmore Academic Press

CHAPTER 19

HE WAS STANDING ON A LEDGE. Just as he had stood all those months ago, a lifetime ago, on Salisbury Crag with his eyes closed and a sense of the infinite just below his feet. Then, slowly drawing dry air into his nostrils, he opened his eyes and felt chills. Below was the Nevada desert, and he was standing on a platform surrounded on three sides by a natural amphitheatre of towering rock, and looking up at him were the blurred ovals of ten thousand faces waiting for him to leap.

Very still he stood, wind blowing through his hair, letting the atmosphere build. Sound moving across the rock, choral music spiralling heavenwards, its wordless strangeness making the hairs on the back of his neck rise. A triptych of screens, reflecting the feedback from constantly rolling cameras. Three phrases—*I see you... I feel you... I need you...*—continuously projected above a huge four-poster bed whose posts were the twisted trunks of the burning tree, the great symbol of life and regeneration, rising, like the axis mundi, from the centre of the stage.

On Calton Hill his voice, unamplified, had carried only to the front few rows then passed along Chinese-whispers-style. But here, the moment he held his arms up, the music vanished and his words came booming over the air.

You have been promised and those promises have been broken. You have been hurt and those hurts have not healed. Yet, when the Void opened, you refused oblivion. You, amongst all others, you, who are the Unchosen, elected to choose.

Energy. That is what he felt as he looked over those ten thousand faces. White hot, thrumming in the air, almost palpable, like the heat that rose from the ground in wriggling columns.

Now is the time to gather together. To find one another. All those sparks in the darkness. Draw nearer. You are not weak or powerless. You are not alone or abandoned or forgotten. Your strength is extraordinary, you, who have faced the Void, the Vacuum, Nihilitatas, Absolute Zero, das Nichtige, the Empty Womb, Sunyata of Inexistence, the Eternal Nothingness of Being, and have not been destroyed by it.

There was a roar. Ellisha had taken her place before the bed. She paused, smiling gently at her audience, and was joined by a gaggle of neophytes all dressed in white.

Perdita had explained it earlier. 'They're all members of the trans community.'

'Really?'

'The group formed after Calton Hill. They call themselves the Soul-Searchers. Formed originally from a chatroom known as the Daughters of Cybele.' To his blank look she had added, 'The Phyrgian mother of the gods. Her priests are rather famous for emasculating themselves then adopting the manners and dress of women thereafter.'

Peter stared anew at a long-limbed blond who had earlier caught his eye, and Perdita asked shrewdly, 'Not a problem, I hope.'

'No, of course not. It's just—'

'You'll have to get used to a lot of this kind of thing, I'm afraid.'

'People from the trans community?'

'Things you don't expect.'

The Soul-Searchers had stopped short of Ellisha and stood in silent adoration. Priestesses of the Soul Mystica. The youngest one had begun to weep, on cue. And recognising his prompt, Peter turned back to his audience.

But it is not enough. Merely surviving the Void is not enough. After all, a coma patient may live for decades, breathing, absorbing nutrients, excreting waste, yet never living at all. In the same way, we can live our whole lives, while Soul withers away inside us.

But here is a new way to be, a new way to love. Not a love that enslaves itself, that bows down and loses itself, but a love that connects and transforms. A love that grows in the forests of the imagination, that raises cathedrals in the middle of digital cities, that links millions and millions of minds across virtual space until those minds grow wings and fly. We are souls in a spiritual realm. Naked and shivering, unformed and uncertain, but we are no longer trapped by the Lie.

Ours is not an easy path to follow. It is not comforting or reassuring. It is a new and, also, an ancient way. And it is a way to heal that deep pain that haunts you, the pain which is the buried, broken part of you that belongs to the Eternal.

From the strange sloping perspective of the stage, he could see individuals here and there, popping out, like tiny random letter 'i'-s jumping off an oddly set page. Here, a woman was weeping. And there, a young man had his eyes tightly closed, his head bowed. And there again, a girl with her head tilted towards the heavens, a look of sheer ecstasy shining from her face. Quite why these individuals chose to reveal themselves in that vast, impersonal crowd, Peter could not have explained. Only that he was strangely moved by them, his cynicism pierced. As if his words were having material affect and the stuff of Soul had gathered inside those individuals and lit them from within.

The music was swelling. They were reaching the crisis point, the moment when the audience still hovered between doubt and desire. Hold back or leap into the dark. He stopped speaking. Here was Elli-sha's moment.

She stepped forward. And though he had not meant to meet her eyes, had agreed beforehand that it was a bad idea—what if it put me off? What if I started laughing?—he couldn't help himself, wanted to share a *this-is-really-happening* moment just between the two of them.

But her eyes were blank. She looked through him, and he saw she was trembling slightly.

He took her hand—it was icy cold despite the heat—and raised it above their heads, turning his face towards her in readiness. She stood, staring out over the crowd, saying nothing. And her silence went on and on, long past the point they had rehearsed. Yet no-one broke it. Ten thousand people waited, mesmerized by the possibility of possibility. Then, just as he began to give up hope, and was in the middle of berating himself that there was no plan to deal with this contingency, Ellisha opened her mouth, and her voice, invisibly amplified, split the air.

Come my angels and avatars, we will build the universe anew, you and I, one soul at a time. We, the dispossessed, the cursed, the overlooked, will bring about the revelation for the Third Millennium. Ignis Dei. The Spark of God. We are the beginning. We are the Unchosen. We are suspended moments in the mind of a sleeping deity. And the notion that God IS Love may be the truest instinct we ever had.

He led her back to the bed, and she stopped, turning her head to look at him and everywhere, infinitely reflected through the camera lens. He held her eyes, drawing strength from them, comforted, yet even so, wanting to protect, feeling cared for yet powerful, a liberation he had not known even in the days of his simple childhood faith when God's love had seemed in many ways a finite thing, easily broken or lost. But now this prophetess of new beginnings held his gaze and said,

Help me!

Help me. Woman in her womaness, she was leaning forward so that her eyes filled the screens' trinity, reaching out to him, to all those millions of fragmented souls who found themselves scattered across the world.

She lay down on the bed. And just before the priestesses drew the curtains about her, he joined her, completing the symbolic recreation of the *hieros gamos*, the sacred union between the goddess and her king.

I see you... I feel you... I need you...

And man of spirit, man of flesh, he responded, wanting to save her, wanting to be saved by her, knowing she was the queen of broken hearts yet certain it was to him, and him alone that her words were addressed, while down below the crowd went wild.

Afterwards there was so much excitement and urgency in their veins that they could barely contain themselves.

'Oh my God! Oh my God! Oh my God!' Ellisha was high as a kite. She was filled with light. 'They liked me. They really liked me.'

Her hands felt hot and dry inside his. 'They loved you.'

She barely heard him, turning to Perdita, who was finishing a phone call. 'What did Phil think? Did he think it went okay? I want to thank him for those flowers in my room. Harebells and larkspur, my favourites. Isn't that amazing? Peter, how did he know?'

Peter kept his smile enigmatic, while thinking, *How did he know? I didn't know.*

'He's very pleased,' Perdita said. 'He sends his congratulations.'

Ellisha looked around, puzzled. 'Where is he? Is he here?'

A flicker so small that only Peter, attuned to the secret treacheries of the human face, noticed it. 'Phil will be taking a back seat from now on.'

'A back seat?' Ellisha glanced from Peter to Mariam to see if they understood. 'What do you mean?'

Whatever crack Peter had spotted had resealed and Perdita's expression was impenetrable. Her phone buzzed and she lifted it to her ear, then frowned. 'I'll be right there.' She nestled the phone against her collarbone. 'It's just how Mr Avery works. His talent is to put extraordinary people together then let them get on with it. He's placing great trust in you.' Her gaze grew intense. 'I hope you appreciate that.'

✖

A limo had been sent to speed them back to their hotel suite. Ellisha, who had been a little subdued since the news that Avery would not be joining them, lit up when she saw the pale interior white leather fittings like the caps of horse mushrooms. Milk colours. Moon colours. Ellisha sat back with a sigh. 'This is nicer than the car that brought us. So peaceful.'

'Mr Avery insisted on it,' the driver said, looking back over his shoulder. 'He says the Prophetess must have white to feel calm.'

'Phil said that?' Ellisha's eyes were wide. 'Wow, I only mentioned it in passing.' She ran her hands over the leather seats, stopping suddenly as a thought occurred. 'You're not the same driver who picked us up, are you?'

'No, ma'am.' The man started the engine.

'I remember now. His name was Jose.'

'Jose isn't with us now.'

'Not with us?' Ellisha's eyes widened. 'You mean he was fired?'

A single shoulder shrug. He clearly didn't want to talk, but Ellisha, Prophetess of the Divinely Dormant, was not so easily put off.

'What happened. I want to know.'

As they turned out on to the highway, the driver's eyes flicked up into the mirror. 'Ma'am, all I know is Mr Avery says you need white. And you didn't arrive in a white car.'

'He got fired for that?' Ellisha turned to Peter in confusion. 'We have to do something.'

Peter nodded, covering his own shock with a display of authority. 'We'll talk to Phil. Tell him what happened.'

'It was Mr Avery's direct order,' the driver said.

'But Phil isn't even here. Peter, how could he know?'

Peter reached for her hand and shook his head, but he was thinking, *Doesn't realise it yet, but there are eyes and ears everywhere; Avery's protecting his commodity.*

Mariam was waiting for them in the hotel lobby. Her intuitive understanding of how the Prophetess should be presented to the world had earned her promotion to Ellisha's PA. Hugging Ellisha, she exclaimed, 'You were AMAZING!'

'I was. I was amazing.'

'No, really. I was watching from the control room. You could feel the energy. I mean it. Seriously, my fingertips were tingling.' They laughed together in that shared way women have, until Ellisha stepped back. 'Well, I'm all out of energy for today. All I want now is another chance at that jacuzzi bath.' She gave Peter a playful tug on his arm. 'Care to join me?'

Mariam's smile vanished. 'I'm sorry. Perdita's called a debrief up in Conference Room One. Peter's to go up straight away.'

Ellisha's face fell. 'Can't it wait?'

'I'm sorry.'

'You could pretend we came in another entrance. Say you missed us.'

Peter put his hand on her elbow. 'Be professional. They expect it.'

Ellisha's shoulders slumped. 'Suck-up.'

'Diva.'

The conference room was on the first floor. It overlooked an artificial lake and smelled of Lysol and beeswax. Peter threw open the door expecting to meet Perdita and perhaps a couple of fawning executives for an informal celebration, and found instead that the room was filled with men and women in dark suits who stopped talking as soon as he entered as though expecting him to make an important announcement. He was taken aback, but hid it quickly with a show of humour. 'I thought this was a debrief, not the Inquisition.'

If anyone smiled in response, he did not see it, and Peter had his first inkling of how little he understood real power. *What people saw out there in the desert, just the shiny façade. This is real. The mechanism running under the surface.*

Perdita stepped forward and took charge. 'I'm glad you could make it. We wanted a chance to debrief. See if we can iron out the kinks.'

'Well, I'm your man when it comes to anything kinky.'

Perdita, whose eyes had formed in the ice age and warmed not a jot since, looked at him coolly and he felt himself grow red. He followed her in silence to the conference table where she urged everyone to take a seat. A quick introduction acquainted him with corporate lawyers, financiers, investors, accountants, e-marketers, and a myriad of other titles, which he heard and promptly forgot, apart from one man in a dove-grey suit and an almost painfully pristine shirt open at the collar, who was sitting at the far end of the table—presumably because he was chain-smoking Sobranie White Russians. 'Christophe Babineaux, Publicity Genius.' When Perdita said this, he took a drag out of one and let the smoke curl from his nose like a disdainful dragon.

'We should get together,' Peter said. 'I'd like to hear your ideas.'

Christophe blew out a thin stream of smoke then said, 'Sure. Why not?'

'I think we want to focus on the outcomes right now.' Perdita said. 'After all, this is a multi-million-dollar project.'

'Of course.'

'Mr Avery is investing a great deal in this project.'

'I appreciate—'

'How do you think it went?'

What is she getting at? Didn't she see it? The crowds. The air throbbing. A triumph. One hundred per cent.

'There was a problem with the sound,' one of the money men said.

'A couple of technical hitches near the start,' Peter agreed. 'But we ironed them out pretty quickly. No sign the audience picked up on it.' A lawyer type was writing something down, and it occurred to him that someone else might be fired that day. He spoke quickly. 'The crowd loved Ellisha. They were blown away by her.'

Perdita nodded in a way that made him feel he had said something rather gauche and obvious. She turned to a tall Eurasian woman with a face like a doll. Peter couldn't remember her role. 'Do we have data from the Big Three yet?'

For answer, the woman leaned forward and took hold of a remote control. A screen, up against the wall, lit up with a series of facts and figures, percentages, deficits, graphs and charts, indecipherable as hieroglyphics. 'The atheist community is pretty polarised. Lot of heated debates on forums. Is this a religion if there's no God? That kind of thing. But we're still seeing the follower numbers rising.'

'Islam?'

She clicked through another set of slides. 'No real data. They're ignoring us for now. The highest conversion rates are coming from Christianity, especially the youth demographic, the under twenty-fives.'

'We would expect that,' Perdita said, glancing towards the money men. 'The young are always more open to new ideas.'

'There's more to it,' Peter said. They broke off and looked at him like adults interrupted by a child. He kept his voice level and explained, 'We're looking at the generation that obtains all its information from the internet. It isn't like in our day—' he held Perdita's gaze deliberately '—where we watched the same TV programmes, talked about the same books as our mothers and fathers. The young live in a world nowadays that's almost alien to their parents' generation. They're accepting, debating, rejecting ideas that we haven't even heard of yet. They feel isolated from traditional beliefs and they come looking. Ignis Dei is tapping into a gestalt. Cyberspace has offered them infinite possibility and Ellisha is what they've found.'

He allowed his gaze to move, searching the faces around him for reaction. *Weren't Americans meant to be emotionally uninhibited?* There was nothing but a flat blank wall. No outpouring of acknowledgement, no spontaneous burst of applause, yet he felt a subtle shift in his favour in the room. Perdita pursed her lips and glanced at a suit. 'What feedback are we getting from the ad campaign?'

'It's early days.' He consulted a tablet. 'The results from the analytics are still equivocal.'

'When will we know more?'

'Never. Because it isn't working.' Again it was Peter who interrupted.

The suit turned towards him, puzzled. 'Care to elaborate?'

'The ads are all focussed on Ignis Dei.'

'Excuse me,' another suit said. 'But isn't that what we're selling?'

'No.' Without realising it, Peter was leaning forwards, needing them to understand. 'Not Ignis Dei. That's just words. We need to sell mystery. Ellisha's mystery.' He thought of Babs' words. *The purpose of religion is to make people feel special, unique, chosen of God.* 'The last thing we should be doing is telling them to join us.'

'What do you propose?'

'Tell them we have something. Something precious. Something incredible. Something not everyone can have.'

'And then what?' the Eurasian woman asked. 'You expect them to just come to us?'

'No.' Peter paused and the sun's light flared in his eyes. 'I expect them to fight for the chance.'

There was a silence. Peter couldn't read the room and his mind manufactured ugly scenarios until Perdita leaned back in her chair and tapped the table in front of him with her knuckles. 'You've given us a lot to think about.'

He relaxed. A victory of some sort had been won. At the very least Perdita had thought him to be one kind of man when he entered the room, and now thought him quite another. Perdita looked around. 'Any further business?'

No-one moved, and Peter was already pushing his chair back in readiness to leave when Babineaux made a small noise at the back of this throat. Perdita turned to him. 'Christophe, you have something you want to say?'

The man shrugged and stubbed his cigarette out in a glass ashtray. 'The Prophetess cannot wear Nikes.'

✖

'You wore Nikes?'

Ellisha was lying on her stomach in a frothing cauldron, head peeping over the edge. 'Peter! You need to get in here. There are little jets.' Her eyes widened. 'Just there. I felt one.'

He ignored her. 'Ellie, we need to talk about this. You went out as the Prophetess of a New Age, in front of ten thousand people, wearing Nikes.'

'My feet hurt.'

'You could have asked for different shoes.'

'You know I hate wearing heels. Really, get in here.'

He tried to remain indifferent to the cool beauty of the place, scented clouds of steam, shadows rippling on the walls. There was a stark beauty about it that was alien to Peter's Scottish soul, which hoarded, rather than hid from, sunlight. But still, that bath. He shook himself. 'This isn't a game. You have to act like the Prophetess.'

'I do.' She blew a string of bubbles at him.

Doesn't get it. Not yet. He came towards her through the steam, thinking how the deepening colour of her skin beneath the water made her look like a silkie returned to her watery pelt. 'Be serious.'

'I am. I'm very serious. I'm the Prophetess. What else can I be?'

He sat down on the edge and trailed his fingers in the water. 'I'm glad you're enjoying yourself.'

'But I want you to enjoy myself.' She reached up and began loosening his shirt. His hands lifted to stop her, found her shoulders, his fingers running instinctively over the feathery branches of her scar. Some distant part of him felt the collapse of his resistance. It had been a long day, and the shadow of exhaustion made him gentle, his lust more governable, so that he explored her slowly with his tongue.

Her shoulders relaxed and the shudders in her belly and her thighs vibrated responsively in his own belly and thighs until he felt the press of her hands against his buttocks as she pulled him towards her.

Suddenly he was a coil wound around and around himself in an ecstasy of agony, desperate to be drawn deep, deep inside her, towards the blessed promise of release.

A knock on the door made them spring guiltily apart and brought Peter's climax to a juddering, unsatisfactory end. Mariam entered carrying a tablet. 'I'm sorry.' She looked directly at Ellisha, unfazed by the sight of naked flesh. 'Perdita asked me to tell you the make-up people will be here in five.'

'Make-up people?'

'You need to be ready for the party.' She held out a towel and Ellisha took it, getting unsteadily to her feet, and wrapping it around herself.

'Whose party is it?'

Mariam gave her a look. 'Yours.'

'Mine?' Ellisha looked genuinely bewildered. 'They're giving me a party?'

She was so pleased and touched, Peter didn't have the heart to remind her that parties were common after big events. He shot Mariam a complicit glance, then slapped Ellisha playfully on the rump. 'Come on, now. Even you can't believe the Prophetess should go out wearing a towel.'

CHAPTER 20

ENCOURAGED BY AVERY'S INSISTENCE THAT they enjoy his wealth, and never considering how potently addictive real luxury can be, Peter ordered a new watch in readiness for the party. His wrist had felt strangely bare since MacCaa had pocketed his previous one. And now, Mariam was before him, a good fairy in glittering green sequins, holding out a velvet-lined box and grinning. 'Open it.'

He took it from her, trying to hide how he was feeling like a child at Christmas, and then lifted the lid. His face dropped. 'What is this?'

'A Breguet Tourbillon.'

'But—'

Ellisha appeared, looking beautiful in a long oyster-coloured dress that shimmered as she moved. 'What's up?'

'I ordered a Rolex Submariner. Mariam changed it.'

'Why?'

'Bit Benidorm, don't you think?' Mariam took the watch and held it towards Ellisha. 'I took an executive decision in the interests of good taste.'

Ellisha studied it for several seconds then shook her head. 'I can't tell one watch from another.'

'Will this help?' Mariam pulled out the receipt, leaving them to goggle until Ellisha gasped, 'We could have bought an apartment—a really big apartment—for that money in Edinburgh.'

Peter croaked, 'And Avery—he's okay with this? I mean— My God, what's our credit limit?'

Mariam's grin could have turned a pumpkin into a carriage. 'That's what's so great. There isn't one.'

~ ~ ~

The excitement was infectious. Later, when Peter and Ellisha made their way to the party, Ellisha exclaimed over everything, charmed and excited as a child. 'Peter, did you see how everyone looked at us when we walked through the hall? … My God, even the elevator looks like a palace… those brass fittings… this dress, all for me. I feel like I'm in a dream.'

And there was, indeed, something of the dream about the whole affair. The elevator stopped at the top floor and the doors glided silently open, revealing entry into a secret world. There was no roof and men and women walked beneath a canopy of glittering stars, glittering themselves like faint jewels in the torchlight of huge burners set about the place. Waiters carrying tinkling trays of champagne flutes moved amongst trees in huge pots and astonishing sprays of flowers, like silent sprites. A garden where no garden had a right to exist. Eden on the first day of creation.

Peter felt a lump in his throat. It struck him powerfully that this was the world he had been seeking entry to all his life. And he wished that JD and the bank manager and all those close-minded, dull-witted, midgie-raking *nids* who had dismissed him and sneered at him and pushed him out into the cold, were there to see this moment when Peter Kelso, daft wee laddie from Findbrae, surpassed their wildest dreams and made it. Actually made it.

Ellisha's nudge brought him back to earth. 'You're grinning like the cat who stole the cream.'

'More like the cat who sold the idea of cream to all the other cats.'

She pulled a face, but he bent down and whispered urgently, 'Remember, they came here for your mystery.'

She frowned, and he was afraid she was about to argue, but their presence had been noticed. Rapturous applause, cheers and catcalls. He took her hand and lifted it victoriously, self-conscious of his cuff moving to reveal his watch, while all around flashbulbs exploded like fireworks.

It was wonderful and delightful and overwhelming and a little frightening. They moved through the crowd, smiling and nodding, keeping their gaze towards the middle distance, as if for all their nearness they were actually far away, untouchable, a product of the same paradox of perception that makes young children reach out to grasp vainly at stars.

From the corner of his mouth he whispered, 'You're doing great.' But it was his hand that was squeezed reassuringly then suddenly abandoned as Ellisha moved to greet Perdita.

Perdita, austerely impeccable as ever in a sleeveless gown which gave her the look of a glamorous nun, came straight to the point. 'I've been talking with Mr Avery and we both think you ought to have some protection.'

Peter and Ellisha exchanged glances. 'Protection from what?' Ellisha asked.

'Trolling. Stalkers. Nasty stuff. But quite expected.' She glanced above their heads. 'Ah, here he is.' Turning, Peter saw a slab of stone bearing the crude resemblance of a man. Duncan MacCaa. A name like the caw of a crow. Memories flashing through his head—near the Playfair steps in his beggar's garb then kneeling before Ellisha on Calton Hill, the man of no God before the child of unrealised dreams…

MacCaa stepped forward. 'Ah'm here tae protect the Prophetess.' He was dressed in a pristine yet understated suit, and for the first time Peter noticed the military straightness of his back, as if he was not unfamiliar with the life of a soldier.

Ellisha was first to recover. 'Duncan!' she cried, and extended her hands.

MacCaa took them and held them as though they were glass. 'Ah'm here tae serve.'

Peter's jaw worked, but no sound escaped, and it was left to Perdita to say, 'That's settled. We'll do the rounds of the Sparks first then we can drill down to the detail.'

'Sparks?'

'It's what they're calling themselves. Your followers. The Sparks of God. We had our social influencers start using the term and it spread from there. You don't like it?'

'No. It's just—it still seems weird to have followers.' Ellisha moved forwards and MacCaa stepped in front of Peter, throwing his shadow over her. But, when Perdita made as if to go after them, Peter caught her arm. 'A word.'

Without speaking, she looked down at his hand around her forearm then back up into his face. He let go. 'Have you lost your mind?' His voice was hard and angry, dropping to that growling pitch only achievable by the men of Scotland.

'I don't know what you mean.'

'MacCaa is an alcoholic who lives in doorways in his own filth. What on earth could he be needed for?'

'Ellisha is in danger.' He blinked. Blinked as a man who has heard words that have no meaning. Perdita looked at him with what might have been pity. 'Danger?' A mirrored response, an echo, still without understanding.

'We're picking up a lot of hate talk on Twitter and Facebook.'

'Who? Who are these people?'

'A lot of anonymous trolls. Mostly from the US. Christian far right. Bible Belters, that sort.'

'What are they saying?' Perdita sighed. 'Peter, we've been through this. It's best that you and Ellisha keep away from social media to maintain your 'otherness'. Your accounts are handled perfectly well by the Soul-Searchers.' There was blackness at the corner of Peter's vision. 'I want to know.'

Perdita didn't answer at first. She glanced towards Ellisha and Mac-Caa, but they were already muffled by a cloud of glitter and laughter. MacCaa was not laughing, but staring down at Ellisha in a way that made him proud and uneasy at the same time. But that was hardly the point. 'Tell me.'

Perdita pursed her lips then sighed. 'Threats. Rape, mutilation, death. A great many racial slurs. Pretty much as we would expect. There was a crude sort of bomb sent to one of the London offices recently.'

There was something unsteady about the ground he was standing on. Peter glanced around wildly. 'We need to do something.'

'Something is being done.'

'With that *addict*—'

'MacCaa has an exemplary record. Iraq then Afghanistan.' Perdita's eyes narrowed. 'Believe me, we check things very thoroughly. There is no sign that he was ever on drugs or even—' her look became intense '—had a problem with alcohol while in active service. Only that he was a deeply spiritual man who became strange after his wife and child were killed while he was away on active duty. But Ellisha brought him back from the Void and now he's evolving his soul by ensuring her safety.'

'Even so.'

'Ignis Dei is all about second chances.' Her look was penetrating. 'Isn't that what you told Mr Avery?'

She had him. A look in Ellisha's direction. She was laughing. He couldn't see MacCaa's face. 'If anything should happen—'

'It won't. MacCaa is the head of a substantial security team. Sometimes they will be obvious; at other times not so much. The point is, Ellisha needs a visible bodyguard, and the image of MacCaa kneeling at her feet on Calton Hill has over seventy million likes. The Sparks love him. He has a spiritual quality that people find authentic. Did you know that his family were once warrior-priests to the kings of the Western Isles?'

He wrinkled his brow. 'There weren't any kings of the Western Isles.'

'I know. That's what's so fascinating about them.' She began walking away as though that was an end to the matter, but he called after her. 'We should have been informed. Ellisha should have been informed.'

Perdita glanced back over her shoulder. 'It was Ellisha's idea.'

He had thought to catch up with Ellisha, but something cosy in the way she was standing, overshadowed by MacCaa's bulk, laughing with tall, successful people made him feel ordinary and excluded. He turned sharply and something bumped his arm. Looking down he found a glass of champagne had magically appeared in his hand. 'No, I—' But the waiter had gone. He glanced about for a place to put it down but, if this was Eden, then garden furniture had been rashly omitted from the plan. Not a single table or flat surface was visible. The stem was growing warm in the cocoon of his fingers, and feeling suddenly awkward, he lifted it to his lips and pretended to take a sip.

It was a mistake. The aroma stirred powerful memories, a field of white flowers, berries twitching on a branch of a rowan, and suddenly homesickness seesawed inside his gut. He thought of his mother for the first time in a long while and felt sick at how long it had been. And to quell the sickness, he took another sip from the glass, a long settling sip that made him feel instantly better. He looked about for Ellisha. But she had disappeared into a thicket of bodies. He went in search of her.

'Reverend Kelso.'

He stopped, surprised. In his head he said, 'Reverend Kelso was my father.' But somehow the moment passed and he was still Reverend

Kelso. There were three of them, very young to Peter's eyes, two boys and a girl. The girl and one of the boys had that Californian beach look, tanned skin and patchwork blond hair, a perfect PDA couple living their lives against a series of stunning backdrops. He wondered what drew such people to Ellisha's light.

The second boy was incongruous in faded combats and hair that flopped into his eyes, but was shaved high above the ear on either side. He looked at the ground, while the girl flashed a toothpaste commercial smile and offered her hand. 'Hi, I'm Andrea, but friends call me Andi.' She pointed to the blond boy. 'This is Jarred.' A hand towards the boy in combats. 'And this is—'

Something bumped Peter's elbow and his empty glass was replaced by a full one. Peter nodded and took a quick gulp.

'You know, we like really believe in the Prophetess,' Friends- call-me-Andi was saying earnestly. 'We were like just drifting until I came across Ellisha's YouTube channel and she like gave us a way to go.'

'Yeah,' Jarred interrupted. 'We were like, woah, we know her. I mean like really know her.'

'Indeed?' *Indeed? Taken my father's title, starting to sound like him now.* 'And how is Ellisha helping you claim your souls?' He felt a tight band around his neck as though a dog collar were being fastened there, and took another gulp from his glass. Friends-call-me-Andi and Jarred exchanged looks, and the boy in combats (whom Peter silently nicknamed Travis Bickle) glanced up shyly. 'Through love,' he murmured.

'Yeah,' Jarred agreed. 'Love is like the key.'

'Before we found Ellisha,' Travis Bickle continued, suddenly animated, 'Jarred and me, we were like, hey, I don't want to know you. We just weren't cool with each other because of, you know... Andi.'

From this, Peter took it that they had been rivals in love.

'But then we found Ellisha,' Friends-call-me-Andi burst in. 'And it all made like total sense. We were sharing a soul.'

Peter, who had been gazing fondly at the gently effervescing champagne bubbles, looked up sharply. *Who said anything about sharing souls? Perdita's right. Expect the unexpected. Freedom of spiritual expression. Wasn't that the underlying principle we agreed, even insisted upon to Avery? No doctrine, no dogma. But even so, how far to allow that interpretation to wander?*

As he was thinking this, he finished his glass and a fresh one was placed in his hand. He felt suddenly comfortable, as though he had finally relaxed into the night and the young people around him were right. Love was the answer. Love would solve everything. He smiled at them benignly. But the conversation had moved on.

Without conscious effort he drifted away, drawn into conversations with men and women whom he had read of or watched in news bulletins, so distant they had seemed fictive, but who now drank champagne with him and listened to him and were charmed by the couthieness of his Scots wit.

Once a woman stopped in front of him and told him that she was sensitive to the colour of Soul particles, and that she could see his glittering fiery red against the night, and he thanked her and told her that she had a gift. She looked at him with such love in her face that he thought she was about to kiss him, but she only said, *Thank you, Reverend Kelso*, and moved on.

The meme of *Reverend* Kelso, once started, had spread unstoppably across the room, so when a tall Eurasian woman with a face like a doll asked, 'What do you think, Reverend Kelso?' he felt no surprise but only embarrassment at having missed the question.

'I—I beg your pardon.'

She smiled. 'I was asking if you preferred Charlie Tan to Amy Schultz.'

'I—' His head swam, not unpleasantly, but it made it hard to think.
She laughed kindly. 'You've forgotten who I am.'

'No.' He flushed. 'Yes. I'm sorry. I have.' He gestured apologetically
with his glass at the room. 'So many people—'

'So much champagne.'

'Trouble with champagne,' Peter agreed, looking past the woman
and out across the city. 'Either goes to your head or bypasses the brain
and sets fire to your gut.'

'You sound like an expert.'

The comment sobered him and he kept his face turned away. 'What
were we talking about?'

'Whether you thought Charlie Tan was the way to go.'

'Of course. You're our—' He searched desperately for the term, a
little afraid he might laugh when he found it.

'Viral Marketing Guru.' She said the words simply and without
emphasis, and somehow they did not seem ridiculous when she said
them. 'I'm only one of several on the team.'

'Of course.' His head was clearing a little, though there was a tightness at the edges where the beginnings of a headache was forming.
Another drink. But his glass was empty and this time it had not been
magically refilled. Wanting to make amends, he said, 'We're very grateful for the role you play in evangelizing Ignis Dei, uh?'

'Constance Tao.' She held out her hand and he shook it, aware that
this was probably the second time.

'Well, you're doing a great job. We need to keep Ellie—the Prophetess—at the forefront of everyone's minds.'

She smiled. 'I like the idea of being able to build my soul digitally.'
She had small even teeth in a delicate rosebud mouth. He liked the
way she was smiling at him.

'It's a kind of magic, isn't it, the ability to make people look at things
a certain way.'

Her smile grew a little wider. 'There's a secret sauce. The real difficulty is keeping the interest alive.'

'How much mileage will you get out of today?'

'A few days. A week maybe.'

'Really? That's all?'

A waiter appeared and replenished his glass. He lifted it to his lips, and made a weak joke about the merits of finding your glass half full. She laughed; she really had the most endearing laugh. While Peter was thinking this, she explained, 'Nothing lasts longer than ten days on the net. A new phenomenon comes along, celebrity meltdown, someone sleeping with someone. Then boom.' Her hands mimed an explosion. 'We've lost them.'

'But you make the most of it, of what we give you, with the social influencers I mean.' He seemed to be standing very close to her. 'That's very important.'

'Of course. We're doing it right now. We've taken the footage from today and it's being seeded. The network is very efficient.'

Peter wasn't sure if they were talking about people or computers. But an uncomfortable thought was occurring to him. 'Ellie—Ellisha—The Prophetess may not have been wearing exactly appropriate footwear.'

Constance answered him, but for a moment he did not understand, repeating in confusion, 'Edited out?'

'Of course. The tech's very complicated, but we have experts in all the latest techniques. Using temporally-based geomes we can change a person's expression—even their mouth movements—if we want to alter the message they're giving. Replacing shoes is child's play. It's called Creative Rendition.'

He was still processing this when a familiar voice said, 'Reverend Kelso?' The voice made a wonderful kind of sense even as the words did not.

'Mariam.'

She looked up at him, abashed. 'Everyone's calling you that.'

'Mariam, this is—' He turned, but Constance had melted away. *Oh well.* He turned back, smiling warmly. 'What can I do with you—I mean for you?' She was frowning at the glass in his hand, and he had a sudden urge to whip it behind his back and beg her not to tell Perdita. But her next words brought him to immediate sobriety. 'It's the Prophetess. I think she's unwell.'

He expected to find Ellisha holding court somewhere on the roof garden. Instead, Mariam steered him to a private lift that took them down one floor to the penthouse. 'Who is she with?'

'Lacey Landi. Her agent's there too.'

He was impressed. '*The* Lacey Landi?'

'Hollywood's number one wild-child, yes.'

'And the rumours about the partying, the rehab, all true?'

'No.'

'No?'

'It's way worse than the rumours.'

At the top, a door was opened a crack and an expensively dressed, youngish man peeped out, finger pressed firmly to his lips. Peter guessed this was the agent. Mariam leaned forward and hissed, 'The *Reverend* must enter.' And perhaps the title impressed because he stepped back and allowed Peter inside.

Still communicating by gestures, he led Peter through an ante-room to a door on the far side, which was partly ajar, then through a series of complicated hand signals he made it clear that Peter might observe, but not to enter. Obediently, Peter looked around the door and came eye to eye with Ellisha. She was sitting very stiffly, left hand creeping towards her right shoulder as though trying to reach the topmost fronds of her scar. He thought at once: *Headache. She's trying to hide it, but she won't be able to. Not for much longer.*

She did not acknowledge him, and he realised she was looking directly at a person sitting with their back to the door, whose presence he only now became aware of.

Lacey Landi was even more waif-like in the flesh, so much so that the term *in the flesh* hardly seemed appropriate. She looked like something very fragile about to shatter any moment. He could see nothing of her face, but she had a low, breathy, slightly whining voice, which she was using to say, 'It's so hard. It's *so* hard. Wanting all the time to be an authentic person. I try. I like *really* try. But there's all this pressure with cameras in my face and stories about me, and everybody wanting to know my next move. I mean you know it, right? Or is this... this Mysterious Soul some kinda antidote to all the dark shit?'

Ellisha said nothing. She had developed a peculiarly Scottish knack for silently disdaining self-pity and her expression was inscrutable. But such nuances were evidently lost on Lacey who, used to emoting before the glassy eye of a camera, mistook indifference for appreciation. 'I mean, I really have a fear deep down inside me that I'm going to die. Do you know what I mean? Every time I have to go out there it's just like so much harder. Then I end up doing more shit. Really bad shit, know what I'm saying? And everyone thinks I'm a total party girl and they're like, *Hey Lacey. You rock.* But they're not looking inside. They don't see how my heart feels like it's going to explode, and how I'm pleading with the universe not to give up on me.' She began to cry, but in a very decorous way, dabbing at the corner of an eye with a long, manicured fingernail.

'The universe doesn't give a shit, you know? So when I heard about you, I thought you *get* me. You understand how all that shit just *borrows* from your soul.'

'No.' Ellisha spoke softly but firmly and Lacey stopped dabbing and stared.

'What do you mean?'

'It doesn't borrow, Ms Landi. It steals. Eats away the precious fragments until there is nothing left.'

Lacey stopped dabbing. 'Then what?'

'Then?'

'What's going to happen to me?'

'Oh. You will dissolve, disappear, become less than a breath of air. Forever excluded from joining the mysterium of Soul.'

'Oh my God.' Lacey began to wail. 'This can't be happening. You said you would help me. You promised. You said—'

The crack of a gunshot made Peter and the agent start. No, not a gunshot. Worse. Far worse. Ellisha had sprung forward and slapped Lacey Landi soundly across her porcelain cheek. In the stunned silence that followed, Peter saw two things: Lacey clap a hand to her face and Ellisha, fiercely unrepentant, step back, hands on hips. He knew he should say something, do something to defuse the situation but his legs felt shaky, as though he had witnessed a car crash without being able to prevent it, and all he could think was, *My God, she's blown it.*

Ellisha was still staring down at Hollywood's hottest property, a look of distaste on her face. Her nostrils were trembling with little puffs of breath, like a horse about to shy, and suddenly she burst out, 'Ignis Dei is not a drug for those who wish a quick "injection" of God to make them feel better or safer or more self-righteous. It is your chance at divinity. Your chance to create an everlasting soul. You can't buy it or ask someone else to do it for you. It has to come from you.'

Lacey glanced from side to side as though trapped, and Peter noticed how her nose ran a little. She wiped it with the back of her hand then asked in a low, helpless voice,

'But what if I can't do it?'

'Then you will return to dust, and whatever remains of your Soul Mystica will be absorbed by the potential of a new life.'

Lacey had hugged her arms around her upper body. Now she began to rock. 'This is horrible. The worst.' She swung around as though recalling her agent was there, and Peter only just had time to duck back before she yelled, 'You said this would help. But the ideas in this screwup religion are total bull.' She swung back to Ellisha. 'They're dark shit, totally fucked up.'

'More fucked up than Hell? More fucked up than holy war or genital mutilation?'

Lacey went quiet. She was biting the knuckle of her thumb. Ellisha let out a long breath then leaned forward to take hold of the girl's hands.

'You can do it, Lacey. Weren't you the little girl who climbed a dangerous rockface to rescue a bird caught in discarded climbing ropes?'

Peter saw Lacey's back stiffen. 'How do you— I never told anyone. Not even my mother.'

'You couldn't tell your mother, could you?'

'No. She wasn't there for me. Not ever. She had her own demons, I guess.'

'So she left you, a little girl with the tiniest fragments of a soul. Fragments that could make her fearless and selfless in the face of another's danger. But little fragments, in need of nourishment.'

Lacey's voice had fallen to a whisper. 'They went out. I'm in the dark.'

'No.' Ellisha's voice was gently firm. 'That is the Void. There's a way out. I promise.'

And something in the way she said it altered the space around them. *Imagination? Or did the room grow cold?* Certainly he shivered, a prescient shiver of excitement and dread, the quiver of the condemned walking up Castle Hill towards the terror of the inferno and the infinite possibilities of death.

❈

A thin thread of yellow light was visible in the east as they headed back. Dawn, and he had barely slept in the last twenty-four hours. He was sober now, the champagne an acid wash inside his stomach. As they entered the elevator, Ellisha had asked, 'Should we go back to the party?' Her headache was forgotten under the analgesia of triumph and she was eager to go on, but there were smudges beneath her eyes and a tired droop to her mouth.

'No.' He put a hand on her elbow. 'Always leave them wanting more. In a less self-pitying mood, Lacey would tell you the same.'

'She wasn't self-pitying. Hollywood's made her into this big star, and underneath she's just a scared kid. One day she's climbing trees or missing school to take care of her car-crash mother; next, the whole world wants to know what she has for breakfast and who she thinks ought to be president. It's a lot of pressure.'

He bent down and kissed the top of her head. 'You were amazing.'

'I was. Totally amazing.'

'Everything you said. The way you said it.'

'Perdita coached me for days.'

'Did she coach you on when to lamp someone in the face?'

'That was pure improv.'

He laughed. 'Well, it worked.' But a moment later he grew sober. 'How did you know?'

'Know what?'

'About rescuing the bird. Did—did something happen?' He searched her face for a trace of that eldritch he had felt when she spoke. 'In the room, I thought maybe…' The words trailed off in the face of her confusion.

'Perdita briefed me.'

'How did she know?'

'Lacey's mother sold her childhood diaries to Ignis Dei. The anecdote was in there.'

Of course. It was the simplest of tricks, the magician's sleight of hand. He felt as though cold water had been thrown in his face.

'Peter, what's wrong?'

'Nothing. I—' Feeling foolish, he cast about and was glad to see Perdita coming towards them. She was wreathed in smiles. 'Ah, excellent job. I've just had a call from Ms Landi's agent.' She extended an arm to Ellisha. 'Now, I've been talking with the French ambassador and he's cock-a-hoop at the chance to meet you.'

'I'm afraid we're off to bed,' Peter said.

'That's impossible.'

'What do you mean?'

'We're at an extremely delicate stage of the process. Ellisha's presence is crucial, I'm afraid. Mr Avery would expect me to insist.'

'Can't you see—' He hesitated. They hadn't disclosed Ellisha's headaches to Avery. Was it too soon to show weakness? 'Ellie is tired,' he finished lamely. 'She needs to rest.' Ellisha's fingers closed on his forearm. 'It's fine, Peter. Perdita's right. I need to be seen.' She gave him a squeeze. 'I'm okay. Really.'

He had lost the battle, and the only option left was to take defeat gracefully. Forcing a smile, he said, 'Guess I could do with a nightcap.'

Perdita looked at him appraisingly. 'Are you sure that's wise?'

He blushed to the roots of his hair. *She knows. Bitch has been watching me.* Perdita put an arm around Ellisha's shoulders and began to walk her away, and he watched this in silence, grinning stupidly and not trusting himself to speak.

During the night—at least what was left of it; Ellisha had not come to bed until after five—there was a price paid for deferring the pain of the headache. He woke up and noticed she was lying curled on her side, her back to him, fingers of one hand resting on her left shoulder along the edge of her scar, her breathing coming in a series of short shallow gasps.

Knowing how the smallest of sounds stabbed like a knife, he sat up cautiously, careful not to touch any part of her. 'Where does it hurt?'

'Everywhere. It's like I have lightning inside my head.'

'Do you want me to go?'

'No.' She pushed herself up painfully, gripping the edge of the mattress, head drooping.

'We don't need to keep this a secret. We can talk to Avery. He has access to the best doctors.'

'There aren't any cures. I've tried everything from aspirin to anti-epileptics.'

'You shouldn't have spent all that time with Lacey.'

'But that's just it. When I was speaking, I didn't feel the pain. Even when I was angry. It was like I was floating. I could see myself doing things, saying things. But it wasn't really me. And the pain just disappeared. I didn't even think about it until I came to bed.'

'Is that possible?'

She tried to shake her head then groaned. 'I don't know. Did Babs mention if heroes touched by divine lightning receive a prescription for painkillers?'

She was trying to be brave and he felt a rush of tenderness towards her. 'Ellie—' Their thighs were nearly touching but separated, as though they sat either side of a pane of impenetrable glass. He risked edging a millimetre closer. She shrank away, pressing her fingers into her temples.

'I don't know if I can do this.'

He stared at her in alarm. 'Of course you can.'

'What if this headache is a sign of something? A sign we're doing something wrong?'

'You're helping people. What could be wrong with that?'

She glanced up at him, but only fleetingly, her gaze moving fearfully around the room as though there was a third, invisible presence. 'What we're doing, it's making me feel things. Strange things. I'm afraid we're crossing some line. I don't know. Like we're contravening some law of nature. Maybe we're offending—' She looked around a little wildly. '*Something!*'

'Ellie, all we're doing is good. Even if we have it all wrong, what deity could be offended by that? You have to hold on to what we're doing here.'

She buried her face in his chest. 'I don't know how.'

'We'll figure it out,' he said patiently. 'We're changing people's lives. Bringing them back from the brink.' He stroked the worry line at the corner of her mouth with the tip of his finger. That she allowed his touch was a sign that the headache was abating and he took heart from that. 'I think you saved Lacey Landi's life tonight.' The worry line did not entirely disappear, and he propped himself up on an elbow. 'We're not doing anything bad. If I thought we were doing something bad, I would end it now, I promise.' He made a vague gesture towards the world beyond their door. 'But the more I see of the good we are bringing about—the good you are bringing about, the more I think maybe we've stumbled across something bigger than ourselves.'

'Something real?'

'Something that lets us make a difference. We have this incredible chance to put an end to all the corrupt, petty misery that destroys lives out there. It would be criminal not to do it. You just have to believe you can do it.'

She let him ease her down and lay on her side, face away from him. He slid his arm around her waist.

'I'm afraid,' she whispered.

'Of what?' He was kissing her between the shoulder-blades.

'Of losing you.'

'You're never going to lose me.'

She gave a little wriggle as though the spot where he had kissed her had irritated the skin. 'No, I mean I'm afraid of losing us.'

'That could never happen. You're all that's good in me. Without you, I wouldn't have found out what Ignis Dei really meant or had the chance to turn my life around.' He felt her relax in his arms. She stifled a yawn which he echoed and magnified into a compelling drowsiness so that he only just heard her murmur, *A-hole,* and managed to form his lips around a soundless *Drama-queen,* before the current of sleep carried him away entirely.

CHAPTER 21

Savary: Thank you, Prophetess for granting me an interview. I believe it is a rare honour.

Ellisha: Not at all. I admire French journalism. Mediapart in particular. May I offer you a drink. Tea, coffee? Perhaps something stronger? We have Remy Martin.

Savary: You know my favourite drink?

Ellisha: We know many things, Monsieur Savary.

Savary: May I smoke?

Ellisha: The ashtray is beside you.

Savary: I see that everything here is white. It is true then, everywhere the Prophetess goes, everything must be decorated the colour of the moon?

Ellisha: I prefer it, yes.

Savary: Why is that?

In the control room Peter glanced at Perdita then leaned forward. He whispered into the mic, 'Tell him you're not here to talk about interior design.' Ellisha touched her ear and nodded absently.

Ellisha: We are not here to talk about my taste in interior design.

'And don't touch the receiver. He'll notice.' Her shoulders stiffened and he was afraid she would look towards the control room and pull a face, but she stayed still, attention on Savary.

Savary: *Where are you from?*

Ellisha: *I'm American, Monsieur Savary.*

Savary: *Where in America? Where were you born?*

Ellisha: *I don't remember. I was very young at the time.*

Savary: *It's a very simple question. Surely you have an answer for me.*

Ellisha: *The truth of it is, I don't remember. My parents died when I was very young and I was brought up by my grand-parents. They weren't the kind of people who spoke much about the past. There was talk of somewhere near Natchitoches, Louisiana, but I was never certain.*

Savary: *Where did you go to school?*

Ellisha: *I was home-schooled.*

Savary: *So, there are no records of you attending school?*

Ellisha: *These questions have been asked before, M. Savary.*

Savary: *Yes. But they have never been answered. You appear, sans prévenir, three years ago on Calton Hill to tell the world that there is no God.*

Ellisha: *'I was working as an archivist at Edinburgh University before that.*

Savary: *They have no record of you either.*

Peter glanced around at Perdita, half expecting an explanation, but she was concentrating on the monitors. *Did Avery have the records wiped? Can he do that? Ask her outright. No, not with Mariam here. Later.* Perdita leaned over his shoulder and spoke into the mic. 'Move the conversation along.'

Ellisha: *You wanted to ask more about our organization?*

Savary: *Yes. Ignis Dei began in Edinburgh three years ago?*

Ellisha: *In February. Yes.*

Savary: *It has been a busy time.*

✖

Busy time indeed. First Nevada then San Francisco, where the audience was twice as big. Then came New York and Seattle, Denver... Angelic voices; sunsets to break your heart; the mesmerizing chanting of the Soul-Searchers; the warm, open hearts of the audiences; nights rushing past, like speeded up movies, as they travelled to the next destination and the next. Everything passing in a blur. And there was a terrible urgency about it all. For every extravaganza there was a counterpoint of human tragedy, a rift that tore Soul apart and let the Void rule supreme.

✖

Savary: *How do you explain the extraordinary rise of Ignis Dei? There has never been anything like it.*

Ellisha: *There have always been new stories.*

Savary:	*But the speed, at which it is spreading, is without precedent. It is as though the world's imagination has caught fire.*
Ellisha:	*Think how much loneliness there has been, so many people left without answers. Without a sense that there was any reason to go on. We came at just the right moment.*
Savary:	*As an attack on traditional religion?*
Ellisha:	*As an alternative. Tradition claims the deity is here, that there is a plan no matter how impenetrable. We claim that the deity is not here yet. It is our deeds, our willingness to work together to solve problems, our goodness, if you will, that brings the Divine into the universe.*
Savary:	*Are you a cult?*
Ellisha:	*Some would say that a religion is simply a cult with good PR.*
Savary:	*You say that God 'is not here yet'?*
Ellisha:	*Yes.*
Savary:	*But there is a strong female element to this—to this—how do you put it—imminent divinity?*

Mariam touched his shoulder. 'She needs to sit straighter in the chair. The dress is bunching.' Peter leaned forward. 'Sit up, Ellie. You look like a hunchback.' The Prophetess coughed into her hand then sat up ramrod straight.

Savary:	*Your priests, for example. They are all trans women.*

Ellisha: Not exclusively. And we prefer the term 'Soul-Searchers' to priests.

Savary: Yet there has been a spike in the number of male to female gender assignment operations in the last two years.

Ellisha: The correlation is not proven.

Savary: But you will not deny that when there is talk of the 'Coming Divine' your followers use the feminine pronoun, do they not? 'She is coming. Our love is Her love.'

Ellisha: Is that so strange? Clerics have been claiming that God is gender neutral for thousands of years. Yet God is father, God is son. Never mother, never daughter. We are simply redressing the balance.

Perdita leaned past Peter's shoulder. 'Don't let him rattle you.' Ellisha sat back, smiled.

Savary: And do you believe that there was an ancient time of peace and prosperity when women ruled? Your followers quote myths from Tierra del Fuego, Western Sudan, and the aboriginal Dream Time, suggesting that the women were privy to a secret knowledge eventually destroyed by men.

Ellisha: Ignis Dei has no doctrine or dogma, monsieur Savary. People are free to discuss what they will. If it comforts them to think of the evolving sacred as a mother, I see no conflict.

Savary: *You use the word 'evolving'. I wonder, is Ignis Dei compatible with Darwinian evolution?*

There was silence. Peter and Perdita exchanged looks then Peter hissed into the microphone, 'Say, yes. Tell him, yes.' But Ellisha was strangely frozen. Perdita made a whistling noise between her teeth. 'He's pushing too hard.'

'What do we do?' Peter tapped an agitated tattoo on the edge of the table with his fingertips. 'Should we pull the plug?' But Perdita was already looking towards Mariam. The possibility of a staged interruption had been rehearsed. 'Be ready.' Mariam moved to the door.

Savary: *Prophetess?*

Ellisha: *Do you believe in love?*

Savary: *Naturally. I am a Frenchman.*

Ellisha: *Then you will have no difficulty understanding that love is the guiding principle of the Ignis Dei universe. All else is irrelevant to Soul.*

Peter found that he was watching through the slats of his fingers. *Did she— I mean she didn't deny evolution, did she?*

At his side, Perdita was shaking her head. 'Fascinating. Mr Avery will be intrigued.' The alchemical summoning of Avery's name made waves of heat pass through Peter's body. *Divert this. Quickly.* Savary's data was scrolling past on a screen set before him. He scanned it desperately then picked something at random. 'Ellie, ask him about his charity work at the *Grand Séminaire de Lyon.*' He watched Savary absorb the question. Clearly he was discomfited by it, but didn't want to show it.

Savary: *You know my connection? Of course you know. You use data to make you appear omniscient.*

Ellisha: *The information is there. I have it. What is the difference?*

Savary: *Yes, I thought to be a priest once. What of it? There is still—how do you put it—an emotional tie. Not even a prophet can provide the human need for community. Do you not have your own temples springing up everywhere? What do you call them?*

Ellisha: *Soulariums.*

Savary: *Tell me about those?*

Ellisha: *The first one was in Andra Pradesh...*

∞

In Andra Pradesh Ellisha had held the hand of a young woman dying of Aids. 'She is Devadasi,' the interpreter explained. 'A sacred prostitute dedicated to the goddess.'

'I thought the Devadasi system was outlawed.'

The interpreter made a sorrowful gesture. 'Yes. Yes, that is so. In nineteen-eighty-eight they passed a law. But you cannot outlaw belief. Families, they believe a child has been called and they dedicate her to the goddess' service.'

'What is she saying?'

'She is saying she knows you.'

Ellisha turned back and squeezed the girl's hand. 'Yes. Yes. You know me. How old are you?'

The interpreter translated and the girl replied. 'Twenty-four.'

Twenty-four? Peter could have believed the skeleton in the cot was a child or a very old woman. But a young woman in her prime? He felt a knot tighten in his stomach.

Ellisha swallowed. 'I want to know her story.'

'It is very sad,' the interpreter said, shaking his head. An old woman nearby said something, and he barked a response then rolled his eyes. 'She wants me to say her story is also very sad. All the stories are very sad.' Shaking his head, he returned to the cot. 'Umarani comes from a poor family. She has no brothers. When she was young, she had fits. There was no money for medicine so her mother took her to a fortune teller. He told her that the fits were a sign that the goddess wanted her daughter as a servant, so she was dedicated when she was ten years old.'

His words were interrupted by Umarani's coughing. A spasm seized the girl's chest and a violent cough emptied her lungs. A deep inhalation. But the air would not go back in. Something was blocking it. Gasping and sucking, eyes wide and terrified then another bout of coughing. Suddenly her back arched and she whipped her head from side to side. The room was silent, filled with the horrified helplessness of the living before the dying. Umarani was with them, there in the room, but also beyond them, drowning in a waterless lake.

Ellisha recovered first, leaning forward and forcing the girl into a sitting position. 'It's okay. It's okay. I'm here. You know me. I'm here.'

Her words became a meaningless litany repeated over and over, but somehow they touched some human part of Umarani not yet ready to flee the cage. The girl twisted around and clung to Ellisha's arm so tightly that, even in the dim light, Peter saw her knuckles whiten. There was the force of desperation in her grip, and Ellisha's eyes widened with pain, but she did not move, reaching down to stroke her hair and fix her sari, which had fallen from her head. 'I'm here. I'm here.'

The intervals between coughs grew longer and their ferocity lessened. A rattle, like the thinnest of trickles, indicated that air was returning to her lungs. Ellisha turned furiously to the interpreter. 'Why is there no water here? Bring water now.'

'Of course. Of course. There must be water.' He turned and barked an order at one of the old women who scurried, head down, from the room. The coughing fit had exhausted Umarani. She became limp, and Ellisha cradled her head.

'We will ensure she has the best medicines.'

Umarani's lips moved faintly and the interpreter bent over her. 'She says it is too late for her. She wants you to help others to find their souls, to be Ignis Dei people.'

Ellisha looked stricken. 'Tell her I will help her.' Fighting tears, she went on, 'Tell her, her pain has increased her soul, not lessened it.'

Peter kept his face very still. *What is she doing?*

'Tell her it's not too late.'

The interpreter listened then frowned. 'She says she is given to the goddess and cannot change it. You must forgive her.'

Ellisha looked at the interpreter with such naked anger in her eyes that the man dropped his gaze to the floor and shuffled back several steps. Ellisha swallowed hard then, in a voice that was stripped of self-pity, she said, 'Tell her that I will build a beautiful temple here in her memory.'

The interpreter translated. Umarani listened but drew her brows down and shook her head with a strength she did not seem to possess.

Ellisha's eyes filled with tears. 'She doesn't want that?'

'Not a temple. No.' The interpreter's ear was close to Umarani's lips. 'She wants a place for Soul to grow, a place where soul is free to seek Soul.'

Ellisha nodded. 'Then that's what we'll do. Tell her I will build a…
a soularium. Yes. That's what we'll call it. A soularium, a place for soul
to seek Soul.' Gently she laid Umarani back on her threadbare pillow.
'Tell her it will be done.' Peter searched the girl's face hopefully for a
smile of gratitude, a radiant, transformative expression that could be
caught on camera. But Umarani's eyes were tightly closed, and she
seemed to be asleep. When he looked up, Ellisha was weeping, Mac-
Caa's arm about her shoulders

✖

Savary:	*You paint an egalitarian picture of Ignis Dei yet, are you not the absolute leader, our conduit to the possibility of God?*
Ellisha:	*I do not claim to be special, only to have seen a little fur-ther.*
Savary:	*Yet people attribute miracles to you. It is claimed that you cured a prostitute dying of AIDS in India. That you appear to people in their dreams. You can cure addictions. You can bring back the dead.*
Ellisha:	*I have never claimed these things.*
Savary:	*But you do not deny them?*
Ellisha:	*Monsieur Savary, you and I both know that the paradox of denying messianic power is only to be believed all the more.*
Savary:	*And what of children?*
Ellisha:	*Children?*

Savary: It is said that they hold a special place in your heart.

Peter pushed himself away from the mic with an angry gesture. 'Damn!' Perdita was watching him. 'Will she cope?'

'She'll cope.'

Ellisha: Let me tell you about Santa Madre.

∝

There was something brutal about landing in a place where all the old primal fears of being swallowed by the earth had come true. Only hours earlier illegal logging had loosened the protective web of roots cradling the earth and the land had begun to slip. Slowly at first, a pebble here, a bolus of dried leaves there, skeletons of discarded feathers, the femur of a tiny forgotten mammal, all moving, churning together and sliding into the water until the Magdalena river sent sixty million tons of mud crashing down on the little village of Santa Madre, effectively wiping it from the surface of the earth.

'Peter!' Ellisha whispered his name on an outbreath, an invocation against the evil they saw in every direction. The mud extended as far as the eye could see: black, oozing filth that engulfed everything in its path. Collapsed houses, broken roof beams sticking up through the mud like exposed ribcages. Hundreds of trees uprooted, as though it was nothing to uproot a tree. A child huddled in a blanket, shivering despite the heat. Behind the child, a row of corpses wrapped in thick black liners.

Mariam appeared. She was dressed in the same protective gear they now wore themselves—jumpsuit and thick boots.

It's not right, he had argued. *This isn't how the world should see the Prophetess.*

But Ellisha's jaw had set in a firm line. *You don't create Soul by watching on the sidelines.* Mariam had brought over an interpreter and they listened to their stories through his words and to the sighs and moans around them that required no interpretation at all.

—Over and over, he is saying, the noise. Snapping. Breaking.

—A rumbling sound. Like the end of the world.

—She says her neighbour's house was there. Gone. Her neighbours were inside...

Standing amongst them, Peter began to understand that distance, achieved by soaring above in a helicopter or observing from the comfort of an armchair, gives tragedy a fictive element: a story of tiny ant people that can be dismissed or switched off when the well of sympathy threatens to overflow. But human scale allows horror to rush in, to become real. His throat tightened and he reached out to take Ellisha's hand, but she was holding the hands of a little girl, not more than five years old, and concentrating on the words of the interpreter.

'This girl's mother is missing. She heard a rumble then it was dark. When she woke up, her mother was not there.'

Ellisha hugged the little girl to her, mud stains and all. 'Tell her we'll find her.'

Smiling at the interpreter, he bent down and hissed in her ear. 'Ellie, what are you doing?'

She pulled the girl tighter. 'I'm doing what you said we would do, helping people.'

He looked at the interpreter. 'Tell her we'll do our best.'

'No.' Ellisha's voice was firm. 'Tell her we'll find her mother.'

'But—'

'Duncan.'

MacCaa stepped forwards. He was flanked by several Soul-Searchers. Wherever he went they seemed drawn to him, as though some primitive masculine element of his makeup called to an essential femininity in theirs. Peter noticed that he now had a small copy of the burning tree tattooed at the corner of his right eye so that the branches dripped like tears. It looked ridiculous, and Peter gave a snort under his breath, hoping Ellisha heard it. But Ellisha had taken MacCaa's hands in hers. 'We need to find this little girl's mother. She's trapped out there in the mud.'

Don't ask him. Peter nearly said it aloud. But the Sparks had downed tools to watch, and many had phones out, recording as the scene unfolded.

MacCaa leaned his head back and sniffed the air. His eyes closed and he began to speak in a clear resonant voice.

'We urnae made tae come into this life alone

We arrive in our mothers' arms

Surrounded.

Nor should we think tae tak leave frae this life as one.

But as part o the Great Beginning

Unbounded.'

There was a long silence then Ellisha nodded. 'You're saying she's out there.'

'Wait!' Peter clutched her arm. 'That could mean anything.'

'No. I get it. It's the way MacCaa sees the world. Not with this—' a tap to her head '—but with this—' a hand over her heart.

'But—'

'No buts, Peter.'

'Ellie, you can't do this.'

She looked at him calmly. 'I can. I'm the Prophetess.'

It was a logistical nightmare. It was a lost cause. The mud was treacherous, and it was difficult to keep upright with the constant sense that your boots were about to be sucked off, but Peter managed to reach the teams who were organizing the digging with his footwear, if not his dignity, intact.

There was a pause when they recognised who he was. And it was startling, and not a little gratifying, to see how shy they became in his presence. He waited patiently while the mutters of *It's him* died down, before saying, 'There's a little girl out there who has lost her mother.' He paused, letting his words sink in. 'The Prophetess wants her found. How can I help?'

That he wasn't afraid to lift a spade and dig made him at once a man of the people, even as they acknowledged that he was not. And, as he worked, he made it his business to engage them in conversation, finding out where they were from and why they had felt compelled to throw up their old lives to answer the call of a faithless faith. And he was good at this, a man who could converse with kings yet not forget his common touch.

He met an oncologist, who said that she had witnessed so much death that it had sucked the meaning out of life until she had seen Ellisha on Calton Hill, and another woman, brought up in a strict religious sect, who had been constantly plagued with the feeling that God was not benevolent. He felt them warming to him, these Sparks who had travelled impossible distances, far from the secure bubbles of their homes, because they had heard the message of a coming God and had responded to it in some deep, occluded part of themselves.

He shared in the triumphs—the miracle of the baby cradled in the branches of a tree—and the crushing disappointments—the old man, who lived only long enough to feel the sun on his face, before slipping away—high fiving and patting shoulders, hugging a young interpreter who was overwhelmed by exhaustion and relentless tragedy, and all the time repeating his message, soul seeks Soul.

He squatted beside a well-built African-American man who was expertly treating the wound on a young woman's thigh.

'You've done this before.'

'Once or twice.' He flashed Peter a quick, friendly smile.

'A doctor?'

The smile vanished. 'No, sir. I was a sergeant with the army in Afghanistan. You learn a thing or two about dealing with a wound out there. Pass me that alcohol wipe, please.'

Peter complied and watched him clean the forceps he had been using. 'What made you come to Ignis Dei?'

'The usual reasons.' A silence followed. Peter was wondering how hard to push, when he heard the man draw a sharp inbreath. He put the forceps down. 'I did things. I saw things. You look into the empty eye socket of a guy you shot thirty seconds ago and you see nothing, no light, no sign that he's gone to Jesus. Nothing but ruined flesh and darkness and the stink of the Void.'

'I'm sorry.'

He stared. 'Sorry?'

'Sorry that you have been through so much pain.'

'Don't be. It brought me here. To Ellisha.'

Peter sat back on his heels, not knowing what to say, humbled by the simplicity with which the man spoke and the profound realisation that he had created something with the power of self-creation. It moved him in a way he was unused to, and he was afraid he might begin to weep. It was a relief when an urgent cry came from one of the Sparks:

'We got sounds.' The Spark was standing proud and tall atop a pyramid of rubble. He tore off his headphones as a king might tear off his crown before combat. 'We gotta hurry. There's life down there.'

Then there was motion, as in a battle a kind of chaos, but the chaos of many individuals impelled by precise purpose.

—Are they responding?

—Just knocking. But it's rhythmic.

—Do we know which sensor?

—Not clear. Could be five or maybe six. Anything from the dogs?

—Can we get in?

—It's six. It's definitely six!

—Beam's fallen. Blocking the way.

—We need the hoist.

—Over by the excavation.

—Bring it over here.

—Hurry! The knocking's getting fainter.

Then a single trembling voice. 'Generator's failed.'

And Peter who had been watching it all with the detachment of a bystander, suddenly found himself at the bottom of a well of silence down which all the Sparks were looking. They were waiting for him to tell them what to do.

'Ah.' His tongue ran along the dry crevices of his lower lip. Whatever he said, whatever he did next was crucial. They had come on the promise that Ignis Dei was the wellspring of its own creation, existence from non-existence, question teased out of answer. And now they were waiting for the proof.

He cleared his throat, playing for time, the sum total of his knowledge of generators amounting to a fat diddley squat. 'What exactly is the problem?'

'There's no power.'

'And you've checked everything?'

An earnest nod. 'The AVR, the circuit breaker, even tried shooting a DC current through the stator for a couple of seconds, everything.'

'I see.' Peter nodded. Desperation trailed his eyes along the site. There were Sparks working in the safety zone on the edge of the mud, their focus on the growing group of trembling survivors. Ellisha was rocking the child in her lap, a dark-skinned Proserpina casting her light across Hell.

And now the Lord of the Underworld appeared in the shape of MacCaa striding towards them as if chaos was his natural habitat. He stopped when he reached Peter, surveying the scene, and Peter held his breath, anticipating those great paws taking hold of the beam and lifting it clean off the ground.

'Huv ye goat a power drill?'

A hesitation then the Spark nodded.

'Ah think ah kin use it tae bump start the residual magnetism.'

A drill was found. MacCaa signalled for the Spark to start the generator and, with surprising gentleness, he pulled the trigger and spun the drill chuck in reverse.

A moment's uncertainty then: 'It's working!' The Spark punched the air. And suddenly the electricity was not only from the generator. Their success crackled in the air, and they stared at each other, bonded by achievement and the feeling that here was something good that was greater than the whole. 'Soul seeks Soul,' one of the Sparks cried and everyone cheered.

The process of reaching the survivors was long and slow. Each brick removed with painstaking care, breath held whenever their dismantling of the matchstick structure set off an echoing creak or shudder. A man was rescued first. Frail, unconscious, he had been hanging upside-down in a narrow cavity between collapsed walls. The medics took charge of him.

Then came a woman. She was small-boned, so thickly coated in mud her age was impossible to tell, but MacCaa pulled her out and held her in his arms, cradled like a little bird, and Peter saw how, like certain men of raw, brutish power, MacCaa was especially gentle with the vulnerable, and Peter found himself remembering that MacCaa had once had a child and wondering what sort of father he might have been.

As they made their way across the glutinous mud to the safe zone, he tried to express some of this new appreciation. 'What you did out there. Great job.' MacCaa glanced down, the gesture absorbed without reaction, light disappearing beyond the rim of a singularity. Peter silently cursed himself. *Stupid. Reaching out to this man. Like seeing emotion in the gnarly bark of a tree or the face of Jesus on a slice of burnt toast.*

The woman's mud-caked lips parted and she began to make small whimpering noises. She rolled her eyes.

'She's in a bad way. Come on. Hurry!'

He tried to hold her gaze, willing her to stay alive, afraid if he looked away, she would slip beyond his grasp. In his urgency, the woman and the sucking ooze beneath his feet became the whole world, and he became so absorbed in the task that he did not notice the moment when they reached the secure zone. Only a sense of solidness beneath his feet and the blur of someone rushing up with a flask of water. Then the woman's choking gasps as she swallowed. Her fingers finding the folds of his jumpsuit. Faintly, '*Gracias. Gracias.*'

'She says—' began one of the interpreters.

Peter cut him off. 'I know.'

MacCaa laid her on the ground and the medics closed in to assess the woman. Peter knew he should return to the rescue mission out on the mud; he should talk about the arrangements for the survivors; he should make contact with the media team, get a feel for the vibe. But he stayed. And the sun, that had been too hot, felt good on his skin. And the pain in his joints did not bother him because it was only a sign that he was real and whole and alive.

He felt, rather than saw, Ellisha's approach. She had the child in her arms, and someone was following behind her with a camera. She did not come up to him immediately, but looked about, confused. And it was only then he understood that he was made anonymous by mud and exhaustion.

'Ellie!'

She turned at the sound of his voice, her face lighting up. 'Peter. You've been gone so long. They keep harassing me to pose for pictures.' She looked down at the woman, whose hand he still held, and her voice softened. 'Who's this?'

But it was the child in her arms who responded, letting go her grasp on Ellisha and holding out her arms. She was saying something, and the woman in the stretcher responded, finding new strength that propelled her up on her elbows.

'What is she saying?' Ellisha demanded.

'Auntie,' the interpreter explained. 'This is her mother's sister.'

The child was struggling in Ellisha's arms, but she did not let go. Peter jumped to his feet. Ellisha was looking at the interpreter. 'Not her mother?'

'No. Her aunt.' And thinking it a matter of elucidation, he added earnestly, 'The little sister of her mother.'

'Ellie.' He was at her side now, whispering in her ear. She stiffened, her arms tightening around the child, mouth falling open to argue. But he reached around and began loosening her fingers. 'Time now. You know that.'

Her mouth clamped shut in a thin line, but her hands were limp. He gently prised the little girl free and set her on the ground. She toddled towards the woman on the stretcher, who promptly burst into tears. Ellisha said nothing, and he saw how it wrenched and tore her. He whispered in her ear. 'One day.' But she only stood there, surrounded by love and feeling none of it.

He was aware that there were cameras pointing from every direction at the Prophetess' face, and it was a relief when MacCaa's bulk came forward and blotted them out. He took Ellisha's hands. 'Ye gied me hope. Gie it tae them.' As he stepped aside, Peter was hurt to see her eyes follow him. But her focus returned to the Sparks and she straightened, before announcing in a calm, clear voice that the Soul

Mystica moved within her. She spoke of how Ignis Dei would buy the land and replant the forest. And not only that forest, but across the world, wherever there were Sparks forests would be replanted so that the great green cathedrals might rise again to herald the age of Soul.

When she had finished speaking she stood very stiff and still, her glance moving across the ruined landscape, and the gesture was so simple and brave and clean it invoked magic. A tiny white-necked jacobin flew between the ruined trunks and landed for a moment amongst her plaits in fleeting coronation of the Queen of the world.

Peter felt he should make some gesture to draw attention to the symbolism of the occasion, but suddenly he was speechless.

Sparks and survivors alike were falling to their knees, like stars at dawn going out before the power of the risen sun.

✺

Savary: Was this ethical?

Ellisha: Are you asking if helping people in dire need was ethical?

Savary: Was it proper for Ignis Dei to attempt a rescue when there are other trained aid agencies who have more experience in this area?

Ellisha: Those agencies were not there. We were.

Savary: How did you manage to get there faster than the professionals?

Ellisha: There is no mystery. As you have noted, we have technology on our side. Virtual cathedrals, digital disciples, all those minds combining into something beyond imagining.

Savary:	*Is this really all it takes?*
Ellisha:	*Much of Christianity's success could be attributed to its administrative efficiency against the background of a crumbling Roman empire. We can mobilize locals and gather experts in a particular field more efficiently than governments or NGOs.*
Savary:	*And you see the internet as a spiritual medium?*
Ellisha:	*Of course. The only way to enter cyberspace is spiritually. We connect with millions of minds every day, and how else could it be done except immaterially?*
Savary:	*It is difficult to see how this is not simply a religion for atheists.*
Ellisha:	*No.*
Savary:	*No? Then how do you explain the contradiction?*
Ellisha:	*We are a religion for people who have lost God.*
Savary:	*Is that not the same thing?*
Ellisha:	*To lose something you thought you had is not the same as denying its existence. You know that, M. Savary.*

Constance Tao had come into the room. Over the years Peter had become used to her presence, High Priestess of Virtual Reality, both she and her team, transmitting Ellisha's message along the silent corridors of cyberspace. She had come in to discuss tweaks to the new AI system they were rolling out, a system that would speak with Ellisha's voice. 'Like Alexa or Siri?' he had suggested when he first heard of it.

Constance had given him a humouring glance. 'Not exactly. It won't simply turn on the TV or switch on the lights. It will guide the user towards the Soul Mystica by monitoring their actions for Soul value.'

She had broken off when she realised the interview was underway, and was studying the data they had on Savary. 'Tell the Prophetess to ask about his marriage.' To Peter she explained. 'He trained to become a priest before renouncing it all for love. We can use it to show how his soul turned from men to seek love with a woman.' But when Ellisha asked he denied it.

Ellisha: No?

Savary: *I was. I was married. I am no longer married. My wife is dead. These facts are known of me.*

Ellisha: *Is it known that you looked into the Void?*

Peter leaned forward. What is she doing? 'Ellie, we need to show his soul seeking the light of another. Steer him back to where he first met his wife.' But Ellisha's jaw set in a way he didn't like.

Ellisha: *What did you see, monsieur Savary, when you looked?*

Savary: *I loved my wife. French men, they have a certain repu-tation. But I loved my wife. She was—how do you say it—my soulmate. Even when she left to be on her own, I never thought of myself as single, never looked at other women. I thought... if I gave her time. I did not—could not imagine that someone so full of life would—*

The data scrolled past silently. The orders for brandy then more brandy. The books with titles that translated as *When your loved-one has depression. Dealing with Loss. Death of the Divine. Use of sleeping pills in suicide rates.* Ellisha looked as though she was about to speak, but Savary continued in a low, savage voice.

Savary: *Do you think you have discovered something because you suffered and could not see beyond it?*

Ellisha: *Have you seen beyond it?*

Savary: *You expect me to believe that, when it comes to the dissolution of an incomplete soul, there is no hope?*

Ellisha: *That is exactly what I expect, Hugo. Because there is no hope.*

It was always a shock to hear that final refutation. Savary looked like a waxwork, and Ellisha reached for the brandy. She poured two sizeable measures and handed one to the Frenchman, who took it without acknowledgement. Sitting back in her chair, Ellisha drew her legs up and relished a long sip. Watching, Peter licked his lips.

Ellisha: *We must mourn those who are gone. But we must concentrate on the way ahead. You are falling, are you not, Hugo? Before Eloise died, you were special, chosen, marked by the universe for love. But you have discovered that was not true. You have seen the empty soulless horror of everything. People, like you and me, Hugo, we are Unchosen, and it drives us to change things.*

When she finished speaking there was silence, the kind of silence that made Peter want to put his hands over his ears. The ash on Savary's Gitane crumbled from the tip, but he did not seem to notice. Ellisha got to her feet. She placed a hand on his shoulder. 'Drink your brandy, M. Savary. And when you are ready, I will be waiting.' She left the room. The lights dimmed. But not before Peter had seen a single tear roll down Savary's sunken cheek.

Constance was the first to speak. 'We can fix this. We can cut the interview before she tries to convert Savary. And if he won't be bought off, there are other methods.'

Peter blinked, as though coming awake. 'This was a mistake. I'll talk to the Prophetess. Sort things.'

But Perdita had her phone to her ear. 'No. Mr Avery has been watching. He says it's time to let Ellisha spread her wings.'

CHAPTER 22

THERE WAS A SALTY, ROTTED smell in the air as they sped across the lagoon towards Poveglia, Venice's island of the damned. Over the noise of the spray, Ellisha said, 'You know they say half the soil is human ash?'

'All the more reason to bring it back to life.' He leaned forwards, squinting a little. 'Look, you can see the hospital.'

Through the haze a low structure was emerging, built from terracotta bricks with several taller structures behind it. 'We had to promise to keep the original façade,' he explained. 'But inside is tech like you wouldn't believe. I want to show you the holographic imaging systems and the AI diagnostics. It's like we're dealing with honest-to-God magic.'

She threw him a look. 'Honest-to-Goddess surely? Just tell me that you haven't forgotten the patients in the midst of this tech extravaganza.'

He affected a hurt tone. 'We've had the best Spark psychologists and designers on the job. Healing colours, lots of light, doctors who care as much about the patient's spiritual recovery as his physical one. Trust me, this is going to be as big a revolution as germ theory or antibiotics. This is the future of medicine. Soul appearing out of the Void; the world healing itself.'

Ellisha pursed her lips. 'Gotta say, I didn't think you'd be able to persuade Phil. All that talk about belief and healing going hand-in-hand. I didn't think he'd buy it.'

'It'd be a lot easier if he would actually attend a meeting instead of relaying everything through Perdita. Doesn't it ever bother you the way he acts like the ghost in the machine?'

She shrugged. 'I guess he trusts you.'

The hospital director, a raw-boned woman with hair that was going grey at the temples, seemed awestruck to meet Ellisha in the flesh at last. Peter felt a stab of sympathy. A legend is not easy to meet. Both less and more.

'We are so pleased … so very honoured— I can't begin to—'

'Thank you.' Ellisha took hold of the Director's hands and the woman fell silent. 'Show me what progress you've made.'

'Of course.' The Director beamed then looked anxious. 'I hope everything will be the way you want it. If you want to see the books, I can make them available to you. We've made careful use of all the funding and—'

'That won't be necessary,' Ellisha assured her. 'I feel the fragments of your soul reaching for the light. We trust you.'

They say it is impossible for an adult to grow beyond the age of twenty. But, there in that entrance-hall, Peter saw that woman increase in stature by several inches. Shyly, she offered Ellisha her arm. 'This way.'

Following, with MacCaa a pace or two behind, something caught Peter's eye. Ellisha's dress, backless as always, the burning tree rippling across the smooth plain of her skin. He had seen it a million times until he no longer saw it. Yet now he looked closer and saw clearly the stiff structure of her shoulder blades, how they pressed against the flesh like nascent wings. *She's lost weight.* It gave her a leaner, more ascetic look which pleased him. Still it was strange. They attended so many functions, state dinners and banquets. *Surely she ate. Or did I simply see the food so often, I went on seeing her eating even after she stopped?*

The Director was speaking to him and he pressed his lips together and nodded to hide his confusion. Pulling a word from instant recall, he said, 'Meditation?'

'Oh yes.' The Director seemed pleased. 'It's an entirely holistic approach. As you know, our doctors and nurses are trained to heal the soul along with the body. And there are Soul-Searchers and diviners on the staff, of course.'

'But you don't only treat Sparks?'

'No, indeed. But you would be surprised how many become interested in learning more once they've experienced our methods.'

They entered a light airy ward where the beds were placed in a series of alcoves separated by tall pillars and frescoed arches. An old man was the first to approach, back hunched over a slender walking stick in a way that made him look like an ancient tree twisted about a vigorous young sapling. 'I have had a thought,' he said softly, so softly that Ellisha was obliged to ask him to speak up. After clearing his throat noisily, he continued on a note of pride, 'My grandson is only five, but there's something about him. I know every grandparent thinks this. But he's my sixth, and he's quite different to all the rest. Talking to him is… well… it's like he knows things…'

'Go on, please.'

'I think he is what used to be called an old soul. But, if as you say, none of us is born with the Soul Mystica, I wondered how this might be?'

Ellisha nodded slowly, as though in deep thought.

'I wondered,' the old man offered into the silence, 'if he might have an unnaturally large potential.'

Ellisha stopped nodding and looked directly at the man.

'Like a musical prodigy?' he added.

'Psychic perfect pitch?'

The old man beamed. 'Indeed. Indeed! That is what I meant. Do you think it possible?'

Ellisha's face broke into a smile and she laid a hand on his shoulder. 'It is possible.'

Glowing, he returned to his bed, dipping his head graciously towards a variety of admiring and openly envious glances.

They continued along the ward, and Peter noticed how eager the Sparks were to share their commitment. One of the nurses told of how she had found the courage to leave an abusive husband and retrain as a healer, and several patients were keen mention that they had made large contributions to their soulariums. But this made Ellisha frown. 'You can't buy your soul,' she said sharply and walked away.

Peter caught up with her and hissed under his breath. 'We shouldn't look down on them for making donations. Giving is their way of helping. And remember what Avery said: money makes all this possible.'

Ellisha ignored him. She was holding the hand of a woman, so frail she could not lift her head from the pillow. The woman's voice was low and whispery. 'I'm taking the Advanced Soul Seeker course,' she was saying. 'It's expensive. My son didn't want me to. But I'm glad I did. The diviner says I might be an adept.'

Ellisha's eyes were full of tears, but she reached out and stroked the woman's hair. 'And you feel at peace?'

'Yes. Yes.' The lips twitched with the ghost of a smile. 'In a way I never knew before. My whole life I've felt like an outsider. Not really understood. But I belong now. I feel Soul calling to me. Like a deep calm ocean, wanting me to be part of it.'

Ellisha started to answer, but a commotion at the nurses' station drew their attention. A young woman was trying to get through, but her way was being blocked by a group of nurses. She was shabbily dressed, and her hair looked unkempt. There was something a little wild about her, as if she might be drunk or high. Peter glanced at Mac-Caa, but he was strangely motionless.

'Ellisha! Prophetess! Please let me speak to you.'

The Director frowned and made a move to guide them out by another door, but Ellisha shook her head. 'No. Let her come.'

The nurses parted reluctantly, keeping close on either side, and she came forward pushing her hair behind her ears with one hand and clutching a jacket, with missing buttons, about her with the other. There were dark circles under her eyes, which looked at Ellisha with desperate, burning hope. 'Save him. I know you can do it.' She thrust a crumpled photograph into Ellisha's hands. Glancing over her shoulder Peter had the impression of a frail bald old man with pain-filled eyes. Then some shift in perception made him look again, and with an inward blench, he understood that here was a child looking up at the lens from a hospital bed.

'Your son,' Ellisha said.

'He's on the children's ward. He has leukaemia. Please save him.'

Ellisha was still captivated by the photograph. 'I have never claimed to have saved anyone.'

'But you can. Everyone knows you save children. You can bring them back.'

Ellisha was shaking her head gently, and Peter felt it was time to intervene. 'We're terribly sorry for your son, but that is not what Ignis Dei is about—'

His words were broken as the woman grabbed Ellisha's arm. 'Please. I don't have money. But you can have anything… anything you want. I'll convert. I'll work for no pay. You are the one with the—the—what-do-they-call-it—*Soul Mystica*. You can do things. Everyone knows this.'

Peter made a rumbling noise, but Ellisha gave a slight shake of her head. 'You do not need to come to me. Your son will live.'

The woman swayed slightly and blinked several times. 'Thank you.' Her lips barely moved and the sound came from deep inside. 'Thank you.'

Ellisha took her hands. 'I haven't done anything.'

A nod. But of agreement? Peter thought not. The woman looked dazed, in the way lottery winners or the survivors of catastrophes look, disbelieving, suspicious of their good fortune. Ellisha stepped back. 'Go to your son.'

Stiff, disbelieving steps took the woman through the wondering, reverent faces of the Sparks. As she passed, one of the diviner's pressed his fingers to his lips, as though kissing the sprig of sage he held in one hand, and a Soul-Searcher tipped her head back ecstatically and moaned. Ellisha waited until the woman had gone before turning back to the Director. 'Now, where were we?'

'Ellisha, we need to talk.'

'We do?' She was sitting on a heap of white cushions at a window seat, looking out over the Grand Canal, and there was something dreamy about her voice.

'You gave that woman hope.'

'What woman?' She turned around.

'You know what woman! The mother of that child in the photograph. You told her he would get better.'

'He will.'

Peter's head began to throb. 'Ellie, you need to be careful. You're taking risks. The investors won't like it.'

A shrug. 'What are they going to do, find a new Prophetess?'

'What if the child dies?'

'He won't.'

'You can't know that.'

'I can. I do.'

'What on earth do you mean?'

The dreamy expression was back in her eyes. 'I can't explain it. Something's happening. Sometimes it's like I'm not me anymore.'

'You're scaring me.'

She tilted her head to one side. 'Why, afraid of your own creation, Dr Frankenstein?'

He forced out a laugh, not because it was funny, but because he felt the first stirrings of fear. 'Be serious. Out of all the children you've met, why choose that one?'

'I don't know.' Her eyes were moving across his face. 'Out of all the men I'd met, why choose you?'

He had no answer to that.

'Poor Peter.' She reached up and brushed her fingertips along his cheek. 'I wish I could let you inside my head. I feel like… sometimes I feel like—' biting her lip '—as though something was gathering inside me. Like I'm growing hotter—' a small shake of her head '—no, that's not it. There are whole nights I don't sleep because I feel as if I'm on the brink of something.'

He leaned forwards, fascinated in spite of himself. 'What? What something?'

'Something that's about to be revealed.'

Dark green walls and ceiling of age-blackened oak gave the room an underwater feeling that made it seem to rock gently, or perhaps the sensation was merely a reflection of the bobbing pontoons on the canal outside the window or the words Perdita had just spoken. 'Mr Avery will be pleased.'

Out of all the reactions he had expected from Perdita, approval was not one of them. He had found her on the phone asking for London, while a steady stream of Sparks hurried in and out fetching and delivering reports. In the background a video of Ellisha in Santa Madre was playing. There was no sound, but Peter noticed that she was a shade taller and that her freckles had been edited out. She was watching the little girl reunited with her aunt, a delighted smile quirking her lips.

'What can I do for you?' Perdita's voice penetrated his distraction, holding the phone against her chest while she listened to what he had to say, then astounding him with one of her rare smiles.

For a moment Peter stared, feeling a burning sensation creep along the tips of his ears. He said angrily, 'You're not listening. She promised that mother. Think of the consequences. What if the child dies?'

Perdita put the phone down and began gathering her papers. 'We have ways of dealing with these situations.'

'What are you saying?'

'I think you understand perfectly well.'

Peter placed his hands on the desk and leaned forward. 'Spell it out for me.'

They locked eyes then Perdita sighed and looked towards a group of Sparks, who were packing up the IT equipment. 'Give me the room, please.' Without question, they scurried away, the last one tentatively making the burning tree salute before she disappeared.

Perdita waited until they were alone before turning back to Peter. 'Everyone has a price, you know that. The mother's silence will be bought. Our influencers will divert world attention for a few days, and the story will sink beneath the surface without trace.'

Every muscle in Peter's face was frozen. He forced sarcasm over stone lips. 'What is a dead child worth?'

'One point two million in our experience.' She looked at her watch. 'If you'll excuse me. There's a lot to do before our next flight.'

Leaden steps took him to the door, where he hesitated, fingers curled around the handle. 'You're wrong.'

'Oh?'

'You said everyone has a price. Ellisha doesn't have one.'

'No. That's why you sold her to Avery. It was the price of having a destiny.'

As Peter gawped, Perdita got to her feet and snapped her bag shut. 'You didn't really imagine we didn't know?'

He walked away feeling furious and insulted and afraid there was some truth in what she had said. It made him pace very fast and decisively, paying no attention to what was around him. When he started up the broad staircase that led to their apartments he was unaware of the descending stranger, until the man's body hurtled past, nearly taking Peter with him. Blind instinct made him grab at the iron balustrade. He cut his hands in the process, and twisted around just in time to see the man land in a contorted heap at the bottom.

'Holy fuck!'

A laugh made him look up. MacCaa and two heavy-looking Sparks stood there. They were dressed in khaki fatigues and, like MacCaa, they had the burning tree tattoo dripping from the corner of their left eyes. It was not MacCaa who had laughed. His granite eyes were on the crumpled figure at the bottom of the stairs.

'What have you done?' Peter bounded down the stairs and knelt down beside the prone body. There was blood frothed about his nostrils and one of his eyes was sealed shut. He didn't seem to be breathing. MacCaa appeared at his side and Peter cried, 'You've killed him.' MacCaa took the news equably, poking the toe of his boot into the victim's ribs, causing him to groan and roll onto his back. MacCaa considered this development then said to no-one in particular, 'He'll no try taking pictures of the Prophetess again.'

'What?' Everything in Peter's head suddenly stopped. He looked down at the man then back at MacCaa, then before he knew it, he was taking the steps, two at a time, to Ellisha's apartments.

He found her more angry than afraid. 'He was hiding in there! In the closet.'

Peter opened the door of the armoire, half expecting to find a dozen paparazzi skulking beneath the hangers. 'Did he threaten you?'

'No. He just wanted pictures. But it was humiliating. I was half undressed.'

'But how did he get in?'

'We don't know. Duncan's very upset.'

'He half killed him. He was unconscious, bleeding. Did you know MacCaa was capable of something like that?' He meant to shock her, but Ellisha only scowled then stormed over to the window. She stood looking out in frosty silence so absolute he couldn't find a way to enter it.

Just as he was wondering if this was a kind of dismissal, she swung around angrily and declared, 'I'm sick of it. Sick of being constantly hounded. Flashbulbs going off in my face, cameras crawling over my skin. Everyone thinking they have a right to know what I eat for breakfast or what brand of toothpaste I use. The endless debating over every little thing I say. Good grief, I can't sneeze without making headlines. It never stops. Photographers, reporters, bloggers, trolls everywhere, waiting to pounce. I need. I need—'

She pressed her hands against her head and he feared she was bringing on another headache. Anxiously, he asked, 'What do you need?'

'I need to go out. Not like usual. Not smothered by security men. Just out. Just me.'

Taken aback, he could think of nothing better to say than, 'Ellie, it's not a good idea.'

It was the wrong tack. Suddenly she was yelling, 'I need to! I'm tired. Tired of everything. I can feel it building up inside me, like… like I'm a thermometer with the mercury rising. I need it to STOP!' The anger left her and she stood panting, her eyes large and accusing. Suddenly she groaned and covered her face with her hands. He approached softly as one might towards a lost child or the criminally insane.

'Diva.'

She gave a sniff and wiped her nose on the back of her hand. 'Jerk-off.'

'Nice mouth for the promise of a new age.'

Down they went through the narrow streets, avoiding the Grand Canal and the main thoroughfares for the tiny anonymous backstreets, so narrow that they sometimes had to go in single file, footsteps echoing up between the lines of laundry strung between the tenements. He had dressed casually, a baseball cap shading his face, and Ellisha had covered her hair with a headscarf and donned a pair of outsized sunglasses. She was fiddling with the knot of the scarf, drawing it closer around her face, and he thought he understood. She was feeling a kind of nakedness.

Outside, like this, they were unnaturally exposed. Like prisoners who fight to be freed from their incarceration, only to find that they no longer know how to behave in society. He tried to express some of this, but Ellisha asked suddenly, 'What month is it?'

'I'm not sure.'

'The trees we've seen don't seem to be in full bloom yet.'

'Spring?'

'I guess.' They looked at each other and burst out laughing. How could they not know? It broke the tension and released something wild. Holding hands, like children, they ran along the paved streets, winding through Venice's dark maze until they came, quite suddenly, upon a tree-lined square. It was empty save for an old man asleep on a bench, and the sight of him made Peter realise how footsore he was. *How far have we come?*

Ellisha had evidently had the same thought, because she slipped free of his hand and moved towards the benches. But it was not, as he had thought, to find a comfortable place to take the weight off her feet. Instead she made straight for the old man, approaching him softly as though there was something about him that puzzled her. And joining her, Peter saw him through her eyes, how his hat sat beside him on the bench and his head drooped towards his chest, and how he was not sleeping as he had first thought, but weeping.

Slowly, Ellisha removed her sunglasses and unwound the scarf from her head. The man looked up through his tears and there was a moment's silence before he whispered, '*Ti riconosco.*'

'Ellie? What's he saying?'

'He knows me.'

'You speak Italian?'

'No. But Italian and Latin are close. I can pick up a bit.' She listened closely then after a moment stood up. 'He's lost. He's lived here all his life, I think. But now he's lost.'

'We should call someone.'

'No. We'll take him ourselves.'

'Are you sure?' Now that they had stopped, the sense of what they were doing caught up with him. *Mad. This was a mad idea.* 'I think we should go back.'

Ellie looked mulish. 'Didn't you hear him? He knows me.'

'Everyone knows you.'

'It's different.'

'How?'

'You didn't notice?'

'Notice what? That this man out of all the people who recognise you is somehow different, specially connected?'

'Didn't you notice he's blind?'

Mouth agape, Peter looked again, and this time saw the milky surfaces of the man's eyes. He felt embarrassed and started to apologise, but Ellisha had helped the old man up and they were already walking arm in arm across the square. She was telling him about the planting of the Soul forests, and of her sadness that she would never see them hundreds of years in the future when they had grown extraordinarily beautiful, green cathedrals and sacred groves, where people might come in search of the lost fragments of their souls. The old man was nodding, though it was plain he understood not a word, and Peter walked alongside them thinking how long it had been since he had heard her talk so openly. *I didn't understand how much the forests meant to her.*

'Peter.' Ellisha's voice interrupted. She was pointing up ahead. 'What is that?'

'I don't know.' It was hard to make sense of what he was seeing. At first he had the impression that he was looking at an ambulatory forest, Birnam Wood approaching Dunsinane. But, as logic resolved the image, he saw a protest march coming towards them, men and women, young and old. There seemed no colour or creed binding them. He spotted dog collars next to hijabs, a gaggle of nuns walking alongside Orthodox Jews, and a number of distinguished-looking men in Sikh turbans. Many were holding up poles with clumsily daubed placards mostly written in English.

HE IS OUR CREATOR!

THEIR LIE IS OUR TRUTH!

As they drew closer he realised that they were chanting in English—GOD IS NOW! GOD IS LOVE!—repeated over and over with growing venom.

'Who are they, Peter?'

'Ellie,' he said in a low tight voice. 'Put your scarf and glasses on. Now!' He pulled the visor of his baseball cap lower. *If they catch us out here…*

He looked about wildly for an escape route, but a shout from the demonstrators cut him off.

'It's her!'

Suddenly they were the focus of a beam of pent-up rage. Reaching behind, he took Ellisha's arm. 'Ellie, we need to run.'

'No. I'm not leaving him behind.' She had her other arm around the old man's shoulders.

'They don't want him. If we go, he'll be fine.'

'I'm not leaving.'

The argument was pointless. For an instant everything was frozen. An image of Peter's old dog flashed into his mind. The way it had chased the neighbour's cat in frothy fury for years until one day against the odds, it caught it. Then the moment of bewilderment. Both animals frozen in the confusion over what should come next.

They don't know what to do. Didn't expect to find us. We need to run. Now!

He tugged at Ellisha, but anchored by the old man, she refused to budge. The mob was creeping forward. '*Ellisha! Ellisha!*' The cry was ragged, hungry. *No reasoning with them. They'll tear us to pieces.* 'Stop!' he shouted. 'We can talk about this.'

But the demonstrators had smelled blood in the water, and they would not be held.

'*GOD IS LOVE! GOD IS LOVE!*'

Instinct made him let Ellisha go then step back to shield her with his body. *One punch. I might get one good one in. Scare them off? Or enrage them?* His temples throbbed and he felt a wave of sadness that everything should end like this. And only faintly did he understand that there was a force felling a path through the protestors, like the wrath of God.

CHAPTER 23

PERDITA AND MARIAM WERE WAITING for them when they returned. Perdita looked wan. Her normally etiolated skin, reminiscent of snowdrifts and ice floes, now seemed ashen, and seeing her like this made Peter repentant and moved to make apologies. But Ellisha was curiously aloof. Once she had established that the old man was safe, she had withdrawn into her thoughts, ignoring Perdita's reproaches and Mariam's hurt expression, and flinging herself down on a velvet fainting couch.

Perdita was fingering the pearls at her throat. 'We were aware of their presence. MacCaa has been keeping an eye on them.'

'But to allow it here—in Venice.'

Perdita sighed and glanced briefly at Peter. 'It's not as simple as you think. We're not dealing with a single entity.'

Peter tried to put his arm around Ellisha, but she was so stiff he let it fall and walked over to lean his elbow against a bookcase. 'What exactly are we dealing with?'

'They call themselves America Follows The Truth. They started as a loosely connected collection of Christian sects, campaigning against what they see as blasphemy. But it seems they have moved to a multi-denomiational ethos. The enemy of my enemy and so on.'

'So they're Americans.'

'Not necessarily. They have global networks. And recently they've become more media aware. It's ironic, but they appear to have learnt from us.'

'But we still have the lead.'

She held his gaze. 'That's debatable'

'What do you mean?'

'I've just had word. Tonight's Reverence has been cancelled.'

Ellisha sat up straight. 'They can't do that.'

'They've made excuses, claiming that MacCaa's men attacked a peaceful protest. But the fact of the matter is, the authorities have caved before the God of Men.'

Ellisha jumped to her feet and began to pace up and down angrily, while Peter, afraid there would be a scene, attempted to calm her. He spoke soothingly of "different approaches" and "tactical withdrawals" until her pacing slowed and she threw him a sulky, slightly mollified glace. Hope flickered inside him, and he started to say something about it being the "smart move" when the door banged open and Mac-Caa barrelled into the room.

There was madness on his face, a wild elemental fury that made Peter think he was under attack. He took an involuntary step back, but MacCaa ignored him, bearing down on Ellisha with his mountainous strength. He took her shoulders and dragged her to her feet, all the time scanning her as though she might have been victim to some invisible, unassailable force. 'Never—never—' He was trembling. And if Ellisha was the good things of the earth, here was the wind that shaped her. 'Tae dae that—'

Peter jerked forward. *If he hurts her.* 'Ellie, stay back!' But Ellisha looked up at MacCaa quite calmly, her head very slightly tilted to one side. 'Oh Duncan.' And MacCaa responded to those two simple words like a melting glacier, rivulets and fissures appearing all over his granite face as tenderness split him open. A tear rolled down his cheek. It was grotesque. It was funny. It was none of those things. It made the words dry up on Peter's tongue, and it was Ellisha who spoke next. 'It won't happen ever again.' She reached up to wipe away the tear. 'I promise.'

'They don't want us here,' MacCaa said. 'We need tae move on.'

'No.' Ellisha's eyes were very bright. 'We stay.' She turned to Perdita. 'And the venue goes ahead tonight as agreed.'

Something flickered in Perdita's throat. 'That's impossible.'

'Nothing is impossible in the age of Soul.'

'The organizers have made up their minds.'

'Unmake them.'

'I'm afraid you don't understand. The situation isn't straightforward. Something has changed.'

'What? What has changed?'

Perdita sighed, pulling out a rattan-backed salon-chair, and taking a seat. 'As we all know, Ignis Dei has been soaking up misfits and drop-outs since the beginning.' She raised her eyebrows until there were general nods of agreement before she continued. 'It's not an uncommon phenomenon for an emerging philosophy. But the data shows that we're now attracting apostates. Grassroots believers are beginning to shift allegiance.'

Ellisha spread her hands in a *so-what* gesture, but Peter took up the thread. 'Changing faith is a big leap, and generally people do it within a context they understand—different sects or at least within branches of the Abrahamic traditions.'

'Quite,' Perdita agreed. 'But we've received reports indicating that churches and temples are beginning to lose their congregations.'

A choppy sea of worry lines appeared on Ellisha's brow. 'Are you saying we've gone too far?'

Perdita seemed surprised. 'On the contrary. The protests here in Venice are meant to look spontaneous, but there's evidence that the thought behind them came from more official sources.'

Peter wasn't sure he was hearing correctly. 'Surely you're not suggesting an ecclesiastical connection?'

'We can't prove it, of course. But it appears that the big players are becoming a little bit afraid of us.' She smiled reassuringly at Ellisha. 'Mr Avery is very curious to see where things are going. He certainly doesn't want to stop.'

Ellisha stood up. 'Good. Then we need to put the Reverence on tonight.'

Perdita's smile froze. 'I'm afraid that's a battle we can't win. The authorities have lost their nerve. Somewhat unsporting, I agree, but there you have it.' She paused to brush away a speck of dust from her cuff as she uncrossed her legs and stood up. 'No time to be lost. We need to fall back before the press gets wind. An announcement that you've taken ill would be best in the circumstances, I think. Constance can handle it.'

'No. Too negative,' Peter said, his ad-man's instincts tingling. 'We need to spin this. Better to suggest something unsaid, mysterious.' Snapping his fingers together to summon inspiration. 'A hint maybe that the Prophetess is experiencing some deeper revelation.'

'That's not bad.' Perdita looked up as Constance Tao came through the door.

'You wanted confirmation that the cancellation has been announced through all channels?' she said.

'I did, yes.' She ignored the furious look on Ellisha's face, and it was left to Mariam to whisper soothingly, 'This isn't your fault.' She was silenced by an *et tu* look by her Prophetess.

'Well, that's settled,' Perdita said, turning to the door. 'I'll make the arrangements.'

'No!'

Perdita froze. Ellisha hadn't moved from the spot yet something had changed. There was a new authority in her voice, and only once she was certain of their attention, did she sit slowly back down and addressed the room. 'Today a blind man recognised me. The Void was all around him. He was in darkness. Yet he believed me when I said I would help him find his path.'

No-one answered. The silence was filled with small, unconscious motions and sounds, chewed lips, a foot tapping nervously, Perdita's calculating eyes. Only MacCaa stood like stone. Ellisha looked from Perdita to MacCaa and back again. 'He believed in me,' she said. 'He believed in Soul. Why don't any of you?'

That afternoon Peter discovered that the Prophetess had a flair for practical politics. She informed Constance that she expected her to gather a team of digital strategists and to rendezvous with her within the hour. Constance's mouth dropped open and she turned to Perdita for guidance, but Ellisha's voice cut between them. 'No. Don't look at her. I am your Prophetess. Look at me!'

Constance looked and there was almost a visible tipping of scales as the balance of power shifted. Perdita's mouth was a thin line, and Peter glimpsed something he hadn't seen before. If Perdita and Constance were cool, stardust women, Ellisha was an earthy goddess of the earth. She stood with her feet firmly planted on the ground and when she stamped she expected the ground to tremble.

'I want every bit of information we can find on the authorities who closed us down. Affairs, false accounting, anything we can use. It can be done? Yes? Yes?'

Constance glanced up. 'It won't be easy.' She began to look around at Perdita then checked herself.

'But you've done this before.'

'Yes. But you have to know what you're getting into. There can be… ramifications that might not be within our control. Are you certain—' She broke off because Ellisha's face told her she was certain.

As soon as the team was assembled Ellisha wanted to know how many Sparks were in the local population.

Constance brought up the figures. 'Between three thousand and four thousand.'

'And the local population is what? A million? A million-and-a-half?'

'Over two-and-a-half-million.'

Shaking her head, she continued pacing the room. 'Not enough.'

'How many of the Sparks, who came for the event, are still here?' Constance looked to one of the strategists. He was young and skinny, popping eyes, a scrawny neck and a gangling disproportionate head which he was constantly bobbing up and down. Everyone called him Chick. When Constance asked, he swallowed his Adam's apple then popped it back out. 'Hard to tell. We have the ticket numbers and we can correlate them to plane or train journeys. But a lot of people were turned around at the station and the airport by the authorities, and others didn't attempt the trip in the first place.'

'Cross reference it with Twitter and Instagram feeds,' Ellisha said. 'I want to know.'

What is she looking for? Peter felt Perdita's puzzled glance and shook his head slightly. *I don't know.* He stepped into Ellisha's path. 'Can we help?'

Her step faltered, and she looked up at him in surprise almost as though she had forgotten he was there. 'Thank you. No. I don't need it.' She was about to resume pacing, when he asked, 'Who are you looking for?'

That made her smile. 'Fragments. All those shards of Soul who are here for me, drawn here by me.' She gave him an almost dreamy look. 'It's funny. We've been growing more and more powerful and yet I didn't really understand. Not until today. It took a blind man to make me see who I am.'

Chick's voice interrupted. 'Trends suggest that the number of Sparks still in Venice is close to six thousand.'

Ellisha's eyes lit up. 'Three per cent. It's enough.'

'Ellie,' he whispered under his breath. 'What are you up to?'

She looked at him calmly. 'Don't you remember Babs saying the goddess has a dark side?'

❌

They lay down. Wherever they were—in shops, at the docks, in a vapouretto—Sparks received word from their Prophetess and they lay down. At first there was bemusement, then there was anger. The carabinieri arrived to move them on, and without protest, the Sparks would get up and a few minutes later would lie down again in a new area. And, while this was dealt with, Sparks from another location would appear and lie down in the original spot.

The authorities attempted to suppress the story, and when that didn't work, they sent out press releases proclaiming Ignis Dei to be a terrorist organization and the Sparks extremists. The words sent a cold knife of fear through Peter's heart, and even knowing that Spark lawyers were already shouting libel, he turned to Ellisha. 'Maybe we're going too far.'

She stared straight ahead, straight-backed, her hands on the armrests of her chair. 'No.'

'But El—'

She looked at him coolly. 'You're forgetting. We control the flow of information.'

Within minutes every airway, every channel, every media site was filled with images of the Sparks receiving rough treatment at the hands of the authorities. A carabinieri dragging a female Spark by the hair. In another, a group of shopkeepers threw several Sparks into the Grand Canal. One clearly couldn't swim, and there was panic as his head disappeared under the surface a second time. Constance showed him what they were broadcasting.

'And this is real?'

'Some of it. We can do a lot with digital manipulation. In some cases it's just careful editing.'

'But it's turning opinion?'

'Oh yes. There are Sparks all over Italy lying down in solidarity, while others are levying accusations at the government that they are trying to suppress freedom of belief. We're getting reports that government mailboxes are already jammed because of the high volume of traffic.'

It was astonishing. Peter looked around the room at the bent heads of the Sparks answering telephones and tapping furiously on keyboards. So many young men and women following the path to Soul, following the words he had written. He felt he should say something inspiring, but just as he opened his mouth, Chick punched the air. 'They've caved. We're on tonight.'

The room suddenly filled with hugs and high-fives. Peter found himself in a manly, awkward embrace with Chick, and tried to share a wry look with Ellisha over his shoulder. She was sitting quite erect in her chair, but her face was absolutely still and quite drained of emotion.

Splendour like beauty fades, becomes characterless when presented with uniform monotony. And there had been so many appearances as they criss-crossed the great cities of the world that memories of them became fluid, formless, like precious jewels liquescing in the fiery heart of a kiln. Yet this night, out of so many, stood out.

There was triumph in the air. Peter looked down on the mosaic of faces covering the sweeping expanse of San Marco's Piazza, and felt how they leaned forwards in their seats, a new fierceness within them at having brought this to pass. Many of them had brought glowsticks or held up tiny wavering flames from lighters so that, as the sky darkened, he understood they were holding out the fragments of their Souls towards Ellisha and the divine imminence she represented.

At his side, Ellisha wore a glittering dress that cradled her breasts like twin moons, but sheered away almost to the split of her buttocks so that her burning scar was revealed when she turned her back to the audience, sending them into thunderous reaction, their feet drumming in unison until Venice shook all the way down to her indirect foundations.

The old man they had rescued was led on to the stage, his blind eyes searching for Ellisha. Watching from the wings, Mariam gasped and clutched Peter's hand.

'Do you know who that is?

Peter looked again. 'No.'

'Only Claudio Donizetti. He's famous. I mean really famous. First violin with the Santa Cecilia. National treasure, that kind of thing. I saw him play at the Barbican.'

Peter felt himself staring until Mariam cried, 'What?'

'You're just so… so—'

'Black?'

The back of his throat burned with embarrassment. 'Young. I meant young… and fashionable.'

She lifted an eyebrow. 'You thought I listened to Beyoncé.'

'No.'

'No?'

He looked at her from the corner of his eye. 'Maybe a little.'

Mariam looked out towards Donizetti, who was opening a violin case. 'Nailed it.'

He was spared further embarrassment by Ellisha's amplified voice announcing to the piazza that Donizetti intended to play for her. And he did. Gone was the shuffling, confused old man. When he played his music seemed a kind of narrative, as though musical notes could be used to describe a person. And somehow a form of Ellisha, made entirely of music, suddenly hovered with them on the stage and held the audience rapt.

How is he doing it? Peter wondered. *The skill of an accomplished musician or the magic absorbed by an instrument hundreds of years old?* It made no difference. When he looked towards Ellisha, he saw that she was glowing, not just from happiness, but because she belonged out there with every fragment of Soul, and also beyond them—as though she was created in the very moment of her own act of creation.

Later, when they lay behind the curtains for the culminating symbolism of the *hieros gamos*, he whispered, 'So, today you saved Venice. Who do you intend to save next?'

She opened her eyes and peered at him, pupils magnified and slightly blurred by the dimness. He expected her to laugh or begin to lecture him. Instead, she answered with a single word.

'Africa.'

CHAPTER 24

A BILLION STARS. SUNRISE SMOULDERING through the darkness. Thin gold-leaf light pressing against the sky. Blue distances of the Virunga mountains. Dust, diesel, a whiff of wild sage, cooking smells, fried okra and earth-scented palm oil, and fat fragrant drops of rain, sizzling where they fell upon hot tin roofs. This was their first trip to the dark continent and it made Peter's bones tingle.

He stood at Ellisha's side, pale northern eyes screwed up against the attack of light and the blinding absurdity of their position. Madness. Madness to come. And yet he felt the throb of a new kind of challenge. *We could make a difference here. We could take Ignis Dei beyond anything we've ever achieved.* He turned to Ellisha, suddenly anxious that she did not share his vision; she hadn't spoken since they landed. Yet there it was: Ellisha's smile, shining like a thin vein of gold. 'Isn't it amazing? It makes me want to burst.'

It was good to see her old open smile. He didn't often catch it now beneath the Prophetess' beneficent expression, and he missed it more than he liked to admit. But here, in Africa, she smiled. And something in that smile reminded him of that first meeting on the Wayfair steps, rain catching in the looping spirals of her hair. She had seemed so mysterious there against the grey, with her wild cherry skin and moss-agate eyes. As though she had stepped out of another world. Yet, here in Africa, she still looked out of place. Too pale to pass for a local, her sub-Saharan heritage blended with the cool tones of higher latitudes. *And what did I think,* Peter thought ruefully. *That I was returning her to her people? That she would look at home here?*

Guilt made him toy with telling her, so that he might suffer the mocking flagellation of her tongue. But he was distracted by the idea that Ellisha would look out of place wherever they went in the world.

It was part of her allure, that mongrel cast of her features that seemed to contain a little bit of everything yet belonged to no-one. She caught him looking, and in that way she had of leaping ahead of his thoughts, whispered, 'You won't find me here, Peter. I was born between stars.'

'Narcissist.'

'Big old racist.'

They visited a refugee camp, a squalid and badly-run place with no running water and little in the way of medical supplies. Listless adults with the light gone out of their eyes sat on the ground, and ragged, malnourished children crowded around them.

From the corner of his eye, he saw Ellisha press her fingertips to her mouth, and knew that her heart was crushed by what she was seeing, and that each new tragedy struck her afresh, and he loved her and feared for her. While he was thinking this, a boy of about twelve, with no hands, pushed his way to the front and held out the stumps of his arms towards her. 'Rebels,' the translator explained. 'They cut off the hands so that he cannot grow up to be a soldier.'

The boy said something and the translator nodded and turned to Ellisha. 'He says he knows you already, that you have visited him before.'

Ellisha laughed. 'I get that a lot.'

The boy grinned and waved his arms, so thin they moved like wands that cast spells in the air. Enchanted, Ellisha moved forward and put her arm around his shoulders. 'Show me,' was all she said. Suddenly she was no longer a stranger from outside but one of them, and soon she was sitting cross-legged in the dust telling stories with grand illustrative hand gestures and trying to learn their songs.

She caught Peter's eye and beckoned him over. He joined her awkwardly, strangely shy, squatting on the dusty ground, painfully aware of the curious stares of the children. *What do they see? A crouching crow of a man, dressed in black, his hair slick with sweat. Unable to reach them because we don't share a language. Words. Always words with me. Without them I am powerless.*

And he saw, with sudden clarity, that this was what set Ellisha apart: her ability to reach under language to older, subliminal forms of communication, a drawing down of universal truths that made people feel that somehow they already knew her.

A little girl had crawled into her lap and was tugging at her plaits. 'I think we're singing about someone called *Nzambi*,' Ellisha was saying to the translator. 'Who is that?'

The translator nodded solemnly. 'It is a very old song belonging to the Bakongo people. *Nzambi* is the great mother, the wife of God. She is Mother Earth. Sometimes the song is about the child she suckles on her lap, which is all mankind.'

'But not this song? It's too wild.'

The translator was impressed. 'Yes. You are right. This song is of *Nzambi* with a sword in her hand, punishing the wrong-doers of the world.'

On their last evening back in Goma, they sat on the balcony dining room of their hotel, with its view of the lake Kivu under a sky the colour of raw sienna, and were served brimming dishes of rice and chicken nestling in green casava-leaf sauce. Peter tucked in with relish, but Ellisha sat swirling her glass, watching the wine tears falling from the rim.

'You don't like it?' He pointed at her untouched plate with his fork. 'We can order something else.'

'No.' She shook her head. 'It isn't that.' An embarrassed wriggle of her shoulders. 'Seeing people living like that. I don't know. I guess it takes my appetite away.'

He was afraid of the faraway look in her eye. 'Headache?'

She blinked. 'What? No. I thought maybe earlier. But Mariam made me some tea.'

He nudged her plate towards her. 'You have to eat.'

'I'm not hungry. I'm never hungry now. Isn't that what you want? The ethereal Prophetess, all filled with Soul. More light than substance.'

Caught out, he swallowed. 'How did you know?'

'I'm the Prophetess.'

'No, seriously.'

'I'm your wife. Of course I know.'

'You have to eat something. For generations Scottish mothers have been telling their offspring not to waste the food on their plates because children were starving in other countries.'

'Seriously?'

'I believe so.'

The laughter went out of her face, but she lifted her fork and took a small mouthful of chicken. Still chewing she added thoughtfully, 'Everyone talks about the extraordinary things we do.'

'They should.'

She looked briefly away then swung round to face him. 'I don't think our vision is big enough.'

He laughed. 'You don't think being the fastest growing phenomenon of the century is big enough?'

'No.'

Something in her voice made him place the rice bowl down and reach for her hand. 'What are you saying?'

'Only that you were right. You were right all along.' She sat back in her seat and her hand slid away. 'With Ignis Dei we can do the extraordinary. Except we don't. Okay, we give water to the thirsty and we feed the hungry. But we're only reacting to pain, as if the creation of the Soul Mystica was just a case of putting a sticking plaster over the Void. Don't you see, we're not really changing anything.'

'Give a man a fish and he will eat today,' he began. But she finished for him.

'Give a man freedom and he might discover he hates fish.'

He laughed. 'How do you propose to do that?'

'Make them eat fish?'

'Give them freedom?'

The question, intended teasingly, hit its mark. Ellisha's face darkened and her eyes slid towards the violet shadows spreading across the lake. 'I'm going to push back the deserts; I'm going to build communities. All over the world. I'm going to free people.'

He was taken aback by this sudden swing of the pendulum. 'I think you might find that the governments have something to say about social planning.'

'Oh, that won't be a problem,' she said airily. 'There are Sparks working on the inside in more than twenty-eight countries, and the number keeps going up.'

Peter choked on a mouthful of rice. He reached for a glass of water and wiped the tears from his eyes with the back of his hand. 'Already? Sparks within the governments?'

'Yes, we have people on the inside.' She smiled with such patience that he felt a rush of confusion. 'It's funny, everyone thinks I'm the innocent, but you still don't get it.'

In surprise he searched her face, but there was no twinkle of amusement, only a deadly seriousness that drained the light from her skin. *Looking at me so strangely. Pupils fixed. As though she isn't quite here. As though she's dreaming. As though she's looking beyond me.*

'We've been such children, Peter. We've been acting as though Ignis Dei were some wonderful toy we were given permission to play with. Phil is daddy and we have to be careful mommy doesn't tell him we've been naughty or careless.'

He smiled. 'I'm not sure Perdita quite suits the nurturing role.'

'Oh, but she does. She tells us how to dress, how to behave, what we can and can't say. You think I don't know how they grill you after every event?'

He stared. 'I didn't think— I mean, how?'

She shrugged then said, as if it were the most natural thing in the world, 'I have my spies.'

'Your spies!'

Her fork stirred listlessly in the cassava leaves. 'It's funny. All along Perdita and Phil have been at the helm.' Seeing his change of expression, she waved the fork at him, like *Nzambi* with her sword of justice. 'Oh, not that they haven't done a great job. Phil wants a slice of immortality and Ignis Dei is his legacy. I get it. But I didn't really see. Not really. Maybe because they didn't want me to see. And I didn't. Not until Venice, not until a blind man looked up and recognised me.'

'Didn't see? Didn't see what?' He was pretending to be amused. She didn't answer at first, turning her gaze out over the healing waters of the lake then she said softly,

'It isn't their power; it's mine.'

They had built before. A digital universe filled with virtual cathedrals and the thrum of gathering Soul. And they had built in stone and wood and brick, the soulariums that sprang up like sacred trees across every continent. But it was different to build a city.

'It must be a city like no other,' Ellisha had said. 'It must be able to rise from the desert or cling to a mountainside or hide in the heart of a forest. And it must belong to the people. To the Sparks. To all the fragments who will come because soul seeks Soul.' The Sparks in the room—architects and engineers, artists and electricians—burst into applause, while Peter looked at Ellisha with a kind of awe, and wondered how you could know someone and not know them at all. From the corner of his eye he saw Perdita lift her phone and leave the room. He looked after her, wondering how she would relay this move to Avery. *A step too far. Too audacious. Out of control?*

But his fears proved unfounded. The sheer magnitude of the technology Avery laid at their feet was overwhelming, and suddenly they talked of nothing else, sitting up long into the nights going over plans for transforming refugee camps, poring over the propositions, arguing over innovations and inventions.

Peter discovered a talent for bringing together the improbable and using it to solve the impossible: Braithwaite mirror technology; water-divining wind turbines; fog-catchers; graphene filters? It was exhilarating and frustrating. For every tiny step of progress, a new barrier was thrown in his way. Permits were demanded where no permits had previously existed. Deliveries of raw materials came up short or proved substandard. Contractors proved less reliable than the spring rains.

Ellisha took his reports with immense patience until the government took it into its head to forget the generosity of the bribes and to ban future Ignis Dei workers from entering the country. Then she called for every resident Spark to lay down their tools and to march on the capital. And they obeyed, coming in their thousands and tens of thousands. They surrounded the parliament buildings and stood there.

Standing next to her watching the news feeds, Peter said, 'The government—they won't take this lying down.'

'I don't intend them to.'

He glanced sidelong at her. 'This isn't Venice. There might be casualties.'

'No.' Not *I don't think so* or *I hope not.* Just, *No.*

'Ellie,' he hissed, but she only stood there, ignoring him, and smiling slightly to herself.

And in the end she was right. The troops came, but they stood, awed by the exquisite expectancy of the crowd who held out their arms to them and called them brothers. And when the commanders raged at them to fire, they did not move until a tall thin boy with burning eyes, who stood at the front, stiffened as though something had passed through him. He glanced over his shoulder at the screaming commander then he stepped forward and laid his rifle on the ground.

A reporter commentating on the scene caught the mood, and with that flair for metaphor, described it as the first drop of rain hitting the dusty ground. And the image was sound, because a moment later came the patter of dozens of other rifles laid on the earth. Then the soldiers left the raging commanders to stand with the people, fragments drawn to the whole, joined by the *Soul Mystica* and a sense of gathering imminence. And, with the whole world watching, the government backed down and Ellisha had her way.

Africa was still Africa when they returned, but everything was changed. They had travelled lightly before, only MacCaa and a handful of security men when they visited the camp on their first trip. But this time they entered at the head of a retinue of aid-workers, government officials and bodyguards, like the queen and high priest of some ancient Kushite kingdom, though a kingdom that replaced chariots and noble steeds with rattling four by fours mottled with dirt and rust.

Glancing over at Ellisha, Peter saw that she was resting her head on the smeary surface of the window, her eyes glassy and blank.

'Headache?'

She nodded slightly.

'We can stop.'

'No. I can control them now.'

He stared. 'What do you mean?' But she would not be drawn, and it felt wrong to push her on their day of triumph, so they rode on in companionable silence, feeling that they were not only on the side of, but were creators of, angels.

The sound of the engine cutting off made Peter start, suddenly aware that he had been half dozing. He looked about for the squat ramshackle buildings and grey-faced people with all the light gone out of them. But his dream had been made flesh. Pristine rows of houses gave way to colourful shopfronts. A broad avenue thronged with stalls and cafes, where relaxed-looking people browsed or sat sipping coffee beneath umbrellas. Try as he might, he could find no traces of the camp.

It's everything I asked for, Peter thought, as he stepped out of the jeep. *Everything I dreamed of. And more. Why does it feel like a dream? All those plans and setbacks and conundrums, just moving pieces on a board. Just a huge intellectual game. Have we forgotten*? he wondered, throwing a puzzled glance in Ellisha's direction. MacCaa was helping her down. *The idea that these were real people with real lives ... I didn't really believe.*

Ellisha appeared at his side and he spread his arms. 'Welcome to Mzazi.'

To her raised brows, he replied, 'It's Kingwana for "mother". They've named it after you.'

And she was so proud and pleased, his heart ached for her. 'Do you believe I'm the mouth of the goddess now?'

He followed, wide-eyed and laughing. 'Ah, you say that. But perhaps you are the devil. Scottish literature is peppered with righteous men who have fallen foul of fair strangers.'

A poke in his ribs. 'That's your national fear of success talking.'

A choir of singing children had come out to greet them, and several officials, who gave lengthy and incomprehensible speeches, which they listened to in the pulsing heat. Peter found it almost unbearable, pockets of sweat gathering under his arms and in his crotch, the light evenness of his complexion turning red and blotchy despite the shade of an umbrella. At his side, Ellisha stood erect in her role of Wise Matriarch, listening without comment to the excited outpourings around her then submitting to the usual barrage of selfie-requests until it was time to be taken on the tour of the shining city.

Before they left, a young man approached carrying a tray of damp cloths to allow them to refresh themselves. 'Take one, please. You will feel better.' He turned to Peter. 'Maybe take two.'

One of the guides, a shy young man who had been introduced as Salehe, was tasked with explaining everything, which he did in a low, mellow voice which was pleasant to listen to. 'You see, Reverend Kelso, we did not want to use your plans simply to rebuild a better refugee camp. After all, it is no longer the case that a refugee will only be in a camp for a few months before moving on. They may be here for years, sometimes generations.'

'This is exactly what Reverend Kelso and I discussed,' Ellisha added softly. 'The idea of turning a camp on its head.'

'And it is working,' Salehe agreed. 'When the indigenous population saw the camp people with better lives and more dignity, they wanted the same things for themselves. What the Prophetess is doing here changes everything. I did not understand at first.' He exchanged a shy glance with Ellisha then brushed away a small buzzing insect that flew near his ear.

'When Reverend Kelso first approached, I said we do not want any of the broken models applied by previous governments and NGOs. No stop-gap remedy. But the Prophetess promised a solution that creates something that is more than its own answer.'

'And that's when we came up with the idea of wandering cities,' Peter said. Salehe nodded eagerly. 'In so many places, climatic and political conditions force people to be nomadic.' He made a sweeping gesture. 'But everything here is modular. It can be torn down and reconstructed at a different location in a matter of days.'

'Incredible,' Ellisha said. She sounded a little dazed. 'The buildings, they look so... fixed.' She pointed to one of the more impressive structures, several storeys high and supporting two slender towers. From one of the pinnacled crests he could see a flag bearing the burning tree emblem. 'Just incredible.' Peter wanted to laugh out loud and punch the sky. Salehe was pleased with his reaction.

'We do not see the place in isolation, but as part of the larger community, a building block in the creation of the country's identity.'

'And, of course,' Peter put in quickly, 'this is just the first city. There are dozens of Ignis Dei-funded cities springing up. Not just here, but in many countries.' He grinned broadly. 'We are changing the face of the world.'

'It's divine insight,' Ellisha agreed. 'So many fragments drawing creation out of the universe, bringing the godhead closer.' Impulsively, she reached out and took Peter's hand. The intimacy of the gesture, almost never seen now in public, burned against his palm. 'Who knows? Maybe the cities of the future will all be like this, able to relocate at the drop of a hat when famine or war strikes. This is our doing. People are alive because of us.'

They had been still long enough for a crowd to gather, kept at a respectful distance by MacCaa and his men. They listened reverently as she spoke, explaining how many of the micro-cities were really not much larger than villages, and that Mzazi was the finest example of their work, and how empowering it would be if, when refugees turned up, they held out their hands, not in desperation but with something to offer. And though Peter heard everything she had to say, he was thinking more of the feel of her hand, and how she still had the power to move him with no more than her touch.

But eventually she stopped in front of the soularium. 'Shall we?'

He nodded. 'But let it just be we two.'

The request took her by surprise. She glanced in MacCaa's direction and shrugged. 'Okay. If you want.'

MacCaa didn't like it. His yellow eyes looked over Ellisha's head at the building then found Peter. 'Ah'll be within earshot,' he said, and it was unclear whether he meant this as reassurance or threat.

Outside the sun had glared down, hard and uncompromising, but the light within the Ignis Dei building had an unexpected warmth, spread from dozens of little spotlights, strategically placed. Ellisha saw him looking and whispered, 'Let there be light.' She kept her voice low, as a sermon of sorts was underway.

At the front of the hall, upon a low stage, stood a small woman with skin the colour of volcanic sand and a frizz of grey curls. She was conducting the sermon in American English, her voice surprisingly powerful for her diminutive size. 'And in days of old,' she was saying, 'we knew we didn't have an immortal soul. We were wise in our lack of wisdom. We were profound in our ignorance. We knew that a soul is not your God-given right. You gotta earn that soul. You gotta reach out into the world and reach down into yourself. You gotta take the power of Soul and drag it into the universe so you can earn your place in immortality. You gotta stop believing the Lie and start believing the Truth. 'Cos that's the only thing gonna save you. That's the only thing gonna draw you whole and conscious into the mind of God when She is ready to receive you.'

She jabbed a finger at her audience. 'What did you believe?'

'We believed the Lie.'

'What does the Lie say?'

'We have an immortal soul.' It was clear that the audience was responding in rote fashion, the English sitting awkwardly on many tongues.

'Who taught you the Lie?'

'Men taught us the lie.'

'Who brought us the truth?'

'Ellisha brought the truth.'

Barely able to tear his eyes away, Peter whispered, 'Who is that?'

'Her name is Violet Bello. She used to be a Christian evangelical preacher, but she joined us when we were setting up the Los Angeles soularium last year. Brought almost a hundred thousand followers with her.'

'She looks so frail.'

'Razor wire looks delicate at a distance. Don't be fooled.' Something in Peter's face made her ask, 'What is it?'

He hesitated. How to put it? That the forgotten Presbyterian in him recoiled a little at the expressive vitality of the tiny woman on the stage. Ellisha was still looking at him, and he mumbled something about surprise at the manifold ways Ignis Dei expressed itself.

Violet's deep voice boomed out. 'Who is our truth?'

'Ell-ish-ah'

'Who lights the way?'

'Ell-ish-ah.'

'Who heals our souls?'

'Ell-ish-ah! Ell-ish-ah! Ell-ish-ah!'

As these last words were spoken the lights grew in intensity, and they found themselves, no longer in the shadows of the doorway, but revealed to dozens of pairs of curious eyes. Violet did not miss a beat. 'Behold, as I promised you, Ellisha walks amongst us this day, the Prophetess of the Unmade God.'

The audience parted and Ellisha walked, straight-backed, amongst them, her honey-coloured dress fanning against the contours of her body. At once the audience closed around her, men and women eagerly reaching out. She disappeared from view, and, afraid, Peter began pushing forward to reach her. He glanced back, wondering whether to call MacCaa.

But his fears proved unfounded. For all their longing, the men and women on both sides stopped short of physical touch. At the last moment they pulled back, hesitant, retracted fingers, afraid that contact with her mystery might burn until, with simple grace, Ellisha joined Violet on the stage. Peter followed some moments later with considerably less elegance.

'Can this be?' Violet boomed. 'That we have immortality amongst us. That here is a human vessel blessed with that precious light. Can you feel how the darkness retreats? How suffering retreats. How pain retreats. This is what it means to hold a piece of God within you. This is what it means to be a living flame!'

The crowd swayed with her words, many of them, Peter suspected, with too little English to understand their meaning, but drawn by the power they sensed behind them. Violet, he suddenly saw, shared possession of that same power as Ellisha, the ability to move under the currents of language. But Violet had more showmanship.

The men and women below the stage might stare agog at Ellisha, but they were listening to Violet. So intently, he began to worry she would overshadow Ellisha's arrival. Indeed, Ellisha did seem to fade next to Violet's exuberance. She was very still, almost ghostly at the back of the dais, a conjured wraith. Anxiously he cut his eyes towards her, but she made no acknowledgement.

Violet's voice had developed an almost musical tremor. 'Ellisha is power. She came here to show us power. And not just to show us. She came to give us power. She is a miracle maker. You hear what I'm saying? A maker of miracles. And not like in the book of Lies. She doesn't walk on water. She doesn't take the water and make it into wine. Her miracles are real! She shows that when we Love, when we partake in the miracle of Love, we make things happen. Us! We have the power of immortality within US!'

She pointed at the audience. 'Do you want to see that power?'

Fierce nods. Violet was not satisfied.

'Do you want to see a miracle? Right here, right now, on earth.'

Cries in the affirmative. Stamping of feet.

'I can't hear you.'

Yells, cheers. Violet cupped her ear. 'I still can't hear you!'

A rapturous response made Peter yearn to clap his hands over his ears. But, at last, Violet seemed satisfied. Waving a hand towards a curtained area, she commanded, 'You heard them. Now, come on down.'

The curtain stirred and a young man, still gangling between youth and manhood, appeared. He froze, blinking in the sudden spotlight of attention, but at Violet's urgings he walked towards them, holding out his hands. No, not *his* hands. Peter looked again. They were artificial, but of startlingly high quality; he had never seen anything quite like them. As if reading his thoughts, the young man touched his thumb to forefinger several times.

'Diallo Bankole,' Violet announced. 'He came to you, two years ago. He had been cruelly mutilated.'

'I remember,' Ellisha said. She spoke softly, making no attempt to compete with Violet's voice.

'But the miracle of Ignis Dei gave him hands.' Violet raised her arms, detonating another thunderclap of applause.

Ellisha spoke to Diallo. 'I sang to you.' She stepped forward and there were tears in her eyes. And suddenly Diallo's eyes were moist too. 'Soul seeks Soul,' he said gravely, and entwined his fingers in a gesture of oneness.

Ellisha reached out and took hold of his hands, gasping when he gripped hers. Diallo's grin took up most of his face. 'I worked hard. Every day I want to know more about the Spark of God.'

A hush had descended. No more shouts or claps. Heads were craning forwards. The whole room was poised. He glanced at Violet and saw that she was about to interrupt. But Ellisha gave a startled cry. And jerking around, he was just in time to see her looking deep into Diallo's eyes.

On an urgent outbreath, he whispered, 'Ellie, what is it?'

'I see it,' she said, still looking at Diallo, and this time her voice carried for all to hear. 'I see your soul.'

They carried them aloft through the streets. And there were fireworks. Where they had come from heaven only knew. But the first confirmed emergence of the Soul Mystica had set off a rapturous response that shot stars into the skies.

After some time the procession returned to the square, where long tables had been set out, and Peter found himself at the top table, sitting between Mariam and Violet Belo. A choir of children were singing a song whose recurrent refrain was *God is coming! God is coming!*

'You seem puzzled, Reverend.'

He turned to Violet, shaking his head slightly. 'I hadn't come across this song before.'

She nodded understandingly. 'There are many ways for soul to understand Soul.'

'Of course.' He reached for a dish of figs on the table. 'But you must find all this strange. In respect of your background, I mean.'

'What background might that be?' Violet looked at him assessingly, and for a moment he had an uncanny sense of recognition. As though he were back in Edinburgh and Babs' penetrating eyes were scouring his face. Strange, the impact that one short meeting had. Violet was still looking at him, and he added hastily, 'From an evangelical calling if I understand correctly.'

Violet nodded slowly. 'You do.'

'And what, may I ask, brought you to Ignis Dei?'

Violet was cutting a piece of fish on her plate. She speared it with her fork before answering. 'The same as you.'

'I'm not sure—that is, I don't—'

'I lost my faith in man, and found it in a woman.'

There was something in the way she said it, some undertone of reproach that made him defensive. 'I don't apologise for it,' he said coldly. 'Ellisha is a remarkable woman.'

This time Violet's laugh was open. 'That she is,' she agreed. 'And a clever one too. Make no mistake about that.' She looked along the table to where Ellisha was listening attentively to her new Soulmate, and her eyes narrowed. 'Cleverness like that is a rare gem. Comes along once in a century, maybe less.'

And she sounded so grave that Peter felt compelled to tease her. 'You almost sound afraid.'

But Violet's eyes stayed on Ellisha's averted head. 'I am,' she said softly.

CHAPTER 25

'MY NAME IS VALENTINA RIVERA. I am sixteen years old. When I was fourteen, I shot three of my friends.'

It was a horrible, heart-wrenching story, and it was so far from being the first time Peter had heard horror spurting from the innocent mouth of a child that its venom should have been powerless to sting. Yet, he felt sickened as she continued.

'I did not want to kill them. But I had been with the rebels ten months and I knew the punishment for desertion. If I had refused, they would have killed me. My friend Elena was crying. She was begging me not to.' A hesitation. Two ideologies clashing behind her blank brown eyes then a slight shake of her head. 'But also, I thought it was right. I thought, if they had been disloyal then they should die for it. I had to.' A quick angry glance in Peter's direction. 'An order is an order. They taught us that.'

The room had no air conditioning, and the heat wrapped around Peter's head unpleasantly, as though damp sheets were being pressed over his mouth and nose. He was forced to take out his handkerchief and dab at his forehead continuously and a dull thudding had begun behind his temples. *Bosquecillo Sagrado* was the newest of the wandering cities and not yet complete. He wished they had waited until the air conditioning had been installed.

He glanced at Ellisha, wondering if the humidity was bringing on a migraine, but she was cool and blank, an idol made in flesh while beside her Mariam was weeping a slow drizzle of tears which she made no attempt to wipe away.

Valentina had finished speaking and there was a smattering of polite applause. Before she left the platform, she fixed her gaze on Ellisha and raised her hand in the burning tree salute. The fierceness of the gesture—the rebel teachings still strong within her—would have been funny in less tragic circumstances. Peter dabbed at his forehead again. He could feel a pulse beating dull inside his skull, and his eyes felt gritty, yet blinking only seemed to make things worse.

A boy had mounted the platform. He was introducing himself, though Peter somehow failed to pick up his name. Great waves of darkness seemed to be blocking his thoughts, and the more he tried to concentrate, the further away things seemed to grow. He was aware of Mariam looking at him curiously, as though she had said something, and he had failed to reply or had said something inappropriate. He had no idea which it might be.

'Excuse me.' He lurched from his seat, almost knocking over an unoccupied chair on the end of the row, and headed for the door. The air was as flat and heavy outside as it had been inside the soularium, but he gulped muggy mouthfuls of it nonetheless. A few stumbling footsteps took him to the edge of the building, where he supported himself with a hand against the stuccoed surface of the wall.

At his feet the surface of the road had cracked, and weeds had already begun to colonize the spaces. He lifted his gaze painfully, and saw in the distance the sharp rise of the hills beyond the river: the vivid, almost reptilian green of the foliage curled around the land and exhaling a drowsy breath of steamy vapour. A paradise, a green world.

His head was spinning. *Everything so busy lately.*

This violent welling of unacknowledged feeling took him unawares, and he lurched instinctively towards the door, towards Ellisha. A small boy in dusty broken sandals was watching him. Embarrassed, he waved in a way he hoped was reassuring, and tried to ask his name. But a sudden sharp spasm in his abdomen made him double over and retch upon the dusty ground.

⚭

From that point on time fragmented, split. Memories became leering-ly large or unfocussed as water-colours running from a page. One of the Sparks' faces, close to his, saying something about meditating on Soul. Trying to listen, but weak as a kitten, sweating, the wall the only thing preventing his falling to the ground. Frowning, the Spark shook his head and said, '*La malaria.*'

Waking up in the Ignis Dei hospital, which was still undergoing completion about a mile from the soularium, he found himself lying in a clean, antiseptic-smelling room, protesting weakly that he did not want to be fussed over. The room was filled with Sparks from the sou-larium. And, for a moment he thought he spotted the silent boy in the broken sandals in their midst.

Ellisha arrived alongside a Spark whose aquiline nose and chis-elled cheekbones would not have looked wrong on the side of a Mayan temple, who turned out to be the doctor. He introduced himself as Santino Tepetzi, a recent convert, who had seen Ellisha on tour in Rio.

'How do you feel, Reverend Kelso?'

'Nauseous,' he admitted cautiously.

Dr Tepetzi wasn't fooled. 'Go on,' he said, tapping a pen against his clipboard.

'Weak. I have pains in my muscles. A bit of a temperature, I think.'

He tapped the pen. 'Hmmmm.'

'I have flu.'

'You have malaria. And I am afraid you have suffered a stroke.'

Stroke? No. For old men. Grandfather, withered right arm, never able to speak again. 'That—that's not possible.'

'Unfortunately, it is well within the parameters of possibility. Any bouts of diarrhoea before today?'

'I—' Why were there so many people around his bed? 'I did expe-rience a certain looseness during our trip to Benin.'

A glance at the clipboard. 'And what antimalarials are you on?

'I don't know. The tablets are called Alaren.'

Dr Tepetzi's dark brows rose. 'That's chloroquine. Didn't you know we're resistant here?'

He shook his head weakly. Ellisha was standing at the bottom of the bed. She turned to Dr Tepetzi. 'Someone mentioned a loss of shadows?'

Peter was following this debate with difficulty, his eyelids drooping and sleep not far off, but at the mention of shadows, his ears pricked up.

'Yes,' Dr Tepetzi was saying. '*Pérdida de la sombra*. Loss of a shadow.'

'It comes from a very old medicinal understanding,' Mariam chimed in. Peter blinked. Had she been there all along?

'That is correct.' Dr Tepetzi was agreeing. 'We mirror Ignis Dei's blend of ancient past and approaching future in all our techniques here. As you know, traditional understandings of healing are respected alongside modern scientific methods. And here in *Bosquecillo Sagrado* we remember the old ways that say that a man has four shadows, and all must work in harmony or the body becomes susceptible to disease.'

'Like the four humors of the ancient Greeks,' Ellisha said slowly.'

The doctor gave a nod of assent.

'A body which fights disease cannot be open to Soul,' Mariam added.

Peter had heard this somewhere before, the idea that the power to achieve the Soul Mystica was impeded by illness. He hadn't liked it, and now he tried to explain his point of view, but sleep was overcoming him. He heard Dr Tepetzi say, 'We'll get Reverend Kelso on a regime of Atovaquone and Proguanil. And I will recommend a decoction from native plants, Estrelle and Artemesia Annua to start, I think.' He tapped the pen against the clipboard again. 'Once we have the fever down, a distillation of Yaje to induce spiritual purification and connectedness with Soul. Then a regime to assess the damage from the stroke.' Remembering his patient, he explained, 'You were fortunate. It seems to have been mild. A warning to slow down. We will get you in a rehabilitation program as soon as you are a little fitter.'

'He will recover?' This from Ellisha. And the real fear in her voice was more remedy than any decoction of native flora. A pitying glance from Dr Tepetzi in Peter's direction did not connect with his eyes. 'He won't like it much. Forcing open the spiritual pathways will not be without a price. But this is the best way to undo the damage both to the body and to the cohesion of the Soul Mystica.'

Ellisha nodded gravely. 'There is no choice.'

'We'll add an anti-emetic into the mix,' Dr Tepetzi said kindly.

'But what of the Prophetess?' Mariam asked suddenly. The thought was clearly just occurring. 'Is she in danger?' He heard Dr Tepetzi's response. But there was something tinny and wrong about the way it played in his head. And perhaps this was the reason he did not query the strangeness of hearing him say, 'A body as ensouled as that of the Prophetess is immune from ailment.'

'I can come with you.'

'You can't.' Ellisha handed him the glass of water he had asked for with a mixture of tenderness and exasperation then stalked over to the window.

'Ellie, listen. I'm fine.' He swung his legs over the side of the bed with an effort then attempted to stand on them. They gave way at the ankles and he fell back on to the mattress.

Ellisha turned and regarded him without pity. 'We can't perform the *hieros gamos* with you starting in the bed.'

'You can't perform it without me.'

'I'll think of something.'

'Dr Tepetzi is talking about six months or more before I'm back to normal. You can't manage it all without me.'

'I'll be fine. Duncan will take care of me. And Perdita will take care of everything else. Just concentrate on getting better.'

He looked at her helplessly. 'Cold fish.'

'Weakling.'

Peter's recovery was longer and slower than he had first confidently expected. The chills and the fevers returned with a terrifying frequency, as if an ancient spirit enemy lay in constant wait to hinder his path. It was a demoralizing time. For a while he tried to keep on top of Ellisha's movements, scanning his laptop for news of her or her works: Ellisha sending fifty thousand Sparks to wrap their arms around the trees of a Soul forest endangered by loggers; a general strike in Ohio after the governor tried to outlaw soulariums; Ellisha thanking the world in a speech for making her the first woman to receive the Templeton prize for progress in religion. But Dr Tepetzi took his blood pressure, and after he had seen the results, announced that complete rest was required. The laptop was taken away.

His one solace was in the familiar presence of Mariam. He had been surprised to find that she had stayed behind. 'Ellisha asked me,' she said, her smile as open and friendly as ever. 'She didn't want you to be alone.' And though there were many times, his teeth chattering and his muscles locked in uncontrollable spasms, he wished her on the other side of the moon, he came to rely upon her constant good nature, the glasses of water or chips of ice from the machine.

It was Mariam who brought books when he could not sleep, and read to him, even when he could take nothing in but the soothing trill of her voice. He had not been read to since childhood, and it struck him now as funny that Ellisha, for all she had been forever buried in a book, had never once thought to share the page aloud. As the days passed and the pain of separation dulled a little, he came to appreciate this cheerful, uncomplicated woman who had been at their side from the first, and whom he had never really taken the time to get to know.

Only once did he see the light behind her eyes flicker out. He'd had a bad night and by the morning a morbid sense of doom had invaded his thoughts. He found himself talking of his night on Salisbury Crag and the face of the Void, and from there he began to probe the reasons Mariam had chosen to throw her lot in with them.

'I don't know. Ellisha seemed really cool. The next big thing maybe.'

'Come on, there must be more to it than that.'

'What makes you so sure?'

'There always is.'

She stared at him very hard then abruptly looked away. 'Do you know what a Dutch Tear is?'

'One of those glass drops that can't be broken?'

'Sort of.' She was brewing him a medicinal tea and had her back to him. 'You can't damage them by any kind of extreme force. But snip off their tails and they shatter into a million pieces.'

He looked at her with renewed interest. 'So your faith was broken by a single act?'

An embarrassed shrug. 'I guess.' She fell silent, and Peter was wondering how to persuade her to go on, when she sighed again and shivered slightly before pouring out the tea and bringing the cup over to his bedside table. She sat down on the edge. 'My parents were Spiritists. I don't know if you know what that means.'

'I've heard of Spiritualism.'

'It isn't quite the same. They believed in the physical reality of life after death in the Spirit world. But they were followers of Allan Kardec, the founder of Spiritism. And he taught that we can have rebirth into this world to learn the lessons that we failed to understand during our previous incarnations.'

'Like Buddhism?'

'A little. But they believed that they could communicate with spirits while here on earth. My mother used to come into my room and tell me she could see my dead sister sitting on the end of my bed.'

'That's terrible.'

'No. It isn't like that. Death walks alongside life. There's none of that modern pretending that *death only happens to other people*. It's liberating in its own way.'

Peter pushed himself further up the bed by the elbows then fell back on the pillows, exhausted by the effort. 'What made you stop believing?'

'A boy. Lee Chesney. He lived in the flat below ours. We were in the same year at school.' She handed him the cup, holding it tightly until he was steady enough to take it.

'You were friends?'

'I didn't really know him.'

'But he was the catalyst?'

'We ran in different circles. I was a little wild. Liked messing about in class. He was very studious. Very serious. Hunched shoulders, big round glasses.' She mimed with her fingers. 'Total nerd really. My mother was always saying, *Look out for that Chesney boy. He's going to get on.* She laughed a little at the memory. 'I think that made me avoid him all the more.'

The tea was hot and slightly bitter. He let the vapours fill his nostrils before asking, 'What happened?'

'He was stabbed outside in the street. I didn't see it. It was all cordoned off when I got home that night. But you could see the blood on the pavement.'

So calm, Peter thought. Perhaps even a little self-mocking. As though she was telling the tale of some childish misdemeanour, a theft of sweets, a ball sent through a neighbour's window.

'It was the gangs, of course,' she said matter-of-factly. 'A boy of thirteen who needed to prove himself. Didn't even know Lee. I don't know why his death affected me so much. It wasn't even the first stabbing in the neighbourhood. The press made a big thing about Lee having a knife on him. Tried to say he was part of the gang culture. But he wasn't. He was never a member. He was just scared.

'I remember going back outside and the blood was all gone. Someone had cleaned it away and there were flowers tied to a lamppost. And I tried to tell myself that he was still with us, only in the spirit world now. And I stood there trying to feel his presence. But I think I already knew; this was different. Different to when my cat was run over in the street, or when that other boy was stabbed, or when a whole family died in the top flat because of a carbon monoxide leak. And I kept standing there because I knew. Knew that the tail of my faith had somehow been snipped off and the hard core shattered into a million pieces.'

She was breathing in rapid ragged gasps, and her fingers had screwed the bedcovers into a painful coil about her knuckles. Peter put his tea down then reached out and took her hand in his. He didn't say anything, and they sat together silently, joined by the memory of pain.

CHAPTER 26

A FEW DAYS AFTER THE first bout of fever had abated, Peter awoke violently with the sense of being observed. Mariam was asleep in a chair, mouth slack and book splayed on her lap like a softly alighted moth, and for a moment, Peter thought he was mistaken. Then a small figure standing at the bottom of the bed caught his attention, the same ragged little figure who had watched his descent into *la malaria*.

The sight of him made Peter want to laugh. He had been convinced that the child was a product of a fever-confounded brain, but now he stood looking up at Peter out of huge, unblinking eyes. A dirty forefinger sought refuge in the corner of his mouth. Not sure how to proceed, Peter said, 'Hello.' And when this did not work, he tried a self-conscious, '*Hola.*'

At that the boy's mouth twitched slightly, but still he said nothing, only stood there, staring until Peter felt compelled to drop his gaze. He was still there a minute later when Peter sneaked a fleeting glance. *As though he wants something from me.* This made him a little desperate. He glanced towards Mariam, but she was snoring slightly, and he didn't have the heart to wake her.

At something of a loss, he pointed to himself and said, 'Peter' in an exaggerated way. The boy watched solemnly, then cocking his head to one side pointed to himself, still without sound. This continued for some time, the boy looking at him, and Peter looking back at the boy. It was like some bizarre game of mirrors, the rules of which he was clearly failing to fathom. Peter smiled encouragingly. The boy smiled back. He still seemed to be waiting.

What to do? Call for a nurse? No, scare him away. But what? What does he want? Eventually, he turned to the only thing he knew, to words. He told him of the story of the Battle of the Birds and the story of The Daughter of King Under-waves. He told him of brownies and bogles, kelpies and selkies, mermaids and giants, and lands that exist beneath other lands or beyond the sunset, and of castles that appear for a brief time only to vanish with the mists. He talked until he was almost hoarse, and throughout this the child listened with rapt attention, as though he understood. Slowly, one faltering step after another, he came up alongside Peter then perched on the edge of the bed.

By the time Dr Tepetzi entered, stethoscope glinting around his neck, Peter was the only one awake in the room, but he was uncertain as to whether this was entirely a compliment to his story-telling skills. Tepetzi grinned widely when he spotted them.

'Ah, I hope Tomás hasn't been bothering you.'

'Tomás, is that his name?'

Dr Tepetzi's smile vanished. 'It's the name we gave him. He's a sad case, our Tomás. We found him three months ago wandering around the forests unaccompanied. We don't know what he's been through, but it must have been bad. He doesn't speak. And we haven't been able to trace any family.'

Peter looked down at the sleeping figure curled at his side, the narrow brown face and stick-like limbs. He might have been one of the Still Folk, that old, old term for the fey. 'What age is he?'

'Nine we guess, looking at his teeth. We guessed he was much younger when we first got him; he was so small. If he's disturbing you, I can move him.'

'No.' Peter surprised himself by the violence of his response. Dr Tepetzi raised his eyebrows then nodded as if he understood. 'I'll leave you two alone for now.'

'Thank you.'

After that Tomás became his shadow. Slowly he grew in strength, aided by a stick, to which he initially objected then secretly came to rather enjoy, feeling that he cut a figure similar to that of Marquis de

Lafayette or Major Thomas Weir, though the latter was perhaps a poor choice as he was a presumed occultist executed for witchcraft.

Nonetheless, on any given day, a visiting Spark might spot the famous Reverend Kelso, cane in one hand, the hand of a small silent boy in the other, walking through the dusty environs of the hospital. They would see him pointing his stick at the construction site, explaining to the boy how the new wing of the hospital was developing. Tomás hung on his every word, as though Peter was a reedy shaft of sunlight and he a small green shoot that absorbed everything. Afterwards, Mariam would be waiting with a pot of her carefully brewed tea. And while Peter often longed for a refreshing glass of beer, he never forgot those small kindnesses: the blanket pulled over him at night while he slept or the damp corner of a handkerchief used to clean the corners of Tomás' mouth.

There was much interest in Peter's bouts of delirium. Dr Tepetzi, in particular, seemed curious about what he suggested was an altered level of consciousness. 'Hallucinogens have been used since ancient times in this part of the world to open the spiritual pathways,' he explained, as he measured Peter's pulse. 'But could they be used to harness Soul, I wonder?'

Peter, who had an innate dislike of chemical enhancement, insisted, with a degree of truthfulness, that he didn't remember any of his fever-fuelled dreams. Yet it was not quite the whole story. One night he awoke from a deep sleep to discover a crow—oil-slick feathers and with fierce intelligence emanating from the one eye it had trained upon him—sitting on the sill of his open window. That this was a bird native to Scotland rather than to equatorial climes bothered him not at all, nor did the fact that it was speaking to him in a language he could plainly comprehend, albeit that the sounds were inside his head rather than emerging directly from its beak.

It wanted him to come with it, that much was clear, and as a fellow countryman he could think of no reason not to oblige. He was out of bed before he knew it, aware that he was dreaming, and at the same time oddly conscious of dreaming that he was aware. It was night-time, yet the room glowed, every object lit up by a Kirlian spectrum of colour. Entranced, he might have stared forever, but the crow wanted to be followed, and it seemed indecorous to refuse.

He was not afraid, despite his folkloric knowledge of the psychopomp nature of crows, those shadowy, inhuman creatures who lead spirits down the eponymous, 'Crow Road' to the land of the dead. Somehow Peter's crow seemed trustworthy, never more so than when he turned his obsidian eye upon him, with what seemed great tenderness, to check that he was following.

They took a route behind the hospital with which he was not familiar, emerging eventually at the gateway of the most gorgeous park. Through the bars he could see glistening lakes, trees bearing all manner of wondrous fruits and even a line of cloud-capped mountains, majestic as white-robed hierophants, gathered in the distance. It was heart-wrenchingly beautiful. How was it possible that he had not known about it? *I could have brought Tomás here to chase the deer. Or to snatch at butterflies.*

But, even as he exclaimed his surprise, the crow, which had alighted upon the curlicued apex of the gate, so that it resembled Grahame's *Piper at the Gates of Dawn*, looked at him sternly, and he knew then that he *had* known. He had always known, but he had forgotten, and only just now remembered.

To his surprise and delight the gates swung open and he entered, following his feathery guide down grassy slopes and along meandering riverbanks until he found himself in a grove of trees. There was no sound of birdsong here. The air was stealthy as if the grove were a gigantic bell, and the smallest motion might make it start to chime.

There was a sense of immanence, of holiness, and a fleeting memory floated through his mind of Ellisha telling him that the first places mankind felt 'otherness' was in forests. *I mean, think about it, Peter, every temple was built with great soaring pillars. And what are pillars, but stone trees?*

As if in response to this thought, the crow leapt from its branch and began to circle above his head. Up, up it went, and he saw that it was night above the grove. He had been unconscious of it till then, but the journey to the park had been gilded by perfect sunlight. The crow was whirling far above his head now, so that it merged with the night, a little point of darkness lost between the spaces in the stars.

And, as he looked, the stars themselves began to move, rushing towards each other, not timeless at all, but living little finite lives from fiery birth to slow, waning death. Beautiful but infinitely sad. Families of galaxies rising and disappearing, a blinding blaze then forgotten. And no-one to witness it but Peter, one tiny fragment of a fragment in all this terrible splendour, an infinitesimal speck moving across the endless pupil of God's eye.

And yet that eye knew him, yearned for him, called to him. No Blind Watchmaker, it drew creation from its creations, as he, and countless others of his clan, had drawn consciousness out of oblivious substance. Divinity, the Soul Mystica, their pinnacle, not the substance of being, which otherwise was nothing but a dance of atoms, base matter, the *koyn mtalla*, a quintessence of dust. The heavens were Peter's because he saw the heavens and they did not see him. Forty-five years ago he had awakened from the lumpen stuff of matter and stretched out towards Soul. And now Soul opened up towards him, and he was unfurling, like a mystic lotus, an immortal rose, the sacred leaves of a burning oak.

'*Bosquecillo Sagrado.*'

He was in his body, but his body was not where he had left it. He was sitting at a small table on the veranda. Mariam was sitting opposite, drinking coffee. Tomás was curled on his lap. By the tilt of the sun, it was sometime past noon. What had happened? *Did I doze off?* His body was certain it was the middle of the night. Yet his eyes still saw the lush enticement of the park transparently: a double exposure fitting badly over the solid contours of the veranda, a lake interrupted by the French doors to his room, the mountains obscured by the dusty unfinished track which led beyond the hospital to a line of trees.

Mariam was looking at him curiously, but not with alarm or dismay. Apparently, his actions had given her no cause for disquiet. And, as he could hardly ask her what he had been doing all morning, he coughed, and said, '*Bosquecillo Sagrado*?'

'Yes,' she smiled, pleased with herself. 'It means Sacred Grove. It's strange. I didn't think of it before. We must let Ellisha know.'

Despite that one strange encounter with the Soul Mystica—which Peter buried deep in the subterranean caverns of his consciousness—and the limitations the illness imposed upon him, the time in *Bosquecillo Sagrado* felt like a kind of holiday. He had been touring and visiting and overseeing for so long that he had forgotten what it was just to stand still and take stock of things. He stopped once to admire a constellation of jasmine growing along a broken-down wall at the perimeter of the hospital grounds and spotted the fragile threads of a spider's web. It gave him a great jolt to witness the fragility of the world. A tug on his arm. Tomás was staring up at him, and he realised he must have gasped. 'It's all right,' he said to reassure him. 'I miss Ellisha, that's all.' And, as he said it, he realised how very true it was. Of course, they had spoken on a number of occasions since her departure, snatched telephone calls at ungodly hours, with one of them always dazed and sleepy.

When are you coming back? he asked as they conducted a fractured conversation across a Skype connection. But she had shaken her head. She couldn't hear him. Then her image vanished in a snowstorm of tiny squares, and through the distortion, he heard a man's laugh.

After that, he found his words to Ellisha filtered through an internal distortion of false cheer. They talked—when they talked at all—in clichés and commonplaces. Ellisha had evidently been warned by Dr Tepetzi that Peter was not to be burdened with what was happening with Ignis Dei. And, despite all his pleading and pouting, she steadfastly refused to reveal anything beyond, *It's all fine. Don't worry.*

He wondered a little bleakly if Ellisha felt the pain of separation as badly as he did, and wished he could explain what was wrong, but then Tomás squeezed his hand so perhaps words were not necessary after all.

That night he sat with Mariam at the little table set for them on the veranda outside his room. It was not late, but the light was going. The shortness of the days was something he could never quite accustom himself to, and he always felt a pang for Scotland with her endless summer light. Tomás was asleep in his bed. He had seemed tired throughout the day, which happened occasionally, as though the horror of his past sometimes reared up in the closed parts of his mind, making him listless and withdrawn.

It had taken Peter a long while to persuade him to sleep, his eyes staring fixedly at unseen demons then gradually darting back, lured by his talk of knights and gallantry, and enchantresses—whose promises inevitably proved to be only illusion and mirage—until gradually his eyelids began to droop and his breathing became slow and shallow.

In sleep, at least, he seemed untroubled, and Peter was happy to leave him and to join Mariam on the terrace, where they sat comfortably in each other's company amongst the endless sawing of cicadas and the lulling scent of night-blooming jessamine. They might have been a little family settling in for the evening.

'Is something wrong?'

He jerked upright in his chair, feeling oddly guilty about where his thoughts had been leading him. 'I was thinking about Tomás. We've been making such progress recently. Have you noticed how he keeps trying to find his voice, little growls and squeaks? Dr Tepetzi says it's quite promising.'

'Yes,' Mariam agreed. 'He's hopeful that he's beginning to form a soul. He wants to talk to you about putting some sweet calomel and virola leaves in his room. To align his inner awareness.'

He made some non-committal noise. He did not like all this talk of energies and alignments. It felt as though the deep spiritual message that Ellisha embodied was being lost in a fug of celestial vibrations and cosmic correspondences. Mariam was watching his face. 'You don't agree?'

He said a little of what he was thinking, and though he had intended to couch things in a reasonable fashion, he suspected his tone was too harsh because Mariam's face fell, and guilt caused him to add hastily, 'Forgive me. I didn't sleep well last night.' This was a lie and immediately landed him in deeper waters.

'I'll ask Dr Tepetzi to prescribe something,' Mariam said, jumping to her feet.

'No. No, that isn't necessary. Please sit down.' Then, to fill the awkward silence that followed, he clumsily complimented her dress. It was a bright yellow shift dotted with slices of melon in pink and green. She had tied her hair in a matching scarf. The ineptness of this flattery should have made his motives transparent, but Mariam coloured and fingered the neckline.

'Oh, I wear it because it's cool.'

'Well, it suits you.' He refilled her glass. For once they were not drinking tea. The distance and dreaminess of *Bosquecillo Sagrado* had encouraged him to make an exception to his vows of temperance. The wine was not the best, but it possessed that warm, melting quality that tends to loosen tongues. Suddenly things which had not previously been funny—a bush shaped like a goat, the hairs on the upper lip of the night-nurse—sent them into spasms of laughter.

'Do you know what they call you here?' Mariam asked, helping herself to the bottle.

'Reverend Kelso?'

Laughter made her spill the wine at the edge of the glass. '*El que anda detrás de ellat.*' He steadied the neck of the bottle as she poured, and their hands touched briefly. 'What does it mean?'

'*He who walks at Her back.*'

He laughed, but suddenly he wasn't sure why.

'Are you ever lonely?'

The question caught him off guard, and he answered, 'Yes. Sometimes,' before he had time to recognise the full truth of it.

Mariam was leaning forwards, balanced on the points of her elbows. 'The world needs someone like Ellisha. She takes dreams, impossible dreams, and makes them happen. But she's always looking to the big stuff. I get it. She has to. But she doesn't have time to see the small things. Not like you—' a hesitation '—or me.'

He was suddenly aware that she was looking at him very intently. He put his drink down and waited for her to go on. But she turned her gaze deliberately, out over the terrace towards the sound of the cicadas. 'Sometimes it's not easy to live in the shadow of greatness.'

'I'm not sure what you mean.' A lie. *That hollowed-out feeling when Ellie looks right through me and out towards the audience. The secret smiles with MacCaa. Thinks I don't notice. Yes, there's loneliness living in the shadow of greatness.* And so deep were his thoughts that it came to him only slowly that Mariam's hand was resting gently on his.

Embarrassment overrode the instinct to jerk away. After all, Mariam was a good woman, a kind and giving soul. *Misled her? Reached out. What could I have done differently? She was there, vulnerable to my vulnerability. Oh, Peter, you selfish shit.*

'I mean,' Mariam was smiling shyly. 'I mean that we live so closely to a powerful soul that we can't help but feel our incompleteness. Like a nagging pain here.' She lifted his hand and touched it to her heart.

And Peter, who had scarcely listened to his father's sermons, was suddenly vividly reminded of the story of Joseph's sojourns in Egypt. He stared at Mariam, as the son of Jacob must once have stared in nervous confusion at Potiphar's wife. The fabric of her dress was very thin, and he could see the swell of her breasts beneath. Every ounce of sense he possessed screamed at him to move his hand yet, he did not. 'Mariam—' His voice sounded hoarse, not at all like the dismissal he intended. He leaned closer. The table between them was small, like one of those tiny round tables found in French street cafes. Fumes of wine from her breath and a pulse leaping in her throat, brief and mesmerising, like the glimpse of a hind disappearing into the bracken.

His mind was spinning. He looked round rather wildly. Was it possible that he was dreaming again? *Free love, so many Sparks already giving themselves up to it. Ellisha preaching, love is power. When we use sex as an expression of love, we take away Eve's shame. After all, polyamorous marriage is a spreading trend. Does Ellisha know? Mariam's staying here with me, her idea. A gift?*

Now Mariam's face was only inches from his face, her voice a soft whisper. 'The Lie is gone. The old ownership of Soul is dead. We are fragments inside a universe, which is longing to become whole, longing to awaken from the broken dream of billions and billions of split minds.'

He recognised the words. How could he not: he had written them. Yet here, with the smell of night jessamine in the air and the constant restless friction of the cicadas, their echo took on a strange potency, as though the words had not come from him, but through him to blossom on Mariam's full, slightly quivering lips. He was aware that he was breathing rather heavily, and of how nice it would be to lie close to someone and feel the warmth of the Soul Mystica expand deep inside him. The sublime mystery of that unexplained moment when sole becomes Soul.

Her fingers tightened, as though she could read his thoughts. 'It isn't wrong.'

'So, this is where you two are.'

They sprang apart. Peter pretending to reach for his glass, while Mariam, eyes wide, stuttered out. 'Soul seeks Soul.'

'Soul meets soul,' Dr Tepetzi repeated. There was a puzzled note in his voice. Formality was not what he had been expecting. Peter sprang up as though doused in cold water. 'Has something happened? Is Tomás okay?'

Dr Tepetzi's smile returned. He pressed the tips of his fingers together, the bringer of glad tidings. 'The Prophetess called to hear of your progress. I have good news. You are going home.'

Part IV

PARADISE LOST

THE DUAL NATURE OF THE Great Goddess is nowhere seen more clearly than in the presence of the elemental deity, Oya, personification of the river Niger. This shapeshifter appears, at times as a nurturing mother of creation, and at others, a chthonic warrior for whom death holds no challenges. Little wonder she has been described as the West African Morgan le Fay, whose double face as healer and bringer of death reflects her mystical skill as an animagus. Able to choose bird or fish or mammal as her disguise, a power which perhaps symbolizes her ability to alter herself when faced with a challenge to her power.

McBride Barbara, The Many Faces of Morgan Le Fay,
Thesis, University of Oxford, (1977)

CHAPTER 27

AS THEY LEFT THE RUNWAY Peter tried to catch a final glimpse of *Bosquecillo Sagrado*. He had told Tomás to watch out for the plane and to wave when he saw it, and he wondered now if he had remembered.

As the earth fell away, he thought of how he had explained that he had to go away for a while. 'But I'll be back. As soon as I can. I promise.' Tomás' eyes, dark and unmoving, had been fixed on his face, and he had been unable to tell how much he understood. Now he looked through the clouds towards the wandering city and wondered how much of himself he had left behind.

He sat back and looked across at Mariam. In the rush to pack and say their farewells to kindly Dr Tepetzi and his staff, they had barely seen each other before the flight. But now she sat opposite, every curve of her body a reproach under a thin vest and linen trousers.

She hadn't mentioned the night before, and a part of him hoped that it would melt away like an embarrassing dream. Nevertheless, he felt it necessary to be clear. 'About what happened. Last night I mean.'

Mariam was smiling. 'I don't know what you mean.'

'I just— I don't want to mislead you.' She was looking at him so frankly that he faltered. Her smile hadn't changed, a broad curve fringed in bright red lipstick. There was something grotesque about it, a fairground mannequin's smile; he couldn't seem to move his eyes from it. At last, he said uneasily, 'I'm loyal to Ellisha.'

The smile vanished. 'Me too.' She turned away to look out at the clouds.

Their landing was delayed. Peter could see the airport below as they circled, again and again, through the gathering heat above LA.

'Is there a problem?' The Spark he asked was a young woman Peter had never encountered before. She looked too young to have been long out of school, but he grinned broadly, falling back on his old trick of establishing himself amongst the ground troops. 'Let me know if I can help.'

The Spark pursed her lips. 'They're making it difficult for us to enter the country. It's been happening a lot these days.' She gave a reassuring laugh. 'Nothing to worry about, Reverend Kelso. 'The lawyers will take care of it.'

'The lawyers?'

But just then the pilot's voice came over the intercom telling them to return to their seats and buckle up, and she excused herself and hurried away.

Frowning slightly, Peter watched her walk down the aisle, but it was Mariam who put his thoughts into words. 'Do you know any of these people?'

He shook his head. None of their old entourage was onboard, not one familiar face. His sense that Ellisha should have come personally to fetch him was curbed by a sense of guilt, which threw up a litany of the challenges she had faced without him at her side. *Oh Ellie, I left you all alone.*

Mariam was looking at him anxiously and he offered her a rueful smile. 'Never mind. We'll be with everyone soon.'

To his surprise, she looked away, biting her lip.

'Mariam?'

'Do you—' She broke off then started again in a small, distant voice. 'Are we being punished?'

The question took him aback. 'Of course not. Why on earth would you think such a thing?'

She gave an embarrassed shrug. 'I don't know.' She lifted a magazine and began intently studying its glossy contents. But there was still a little "v" of worry between her brows which troubled him.

'Worrywart.'

She looked up, startled. 'Sorry? What?'

'Nothing.' He sat back, feeling foolish and missing Ellisha more than ever. 'We'll be home soon.'

Once landed, their documents were checked by assigned officials before they were escorted through the airport. It was impressively orchestrated. Not a single member of the press was waiting as they crossed the tarmac to their waiting car.

At the sight of the white limo, its smoked-glass windows etched with burning tree emblems, Peter felt his heart give a jump of excitement. In the wandering city existence had been simple, uncluttered. Things mattered only in as much as a man might take the time to give them meaning, stopping to stare at a drop of dew on a rose or passing by without comment. It was, he realised, a kind of dreaming.

The world, the real world to which he was only now re-awakening, called to the complexities of his nature, wanting, needing, begging to be fixed. He felt the giddy rush of adrenalin in his veins and, despite the walking stick, squared his shoulders and walked a little taller. By the time he was seated in the car, he had shed a skin.

He sat in the back with Mariam, looking out of the window and enjoying America's trick of luring European eyes with a false sense of familiarity—neat little rows of houses, mowed lawns, picket fences—only to throw up a giant fibreglass doughnut atop a restaurant roof or the improbable glacial spires of a glass church. The journey was a long one. But, when the chauffeur turned east on the 405 he leaned forward and addressed the Spark riding up front with the driver. 'Aren't we staying at the Marmont?'

'No, sir. We're going to the Cathedral.'

'I don't think I know that.'

The driver was looking at the road, but Peter saw him jerk his eyes up towards the mirror. 'The Grand Soularium, sir. The opening was all over the media. About two months ago.'

'Of course, yes. Remarkable.' Peter sat back, but not before he shot a questioning glance at Mariam, who shook her head. My God, he thought. How long have I been away?

The next thing he knew, someone was shaking him awake.

'Look!'

A final tug on his arm threw open the shutters on his slumbering self, and he jerked into a sitting position, surprised to find that his forehead was pressed against the window. 'What is it?'

'We're here.'

He looked past the driver's head and could only see a pair of gigantic gates, which opened automatically as though recognising them. They drove through into the grounds of a vast estate, following a curving driveway past lines of trees strung together with lines of little coloured fairy-lights.

As they passed an immaculately clipped lawn, a fountain suddenly frothed up from the centre of an artificial lake, and a garden of statues could be glimpsed through the drapery of water. But his eyes were drawn beyond, to three irregular pyramids of glass, inwardly glowing, immense yet at the same time insubstantial a mountain-range, a butterfly's wing, neither and both.

'What is this place?' He knew. Of course, he knew. But he had to hear it in a voice that was not his own.

'It's the Cathedral, sir. The Cathedral of Soul.'

The dry earthiness of the air prickled in his nostrils, making him think of herbs, of sage or achiote, the moment he stepped out of the car. *It can't be. Can it?* His head whipped around. *This is the desert.* The last of the line of trees was behind him, and suddenly he appreciated the audacity of what he was seeing. Not simple ostentation, but defiance, a boldness that pushed aside nature in a way that made him think of ancient Petra hewn out of a cliffside or the sprawling subterranean churches of northern Ethiopia.

With Mariam beside him, he walked up the white marble steps in awed silence, while his brain, rusty with lack of use, tried to crunch the numbers. *Six months. Impossible. I was only away six months. The planning, the building. Even with our resources. Impossible.*

At the top a glass door slid open, and they stepped into an immense, unreal space. A hall, three storeys high and full of echoes. White reflecting white; he couldn't see the edges, vanished boundaries, huge snowdrifts of light; his eyes, trying to find the ceiling, wept out dazzled stars. *Where is she?* He was making his way forward, his cane tapping on the floor like a blind man, when a high harrowing note pinned him to the spot.

One by one gigantic screens leapt into life until he was surrounded by a semi-circle of reflections, each one displaying a tiny bewildered man turning his head from side to side. A noise from the opposite side of the hall made him squint through the glare, and his adjusting sight found a staircase. It rose to a gallery at the height of the first storey and, as he watched, two figures appeared at the top. They stopped, when they noticed him, but were too far away to make out, even with his hand held to his brow.

It wasn't necessary. The screens changed perspective and suddenly she was there: Ellisha, wearing a saffron-coloured dress so fine it appeared to be flowing over her, and the sight sent a jolt through Peter's heart, as though he had been electrically shocked, as though he had been struck by lightning.

I forgot. Only six months and I forgot.

Forgotten what it was like to come upon her for the first time, to see that small, composed woman with something of the faerie about her. Not those mawkish spindly creatures of Victorian sentiment, all sticks and cobwebs. But in the old sense of the word, Titania awakening in the forest. Dryad, stepping from the woods, skin like a sapling of sleek rowan, eyes of moss agate.

At her back stood MacCaa. Not wearing his usual khaki fatigues, but an expensively tailored black suit, hands lightly resting on her shoulders. They stood there, the only sun and moon in a vast sterile sky as banners in nine different languages rolled across the screens. The one in English read, *The Prophetess and her consort greet the First Follower.*

The shock of this propelled Peter forwards, while the screens turned their collective eye on him, recording his progress.

'El—'

The sound from his lips echoed from every screen. *El—El—El—*

Above his head great slabs of shadow were appearing as the roof dimmed. He could see better now. There were viewing galleries on the second floor, where white-clad Sparks—technicians and spirit-therapists and diviners and Soul-Searchers with painted faces—were leaning over the balustrades clapping or making the burning tree sign. The eye of the cameras swept across the crowd then zoomed in on Peter. He saw himself as the world was now seeing him, a haggard-looking man, stumbling towards redemption. It was a part, a role written for him without his knowledge, but he was shrewd enough to know that eyes were watching him, eyes that wanted to see how he would play it.

He wiped his face of expression and continued the faltering progress towards the stairs. Ellisha was coming down them, half running, dress billowing behind her. And as she came, an anthem of voices spiralled up from nowhere, rising and fading in wordless beauty, like the notes of a Gregorian chant or a choir of invisible angels. The clapping died away and was replaced by a poised, inward silence until the atmosphere swelled on an indrawn breath, as they drew near.

Ten paces from his Prophetess, Peter threw down his stick—he wouldn't have been surprised if it had turned into a serpent—and forced himself to walk the last few steps unaided.

And now they were face to face. Alone, despite the eyes of the world upon them, searching each other's faces the way strangers do when they sense that they have met a long time ago in some half-forgotten place.

A growing sense of anger had propelled Peter thus far, his head spinning with caustic lines ready to crack the atmosphere's careful construction of awe. But now she was here and he had nothing to say. Her presence extended towards him, curving the space between them as she reached out and took his hands.

'Welcome home.'

He felt a shudder go through him, and had to fight back tears. Wanting to kiss her, he began straightening his body in a move to draw her in, but she pulled back to face the cameras. He saw her reflected on the screens, poised and aloofly radiant, and though their bodies were almost touching, he felt a sense of abandonment.

'Ellie.' He whispered her name as softly as his voice would allow. 'We need to talk.'

'I'd like that.'

'Now?'

'Soon.'

Several Sparks were coming towards them, carrying two golden chairs. They were led by MacCaa, who stopped in front of them and cleared his throat. Then, spreading his arms like the limbs of a great oak, intoned, *We bless the seed that is the fruit that is the fragment on the branch that is the tree that is the Woman who turns the axis of creation.*

Cheers rose like orisons, and Peter heard his name chanted over and over as he and Ellisha were each placed on a chair and lifted aloft. Sparks were flooding into the hall and soon there were so many people crowded around that he lost all sense of them as individuals, and felt only the feathery touch of fingers or caught the gleam in eyes or grinning mouths. The noise was overwhelming. Violent percussive energy, palm struck upon palm, feet pounding marble, an ovation of sound that carried them out into the quieter chambers beyond.

Perdita was waiting on the other side of the door. 'Welcome back.' She extended her hand and he felt her fingers briefly brush against his palm. MacCaa had come in with Ellisha and was standing behind her. The sight gave Peter a sick feeling at the pit of his stomach, and he stared into MacCaa's face, hoping to convey some sense of menace. MacCaa returned his gaze, the pupils of his eyes, like collapsed stars, absorbing everything but emitting no light. Ellisha stepped between them. 'Peter, you're very pale.'

'I'm Scottish.'

She didn't laugh; a tiny frown formed between her brows as she studied his face. 'I shouldn't have kept you up. The 'welcome' ceremony could have been done tomorrow.'

'Unfortunately, all the metrics pointed to immediacy,' Perdita said, coming into the room. The ruthless efficiency of the observation made him smile. *I'm really back.* He beamed down at Ellisha. 'I'm fine.' He hoped she did not notice that he was starting to tremble slightly. Throwing away his stick had made for visual spectacle, but it had come at a price. With a meaningful glance at MacCaa, he asked, 'Can we talk alone?'

'Of course.'

He started to smile, but she added, 'Soon. It can't be now, I'm afraid. But soon.' Her glance shifted to Perdita. 'Will you show Peter to his quarters?'

'Of course.'

She turned back and, in the curve of her lips, he saw a fleeting, impish change of expression. He half expected her to mouth *A-hole* or *butt-head* at him, but she only lifted her hand and touched his cheek. 'We'll talk soon. I promise.' Then she was out the door, MacCaa following, like Greyfriars's Bobby, at her back.

Something of him left the room with her and he felt his shoulders slump. He had no idea what hour it was. *Did I lose time or gain it?* Perdita was studying him and he straightened guiltily.

'If you'll follow me.' She was gesturing at the door. They stepped out into a long, cool corridor with something of the cloister about it. But if the intention was to calm, it failed in its purpose. He blurted, 'MacCaa's the consort?'

'Of course.' Perdita was moving ahead, a little faster than he found comfortable.

'Am I missing something? Did the world stand on its head while I was away?'

'I don't know what you mean?'

'I mean, how did that brute take my place?'

'You weren't here. The Reverences had to go on.' She glanced back at him, brow arched. 'It was what the Prophetess wanted.'

What she wanted? The muscles in his face clamped, cutting off the direction of his speech. *We talked about this. We agreed.* He waited until he had his breathing under control before saying, 'Even so, to let MacCaa perform on stage.'

'The Sparks like him. He has a spiritual quality that people find very authentic.'

She began walking again and he all but ran after her. 'But the Hieros Gamos—'

'It's a ritual.'

'A sex ritual.'

'Surely more than that. It's symbolic. The Hieros Gamos represents divinity coming into the world. Ellisha is simply the lens—'

'Who invites strangers into her bed?'

'If you like. I was going to say, *Who focusses the Coming Divine.*' Up ahead there was a cleaning party, a dozen men and women down on their knees scrubbing the floor. Peter braced himself to make polite greetings, but they scattered, timid as wild deer, the moment they sensed his approach. He stared after their vanishing heels in puzzlement, but Perdita had summoned an elevator and the doors were already opening. 'You must remember,' she was saying over her shoulder, 'the Sparks see the consort merely as a vessel, an imago awaiting transformation. The more flawed the better.' She stepped inside and turned to face him. 'To them, it's confirmation that the power of creation can be drawn into anyone.'

Peter didn't move. 'They believe that?'

'Of course.' Her eyes narrowed. 'Don't you?'

CHAPTER 28

'GOOD MORNING. HOW ARE YOU TODAY?

His eyes struggled against gravity, failed then resumed their struggle behind the cocoon of their lids.

'Reverend Kelso, sir. You need to wake up.'

He pushed himself into a sitting position, eyes still welded shut. 'I— What time is it?'

'Six o'clock, sir. I brought you coffee.'

He felt a cup nudging against his hands and managed to grasp it. A powerful smell of ground beans flooded his senses and his eyes opened a slit. He was in an unfamiliar room sitting on an unfamiliar armchair. His clothes were rumpled and there was a distinctly sour smell that was not entirely masked by the fresh smell of the coffee beans. The Spark hovering anxiously over him was also unfamiliar. He clocked the features: slight build, wavy hair, narrow epicene face.

The Spark thrust a hand forwards. 'What am I thinking? I'm Leonard Glass. But you can call me Leo.'

Peter took the hand, which held his fleetingly then was surreptitiously wiped against a trouser leg.

'I've taken the liberty of running a bath for you, sir. May I call the chef and let him know what you would like for breakfast?'

His thoughts were tarry and wouldn't separate. He made a supreme effort. 'Where is the Prophetess?'

A pause. A show of consulting a tablet. 'I believe she's in her own apartments.'

Her own apartments? He rolled with the blow, not wanting Leo to see his confusion. 'Arrange a meeting. As soon as possible.'

Leo's teeth glowed in the blue light from the tablet. 'Of course. I would love to do that for you. But, please, you must get up now.'

At seven-thirty, he was introduced to his new staff, none of whom he had met before. Leo Glass was there, apologising profusely for not having introduced himself properly. 'I'm your new PA. And I want you to know, it's an absolute thrill to be working for you, Reverend Kelso.'

Peter put a hand to his newly shaved cheek. 'Mariam Kingsley is my current PA. We arrived together.' Leo looked crestfallen, and he added hastily. 'Of course, she may have gone back to work for the Prophetess. But the choice should be hers. Can you ask her to make her wishes known?'

Leo beamed. 'It would be my great pleasure, sir.'

'Good. Let's see what projects I'll be working on.'

His office was filled with box files, reaching from floor to ceiling, and more were stacked up outside in the corridors. Peter looked at them in dismay. 'I thought it would all be held digitally.'

Leo nodded sympathetically. 'Most of it is. These are a few additional items.'

'I see.'

Leo did not move, as though he suspected Peter might cave before a task with mythic proportions, but Peter drew in a deep breath and walked over to the desk. 'Better get started.'

As soon as he was alone, the fight left him. Just the thought of starting set off a kind of internal trembling throughout his body. *Weak. Not the man I was? Not up for the job? Is that what she thinks?* As if in response, his leg ached painfully and he was forced to spend some time massaging it. The pain did not diminish, but gradually a manic anger took hold of him. *Let her down. Forced her to look elsewhere. Prove myself. Turn the tables.*

He began to work, a look of tense concentration on his face. The projects were diverse, but after several hours he began to notice a certain common thread. Each venture had stalled on the point of some crucial decision. In Bolivia the construction of a wandering city had halted over the question of whether to increase the bribes to local officials or pull out altogether. Another file revealed that the global adult literacy program was failing. But it was a flagship project supported by the Prophetess. Should it be scrapped, leaving thousands disillusioned and out of work or might the figures be massaged to show more favourable trends?

He was reading about the governor of Ohio when Leo Glass reappeared. The governor had backtracked on closing down the soulariums, but was now putting himself forward as a presidential candidate running on an anti-Ignis Dei platform. Peter had considered diverting funds into a promotional campaign backing his rival, a prominent Spark. Then again, the campaign had funding issues and the gurus had uncovered the fact that the governor's son attended an evangelical university.

Leo's arrival interrupted his thoughts, and he said aloud, 'There's a report here suggesting that the Ohio governor's son got a girl pregnant and she subsequently had an abortion.'

'That is correct, sir.'

'Is it true?'

'Not in the least. But, if you give the word, the internet will be alive with rumours by the end of the day.'

Peter took a moment to digest this. Eventually he said in a voice not quite his own, 'That's not how we do things.'

'I don't know what you mean, sir.'

'I mean—' What did he mean? It wasn't unusual to distort, deflect, spin the story. But all with the sense that underneath there was truth. A means to a greater end. That moment in *Bosquecillo Sagrado*, his vision so clear. The crow whirling above him and the purity of Ignis Dei revealing itself. Suddenly he felt invigorated, floating almost, as though invisible weights attached to his extremities had finally fallen away, and he wanted very badly for the cleanness of his vision to become a cornerstone of the future.

Leo was still waiting. 'I mean we are going to do things differently. Get John Rockwell on the phone.'

'You want the Ohio governor on the phone?' Leo looked aghast.

Peter had opened the next file and was looking down at it. 'I believe that's what I said.'

Rockwell was a long time answering, presumably fearing that he was dealing with some kind of hoax. But eventually he was on the line and Peter took the call. 'Hullo. I'm Peter Kelso.'

'John Rockwell.' The voice was suspicious yet somehow conveyed the kind of physical confidence of a man who had played college football.

'Mr Rockwell, I have a proposal.'

'Yeah?'

'We'd like to make a donation to your campaign.'

There was a snort from the other side. 'I think you have the wrong candidate, Reverend Kelso.'

'No mistake. But I won't lie to you. I intend to fund your rival as well.'

'Is this some sort of joke?'

'No joke, I promise you. We want to level the playing field. Make it a fair fight.'

There was a sharp intake of breath then Rockwell asked in a cold voice, 'Why would you want to do that?'

Peter regretted that they hadn't met face-to-face. It meant trying to inflect sincerity into his voice. 'I know this is hard, John. May I call you John? But I looked death in the eye recently and it changed me.

It changed how I thought about things. And it made me realise that we're not going to make this world fairer until the people with power start acting fairly.'

There was a long pause. Rockwell said, 'Oh, I get it.'

'Get what, John?'

'You think you can buy me. Make me another Spark zombie beholden to unAmerican values. Do you know what happened when your 'prophetess' called the strike?' Without waiting for Peter to go on, he snarled, 'Manufacturing was brought to a standstill. Jobs were lost. Money was lost. Good people lost their homes. We had so many out of work we couldn't cope. Do you know where their people are now, *Reverend* Kelso?'

'I—'

'Let me tell you. They're in Ignis Dei-sponsored housing with their kids at Ignis Dei schools and their sick treated at Ignis Dei hospitals. Their heads are so full of mother goddesses that aren't even here, that they don't even know what they've thrown away. You didn't give them their souls, Reverend Kelso. You bought them.'

'John, if you'll just listen—'

'No, you listen. I am a religious man, a Christian man. And I say, without shame, Jesus Christ is the centre of my life. It's time for men like me to stand up to those who deny that we are the children of God, to those who peddle false religions that reject our fundamental right to let God's love into our hearts and turn us against our homegrown values and freedom.'

'John, we're on the same side, if you'll only—'

'The hell we are!' The line went dead. Peter sat back, biting the knuckle of his left hand until a slight clearing of the throat reminded him that Leo was still in the room.

'I guess we'll have to chalk that one up to the dissipators, sir.'

'Dissipators?'

Leo looked surprised. 'It's what we call those who turn their backs against the possibility of Soul.'

'When did this start?'

'I really couldn't say, sir. Haven't we always done it? Now, is there anything I can do for you? Another cappuccino perhaps?'

'No. Thank you. Has the Prophetess called?'

Leo flourished his tablet and ran a manicured finger down it. 'I'm afraid not. Would you like me to contact her office again? I can do it right away for you, sir.'

'Yes, do that. No, wait. Has Mariam got in touch?'

'Yes, sir.' Leo consulted his notes. 'She has decided to take some time off. To meditate on her gathering soul.'

'Mariam said that?'

'I have the quote right here, sir.'

Without even saying goodbye. 'I see.'

Leo lifted his tablet again. 'Shall I have the funds diverted to the governor's rival?'

On the point of giving a dispirited nod, Peter found himself saying, 'No. Send the money I promised to Rockwell.' Leo's eyes grew round, but he recovered himself quickly and nodded. 'Of course. It's my pleasure.'

The next morning, he woke to find Leo's teeth glowing in the dark above him. 'Good morning, Reverend Kelso. How are you today?'

'Wh—what time is it?'

'Five-thirty.'

'You woke me at six yesterday.'

The glowing curve of Leo's smile stretched wider. 'There's a delegation in from Estonia. They want to meet you before they go on their official tour.'

'Why?'

'They said it would be an honour, sir.'

'Has the Prophetess called?'

'No, sir. Would you like me to try again?'

His days began to take on a certain uniformity. Glass woke him each morning with another excuse as to why he could not meet with his wife. *The Prophetess has been unavoidably detained. The Prophetess sends her apologies.* Yet his hope was kept alive by a string of broken promises, like the fairy-lights strung between the trees outside, winking out one by one as soon as you reached them. He often dreamt of Cheshire cats.

All through his day everywhere he went, Ellisha was there. He saw her in the corridors, reflected on giant screens, where her appearances were broadcast, Twitter messages scrolling along the bottom from Sparks who were participating live all across the globe. He saw her at receptions, surrounded by official delegations and the press and, of course, MacCaa's hard-faced men, tattoos dripping from their left eyes. At these times he often stood right next to her and joined in the hand-shaking. But there was no opportunity to speak, and he stood there, his public mask pulling so tight there were times he felt he couldn't breathe.

In the end, it was the spectacle of the reverences that broke any illusion that Ellisha was coming. One night, he awoke in the wee small hours, a vision of MacCaa bending down to whisper something in Ellisha's ear and her responding laughter hovering behind his eyelids, and suddenly he could not bear the thought of staying another moment in his lonely bed. He dressed hastily and hurried along the corridors.

Light followed him everywhere and it was clear that there were conferences and debates and hallowings taking place even at this late hour. *Like a hive that never sleeps.* His legs began to grow tired and he wished he had brought his stick. Even after a week, he had not fully got to grips with the vast scale of the Cathedral or the labyrinthine convolutions of corridors or walkways whose layout seemed based on some strange notion of beauty rather than any principle of logic. And in trying to find Ellisha, he found himself, instead, outside Perdita's quarters. He banged on the door, too tired to go on searching.

There was a long pause, then the door opened a crack. He saw a sliver of face above a sliver of grey coverall. 'Is Perdita there? I need to speak with her.' The single visible eye grew wide then vanished when someone spoke behind it. A moment later the door was thrown wide and Perdita appeared. There was an instant of mutual astonishment as she noted his dishevelled appearance and he noted the grandmotherly quilted dressing gown she was fumbling to tie. Perdita was first to recover. 'Peter? Is something wrong?'

'I want to take my place as consort.'

'Ah.' Perdita glanced sharply at the figure in the grey coverall, who grabbed a mop and scurried, head down, from the room. 'You had better come inside.'

She led him to a white leather sofa where he slumped, trying hard not to show that his leg was troubling him.

'You don't look well, Peter. Are you sure you've quite recovered?'

He snapped upright. 'I'm fine, thanks.'

She waved a hand in the direction of a well-stocked cocktail cabinet. 'Drink?'

He shook his head, scowling a little.

'Of course. Very sensible.' She went to the liquor cabinet and poured herself a large measure of brandy, before taking took the seat opposite him.

'So you want to be consort?'

'Yes.'

'Do you imagine it's that easy?'

'Of course it's that easy. I'm the fucking husband.'

Perdita stared down into her drink for several seconds before saying, 'Things have changed since you've been away.'

'I don't know what you're talking about.'

'No, you don't.' She got to her feet. 'Come and see for yourself.'

CHAPTER 29

SHE LED HIM THROUGH TO her private office, where there were tall bookcases lining one wall and a glass-topped Le Corbusier desk in the centre. Perdita opened her laptop then glanced around at Peter. 'Best take a seat,' she said indicating the single office chair. And when he hesitated, she added, 'You should hear this sitting down.'

Finding no grounds to argue, and afraid to admit how much his leg hurt, Peter sat down, jutting his chin and folding his arms across his chest. 'Tell me what's going on.'

'Just a mo.' She left the room and came back with her brandy. 'Nearly forgot.' She took a swig and savoured it before getting down to business. 'You may not know it, but a few weeks after your disappearance, something happened. I suppose you could say that we hit a kind of tipping point. The conversion rate rocketed. Churches, mosques, meetings of Communist party youth, they all started emptying. Overnight, Ignis Dei transformed from being puzzling phenomenon to something rather dangerous.'

Peter ran a hand over the back of his head. 'But there's always been negativity. Think of Venice.' Perdita was looking at him in a way that made him blurt, 'What? What is it?'

'This.' She leaned over him and began tapping on the keyboard. Fumes of brandy wafted from her breath and made saliva gather at the back of his throat. He swallowed hard and tried to concentrate on the information she wanted him to see. A 3-D graphic of the earth was slowly revolving, and country after country exhibited Ignis Dei's rise in impossible shooting-star trajectories.

'We outstripped Islam five weeks ago,' Perdita said quietly. 'That means that one in four people on the planet now belong to Ignis Dei.'

Peter ran his tongue along his lower lip. 'That's great. Isn't it?'

Perdita tipped her head to one side. 'I know what you're thinking. Ignis Dei is simply stepping up as a major faith. But it isn't quite so straightforward.'

'What do you mean?'

'Traditionally, the powers-that-be don't pay a great deal of attention to major faiths. They don't have to. Too much infighting and bickering to really make a difference.'

'Even the atheists?'

'Have you ever seen two atheists agree?'

He conceded the point and she continued, 'However, unlike our rivals there are no schisms or sects fracturing our unity. The energy of Ignis Dei is a pure unadulterated beam. And that's what frightens them. Think about it, a quarter of people on the planet potentially might do anything Ellisha tells them, irrespective of country or government.'

Peter became aware that she was looking at him as though she expected him to say something. He cleared his throat. 'Ignis Dei has never been involved in any kind of violence.'

Perdita shrugged. 'An organization as big as we are has its outliers. There's no doubt that there have been some questionable acts from time to time. The dissipators believe they have enough ammunition against us. And what they don't have they're willing to make up.'

'You make it sound like a war.'

'What else should it sound like?'

To cover his confusion he stood up and, despite the pain, paced back and forth. After a few fruitless moments he could think of no better riposte than to mumble, 'It doesn't have to be like this.'

'No?' Perdita was leaning against the bookcase, taking her weight on her elbows. 'How would you do it? Through love? By offering the hand of friendship?'

Peter stopped pacing. *She knows.*

Perdita levered herself off the bookcase and walked back to the sitting room. He followed and found her refilling her glass. 'Tell me, Peter, how is your interfaith conference going? You invited the Chief Rabbi, the Pope, the Ecumenical Patriarch of Constantinople, the Grand Mufti and apparently even the Moderator of the Church of Scotland.'

'Amongst others,' Peter said through gritted teeth.

'And what was the response?'

His jaw was locked and he wanted to scream, *You know the answer!* But he swallowed hard and took it like a man. 'They all refused.'

'On the grounds that they did not recognise Ignis Dei as a faith,' Perdita finished for him.

On the point of defeat, he felt a sudden rushing anger. 'It's hard to explain, but my way will work.'

Perdita put her drink down. 'Why? Because you had a revelation while you were in *Bosquecillo Sagrado*?'

She can't— It's not possible.

'Understandable, of course. The isolation, the drugs. You were in a vulnerable position. Hardly surprising that you should find redemption.' She raised her eyes, and he felt the hairs on the back of his neck prickle.

'Are you trying to tell me I imagined the experience?'

'Not in the least. In fact, you are stronger for it, aren't you? Strong enough not to fall for Mariam Kingsley's charms.'

'Nothing happened.'

'Of course not.'

'Have you spoken to Mariam?'

'Mariam has chosen to go on a journey of self-discovery. The Prophetess thought it best. A clean start for you both.'

A horrible thought was occurring to him. 'You were watching me.'

'We kept you under surveillance, yes. A necessary precaution. Rumours about your disappearance were everywhere. That you had fallen out of favour, that you were being held at an unknown location against your will. Even that an assassin had been sent to kill you on the orders of the Prophetess. That last one proved to be true.'

Peter stared. 'True?' he repeated faintly.

'Not the bit about the Prophetess, of course. But an assassin was sent to kill you.' She opened a drawer in the desk then lifted out a report, thumbing it gently. 'A porter called Mateo Lopez.'

Peter felt his face slacken. Mateo Lopez. The porter who always seemed to be sweeping the floor outside his room. His friendly face wrinkling up whenever Peter came out, making a point of saying *good day*, and smiling in a way that made his eyes disappear. Peter shook his head. 'He seemed so … harmless.'

'Rather a prerequisite of being an assassin, don't you think?' Perdita brushed her hands briskly. 'It told us the dissipators were serious. An attempt like that was audacious. We knew then that the forces gathering against us were more than disparate conspiracy theorists and trolls. It was a signal. And you were our canary, so to speak.' Perdita was looking at him, evidently expecting a response. When he didn't give one she prompted, 'You can see why this was a turning point?'

He stared at her helplessly. In *Bosquecillo Sagrado*, his vision had been so clear. He had felt the purity of Ignis Dei and all the love that they had brought about and offered to the world. And how had the world reacted? Sending a man to kill him in his sickbed. *And my death not even the worst of it. Using me as a tool to crack open the ribs of our vision. Fingers pointing. Ellisha exposed as murderess and traitor. Her dark heart revealed, and everyone asking why the queen of heaven had killed her lover.* It was the old question, old as memory, and they had turned it into a weapon.

He squeezed his temples between thumb and forefinger, enjoying the simplicity of the pain. 'I need to be at her side. To be consort again.'

'It's not that simple.'

'It's exactly that simple.'

Perdita sighed and began putting the report away. 'The data's against you.' She shut the drawer with a click. 'You're a clever man, Peter. Don't choose now to play the fool.'

'I'm not.'

He saw her shoulders stiffen, and when she turned there was something subtly altered in the way she looked at him. 'MacCaa has the better story, plain and simple. A love story.'

He felt colour draining out of him. Not blood, not emotion. But actual colour, leaving him bone white, stone white. 'Are you— Are you saying—'

Perdita's brows rose in surprise. 'Gracious, no. It's the chase that mesmerizes. You know how it is, Peter. Every great love story dies with the first kiss. MacCaa's relationship with Ellisha fascinates because of its possibility. Chivalry and courtly love. *Amour courtois*. Will they? Won't they? There's no mystery in a husband standing next to his wife.'

'But MacCaa.'

'I don't know what to tell you. He has a huge following. Men look up to him. Women adore him. There's something elemental about him. Do you know someone did a piece on the etymology of his name? Apparently, it means 'the champion', and now we're picking up indications that people are calling him *the* MacCaa. Extraordinary.' There was a silence, then Perdita added almost gently, 'You can see why this has to be, Peter. For now.'

In a savage voice, he said, 'If the world's turning against Ellisha, she needs protection.'

There was a knock on the door and a Soul-Searcher entered. She was well over six feet tall and spoke in a raspy, commanding voice. 'The Prophetess is here to see Reverend Kelso.'

He felt his heart lift. In the secret parts of himself he had been afraid she would never come. But there she was, standing on the threshold, smiling that enigmatic, Mona Lisa smile so that he didn't notice the strangeness of Perdita's murmur at his back. 'Who's going to protect the world from Ellisha?'

He followed Ellisha down the milky corridors, feeling so impossibly angry that it became a kind of tenderness until she turned around and asked, 'What's wrong? Don't you like my cathedral?'

'It's—' He spread his hands. What words could describe it? 'The planning, the building. How did you manage it?'

Ellisha's smile was the widest he'd ever seen. 'It's been a long time,' she conceded. 'But Phil and I have been talking about this from the start.'

'You talked to Avery about this?'

'Of course.'

'I mean, you and Avery. You talk?'

She looked at him in surprise. 'I told you.'

'No. You never mentioned it.'

'You've forgotten.'

He started to say that she had done no such thing, when Ellisha grabbed his hand and pulled him towards an elevator. 'Come on. I have something to show you.'

She took him to a cloud of a room, white billowing drapes, a single linen-spread table, silver set. Two ghost chairs of transparent resin. 'Do you like it?'

He nodded, bemused. 'What is this?'

'Dinner.'

'It's the middle of the night.'

'Is it?' For a moment she looked confused then her face relaxed. 'Time moves differently for me now.'

'What are you saying?'

'It's hard to explain. Duncan understands.'

He said nothing, but her words burned him in the way ice burns or frost bites. A knock on the door distracted them, and a Soul-Searcher entered carrying a silver tureen. She served them a pale mushroom soup in thin alabaster bowls, bowing to Ellisha, before leaving the room.

Peter found he was hungry. But after a few mouthfuls, he paused with his soupspoon halfway to his mouth. He was looking at Ellisha over the rim, consciously noting the deep hollows at her clavicles and the flat way the material of her dress hung from her chest. 'You've lost more weight.'

'Have I?' She frowned. 'Perhaps. I never seem to be hungry these days.' She sent her spoon in a lethargic path around the bowl. Silence crouched between them. Peter cleared his throat several times. The Soul-Searcher came in and cleared their plates then served a stew of vegetables, Jerusalem artichokes and jicama with tiny pearl onions. It smelled delicious, but Peter gave it a tentative poke with his fork. 'I think the chef has a theme.'

'Really?'

'You don't see it? Everything's a whiter shade of pale.'

'I only eat foods related to the moon now.'

He waited for her to laugh, to call him an asshole or a meathead. After a while he said, 'You're not serious.'

'A lot changed when you were away, Peter.' She was slicing a bit of artichoke into smaller and smaller bits. 'I didn't want to tell you. You won't understand.'

'Try me.'

'I became more spiritual.'

'Oh?' He tried to keep his voice neutral, but she pushed her plate away with an angry gesture. 'You don't believe me. Duncan said you wouldn't.'

'Duncan said it, did he? Because he's a champion, I suppose.'

'Because he's a soldier. Because he's looked at death so often it burned everything away, right down to the core. It carved rhymes on his bones.' She stopped speaking, but the muscles in her face tightened, as if she was trying to draw away from him without moving.

He fed a small piece of jicama into his mouth and chewed far longer than necessary to stop himself speaking, and only when he was in control, said carefully, 'I'm sorry.'

'Sorry?'

'Sorry for leaving you. These last months. You've been all alone when you needed me.'

She started to laugh then choked it back. 'Have you seen you?'

He had. The papery skin, the dark circles beneath his eyes. Yet, he was grateful for the sarcasm. There was something healing in it. 'You know, I almost brought something back for you.'

Some of the tightness around her mouth eased. 'What was it?'

'Not *it, who*.'

He told her about Tomás, describing in detail his funny little quirks—the frown of concentration between his brows when he listened to a story; the way he had of sneaking an extra treat from the table when he thought no-one was looking—sure that his description would make her love him the way he did.

But there was no reaction in her face. She was utterly silent. He had not been expecting this, and pressed on with heightened urgency. 'We could bring him here. It wouldn't be easy. We might have to use nannies. But royalty and celebrities manage to be public figures and have families at the same time. Why not us?' He leaned forward, his enthusiasm bubbling over. 'This is a godsend. A new story to capture the world's interest. A sacred family? You, me, Tomás. He really is the most amazing little boy once you get to know him.'

Her eyes were so sad. It was as though he were betraying her. 'Ellisha,' he said desperately. 'Isn't this what you want, what you've always wanted? To be a mother?'

For a moment he thought she might cry. She put her head back and blinked several times. Strange little noises escaped her throat, and it took him a second to realise that she was laughing. 'You don't see, do you?'

'See? See what?' He was irked by her levity, but it only seemed to amuse her more. She patted her abdomen, and he heard—inside his head he heard—the hollow echo of her womb.

'Haven't you realised, I am mother to everyone.'

Afterwards, they visited an observation deck at the top of the first pyramid. It was still dark outside, save for the canopy of stars. Ellisha put her head back and said, in enough of her old voice to make a poignant lump form in his throat, 'If you stare up long enough it's like falling into space. Come on!' She tugged his arm, drawing him towards a huge circular bed in the middle of the room.

He stepped forward eagerly, if a little mechanically, curiously aware of the automatic tread of his feet. His whole body aching yet somehow feeling unreal. A part of him stood outside of himself and observed the beauty of the woman who led him across the room towards the bed, her bones moving beneath the delicate ivory dress like the frail skeleton of a bird below its plumage.

Everything was perfect—the view, the stars, the bed set like an altar—yet he felt more artifice than charm. A thousand times he had stood on stage weaving illusion before watching eyes, but this felt less real, a technically brilliant movie set with an unconvincing script. He lay down next to Ellisha, shivering slightly and waiting for the magic to happen. In his ear, her breath came softly, 'Did you miss me?'

'Not once.'

'Jerk-off.'

'Jezebel.'

The insults hung in the air, but still he felt cold. The slither of her fingers on his thigh, then a pause. 'What's wrong?'

'Nothing.'

'I want you to love me.'

'I do. I will.'

She sat up, drawing the sheets around her shoulders, as though she could feel his chill. 'You don't love me.'

'Ellie! That's not true.'

'Not the way you used to.'

Her weakness strengthened him. Gears released beneath the surface and his hands came up, tearing away the sheets. But he could not quite let go the feeling that nothing was real. He stroked and kneaded and pounded his way across her body until blood-red skies edged with black began to throb behind his temples. Sweat formed on his forehead and his jaw was clenched so tight his teeth ached. Yet no matter how often she bucked beneath him or cried out, he was unable to possess her; something lonely in her voice kept shutting him out.

He felt himself softening and grunted and tore and held her struggling limbs until she managed to squirm away from him. 'Don't. You're hurting me.'

'Ellie. God, I'm sorry.' Reduced by shame, he pulled back, rolling over to sit up, hand over his mouth.

'It's okay. You didn't know.'

'It's not okay,' he said savagely. He felt a light hand on his shoulder and pulled away, unable to allow himself her understanding because he had known he was hurting and had enjoyed the sensation.

She was silent for a long time then she said softly, 'We've been apart too long. So much has happened.' Her hands found his shoulders and this time he didn't pull away. 'It's not your fault. You don't understand. You can't.'

He took a deep breath. 'What if I could?'

'Peter?' She reached around and put her hands in his, and he was aware of them, small and pulsing as though they were two quite separate creatures with heartbeats of their own.

He looked into her eyes. 'What if I could understand?'

She searched his face, then her eyes grew round. 'You've seen it too?'

'In *Bosquecillo Sagrado*. One night, I saw a crow. I think— I thought I dreamed it. But I wasn't dreaming. And I felt something. A presence.' Words inside his skull. *What am I doing? Do I believe what I'm saying?* Shaking his head: 'I don't know. It isn't the sort of thing you can put into words.'

He felt weakened by his confession and was just about to say, *Forget it, Ellie, it was all just a dream*, when she reached up and drew his head down to rest on her breasts, an old gesture that spoke, not to the man, but to what had come before the man, a language inscribed in flesh and symbol, and the sense of belonging to a universe that is utterly, sublimely within grasp. *Is this the secret of her magic?* he wondered? *An ability to make people feel loved.* He thought of asking out loud, but an immense peacefulness had descended upon him and, still wondering, he fell into a deep and kindly sleep.

A loud knocking on the door. Peter jerked out of a dream and flailed his arms towards Ellisha, who awoke with the startled jerk of a small animal. 'Who is it?' The door flew open and MacCaa stood on the threshold, motionless, as though some unnatural law prevented his crossing. His eyes darted straight to Ellisha.

'What is it, Duncan?'

He had that faraway look that usually augured poetry. 'The vagrant child lies bleeding in the burning hearth, an' the place o' reckoning is now a grave house.'

Peter squeezed his eyes shut, trying to establish whether some part of him was still dreaming. 'What?'

But Ellisha was sitting bolt upright, the sheets bunched in her fists. 'Didn't you hear? Mzazi has fallen.'

CHAPTER 30

THEY LEFT WITHOUT CEREMONY OR warning. 'What about Perdita?' Peter asked.

'She'd try to stop me.'

'And she'd be right. It's dangerous, Ellie. MacCaa would say the same thing.'

'Duncan is on my side. Are you?'

They left from a small private airport situated a few miles from the Cathedral and hidden by a natural outcrop of rock. The take-off was smooth but a short time later a worried-looking steward approached. He was wringing his hands and seemed unable to work up the courage to speak until Ellisha snapped, 'Spit it out.'

'I don't know how to say it, ma'am. The pilot, he says—'

'Yes?'

'He says Perdita has contacted him by radio. She's— I don't know how to tell you. She's ordered the plane to turn back.'

Something retreated from Ellisha's face and she spoke with an eerie lack of emotion. 'Go back and ask the pilot a question.'

The Spark was frightened, but he nodded eagerly. 'Yes, ma'am.'

'Ask him if he answers to Perdita or to me?'

'Ma'am.'

The Spark hurried away and the flight continued without interruption.

Once on the ground they travelled in convoy, heavily armed trucks on all sides. And for most of the journey there was a strange jarring sense of normality to everything. It was the Africa of Peter's memory, the Africa Ellisha had helped to build. Except that Ellisha sat stony-faced beside him. No sunburst dress this time but a Kevlar vest and a helmet held on her lap.

They were less than a mile from Mzazi when they saw it: a pall of smoke and below it a ragged outline, like a row of broken teeth snarling at the sky, which was all that was left of the shining towers. The sight filled his eyes and made his stomach constrict. But it was the smell more than the sight that made all other thoughts impossible. It hit them as they pulled up to the entrance of the city.

Acrid, the scent of scorched things and ruin, then something sickly under it all, almost familiar—burning sugar, popcorn, candyfloss— but underneath that lay rot and decay, sulphur, ammonia, cadaverine, putrescine, copper and iron, blood smells, death smells. Soul had been murdered in this place. Peter's gorge rose as though ambushed, and he grabbed for the alcohol wipes. The bodies. The order to clear them countermanded. *No, Peter, I want to see them. I want the world to see me seeing them.*

They made it through the broken entrance. Ellisha wanted to drive straight to the soularium, but there were too many bodies littering the road. The convoy was called to a halt and slowly they climbed down, the guards forming a ring around them, assault rifles slung from their shoulders. They were hard-faced boys, picked for their combat experience, and they were fanatically loyal to MacCaa. Good men, Peter told himself. We will be safe with them. But the air pulsed with evil, and he had a primitive desire to be inside.

Up ahead there was a door, still strangely intact while everything around lay smashed and defiled. Ellisha took a step towards it, but Peter put out a restraining hand. 'Wait till MacCaa clears the area.'

The sun grew hotter. A photographer pointed his lens at Ellisha but Peter made a cutting motion with his hand to arrest the motion. *She's not ready.* He could see beads of perspiration on her forehead.

And when she glanced up at him and said brokenly, *I can't*, it was no more than he had been expecting.

'You can.'

'I don't have that kind of strength.'

He wanted to say, you do, you just don't know it. Instead, he said, 'Remember the tree? The old hawthorn they cut down near the university?' A blank look then a nod. 'Remember how you felt?'

'I wanted to kill them with my bare hands for their ugly stupid blindness.'

'Then how do you feel now that they've cut down Ignis Dei's burning tree?' Before she could respond, MacCaa's shadow fell between them. 'Did you find anything?' Peter asked anxiously. MacCaa's face expressed nothing, but he fell to one knee before Ellisha, head bowed.

'Duncan!' She took hold of his shoulders and raised him up, looking at him with a half-formed smile, while Peter watched, a fierce pain in his heart, wondering if MacCaa truly understood that his role as consort was symbolic. But all MacCaa said was, 'Nae shame in turnin' aboot.'

Ellisha was biting her lip and her eyes were moving rapidly. It was clear that she was being pulled in opposite directions and she was blind to either end of the rope. He watched tensely for the moment of her decision, heralded by a contraction of the pupils and a little shake of her head. She looked up at MacCaa. 'We go in.'

'Right.' MacCaa saluted. 'Follow me.'

With MacCaa in the lead, they began to pick their way across the bodies towards the deeper horror that lay ahead, and Peter found fragments from his father's pulpit running through his head. *Yea, though I walk through the valley of the shadow of death, I will fear no evil.* The words did not comfort. The Old Testament scribe, writing a millennium before Christ, had envisaged a dark, sombre place, the antithesis to light. But in this place Hell was glaringly, blindingly bright, so that all around the air felt like a white scream that bleached out the red details of death and shrivelled the twisted fallen bodies into shadows. He found it impossible to step over them without thinking, *So little am I.*

A glance at Ellisha showed every muscle in her face was taut. *What is she thinking?* He tried to take her arm, but the rigor of her muscles made it like touching marble, and his fingers slid away.

Progress was slow and tense, the guards with their fingers near the triggers of the assault rifles, the smallest sound making everyone jerk to a wary standstill.

They neared the body of a young woman, face-down, her limbs splayed as though she was trying to swim into the red earth. And as they looked, there was a wild cry like a shriek of death over their heads. MacCaa pulled Ellisha behind him and the guards trained their guns on the sky. But it was only a pied crow frantically beating its wings as it rose from the tangled folds of the woman's headscarf.

Shit! There was uneasy laughter amongst the guards as they lowered their guns.

'Thought we'd caught ourselves a bit of Soul trying to make a run for it.'

The Spark, who made the comment, was only a boy, big and dumb-looking, but Ellisha turned on him with such silent fury that he cowered like a whipped dog. When the party moved on he lagged a little, head bowed with shame.

There were no bodies inside the soularium, but a cold, heavy smell of death hung about the place. The furnishings were all gone or smashed, and the roof had partially caved in, but at the far end of the room an old man was sitting on a broken chair with a portable desk on his lap. As soon as he saw Ellisha, he rose painfully to his feet and shuffled brokenly towards them, blinking in the light of the torches the guards had trained upon him. Peter stared without recognition.

But Ellisha moved forward at once and took his hands. 'Salehe, you're alive.'

Salehe? Peter glanced from Ellisha then back to the man. He recalled him now as the interpreter who had first guided them around the camp. But he was a young man, surely. Looking more closely it was there for the seeing. Not grey hair, but hair streaked with ash, those lines, smears of dirt and sleeplessness. A distillation of horror had heaped decades on his head, and the lop-sided grin he bestowed upon them now was interrupted with the gaping holes of missing teeth. His words came through them in a hoarse whisper.

'I still hear.'

Ellisha frowned. 'Hear what? What do you hear?'

'The screaming.'

Ellisha took his hands. 'Where are the survivors? Are they here? Are they hiding?'

Salehe's jaw worked, grating back and forth until he choked out, 'Not many. A few. They ran away.'

'And the authorities? What are they saying?' Ellisha glanced back over her shoulder. 'We passed the government office, but it was empty.'

'No-one sees him. For two days, he is not there.'

Peter glanced at MacCaa, but his face was closed. Ellisha was breathing very hard. She opened then shut her mouth several times before asking, 'Where is Violet? Violet Bello?' And, when he still did not answer, she waved her hand at the stage. 'She gave sermons in this building.'

Slowly, he shook his head. 'She was a good woman, but they cut her down.'

Ellisha went rigid, but controlled herself. 'Diallo,' she said, and it was not a question. Salehe bowed his grey-streaked head with the shame of the survivor. 'We thought his Soul is going to save him, that maybe he could save others.'

Salehe started to tremble with the memory, and pity drew Peter closer. But MacCaa, who was nearer, laid a hand on the man's shoulder. No words were said, but Salehe recovered himself sufficiently to speak.

'We knew things were getting bad. We heard things. Rumours. In the churches and the mosques, they are condemning us. They are saying we are godless liars. A good friend came here, to Mzazi—I knew him because he came here to trade horses—and he came to me and said, "I have to tell you, Salehe, you are all going to die." When I hear this, I cannot breathe. But I knew he was telling the truth. He is a rich man and he knows people in the government. He said to me, "Ignis Dei people are not liked. They are growing too powerful. They want to change things. They will not let you change things."'

His eye twitched and he rubbed it absently with the back of his hand as if brushing away an annoying insect. It was clear to Peter that Salehe was very near collapse. *But he wants us to know, wants to paint a coherent picture of an event that defied all definitions of coherence. Poor man. Poor man.*

'I went to my wife,' Salehe continued. 'I said to her, what shall we do? And she says we must go to Diallo. A man with a Soul will know what to do. Diallo, he tells us we must be strong, that Ellisha will not let bad things happen. But Violet hears and she says a Soul is not a weapon. It is something to be protected. She says she will make calls.'

'Calls? Who did she call?' Ellisha asked.

Salehe shook his head. 'I don't know. But it was too late. They came that night. Many men, and there were soldiers and policemen with them. They called us out. They let the ones who said they were Christians and the ones who said they were Muslims go. But the rest of us, they made gather outside the soularium. There were many women there and children too.

'Violet came out with Diallo, and she asked them who they were? She asked them what authority they had? One of the soldiers told her that they were the Dhdimwanamke.'

Ellisha glanced swiftly at Peter to see if he understood; he shook his head. Salehe rubbed his eye again. 'We did not know them. The word is made up. It means something like *against-the-woman*. And the soldier said that they were here on the authority of God, and that we were renouncing God.

'Violet spoke to him very softly. She asked them how we could renounce what had not yet come to pass? And Diallo, he said to him, "Why don't you come inside, my brother? We will talk." But the man started laughing and he said he did not talk with women-worshippers. And suddenly they were cutting and clubbing people. There must have been a signal, but I did not hear it. Just the screaming that became like one long scream. They cut down Violet and then they were everywhere, and the people were running. But they had us surrounded.

'I lost my wife. She disappeared. Then something hit me on the head. I fell and it was black. And when I woke up everything is very still. The men are gone. There were two bodies on top of me, and I know I have been very lucky. They saved me.

'I got up. And everywhere there are bodies with their skulls broken. I think in their minds the Dhdimwanamke thought they were crushing our souls.' He broke off and licked his lips.

There's more, Peter thought. *Please, don't let there be more.* Salehe was trembling, in deep shock. *Thought himself free of the Void, poor bastard, and now it's reared up and swallowed him.*

Salehe breathed in deeply several times. 'This morning. I try to take an accounting of the dead. Many I cannot recognise, but I try. Sometimes you remember a man's ring or—or—' He broke off to fight an internal battle. And, just as Peter thought he could not go on, the words came out in explosive spurts, forcing their way through an air-lock of grief. 'Or I remember a woman's shoes. Red shoes. I bought those shoes myself. Because my wife has never seen anything like them. Parisian shoes here in Mzazi. She likes to joke. She called them her "sole miracle". Then, today, I see these shoes—'

He drew his hand over his face. Beads of perspiration glistened on his brow, but he shivered and continued, 'Today I find my wife. Her skull is smashed. I cannot look at her face. But she is still wearing her shoes. I stayed with her a long time. And I am thinking—' he looked hopefully into Ellisha's face '—surely the parts of Soul she has gathered are not ready to be taken to the Void, and that they will come to me and I will feel her inside me. But she is not here.' He thumped his chest with a closed fist. 'Nothing. Soul seeks Soul. You said that. But where is she? Where is my wife?'

They stood, facing this man's grief, and listened to the last echoes of his words dying away in that hollow room, until they were standing in the great vacuum of their own silence. Peter cut his eyes towards Ellisha, but she made no move to speak. MacCaa stood erect and expressionless. And it flashed into Peter's mind that here was a man who had been a soldier, who had killed and only thought it part of a day's work. Then, looking at the shadow of horror on Salehe's face, he was suddenly glad MacCaa was with them.

Salehe had begun to sway slightly. The silence had woken something desperate in him. 'Where is my wife?' he asked again. Then louder. 'Where is my wife?'

Ellisha looked sick. Tears filled her eyes, and she turned to Peter, as if she expected to find the answer written on his face. There was accusation in her look. *Did we do this? Is this our doing?* All the empty words he had been about to say died in his hollowed-out heart, and Ellisha watched their whimpering extinction, jaw clenched, before she turned and fled the building, hands pressed against her mouth.

He went after her, closely followed by MacCaa and the rest of the young soldier Sparks. 'Ellisha! Ellisha! Where are you going? It's not safe.'

She kept walking.

'Ellisha?'

A look thrown over her shoulder. 'I'm going to address the world.'

∞

For a city designed to be torn down and moved in a matter of days, the door in front of Peter looked remarkably solid. Nevertheless, he reached down and shook the door handle. 'Ellisha, let me in.'

Ellisha had climbed to the highest point of the most intact tower, barricading herself inside a small room at the top, while Peter pleaded with her from the staircase.

'This is a mistake.' he rattled the door handle again. Inside he could hear the scrape of metal on wood. Ellisha was setting up the equipment for broadcast. She had gone outside only long enough to demand that cameras and laptops be fetched from the convoy. MacCaa didn't like it. He wanted his Prophetess on a plane far from harm, but Ellisha had silenced him with a look that would have scorched Peter to ashes but only narrowed MacCaa's eyes and turned him about to do her bidding.

Peter drummed his knuckles against the door. 'Ellie!' In a calmer voice he tried reason. 'This is not worse than Andra Pradesh or *Bosquecillo Sagrado*. This is just a reminder that our work with Soul is more important than ever.' Near the top of the door he spied a crack in the plywood. On tiptoe, he pressed an eyeball against it and squinted through vision rimmed by the skewed edges of the peep-hole. Ellisha was sitting at the centre of a tiny room, laptop perched on a rusted folding table, which must have been the scrape of metal he had heard as she dragged it into place. Bright knives of light, filtering through from the smashed roof, held her in a luminous cage where she sat hunched, head bowed, hair covering her face.

'Ellisha, please.' *What have I done, bringing you here? Have I broken you?* 'Ellisha. Ellie. This was a bad idea. Come out, please. Let's go home.'

She looked up, hair opening like a curtain, and he thought she was looking at him. But the camera was between them, and the eyes he thought were seeing him were staring blindly out into the world. Her ribcage swelled on the verge of something, and he tensed for the unexpected. It came. She lifted a packet of Marlboros from the table—*Where did they come from?*—and tapped it against her palm until one fell out.

'What on earth are you doing? You don't smoke. You hate smoking.' *Didn't she?* Detested it as much as he did. Yet, now he thought of it, once or twice catching the biting scent of tobacco on her skin and in her hair. Light-hearted enquiries met with a shrug. *So? Musta been a smoker in the room.*

He watched as she took a long drag, letting the smoke slowly escape her lips. Bars of light and shadow striped her face. *What is she doing, calming herself down, psyching herself up?* With a start, he realised that the camera was already rolling. This was deliberate. No remoteness clouding her manner now. Her whole face was a wound. This was the hidden face of the deity, the dark side of the moon.

'Ellisha!' He said it one last time. The susurration of the sound barely audible, but she looked up and, for a split second, he felt her waver. Details magnified: the faint whirr of the laptop, the shadows, like cave paintings, on the wall. Then the dam bursting. His priestess of the Slumbering God opening her mouth and outpouring a wild torrent of white-hot fury.

'You think I'm here to cry, to weep and beat my breast about Mzazi? You think I'm here, as a mother, breaking her heart over her dead children?'

She glanced down to flick a furry tail of ash into a receptacle below his eyeline then looked squarely into the lens. 'I can hear your thoughts.' A finger stabbed at her temple. 'I can hear them in here. You're thinking, it's gone. Destroyed. I killed it. You think you can come here and destroy Soul? Is that what you think? That you are doing God's Will? That you are making God proud? That you have become His Will Made Flesh?'

She took another long drag. Blue involutions of smoke curling from the corners of her mouth. And when she spoke again her voice was hoarse with pain. 'Come back. Back to Mzazi, if you dare. See what I see. Dead children. Was that God's Will? Burned buildings, smashed walls. God's Will? Bodies rotting in the sun. HIS WILL?

'This wasn't a Divine Directive. A command from the clouds. You didn't act for God when you came to Mzazi with your knives and your machetes and your blazing torches. When you tore down the sacred grove. When you smashed the temples. You weren't fiery angels. You weren't on His Side. You men of God, who don't even know how to be human. You were destroying the gentle, good, righteous vessels of Soul. You were destroying God.'

Again a pause, the Marlboro held between her fingers, like a tiny sceptre. She tilted her head slightly, as though listening. 'But I can feel them. I can feel all the broken fragments you scattered on the winds over Mzazi. And it isn't just me who feels them. All over the world, every Spark, every living being with an ounce of Soul hears them screaming.

'But, here's the thing, here's what all you Soulless heaps of empty flesh, don't understand. You can't destroy Soul. Soul is the dark energy of the universe. It's there whether you want it or not. You can't smash

Soul or burn Soul or tear Soul to pieces. You can choose to live without Soul, but you can't stop Soul gathering. You can't hold back what's coming.

'Soul's out there, opening like a flower in the darkness. Out there, in time out of mind. The Spark. Igniting the fire that burns in the chemical reactions of every living creature that crawls out of the mud, eyes upwards to behold the awakening universe.'

She drew in a shuddering breath. 'You think you can stop that?

'Go on! Call to your God-Who-Is-Not-Here. He can't stop us. He can't save you from the annihilation that's coming. He can't save you from the Void. You, who have shut out Soul. You, who have turned your backs on the Eternal. You will crumble. You will sink back into the mud, forgotten. And we, who have felt Soul, and opened up to Soul, and drawn Soul towards us, will dance upon your bones.'

CHAPTER 31

THEY WAITED FOR HER AT the bottom of the broken steps, Peter, MacCaa and Salehe, three silent men standing amongst the dust motes and the stench of death. Salehe's troubled eyes made a constant journey between the floor and the topmost step then back again. Ellisha had stopped talking about an hour ago and the silence was more appalling than her wrath. Peter tried to imitate MacCaa's grizzled grey-wolf stoicism, but he was a man made for movement and after a few moments he began to pace.

Something crunched under his sole. Glass? But there was scuttling at the perimeter of his vision, and he pulled his foot back with a sharp cry. On the floor, illumined by a shaft of light, was a greenish gold mess.

'Scarab beetle.' MacCaa said. 'They feed aff the deid.'

Before Peter could ask him how he had obtained such knowledge there was the scrape of a door at the top of the stairs, and all three men trained their vision on the staircase. Ellisha came down slowly. Her steps were heavy; she seemed exhausted, yet there was a radiance about her as though strange energies were moving under her skin.

Peter's brain was so crowded with everything he wanted to say, he managed only to murmur, 'Oh, Ellie.'

She looked at him strangely, almost coldly. *I let her come here. I let her do this.* But she only looked over their heads and said, 'Oh, hi Perdita.'

'What is going on?' For a split second Perdita's angular figure was outlined in the doorway, then she strode across the room, sending dust genies flurrying at her feet. An entourage of assistants, techs, lawyers, trouble-shooters, Soul-Searchers and security men followed her into the room. 'Who organized this?' Perdita looked from face to face.

Ellisha opened her mouth, but it was MacCaa who stepped forward. 'It wuz me.'

'Thank you.' Perdita's nostrils gave a delicate quiver. 'You're fired.'

Just like that. Another career severed by the blade of Perdita's tongue. Peter had witnessed it before. The second where a droplet of time hung motionless from a branch. The limb severed and cauterized before the patient had time to acknowledge it was gone. Perdita was already moving on when Ellisha said softly, 'No.'

Perdita froze. 'No?'

'Duncan stays.'

'I'm afraid that's impossible. MacCaa has put you in danger. Mr Avery would never allow it.'

There was a terrifying calmness in Ellisha's face, a new unrecognisable expression that had not been there before. It penetrated her voice and made the words burn. 'I don't answer to Phil. I answer to Soul.' She put her hand gently, lovingly on MacCaa's arm. 'Duncan stays.'

Perdita's expression froze, but Peter sensed there was movement below the surface, dark shadows flowing under ice. She glanced up suddenly, looking from MacCaa to the security men she had brought with her. Peter tensed. *Are they going to drag him away? Here? In front of Ellie?* There was something of legend about MacCaa, but even he couldn't take ten men. Ellisha looked sick, but she held her ground and finally Perdita's face relaxed. Her smile opened, like a slit, and she said, 'I see. Well, we had better secure the area.'

'We huv men here,' MacCaa said. 'And ah kin have more boots on the ground in an hour.'

They made a table out of planks, balancing them on a couple of old crates that Salehe pulled from the back. That the man was at breaking point was clear from the violent trembling of his hands, but he refused all offers of help with a shake of the head—*Soul is in more pain than I am*—and Peter was impressed by his quiet dignity and refusal to wear the garb of victim.

Once the table was ready they sat on the floor. There were no cushions to be had and all the benches had been smashed. Perdita gave Peter a quick, unreadable look and murmured, 'For God's sake, let us sit upon the ground and tell sad stories of the death of kings.' Then she calmly lowered herself to the dusty floor.

When they were all seated, Perdita took the lead. 'I think we can agree that the latest broadcast by the Prophetess went astonishingly well.'

There was only the tiniest of hesitations before unanimous agreement, nodding heads, a titter of applause. Perdita allowed it to fade away before adding, 'Of course it will take some time to absorb the shock. To see first-hand that you are not—how shall we put it—universally loved.' She made a gesture with her hand as though words were insufficient.

'I was never that naïve,' Ellisha said tightly. Her nails were digging into the edge of the planks.

'Ah.' Perdita sat back. 'You've come to terms with the collaboration.'

Collaboration? Amongst the Sparks? Unthinkable. Ellisha didn't speak, but her eyes threw themselves wide with shock, and she turned to Peter with such a look of betrayal that he was forced to shake his head violently. *I didn't know. Oh, Ellie, you can't think I knew.*

Ellisha was looking back at Perdita. 'You're wrong. You've got it all wrong.'

'I'm afraid not. Do you think it was coincidence that the government official was nowhere to be found two days before the attack? That Security were given an order to disband? Clearly there was inside help.'

There was a low groan from the end of the table. Salehe had his head in his hands. 'We saw these things. We did nothing. We did not listen to Soul.'

Peter felt the urge to get up and comfort the man, to reassure him, but he couldn't move. Ellisha was ashen, and he felt his anger flare. *What is this? Some cruel game?* Very deliberately he took control of the conversation, explaining his strategy, favouring a diplomatic approach involving the government. 'We don't want things to spiral out of control.'

Salehe interrupted. 'But the government is broadcasting lies. It says this is a flare-up between ethnic divisions within Mzazi. They want people to think minority groups and intertribal politics are to blame.'

Peter nodded. 'They're frightened. The world is turning upside down. And the Prophetess is the cause. They've lashed out because they feel cornered. Because they feel they're losing power.'

Ellisha hadn't spoken, and when his own voice fell silent, time hung quivering between them. He waited for it to dissolve, waited for the hardness to leave her face, but she only shook her head and said in a puzzled voice, 'Soul turned against Soul?'

It was not the encouragement he had hoped for, but neither was it an outright no, and so he set about discussing how an approach might be made. There were innumerable difficulties facing them if they were to base themselves in Mzazi, and his first thought was to relocate, but Ellisha had left the table, claiming the need to "clear her head", taking MacCaa with her for protection, and he sensed the danger of pushing her.

Instead he worked on a plan with Perdita and found, to his surprise, that they were of a mind. There would be sanctions. Concessions would be demanded. And, beneath the "show of force" there would be the usual bribes; certain individuals would find themselves removed; the waters would close and the river would flow on.

Running footsteps. Peter looked up, startled. One of the Soul-Searchers burst in, robes tangled with running. 'The Prophetess. She's unwell.'

Perdita and Peter rose as one and went to investigate. They found Ellisha in the next room, slumped in MacCaa's arms. She turned at the sound of their entry and tried to stand up, but her legs buckled and MacCaa caught her. There was no need to explain. 'Headache?'

Her eyes were scrunched shut, but she nodded and said faintly, 'A bad one.'

'We need to get her to a hospital,' Perdita said briskly. 'I'll arrange a helicopter.'

But seeing how Ellisha's hands made rigid fists forcibly grasping the pain and trying to keep it outside her body, Peter shook his head. 'We can't. She can't be moved.'

Perdita stared at him through the dust-filled light, nose wrinkling at the pervasive stench of death, but she nodded. 'I'll see what can be done.'

✖

Perdita found a doctor, a Spark from God-knows-where, but he was there within the hour, a small, dignified-looking man who had been fortunate enough to be visiting family when the attack took place. Peter waited for him by the smashed gateway that had once opened to welcome people to Mzazi. On top of the broken columns, MacCaa's men were stationed. Their weapons were out and at the ready and they constantly scanned the landscape.

The doctor, whose name was Boro, arrived in a beat up four by four driven by another man. Dr Boro jumped down and the driver sped away. Peter hurried towards him, but two of MacCaa's men arrived first. Guns pointed, they made him open his bag then take off his jacket. Peter broke into a run. 'Wait! Stop! He's with me.'

The younger of the two Sparks glanced towards him, but they continued their search. Raising his voice, Peter repeated, 'He's with me.'

'The MacCaa's orders, sir.'

When it was finished, Peter apologised. 'I'm sorry. Everyone's on edge.'

Boro didn't answer. His eyes were wide, but his mouth had pulled into a tight, grim line. The Void was not new to Dr Boro.

They found Ellisha lying on an improvised bed of blankets. Her eyes were squeezed shut and she was clutching MacCaa's hand. Peter felt hot tongues of jealousy licking inside his chest, but MacCaa gently extricated himself and left the room without a word. Boro's eyes followed him with the first look of surprise he had evinced so far.

Ellisha gave a moan. 'Peter?'

He fell to his knees. 'I'm here.'

'Where's Perdita?'

'I don't know. I think she must have moved the Sparks to another location.'

'Find her. I want to know what's going on.'

Dr Boro had crouched down on the opposite side and was taking Ellisha's pulse. He looked up at Peter and nodded. 'It would be best to give me a few moments alone to examine the Prophetess. I will find you when I am done.' His voice had a quiet kind of reverence about it that Peter felt he could trust. He nodded and, with a quick squeeze to Ellisha's hand which made her wince, he took his leave.

He found Perdita alone in the remains of Violet Belo's sitting room. She was looking out through the smashed panes of a window, and Peter watched her from the doorway, something rooting him to the spot, until he cried out, 'We did this.'

Perdita didn't turn around. 'You mustn't think that way.'

'Why not?'

'Because it isn't true. Ellisha is a far more powerful person than you give her credit for.'

'But it was my doing. I let her come here. I persuaded her to stay.' He gestured helplessly and Perdita turned to face him, resting her hands on the sill and leaning back.

'Don't be too sure of yourself. Not every version of a person is the direct consequence of external influence. Ellisha has vast hidden depths. Depths she's only just beginning to explore.'

Something in the way she said it made Peter blurt, 'You wanted her here. You wanted her to see she'd been betrayed.'

'Did I? As I recall, you brought her here. I knew nothing about it.'

Dr Boro appeared, and Perdita and Peter turned to him expectantly. Unable to wait, Peter burst out, 'How is she? Can I see her?'

'She is resting. I gave her a shot of Dilaudid, which I was fortunate enough to have in my bag. I thought to use it here on the survivors.' Boro's eyes wandered to the door then he shook his head sorrowfully. 'But there is no-one… no-one.' He appeared to become aware that his pain was showing and drew it back into himself. His face became stiff, professional once again. 'But it is, of course, an honour to help the Prophetess.'

'Quite,' Perdita said. 'Perhaps you could tell us more about her condition.'

Dr Boro nodded, but it soon became apparent that his talents lay more in his technical knowledge rather than his bedside manner. He faced them tensely and launched into a long and convoluted explanation that contained terms such as temporary paraesthesia of the right arm, left superior temporal gyrus, medial prefrontal cortex in peri-ventricular areas and Glasgow coma scale.

At a certain point Peter found himself saying, 'Voices?' in answer to a question he barely knew he had been asked.

'Has the Prophetess ever mentioned hearing voices?'

'What? No. Never.'

'Visual disturbances?'

He hesitated. Should he say? It was nothing. Something they rarely spoke of. Something to make fun of. He took a breath. 'Sometimes. She's mentioned it.'

'How would you define sometimes?'

'I don't know. Now and again.'

'Monthly—' when he didn't answer '—weekly?'

'I—'

'The Prophetess has described an increase in the episodes over the last few months,' Perdita said.

Peter stared. 'She told you?'

'Why wouldn't she?'

Dr Borro clasped his chin and nodded to himself. Peter noticed that the nails on his hand were very clean but bitten down, small bulbs of flesh protruded beyond them. 'Did the Prophetess describe what she was seeing?'

'Shadows mostly. Sometimes a figure, human in shape.'

'But not human?'

Perdita shrugged. 'It was hard for her to say. Less than human, but also something more. She couldn't put it into words. There was a feeling of presence. Of something revealing itself.'

'She shouldn't be eating only white food,' Peter interrupted angrily. 'There aren't enough nutrients. It's making her ill.'

'The Prophetess' diet is carefully monitored,' Perdita replied. Her eyes were still on Dr Boro.

'What does it mean? What's happening to her?' Peter heard the distressed edge of his interjection. Dr Boro heard it too; he pulled his lips in and raised his brows then surprised Peter by turning to Perdita and saying quite harshly, 'There is something you are not telling me.'

Perdita held his gaze for several seconds, before turning and going over to the door. She opened it, and for a moment Peter wondered if she was simply going to leave, but she stared into the corridor, satisfying herself that it was empty, then closed the door and turned briskly back to face them.

'What I am about to tell you has the highest level of classification.'

Dr Boro nodded gravely and, after a moment's hesitation, Peter followed suit.

'Good.' Perdita held them in suspense a fraction longer then said, 'You should know that the Prophetess underwent a thorough physical examination a few days ago.'

Peter stiffened. *We had dinner; she didn't say a thing.* He felt Perdita watching his reaction and forced himself to say, 'Go on.'

'A number of brain scans were done and the findings were interesting to say the least.'

'In what way?'

'There are certain structural abnormalities which are inconsistent with the original scans taken in Scotland.'

Peter recalled those scans. A formality, Avery had called them. Necessary medical checks to ensure that they were fit for the rigours of being on the road. But Perdita was still speaking and he forced his mind to focus.

'There is a small but significant reduction in the length of the PCS.'

'PCS?'

Perdita made a deferential gesture towards Dr Boro, who explained. 'A brain structure called the paracingulate sulcus. It is the extreme frontal area of the medial prefrontal cortex.'

'Meaning what?'

Perdita's thin lips lengthened in a rare smile. 'We believe that it helps individuals monitor and regulate reality. Research shows that

Vietnam veterans who had been injured in this area often reported experiences of a mystical nature.'

The chambers of Peter's heart were filling with icy fluid. Barely able to form the words, he said hoarsely, 'Are you implying that Ellisha is delusional?'

A fleeting glitter lit Perdita's eyes. 'Changes are not necessarily indicative of deterioration.'

And Dr Boro said cautiously, 'You are saying there is more to it than pathology?'

Perdita walked over to a sofa haemorrhaging its entrails across the floor and perched on the edge. She folded her arms across her chest. 'There has been a lot of research on this subject, Ignis Dei-funded research. Of course the findings are still in their preliminary stages, but there are certain signs… certain indications that alterations in this area of the brain may open what might be called, a "door of perception". A pathway giving the individual access to a kind of consciousness not accessible to normal people.'

Peter massaged his temple. 'You're saying we don't understand what the Prophetess is experiencing?'

'No.' Something altered in Perdita's face, a strange look that made the back of his neck prickle. 'I mean that we can never understand. This might be a sign that she's evolving. That she's going beyond us.'

CHAPTER 32

FOR THE NEXT HOUR PETER paced up and down, unable to settle. He wandered the broken streets of Mzazi, even though he had been warned not to do so, haunted by Perdita's words. From the outset his belief had been lukewarm. What did it matter if any of it was real, if he gave people hope and the ability to step back from the Void? *But I felt something in Bosquecillo Sagrado. And Ellisha is changing. There's no denying it any more.* He stopped short, afraid of where his thoughts were leading him.

A group of Sparks with burning tree tattoos marched past him. MacCaa had made good his promise to put boots on the ground. Wherever he went hard-faced young men and women were already occupying all the high points, assault rifles pointed and at the ready. But still, he felt death following him as he made his way across the small plaza, stopping for a moment to get his bearings outside the remains of the school.

Diallo had taken them around it. He had been so proud. Peter remembered him waving his prosthetic hands at the neat, well-equipped classrooms. 'We are making Soul stronger here.' Then he'd laughed, a young man with his whole life ahead of him. The memory hit Peter viciously in the solar plexus, taking the wind out of him, and he grasped at a broken doorframe trying to regain his breath. As he stood there, two armoured cars rolled past. He followed them uneasily with his eyes until his toe, scratching in the dust, unearthed something. A discarded cigarette butt, presumably dropped by one of the Sparks. But it brought to life Ellisha's face in his mind's eye, plumes of smoke escaping the corners of her mouth, a modern-day Pythia shrouded in fumes. *I'm missing something,* he thought, but couldn't explain why he thought it.

'Reverend Kelso.'

Dr Boro appeared out of the dazzle of light.

'El—The Prophetess, is she all right?'

'Yes. Yes.' Dr Boro's hands, with their bitten nails, came up to placate. 'She woke in some discomfort and so I have administered another shot. She is sleeping for now and I thought you would wish to sit with her.'

On entering the room, he became aware of two things. The first was Ellisha. She was now lying on an army-style cot—which had been brought in from God-knows-where—looking lost against the sterile whiteness of the pillows and sheets, a plaintive shadow falling across a drift of snow. And the second was that MacCaa had been in the room. How he knew he could not have said, but some instinct warned him of the man's presence. A ghost of the scents which always hung around MacCaa? Mist and dampness and rotting leaves. But he was not there now, and so he crept across the room and sat down on the single chair at Ellisha's side, not daring to say her name.

She was asleep, her arm attached to an IV bag which darted a shining tentacle into one of her veins, and he sat by her bed quietly waiting. He lost sense of the passage of time, marking the hours only by the cramping in his legs and listening to her soft whimpers and half-realised groans. He started up whenever they drew together into something like speech, pressing his ear close to her mouth and trying to hear what she was saying. But only a sibilant hiss of nonsense leaked out, and the meaning remained alien and impenetrable: Elvish, Atlantean, Syldavian.

He watched the rise and fall of her chest until, hypnotized by the movement, it became impossible to look away for superstitious fear that it might stop. He had a great desire to be doing something useful, and yet a terrible sense of inertia held him in place, preventing him even from pacing up and down. And slowly, numbness descended upon him, little by little, drifting down like snow, until he slipped over the rim of consciousness into a twilight world that was neither waking nor sleeping.

Darkness fell. Then came light. He remained in the chair. Nothing changed. Without Ellisha everything froze. Time stood still until, awareness slowly dawning. He realised Ellisha's eyes were open and she was looking at him.

Startled from perpetual anticipation, he sat rock-still, a stone man trapped on a plinth. Her expression was glassy; she seemed to be looking at something further and beyond that he couldn't see. He watched, hardly daring to breathe, while her pupils gradually gathered awareness and it was once again Ellisha looking out through them.

He leaned forward and stroked her hair. 'How are you?'

Her voice came out painfully. 'I'm not sure. I don't know what's happening to me.'

Reaching for one of her hands, he found it limp and unresponsive. He had to squeeze it to be sure it was there. 'It was too much. All that pain and death.'

Her frown silenced him. 'No, that wasn't it. I've seen as bad, worse even. But it made me feel strange. It made me feel a way I'd never felt before.'

'You were angry. It was an attack on everything we stand for.'

But she cut him a look. 'I've been angry before. And being angry brought on headaches. But not like this.' She retreated a distance into herself. Finally, she said, 'I saw things.'

'What?'

Her eyes had grown hot and bright. 'I don't know if I can explain. At least not yet. It was luminous … Numinous.' Her left hand moved in agitated patterns on the white sheets. 'I don't know how to explain it. *Can* you explain the sky to a blind man or Mozart to the deaf?'

'Ellisha,' Peter said cautiously. 'You've been under a lot of strain. And the doctor gave you powerful drugs. You're bound to feel strange.'

'It's more than strange. I felt as though I was filling up with something. No, that's wrong. I felt… as though I was on the brink of something. That something was going to be revealed to me. Soon.'

His scalp prickled. 'What kind of thing?'

'I don't know. A strange thing. Something I've known all along, deep down. I thought someone was here, talking to me about it. And I knew who it was—' a frown— 'But now I don't.'

Peter's joy was rapidly being replaced with alarm. Carefully, he said, 'Ellisha, do you think you were dreaming?'

Her frown deepened. 'A dream?' She turned away from him and looked down at her hands. After a while she said uncertainly, 'I suppose… a dream?' She closed her eyes.

He bent forward and kissed her on her forehead. The skin was clammy. 'You have too big a heart. You have done too much. Tried to save too many.' He stroked her face. 'You need to rest.'

A sharp rap at the door and Perdita entered. Her eyes met Ellisha's and, for a split second, something unguarded looked out. Then she said quickly. 'Soul seeks Soul.'

'Soul seeks Soul,' Ellisha responded weakly.

'I'm glad you have recovered. I'm afraid I need to borrow Peter for a bit.'

'I'm not going anywhere.'

'You need to see this.' And something in her tone made him force himself out of the chair and follow her from the room.

Perdita had set up a communications centre in one of the broken classrooms. Dust and debris had been swept away and someone had managed to get the power working. A huddle of Sparks were already tapping on laptops and talking into mouthpieces. The talking did not stop when Peter and Perdita entered but became more muted and circumspect. Perdita walked over to a young man who was under one of the desks so that only his rump was visible. 'What's going on?'

His head appeared, awkwardly tucked under his arm. A cable dangled over his shoulder. 'Power surge. Tripped one of the circuits. Be back in a moment.' He looked anxiously at Perdita, and Peter said reassuringly, 'I'm sure Soul is safe in your hands.' His words were a charm. The lights came on to a muted cheer. On the opposite wall a clumsily stacked bank of screens flickered into life and Peter's smile died.

In front of him, from a dozen different angles he saw, carved in flesh, the warning of the Dark Prophetess of Soul.

A rolling banner at the top of one of the screens read, Kajoru. He recognised the name, a medium-sized town roughly three kilometres from Mzazi, where life was hard yet Ignis Dei offers of help were steadfastly rebuffed. He knew the place and, at the same time, he did not know it. Terror had remapped its contours. Black hillsides of rubble and ash, tributaries of blood worming their way through the dusty earth, the inky scrawl of smoke rising from wreckage in the handwriting of a vengeful goddess, the message unmistakable: *Do not defy me.*

He watched, transfixed, until the images began to jumble inside his head, mixing a strange numbing feeling like the dull throb of jet engines and the inability to accept what he was seeing as real. He kept thinking: *He's gone mad.*

MacCaa had moved fast. The news reports were just beginning to trickle in, but there was no mistaking the imprint of a professional military operation. This was no rushed counteraction, no hot-headed response to the shock of an attack. This was a precise operation, led by a man who already had an army at his disposal.

'These men were armed,' a broadcaster from CNN was saying. 'Reports suggest that they were not locals, and there's talk amongst the survivors of rebels or even of hired mercenaries. They—'

The camera zoomed its focus on a body facedown in the dirt. Peter felt a jolt of recognition. There was a sickening kind of symmetry to everything, a mirror reflection of all he had witnessed in Mzazi. His eyes trailed the other screens, following horror across camera angles, while fragments of reports forced their way into his helpless ears.

'There are denials from all sides. Yet this atrocity bears all the hallmarks of the attack on neighbouring Mzazi, a refugee facility run by Ignis Dei...'

'This was an organized attack, an attempt to instil fear into the local populace. And it's certainly managed that. Nobody's talking...'

'No representative from Ignis Dei was available for comment.'

'A spokesman for the government refused—'

Slowly, he pulled his gaze away. Perdita was watching him, arms folded. He tried to speak, but his words could not catch up with his thoughts.

'Take your time. It's a lot to take in.'

'She didn't know.'

'How could she?'

'She didn't.'

'Naturally.'

'Stop saying it like that. She didn't.' His eyes returned to the screen. A camera panned along a row of corpses wrapped in thick black liners. One of them so small it seemed to huddle against the others for protection. The camera changed angles, but he could still see it, a melting tar-baby sinking back into the earth.

And it began to seep out of his bones, the toxic knowledge of all that he had hidden from himself: the compromises and concessions, the settlements made out of court; the bribes to men of dubious morals, the unsavoury deals that had been struck, the digital manipulation, the threats, the lies, the carefully spun stories, and all the quiet sordidness that he had simply ignored or looked the other way or told himself was justified for the coming of a greater good. He tried to stop it, to shut down his mind, but it gathered force, a great black wave that rose in his throat until he ran from the room and vomited on the ground.

✖

Ellisha was sitting up, drinking something that Dr Boro had just given her when he stormed into the room. 'He's gone too far. This time he's gone too far!'

Ellisha turned to the doctor. 'Leave us, please.'

Boro glanced at Peter then gave a small curt bow. 'Of course.'

He was barely out of the room when Peter burst out, 'Ellisha? You don't know what's happened. MacCaa has gone mad. People are dead.'

He didn't know what expression he had expected to see on Ellisha's face: shock, sadness, anger even. What he was not prepared to find was that she was smiling. It was a strange, sweet, dreamy smile that did not show her teeth. It made him afraid. And when he spoke again his voice seemed to come from a place that was not his throat, so he heard himself say, 'Did you know? Did MacCaa tell you what he was going to do?'

'MacCaa was carrying out Ellisha's orders.' It was Perdita who spoke. She had come into the room behind him, and now she turned to shut the door. 'MacCaa has been building a PMC for some time.'

'PMC?'

'Private Military Company. They're more common than you might think.'

A sudden queasy drop inside his heart took Peter unawares. He glanced at Ellisha. She wasn't surprised by this information; she knew. Suddenly he was adrift, displaced, as though he had been transported to some inverted world: Atlantis, Avalon, the dark side of the moon.

A dozen conflicting voices chattering inside his head made him fall silent, and Perdita began talking of point-growth and reach and liabilities and plausible deniability and something called, *non liquet,* until he shouted angrily, 'Have you lost your minds?' Perdita broke off. Both she and Ellisha looked at him.

He tried to speak and found that his heart was beating so fast he was almost panting. 'This isn't about how many converts we can count on. People died. Do you understand that?'

'People, yes,' Ellisha said. Then she added softly, so softly he almost missed it, 'But not Soul.'

Gooseflesh on the back of his neck. 'You don't mean that.'

'Soul can neither be created nor destroyed.' She took a sip from the glass.

'Don't quote words at me as though I don't know what they mean.'

'They came from Soul.'

'Ellisha, they came from me. I wrote them for your broadcasts, but to use them to justify this is a distortion and—'

Something in her expression brought him up cold. He had not expected her to immediately back down. There was too much fire in Ellisha for that. He was prepared for obstinacy, even the lightning flash of anger. But not for pity. He was not at all prepared for that. His jaw slackened and the words fell away.

'Poor Peter,' Ellisha said gently.

But he would not take that. 'Ellie,' he said firmly, deliberately. 'I did not create Ignis Dei to justify killing innocent people.'

Ellisha was staring at him steadily. 'You did not create Ignis Dei at all.'

Magna Mater. The maternal awakening. Memory out of nowhere, suddenly vivid before him. A mediaeval bestiary He had seen it in Paris years ago on a school trip. A coppery vixen painted in iron gall ink. Her snarling head with its rolling human eyes looking at the reader, while she tore apart a wild dog with designs on her cub. It was some allegory of Christ's sacrifice, but he remembered reaching out a finger, tracing the vixen through the glass that protected the book, sensing the white violence hidden deep inside that feminine heart, a fury that made the vicious ape inside men seem a small and docile thing.

He waited through five beats of silence then drew himself up so that his words came from a deep well of certainty. 'You're not thinking straight. We need to take you home.'

'No.' She lay back with her eyes closed.

'Listen to me. We have to go. We cannot—must not be a part of this.' There was no reaction. Nothing. A dead silence called his bluff. Something other than will propelled him across the room. He began tugging the sheet back. 'We need to get out of here.' But she shrank away from him. He tried to reach her, to reach under her, leaning forward, whispering urgently, 'We can't be part of this. Don't you see? What MacCaa's done—it could ruin everything.'

Her eyes opened. For a split second, he thought he had won. But she looked at him blankly, like someone who knows in their heart of hearts that they are asleep, and who chooses to go on dreaming. 'Ellie!' He felt his anger flare. 'What's wrong with you? Do you hear me? MacCaa has to go!'

She neither nodded nor shook her head, only went on looking at him utterly still, and he knew the answer was *no*.

He drew himself up then along a stiffening spine of righteousness, the wronged lover, the cuckolded husband. But it was the melting tar baby image behind his eyes—Tomás' body, his skin, his bones, folded up inside that claustrophobic, rubber-smelling dark—that pushed him to gamble everything on a single roll of the dice. 'I won't say this twice. It's him or me!'

It was done. The room scintillated in the balance. And though her answer was quick, he knew a split second before how it would be. And, when she closed her eyes and turned her head away, it was almost as if he were watching it for a second time.

Something landed on his shoulder. A hand. Perdita had come up behind him and he suddenly had the impression that he had been standing staring down at Ellisha for some time. He felt he should say something, but he didn't know what, and instead it was Perdita's cool tones that blew across him. 'Seems she's made her choice.'

His act had been one of defiance, of cleanness even. He had responded as a man who threw down his gauntlet no matter the price, and as he stalked out of the room he kept his shoulders straight and his eyes ahead. But once outside in the pitiless light he felt the prickle of agitated energy. He couldn't focus it and wandered about, rudderless through swelling tides of bewilderment and directionless rage.

The scrape and heave of heavy activity coming from a collapsed row of homes drew him closer. Six or seven Sparks were combing through the debris, separating what might be used from the irrevocably lost. They did not pause and straighten themselves when he came in and he thought, at first, that his presence had gone unnoticed. He was relieved; it gave him time to paint on his forgotten smile. 'Hey there. How can I help?'

There was a moment of awkwardness, as though he had barged into a room where secrets were being shared. The tallest of the Sparks, a ruddy boy with dusty yellow hair, looked not at Peter, but into some indefinite space between them. 'No need to trouble yourself, Reverend. We got this.'

On the point of dismissing his dismissal with jocular asides, he noticed something in the atmosphere of the room, the turned-away shoulders, the downcast eyes. A female Spark, with a high forehead that would have made her a beauty in mediaeval times, was watching him with silent appalled eyes, a mobile phone dripping from her hand. *Instant communication.* Knowledge of his fall had preceded him.

Footsteps at his back had him turning. One of MacCaa's men stood there, the burning tree tattoo weeping from his left eye. 'Your car's waiting, sir.'

'My car?'

'To take you to the airport.'

So that's how it was.

His smile was so wide he felt the corners of his mouth crack like broken plaster. 'Very good. Lead the way.'

CHAPTER 33

HE BARELY REMEMBERED THE TRIP back to the Cathedral, waking up only briefly as he made his entrance flanked by MacCaa's men. For an instant he wondered if he would have to face the chilly atmosphere he had encountered in Mzazi. But, no. His welcome seemed genuine. He returned to his offices, sat down behind his desk and drummed his knuckles against it, filled with a strange sense of anti-climax.

His laptop was waiting for him, and he opened it with a violent sense of purpose, typing almost before his thoughts were complete. *MacCaa is weaponising Ignis Dei. We must act at once to have him stopped.* Then he paused abruptly and began scanning news websites. The evidence was there. The world had seen what MacCaa had done.

But the world's memory was short. Bombs had gone off in Berlin and Paris, a newspaper targeted, hostages taken, amongst them a pregnant woman. And it was not just tragedy that had stolen the limelight. The story of a prominent Hollywood actor, who was cheating on the wife he had cheated on his first wife for, was headline news and the internet was chattering about it.

Of Ignis Dei, there was a new story that made his eyes grow round. A few kilometres east of the Cathedral lay the Old Woman mountain range. He had thought of it wistfully at times, wishing he and Ellisha might be ordinary people for a while, losing themselves as they used to on a trip into the world's quiet places. But it was quiet no more.

If his eyes did not deceive him, an entire mountain was to be carved into an image of the Prophetess. An artist's impression showed a granite Ellisha standing hundreds of feet tall shaded by the curved branches of the burning tree. The project was under way despite the objections of a number of native American tribes. And the head of the

Prophetess was already visible, morphing out of the crude outlines of the tree. The eyes—purportedly seventeen feet wide—stared blindly at Peter from the screen. It gave him the strange sensation of being seen yet unseen. He stared at it for a long time then gave a start, suddenly aware that he had forgotten what he was looking for. The intentional magic had worked. Ignis Dei had diverted his focus and left Kajoru buried in darkness.

He jumped to his feet, poked his head around the door and called to Leo Glass. 'Call a meeting of the Executive.'

Leo put a report down he had been reading. 'I would certainly love to do that for you, Reverend Kelso, but the Executive doesn't meet until Wednesday.'

'Call an emergency. I want to meet today!'

'I'm afraid it's not possible, sir.'

'What do you mean?'

'Without the Prophetess or the Consort, the executive is not quorate.'

Peter's hands clenched tightly. 'I am the Consort.'

'No, Reverend Kelso. You are the First Follower.'

'That was a temporary measure.'

'I'm sorry, sir, but you were never reinstated.'

Peter felt anger crouched and waiting inside his chest. Keeping his voice deliberately steady, he said, 'I am telling you, as the husband of the Prophetess, that I wish the Executive to meet.'

'Absolutely, I would love to do that for you Reverend Kelso, but—'

'But?'

Leo looked uncomfortable. 'They don't recognise your authority.'

'I see.' The two men looked at each other. The air thickened. There was a buzzing in Peter's ears and suddenly he was sitting back in his chair. 'I want to know the minute the Prophetess returns.' He avoided Leo's gaze as he said this, opening a spreadsheet on his laptop and staring at it blindly until he saw the younger man's legs move across the room and the door open then shut.

⚭

Three days later he made his way to the central pyramid and took an elevator to the seventh floor. Ellisha had returned the day before. And though he had asked several times if there was a message for him, and had left strict instructions that he should be interrupted even if he was in a meeting, the only thing that came from the inner sanctuary of the Prophetess was a deafening and deadening silence.

He took this rejection in a deeply Celtic fashion, holding it curled inside his chest, a savage thing not to be approached. But eventually it grew too much to bear, and he let it propel him across the great marble hallways and into the golden elevator that led to his wife's apartments.

At the top the elevator doors opened and he found himself looking into an immense semi-circular hallway. There was so much light pouring in from the sloped windows that he had to lift a hand to shield his eyes, but he made out niches containing antique statues, *Inanna, Persephone, St Faustina… the female divine. No, something more. Some thread that links them.*

'They all came back from the underworld.'

He started, half expecting to meet a winged sphynx, but the glare resolved itself into Perdita, who was sitting on a window seat observing him. She was dressed in a sleeveless white trouser suit with a high severe collar. There was something of the Mediaeval abbess about her.

'The Prophetess wanted to remind us that we have to go down to go up.'

'Is that what she's doing? Reminding me?' Instinctively, he glanced towards immense double-doors of frosted glass at the far end of the hall. Two of MacCaa's men stood guard. With a sigh, Perdita swung her legs down and got to her feet. 'She won't see you.'

He tried to match her coolness, snow settling on ice. 'We need to put a stop to this. Call a meeting of the Executive.'

'The Executive have voted to support Ellisha. The vote was almost unanimous.'

'But someone was against it.'

'I'm afraid that was you.'

'I didn't vote.'

'You made your position patently clear in Mzazi.' She gave him an appraising look. 'Unless we've misrepresented you?'

'No.'

'Then there's really nothing more to be said.'

A flicker of movement caught his eye. Something, a shadow, had moved beyond the glass. 'Ellisha!' He bounded over to the door. 'We need to talk.'

The guards made no attempt to stop him. There was no need. It was firmly locked. 'Open the door! Ellie, I know you can hear me. We need to talk!' The figure on the other side was listening. He rattled the heavy handles. 'Ellie! This is insane. You've let MacCaa inside your head. Open the FUCKING door!' The figure turned and began to walk away. In panic, he shoulder-charged the glass, achieving nothing more than a feeling of humiliation and a searing pain in his neck that made his teeth ache. 'Ellie!'

A light touch on his elbow. Perdita was at his side. 'You should go.'

He turned to her and said in a low, barely controlled voice, 'You knew.'

An arching of the eyebrows. 'I don't know what you mean.'

'You knew what would happen in Mzazi. Knew what would happen if Ellisha got there, saw it up close.'

'On the contrary, I had no idea. You were the one who took off with her. Quite against my orders that you return immediately.'

He stepped back, nodding slightly then lifted his hands and drew them together in a slow, insolent clap. 'Well played.'

Walking away from the central pyramid he felt like a man who has survived a plane crash and doesn't yet know how injured he is. The beating of his heart was a bright blade stabbing inside his chest, but the rest of him felt dead. *Turned her back. Walked away from me. From ME.* His brain began to gather threads, to weave patterns. *Doesn't understand what's going on. MacCaa's done this. MacCaa and Perdita. Turned her against me. Yet—*

She gave the order. Looked at me and said, people died, but not Soul. It was the drugs or the headache. The drugs and the headache. They made her strange. Secretive. But there was a deep core of honesty within him that was not fooled.

Not the first time. All the secrets she's kept. The smoking, the Cathedral, Reverences with MacCaa. She's been changing. What did Perdita say? A reduction in the paracingulate sulcus. Visions and perceptions we know nothing about. She's confused. In a day or so she'll miss me. Start asking questions…

He returned to his office and stood before his desk, fingertips resting on the surface, almost sniffing the air like an animal sniffing for subtle disturbances. Though there was nothing to suggest it, he was assailed by the unfounded fear that MacCaa had been there in his absence. His laptop was still open, the lock screen displaying an image of Ellisha addressing the crowds on Calton Hill. And next to it, his mug of coffee lay, half-drunk and cold now. Even the shadows looked the same. Nothing had changed. Everything had changed.

He sat down to work, and noticed for the first time that there were several brownish rings on the surface of the desk where a carelessly placed cup had been left. That was odd. In the pristine atmosphere of the Cathedral such an oversight seemed almost calculated. Where were the grey-suited cleaners? He thought back to his apartments. *My bed. Unmade when I arrived home. The towels in the bathroom still on the floor.* Lifting his phone, he rang for one of his secretaries, and was startled a moment later when Leo came in. 'How can I help, Reverend Kelso?'

'I rang for Libby.'

'Libby? Oh, I'm afraid she resigned this morning.'

'Did she give a reason?'

'Only that she felt it was her duty to follow her soul.' There was a pause while Peter processed this information, then Leo added helpfully, 'Is there anything I can bring you? Tea? Coffee?' A hesitation. 'Something stronger, perhaps?'

Peter glanced at him sharply. *A mistake? But his PAs were always briefed. Reverend Kelso does not drink.* Drawing his lips back in a smile, he said, 'I want you to get hold of a Spark I used to work closely with. Her name is Constance Tao. She handled media circulation on the Prophetess' team, but I believe she heads a soularium in Frankfurt now. Tell her I need to speak with her.'

While he waited, he planned his strategy. *Charm offensive. Call in favours. Form an opposition. Play MacCaa at his own game.*

Leo came back into the room. 'I'm afraid Ms Tao isn't available.'

'Did she say when she would be free?'

Leo clasped his hands together. 'She said she would prefer it if you didn't call back.'

So that's how we're playing it. 'Thank you, Leo. I'll handle the calls myself.'

Once he was alone he took out a notepad and wrote a list of the likeliest allies to his cause: Sparks in prominent positions, ones who had sometimes voiced dissent or who owed him for a personal favour.

The list was shorter than he would have liked, but he lifted his phone and began to scroll down the contacts.

The refusals came back, flat and dead. And by the time he had called three numbers, he knew he would have to go in person. He thumped one hand against the desk in an old unconscious gesture dating back to his ad-man days. A strange new wind was blowing through his mind and he was ready to sweep into action.

Leo looked up as he came into the outer office. He seemed surprised to see him. 'Reverend Kelso?'

'I'm going to Frankfurt. Find out how soon one of the jets can be made ready.'

Something altered in Leo's face, a small betraying tic that prompted Peter to ask sharply, 'Is there a problem?'

'I'm afraid the private jets are not available at present.'

Peter's eyes grew round then he said chokingly, 'Does this apply to everyone or only to me?'

Leo's silence was all the answer he needed.

He spent the rest of the morning trying to find a way out of the Cathedral. He tried to buy tickets online only to hit a wall when he was faced with entering his payment details. He sat looking at the blank place where his credit card number should go. He didn't have a credit card, not even a simple bank card. *When was the last time I bought something?* He couldn't remember. Everything he desired came with a click of his fingers. He could lift a phone, call Leo, but he already knew what the answer would be. Ellisha had cut him off. He felt a chill at his back. *What do I own? The clothes on my back. Not even those.*

A question was forming inside his head and it made a cold sweat break out on his forehead. *Where is the money?* He had no idea. *All this time, living like a king, the first man of Ignis Dei taking for granted everything this earthly paradise had to offer—the limos, the Lamborghinis, the Suite Impériale at the Ritz, the royal suite at the Corinthia, the grand penthouse at The Mark, Savile Row suits, leather brogues from Crockett & Jones, the Eton shirts with diamond cufflinks.* The chill at his back grew colder.

Some time later Leo came in with some papers to be signed. Peter didn't acknowledge him, sitting in an odd stiff posture, a cadaver's folded arms, wide unblinking eyes. Leo put the papers on the desk and hurried from the room without saying anything. Peter didn't care. All he could think about was how he had been flying high. Too high. His wings nothing but feathers and wax. Higher and higher, all the way into the sun, and she had sent him crashing down to earth filled with the knowledge that Ignis Dei had made him the richest pauper in the world.

His fall from grace was a slow one. He was not denounced or turned out. No poison chalice was brought to him on MacCaa's orders. Rather it was a gentle abandonment. A fading celebrity forgotten by a new generation, a generation who awoke to AI systems that spoke to them with Ellisha's voice inside their homes; who carried the Prophetess with them wherever they used apps on phones and tablets and laptops, who chatted to each other and learned about the world through Ignis Dei-controlled channels; who spoke Ellisha's name in whispers and talked of *the* MacCaa with reverence.

Over the coming weeks, three more Sparks resigned from Peter's staff. His schedule dwindled to almost nothing; he was not invited to meetings; his opinion was not sought. And still Ellisha made no contact.

He called Dr Tepetzi to inquire about Tomás. But Dr Tepetzi informed him that Tomás had been placed with a foster family, and was settling in well. He heard the reproof in the doctor's voice and made a clumsy apology before putting the phone down.

Afterwards he tried to reign in his disappointment but, against his will, his mind kept throwing up images of the little family that was not to be. Would never be. With a sinking sense of shame, he tried calling Ellisha again only to find that his number had been blocked. Shortly afterwards, the funding for his projects was discontinued. He went to have it out with Perdita, but she too was unavailable; later, he heard rumours that she was not even in the Cathedral. 'Away on private business,' her PA said and would say no more.

His days grew emptier. He became careless in his dress and sometimes forgot to bathe. For something to do, he grew a beard until he barely recognised himself. Yet, his awareness that his star had fallen was not complete till the day when a Spark, new to the Cathedral, stopped him to ask directions and thanked him with the bland gratitude of someone who had no idea who she was speaking to. After that he took refuge in his office and watched with bitterness Ellisha's light spreading across the world.

It was not a benign light. He read, ice crystals forming in the liquid parts of his body, that the UAE had passed a law making soulariums illegal. Ellisha's response was eerie in its swiftness, her words travelling instantaneously through the invisible channels of cyberspace. She spoke gently, a mother pleading with her wayward son, but he felt the menace shimmering beneath them, and wondered why he was alone in hearing it. There was talk of war amongst the Sparks. He heard it whispered in the corridors of the Cathedral, but could not get to the heart of it. When he confronted them, they looked at him blankly or said he'd been mistaken.

He was haunted by the thought of another Kajoru; rivers of blood flowing through the unsolvable maze of his dreams. And he awoke determined not to allow it to happen again. *Not this time. Not while I draw breath.* He tried again and again to contact Ellisha, sending a barrage of emails that went unanswered; cornered her PAs, first demanding then begging for an audience, even went as far as standing outside her apartment, refusing to leave until he was forcibly ejected by MacCaa's men.

He made attempts to reach the outside world, endeavouring to initiate meetings with politicians and diplomats, men he had sat down with to discuss putting right the wrongs of the world, who had solicited his opinion and acted on his advice. These same men now ignored his calls or sent curt messages saying that they had no time to meet.

He approached the newspapers. No-one was interested in his story. He tried writing a blog, which disappeared as soon as he put it online. A ray of hope appeared when a freelance journalist contacted him, an intense young man who listened attentively and said things like, *this is big. This is huge!* But the story never appeared and the journalist's personal number became unobtainable; his media presence vanished.

Out of ideas, Peter sat despairingly at his desk, feeling like a divorcee who discovers that all his friends have sided with his wife. And as he sat, Ellisha rolled out her justice.

CHAPTER 34

THERE WAS NO BLOOD THIS time. A simple request went out and, across the world Sparks stopped driving to work, they cancelled train and plane journeys; they did not heat their homes; they ate only uncooked food. Peter read of pilots who landed their planes and refused to fly again; of sailors who forced their ships to dock then abandoned them. The media broadcast aerial shots of lorries lying shipwrecked at the side of roads. The rest of the world looked on in bemusement. Headlines chattered at each other, answering questions with questions. *WHAT IS GOING ON? WHAT ARE WE DEALING WITH? WHAT'S SHE UP TO NOW?*

But within days the first shortages began to bite. The media reported that there was no bread in the shops. Government ministers issued reassurances that negotiations were under way and that progress was being made, but there was panic buying; fights broke out and were quelled with teargas and water cannons. Denmark, Sweden and Canada closed down their soulariums as an act of solidarity. Then the oil price plummeted.

Fear rippled around the world, gathered itself together then lashed back in anger. Christian, Muslim and Jewish leaders released statements denouncing Ignis Dei and warning of terrible retribution for those who followed "the False Faith". China began locking up Sparks. Iran threatened an escalation in its nuclear program. There were reports from Britain that the sacred groves, planted in Ellisha's honour, were being torn down. Only Russia stood aloof, neither criticizing nor approving the situation.

At night Peter paced the Cathedral's pale corridors, his thoughts a constant rebuke. *She's changed. Been changing. Since the beginning. Since the creation of the myth. Between us. But she's been drawn deeper in, dreaming the dream of herself. Chosen. Elect. She doesn't feel human any more. You can see it. See it in the way she acts. In the way she talks. We did this. Avery with his vast power, Perdita's cunning, the blind faith of millions and millions of lost souls. Even me. We all colluded in the illusion and now the legend believes in itself.*

From her glass tower Ellisha watched silently as the storm raged. Then she cut the world's drug production by half. The oil price continued to fall. There were riots in the streets. The Qatari government fell, followed by those of Turkey, Italy and Spain. Peter made another attempt to meet, only to see the director of the FBI being escorted into the central pyramid by MacCaa's men. Several hours later he re-emerged, looking shaken, and the same day sanctions were announced against the dissenting countries.

The rhetoric spilled into violence. There were attacks on soulariums and reports of dozens of Sparks being killed. A soularium in Mumbai was blown up in a terror attack. Ellisha remained immovable. She seemed to be waiting. Then, on the twentieth of the month, the next American president was elected and, before the world, declared himself a soul-fearing Spark. The circle of Ellisha's power was complete.

In the days that followed a hush fell over the Cathedral. There was no discernible difference. Business continued as usual. Lectures were given, hallowings took place. There were no reverences, and the Sparks seemed to accept this, their faith unchallenged. Yet Peter felt a change in the atmosphere. Ellisha had won. With a few face-saving manoeuvres the soulariums had been re-opened, the anti-Ignis Dei laws repealed. But something had shifted, and even the Sparks were awed and a little afraid of the naked and terrible face of Soul. There was a sense that things were not finished, that there was more to come.

Peter thought this, and at the same time, watching a group of Sparks ardently discussing the theoretical speed with which a soul could be unified or the best colour to paint a bedroom to promote spiritual release, he wondered if it were only his own isolation that made him see the shadow that lay across everything. Perhaps the rest of the world no longer cared.

One day he went to his office and found he had nothing to do. With no access to funds, the few sickly projects he still had a hand in had withered and died. What use was his help or advice when he had neither power nor influence? His staff had melted away. There was no work for them. He sat down at his desk, opened his laptop and found that his inbox was empty.

A hollow laugh squeezed out of his tight chest. *Is there a more modern metaphor for the social outcast? What need to drive a man from the tribe when you can simply stop emailing him?* Suddenly he couldn't stand to be in his empty office. And before he had a conscious weighing of his actions, he found himself stalking the corridors of the Cathedral. It was early. Diffuse light, pools of shadow. The eerie echo of his steps on the marble floor.

He walked on blindly, missing Ellisha and finding his thoughts lonely and dangerous. Nothing seemed real. *A dream? Could it be? What if I never left Salisbury crag? My body lying there, broken and paralysed, on the rocks below. And all this—Calton Hill. The reverences. Making love to Ellie. Tomás—nothing but a dream. A life lived in seconds dreamt up by a brain drunk with dying?*

Looking down, he found his stick ominous. A symbol of his body's frailty. An attempt to waken his opiated mind to its own betrayal. And something like a moan, manufactured from the gathering of all his pain, began to swell behind his lips and might have escaped if he hadn't noticed the mop.

In another setting such a detail might have gone overlooked. But this was the Cathedral, gleaming immaculacy from every corner, and a dirty mop was as astonishing a sight as a lamppost growing in the middle of a grove of trees. Without meaning to, he crossed the floor, and was just reaching out to touch it—half convinced it wasn't real—when hurrying footsteps stayed his hand.

He turned sharply. It was a cleaner, one of those ghostly grey-clad figures only ever fleetingly glimpsed scurrying from sight. The woman approached, head down, and did not see Peter until she was almost on top of him. They nearly collided, but the woman sprang back at the last moment. She seemed dumbstruck, but Peter blurted out. 'Mariam!'

The exuberant afro was gone and her hair was shaved a quarter inch from her skull, a practical, manual worker's cut. Devoid of make-up, her face looked strangely naked. He slid his eyes down. Grey boiler suit, heavy workman's shoes. It was so incongruous his mind rejected what it was seeing. 'Mariam,' he said again. 'I didn't know you were back.' She wasn't responding, but it was so good to see a familiar face that he could not stop blithering. 'Come back with me. You can tell me all about it. I'd love to hear.'

She threw a nervous glance over her shoulder. 'I need to get back.'

'Nonsense. I insist.'

They returned to his office and, for the first time, Peter was glad that it was empty. 'Sit down.' He indicated the sofa and took a comfortable armchair for himself. Mariam perched on the edge, head lowered. Peter became conscious that Mariam's jumpsuit was a little short at the wrists and ankles. 'Still,' he said with a little forced laugh, 'I didn't expect to see you working as a cleaner.'

'No.' Mariam was staring at the floor.

'Can I get you something to drink?'

'No thank you.'

They were both avoiding the obstacle of an ugly truth. Eventually Peter cleared his throat and said, 'I heard you'd gone to meditate on Soul.'

A nod.

'Where did you go?'

'Consoulation.'

'I don't understand.'

Mariam looked up slowly. Peter said again, 'I don't understand.'

There were dark shadows under her eyes and an expression that said, *But you do.*

Silence clotted around them until Peter asked in an altogether different voice, 'Is Consoulation a place or a state of mind?'

Mariam shrugged. 'Neither. Both. It's in your head. Three stages: Desoulation, Consoulation and Soulace. There's a place too.'

'Where?'

'Not far from here. There's more than one. But I was sent there. It's out in the desert. Underground. Built under a ruined casino maybe.'

'I didn't know. I knew nothing about it.'

Mariam said nothing, only kept on looking, and Peter thought, *Did I know? The disappearances. The grey boiler suits. Never meeting your eye. Scurrying off into the shadows. I didn't know. I didn't want to know.*

'Why? Why were you sent there?'

Mariam looked away. 'I let down Soul.'

'I can't believe that.'

She didn't reply, but such a raw look flickered across her face that Peter got up and called for Leo, saying when the man entered, 'Bring me brandy.'

Leo's eyes flicked to Mariam. 'It would be my great pleasure. Two glasses?'

'One will do.'

Leo returned with a bottle of Remy Martin and a crystal glass. 'Shall I pour, sir?'

'Thank you, no.' With his back turned to the hunched figure on the sofa, he poured a sizeable measure and held it for a moment. It was fine quality and his hand trembled on the glass but he lifted it resolutely and took it over to Mariam. 'Here. Take this.'

'I should be getting back. I have work to do.'

'Drink. I insist.'

She took a sip, shuddered then several gulps. Peter watched as she closed her eyes and nodded slightly as though at the awakening of an old memory. *Oh, the alchemy of alcohol.* Peter sat down again, and when Mariam opened her eyes, he said gently, 'Do many people go to—to that place?'

'We all seek Consoulation at some point.' This was clearly worn-out piece of dogma, and Peter dismissed it with a look. There was a long pause then she added, 'People go there. People who've done stuff.'

'What kind of stuff?'

She began twisting her hands around each other. 'There—there was a man, I worked alongside, who thought his soul portion had developed specially to understand the Prophetess. He had a job in communications.' Mariam looked down at her brandy then swallowed the dregs in a single gulp before going on. 'He released an uncensored statement from the Prophetess saying that suicides weren't real people.'

'Not real?'

'She said there was no point mourning them; it was just Soul escaping a vessel too weak to contain it.'

'I see. What else?'

'I—I don't know. There were so many. That Soul is pure energy. Once you have unified your soul, you don't have earthly needs. Your bodily functions stop. You don't need to sleep or eat. Hate, love. Dark, light. It all makes sense. It all becomes one. He put those claims on the net and apparently the number of anorexics increased exponentially the following week.'

Finding it difficult to speak, Peter croaked, 'And he was sent to Consoulation as a punishment?'

'As a cleansing. Going there gives you a chance to repair the Soul Mystica.'

'In a place where they keep you underground? Make you work as a cleaner?'

'Yes.'

'You never tried to leave?'

Mariam didn't look down this time, only went on looking at Peter, and her expression said, *where would I go?*

The look was not a surprise, yet it shocked Peter. *The conundrum. No going back once you've seen the Void. Wasn't that the whole point? Ignis Dei the refuge of the hollowed-out and despairing men and women of the world. Or have we trapped them? Cut them off from their chance to heal?*

Mariam was still looking at him and he felt he should say something. His hand, he discovered, was across his mouth, and he drew it down saying, 'This is my fault. All my fault. But I can help you.'

She didn't believe him. 'No.'

'I can. I'm still a powerful man.'

Mariam gave him a look that made Peter sad and angry at the same time. He jumped to his feet. 'You'll come and work for me. I'll arrange it.' He pulled out his phone. 'Everything will be fine. I promise.'

Mariam started to say something, but a furious knocking on the door interrupted her. It flew open before he had time to respond and one of MacCaa's men was standing in the doorway, a big brute with a scar that puckered his top lip so that his teeth showed through in a kind of paralyzed snarl. Peter stepped in front of Mariam and spoke with authority. 'She's not going anywhere.'

The brute glanced briefly at Mariam, in the way he might have glanced at a beetle just before stepping on it, then shifted his gaze back to Peter. He spoke in growling Glaswegian. 'No her. You!'

'Me?'

'Aye. You're wanted. By the Prophetess.'

He approached the central pyramid in the shadow of the snarling brute. Perdita and MacCaa were nowhere to be seen. In front of the door was a massive bull-necked guard, who moved slowly to one side, giving Peter the unpleasant vision of a boulder rolling away from the mouth of a tomb. There it was, the entrance to Ellisha's inner sanctum, the place he had never been invited. The snarling brute stood aside, and he was left to walk through alone.

He found himself in a corridor. It had a surprisingly low ceiling and chalk-coloured walls. But what struck him most forcibly was the silence. As soon as the door clicked shut behind him, all sound disappeared. Everywhere in the Cathedral there was a sense of animation, of scurrying, of purpose, of life. But here, it was like being plunged into a deep, dead pool.

At the far end of the corridor was a door. He began walking towards it. *What is this place, Ellie? Why keep me out?* The silence made him hyper-conscious of his own reactions, the shallow peaks and troughs of his breath, the clockwork tick of a pulse behind his ear. Inside his head, he was repeating, *That's Ellie in there. Ellie, who pulls the covers over her head, who eats the last chocolate in the box, Ellie who weeps when they cut down trees.* But he didn't quite believe it, and his sense of crossing worlds grew.

When he reached the other door, he hesitated before knocking softly. There was no answer. He waited then knocked a little louder. Again nothing, and growing impatient, he tried the handle. It yielded to the pressure of his fingers. The door swung open slowly revealing the holy of holies in an expanding parabola of light, and he saw for the first time what Ellisha had been hiding.

CHAPTER 35

FOR A LONG TIME HE stood there, astonishment draining the strength from his muscles. *What was I expecting? Rippling columns in the air? Ellisha hovering two feet off the ground in the Lotus position? Not this. Never this.*

He had returned to Edinburgh, and now stood in their old apartment on North Junction Street. The very first one they had rented together. All those years ago. As his paralysis left him, he began to explore, touching the artefacts of his past life. A shelf of forgotten novels, glossy pebbles picked up from the beach at St Andrews, fairy lights strung across bare oak branches.

The centrepiece of the room was a lumpy old sofa, sagging in the middle, the pattern of tea roses faded almost beyond recognition. He ran a hand over the seat cushions, pulling back sharply when he found the broken spring. *Impossible. I carried it to the dump myself. And that rug. The one we got at Leith market. Still with the wine stain where I dropped a bottle of Merlot on it at Hogmanay. Ellie down on her knees frantically scrubbing.*

—It's never going to come out.

—We could spill wine over the rest of it. Make it look even.

—Are you serious?

—Witch!

'Jackass!'

He stiffened. The word had come out of the past but was also in the here and now. His adjusting eyes found Ellisha on the edge of this strange milieu, perched on the window seat. She was half-hidden by the old-fashioned brocade curtain, and though she was looking at him, her smile was distant as though she was not quite there. It filled him with the strangest feeling that they were dreaming each other.

Some subtle shift brought animation back to her face. 'Peter!' She swung her feet down and ran across the room, pulling herself up just short of reaching him. 'I didn't think you'd come.'

He bit down a retort that he had done nothing but try to see her these last weeks. 'I'm here now.'

She started to smile, then something anxious came into her expression. 'Are you?'

'Ellie, what's wrong?'

'Nothing. Everything.' There was something a little hectic behind her eyes. 'I don't know. I thought you were here before. But it wasn't you. Was it?' She lifted her hand as if to touch him then drew it back. 'Was it Babs? Was she here? I think she wanted something from the archive.'

He tried to take hold of her, but she cringed away. 'I'm tired.'

'All right.' There was a determined gentleness in his voice. 'Why don't we lie down for a bit?' There was a door leading off the lounge. 'Is that the bedroom through there?'

Suddenly she was her old self again, giving him a look. 'Don't you remember?'

The reconstruction of the bedroom was less faithful than the sitting room. Certainly, the walls were papered in the old-fashioned chinoiserie wallpaper he recalled, windsong cranes and tiny pagodas. And the ancient broken-down bed was there too. Peter could almost hear the groan of the iron frame. Above it were quotes stencilled by Ellisha, *Amor Vincit Omnia* and *There are more things in heaven and earth*. His heart gave a painful squeeze when he read them. But apart from these familiar things there was a layer of chaos that was entirely new. Everywhere books and papers piled in untidy heaps. The bedding rumpled and unclean-looking. And a blue haze of cigarette smoke thickening the air.

'Ellie,' he said, taken aback. 'You don't sleep here?'

She frowned and the distance came back into her eyes. 'Sleep? No. I don't sleep. Not anymore.'

'What on earth do you mean?' He caught her wrist and pulled her close, intending to mutter words about being worried or the importance of never losing sight of one another, but instinct made him pull back, wrinkling his nose. 'Ellisha, when did you last bathe?'

She was wearing an oversized sweater that dripped over the ends of her wrists; she twisted the sleeves defensively. 'I—I am not sure.' Looking about the room, shaking her head. 'Yesterday maybe?'

'Not yesterday,' he said firmly. 'Nor the day before either, I suspect.' He followed her gaze. Half-drunk cups of coffee, plates of rotting food. 'What on earth have they done to you?'

'No. It isn't like that.' Some of the vagueness left her eyes. 'I made them. I insisted.'

'For pity's sake, why?'

She pulled away from him. 'It's the Revelation.'

'The—'

'It's Ignis Dei. Codified. Clarified. So that people can read it and understand it.'

'But we have soul-weavers and spirit-therapists and diviners for that sort of thing.'

'No.' She began to pace in an agitated manner. 'This is important. I need it. I have to leave something behind.' She glanced round at him, as though she expected him to understand. And, when he looked at her, uncomprehending, she sighed and turned away. 'Since Mzazi, I've felt so strange. As though things were speaking to me... speaking through me. I write things, things I know aren't true. But after I say them I know they are true. Like I'm being guided.'

She was wringing her hands as she spoke and he saw her shoulders tensing. 'I know how it sounds. But I woke up in Mzazi. I understood about things. How things have changed.'

Something icy gripped Peter's heart, but he forced himself to say calmly, 'What do you mean, changed?'

She had lifted a crumpled cigarette and was listlessly stirring the contents of an ashtray with it. 'I am the mother of God.'

She was still looking down at the ashtray when she said this, and her words were spoken so softly, her lips barely moving that, for a moment, he was convinced that he hadn't heard correctly. But she turned her head towards him, and even through the blue haze, he saw how brightly her eyes burned. 'The *Theotokos*,' she said, as though speaking in an ancient tongue might help clarify the situation. 'The *Dei Genetrix*.'

'Ellisha.' He took a step towards her. *Take hold of her. Reassure her.* To his dismay, she shied back, wrapping her arms about her stomach. 'You don't understand. Duncan said you wouldn't.'

The barb wounded him, but he controlled himself, asking, 'What do you mean?'

'Before. I was in pain, Peter. Nearly my whole life. It was like thousands of needles stabbing me all over, every second of the day. And I didn't understand why. Not really. Not what it meant.'

He could not help himself. 'Even when you were with me?'

'Oh, Peter.' Suddenly she was in front of him holding his hands, her fingers thin and brittle-feeling, winter twigs easily crushed. She went on, 'You dulled the pain more than anyone I've ever known. But—' biting her lip '—it never went away. Not entirely.'

'I thought Ignis Dei was the way to stop the pain?'

'And it is.' Her eyes were luminous. He thought of what she had said in Mzazi. Luminous. Numinous. But there was more. He searched her face. 'Yet?'

She let go his hands and began to pace. 'I didn't understand. Not at first. I thought I could make up a story, and if I shouted it loud enough it would drown out the hurt.

'But it made it worse in some ways. All those people looking at me, as though I, out of all of them … I, alone, was complete. And I wasn't complete. I was empty. Void. Literally hollow.' With both fists she punched herself in the abdomen roughly at the level of her ovaries.'

'Ellisha— Don't!' Alarmed, Peter tried to grab her hands, but she shook him off. 'It doesn't hurt. You can't hurt what isn't there.'

He was struggling to process what was happening. 'Ellisha, if this is about children. There are options, adoption, surrogates. Tomás—'

'No. No. You don't see. You don't see at all.'

'That is certainly true.'

'The headaches. They were … given to me.'

'The headaches are probably the result of the lightning strike.'

She looked at him sharply. 'It doesn't matter what the mechanism is. The point is, it came to me. The fire. Cleansing. Purifying. This is the way it happens. Through flame. Your father was a minister, Peter. You know all about divinity revealing itself as a column of blazing light. The prophets speaking with *tongues of flames?* They know it here too. In America the Anishinabeg Indians talk of the *Seven Fires Prophecy* which mark out the great epochs of the universe.'

She lifted her chin, and he saw heat rising under her skin. 'Don't you see, I was burned because I am the first point, the singularity, the Wellspring, the *Qaniyatu 'ilhm*, the *Creatrix ex nihil!*'

'Ellisha, you are not making any sense.'

'From me all else flows. I am not a mother, here on this earth, because I am *the* Mother. Divinity is my sacred child. I am—' She broke off and began lifting balls of paper, smoothing them out then discarding them. 'You will understand. When it's all written down. Then you'll understand. I had it here somewhere, a minute ago. I'm writing it all down.'

'Enough!' He grabbed her shoulders and spun her around. He was holding her too tightly, hurting her, but she felt insubstantial, and he was half afraid she might dissolve, like a fairy-tale creature, into shadows or the beating wings of crows. She was limp as though the life had gone out of her, and he thought desperately, *What have I done?* 'Ellisha?'

She lifted her head slowly, and to his astonishment, burst out laughing. 'Oh, Peter. Your face.'

A joke? An elaborate prank? His hands fell to his sides. He could imagine the horrified expression that must be contorting his features, and shook his head ruefully. 'One of us is being foolish here.'

Her laughter faded. 'I'm tired, Peter.'

'We must get you out of this place.'

'No. I— There's so much to do. The Revelation—'

Having heard Greek, Latin and even ancient Phoenician coming off her tongue, he was sorely tempted to make use of some choice Anglo Saxon to tell her what she might do with her Revelation. Instead, he drew in a breath and, taking hold of her more gently this time, said in a voice that brooked no argument, 'The only thing you must do now is take a bath.' She slumped against him, and he lifted her into his arms and carried her out of the room.

The bathroom was just off the bedroom, and here at least there was no attempt to relive the past. The walls and floor were cool green marble. He placed Ellisha on a padded bench, where she sat unprotesting, in a wilted-flower, head-on-chest pose. He turned on frothy jets of water to fill the bath, and while the room filled with sweet-scented steam he knelt at Ellisha's feet and began to strip off her clothes.

The woollen jumper first; it came off easily over her head. Underneath, she was bra-less, and the sight of her brown nipples, darker than the brownness of her breasts, made the blood course through his veins. Even her musk aroused him. Such a long time since his fingers had teased and tickled and bruised those buds into life, since his lips had closed around them. He felt a huge ache inside himself, and had to fight to keep his hands steady as he completed the job and lowered her into the bath.

The water felt cool against his skin because he was burning inside. She leaned against the back, eyes closed, while he rolled up his sleeves and gently soaped her. At first, she was inert, and he feared she had retreated too far for him to reach, then a soft moan and her chest rose a little. Bubbles, little trails of bubbles slipping between her breasts—

'I'll grab you something to eat.' He pushed himself up violently and hurried from the room.

When he returned, his mind was so full of thoughts of how to tempt Ellisha's appetite that he did not immediately acknowledge that she had risen to her feet.

'Peter?'

Her skin was wet, and streams of bubbles ran down her stomach and over her thighs. Venus teetering on her scallop shell. She was painfully thin, her collarbone, her elbows, her knees too sharp. But Peter saw only her lightness and how the little belly that nestled between her hips had somehow retained its roundness.

'Ellisha.' He was hoarse. 'You don't—'

As words failed him, she stepped from the bath, and began closing the distance between them.

'I want to.'

Be strong. Tell her, no. 'You need rest.'

She reached up and began undoing the buttons of his shirt. He caught her hands in his own. 'Ellisha, no.'

'Please.'

The unbearable sweetness of that request. He closed his eyes.

'Please!'

Lips parted, head sinking into the secret nook between her neck and shoulder. Her butterfly touch on his crotch. He let out a groan, lifting her up in the same breath. And she came, in her new lightness, limbs winding like ivy around his waist. Her mouth over his mouth. She tasted unfamiliar, of coffee and strong cigarettes, and he wanted deeper in, to where the real Ellisha, his Ellisha, lay.

He turned and slammed her back against the wall, absorbing her gasp on his tongue and thrusting up through the warm folds of flesh with an urgency that made her dig her fingers into his back and arch her spine. A voice that might have belonged to Ellisha or simply been the raving of his own head was calling out over and over, *Slow down! Stop!* But he couldn't stop. Couldn't take the gentler path. He wanted to feel her battle against his thighs. Wanted her to writhe and buck and scream. Wanted MacCaa—wanted the world—to know that he was unlocking the Woman's mystery.

Trying to slow himself down, he lifted his eyes and drank her in— head thrown back, like a dead girl, the fragile rhythm of the pulse at the base of her throat—until, with his senses overflowing, he felt it coming. The shadow passing through them. Wings beating overhead. Electric currents sparked down the dim corridors of his veins, concentrating his being into a single tortured point, until he felt and knew and breathed the words, *With my body, I thee worship.*

Ellisha gave a cry that shuddered through him, like the crack of Creation, and he exploded, a burning star leaving fiery trails across the velvet blackness behind his eyes.

They lay together on the floor, their limbs tangled like the trunk of a split sapling, facing each other until guilt made him say, 'I hurt you.'

She reached out and wiped a damp tendril of hair from his forehead. 'I wanted you to.'

'Ellisha!' He drew back. 'You don't mean that.'

'Don't I?' She wriggled free and sat up, drawing her knees towards her chin. 'No,' she said after a moment. 'Of course not. Only sometimes it gets so hard. Every day that passes, every hour, I seem to drift further away from everyone and everything. The way Perdita and Duncan look at me, I feel as if they're waiting to see if I'll sprout wings or start firing bolts of lightning from my eyes.' She wiped the back of a hand across her forehead. 'It's like I'm filling up with ideas and thoughts until I'm so… cerebral that I might float away. Just now, I wanted to be covered in sweat and cum and pain because I can't feel the earth under my feet.' Biting her lip. 'I can't be normal anymore.'

'There's nothing normal about a woman who can come like that.' He gave her nipple a playful tweak. But she threw him an infuriated look and pulled away. 'What is it with men? Women are always mindless whores or flawless goddesses. Why can't any of you see us as we really are, just messed-up humans, like the rest of the world?' She began tugging on her clothes. 'You have to go now.'

'Ellie, don't be like that.'

She was looking at him so coldly that his nakedness became uncomfortable, and feeling vulnerable, he made a grab for his trousers.

'I'm not going anywhere.'

'You have to. You must.' He struggled to his feet. 'Are MacCaa and Perdita making you do this? You don't have to listen to them. They don't own us.'

His words bounced off some impervious barrier that had sprung up between them. Ellisha was standing at the door. She held it ajar. 'Thank you for coming.'

'Ellie, don't be ridiculous.' She didn't answer, only glared at him with cold fury, as though by the flicking of some inner switch they had become strangers to each other. And feeling his own fury he snarled, 'What was this— ' his hand describing the rumpled towels, the smeared patch of steam where their bodies had pushed against the wall '—a booty call?' Then more quietly, more dangerously. 'But you don't need me for that, do you?' He took a threatening step towards her. 'Do you?' Nothing. His words echoed against the tiles. It was as though she had already gone and he was yelling at an empty room.

A knock at the door. Ellisha called *enter* and one of MacCaa's men came in carrying a tray. His eyes went to Peter then cut to Ellisha. She didn't move. She didn't need to; the stiffness of her shoulders, the angle of her head: her posture was nuanced with rejection. MacCaa's man looked back towards Peter, awaiting instruction at the pleasure of his Prophetess, and there was a moment of almost perfect tension before Peter snatched up his jacket. 'Never mind. I was just leaving.'

CHAPTER 36

THE OFFICE WAS EMPTY WHEN he returned. Mariam had gone. He summoned Leo. 'Where's Mariam?'

'Mariam, Reverend Kelso?'

'Mariam. Mariam Kingsley. You know who I mean. The woman who was with me earlier.'

'I would love to help, but I'm afraid I don't recall.'

'Don't give me that. I need to speak with her.'

Leo had pulled out a tablet and was typing on it. 'There are currently fifty-two Sparks with the name Mariam Kingsley, but none within a hundred-mile radius.'

'That's not possible—' Peter started to say then a thought occurred to him. 'She was with the Greys, staying out in the desert, at Consoulation.'

'I'm afraid you've lost me.'

He knows. Of course he knows. But he won't say. Not to me. They faced each other across impasse. Leo's face was a study of concern. 'Is there anything else I can help you with?'

'No. Nothing. Thank you.'

'Very good, sir. Might I remind you that you are giving a lecture at two thirty in the small auditorium.'

Peter nodded, though he had forgotten. Leo left the room, but he went on staring at the space the man had occupied, vaguely conscious that his hands were trembling. For a good half minute he did nothing and thought nothing. He was still, locked in, a stone man with his brain derailed.

At two-thirty he mounted the lectern and stood facing an empty auditorium. He had braced himself, smile broad, shoulders back before entering the stage, expecting it to be standing room only. But now, as he surveyed the semicircular rows of empty seats, a great wave of silence engulfed him and, when it drew back, he was no longer smiling.

There was a single exception to this desolate reception, a plump young woman sitting near the back, hands folded in her lap. He noticed that she had unkempt hair the colour of dried seaweed.

Unsure how to proceed, he glanced toward the main entrance doors; they remained obstinately shut. Embarrassed, he stole a look at his watch, cleared his throat, took some notes from his portfolio and arranged them on the slope. He tapped his foot, glanced at his watch again.

A minute passed, then five. Somewhere in this time an invisible line was crossed that made leaving impossible. He was noticing things, small details—one of the ceiling spotlights was out and a display of *boule de neige* roses contained a single rotted flower. He wove then unwove his fingers, repeating the action before eventually darting a furtive, sidelong glance towards the Spark. *Should I say something?*

His mouth was dry. He reached for the glass of water that should have been placed at his side, only to find that it wasn't there. Oversight or insult? A surge of anger made him think, *What is it they say, every revolution begins with a single thought in one man's mind?* Placing his hands on either side of the slope, he opened his mouth to speak, but the scrape of the main doors opening cut him off.

Two, then three, then over a dozen Sparks filed in. Gratitude and sadness welled up inside him; gratitude that they had come, and sadness that they should come in such hesitant, pitiful numbers. Yet, as he watched them take their places, it was strangely like seeing them for the first time, a sudden and new way of seeing. *They're tired. The sheen on their faces as much exhaustion as ecstasy. Why have I nev-*

er noticed? His mind, turning archaeologist, excavated images of the countless thoughtless times he had demanded attention no matter what the time of day, paying no heed to the haggard face of the Spark who came to answer his call. The constant bustling busyness of nearly two billion people yoked to a single cause, and he had taken it all as his due. Wasn't it his standing joke that evolution taught fish to walk and Ellisha taught Sparks to run? At some long ago unnoticed moment, he had stopped thinking of them as people. They were numbers, statistics, faceless drones, worker ants who had lost their humanity to a man who had needed a story to tell and a woman who had believed it.

For a moment, he thought he could not go through with it, but some unconscious gesture on his part sparked a watery trickle of applause, and he burst out, 'Friends. Have things not become very strange?' He paused. Nothing. Not even the faintest ripple. He almost lost his nerve but forced himself to press on. 'Perhaps you find yourself querying the direction Ignis Dei is taking. Wondering how the people of Soul could find themselves at war with the rest of humanity.'

He paused for a response, but they stared at him with the open, uncomprehending faces of young children. A little desperately, he pointed at the woman with the seaweed hair and cried, 'Have you had doubts?' She looked at him as though he had spoken in a foreign language then squeaked. 'I haven't done anything wrong. I've attended all the introductory courses, and I'm saving up for Intermediate Level One.'

'Of course. I only want to hear your thoughts. Tell me what you think.'

She darted a frightened glance from side to side then set her jaw firmly. 'I think about how to gather my Soul.'

He controlled his impatience. 'Naturally. Yes. And it does you credit. But, think about it. Are we... I mean, is Ignis Dei giving you the best chance to achieve that?'

Her eyes grew wide and she drew in a breath, as though her brain had been penetrated by something new and sharp. He leaned forward hopefully. But she shuddered visibly and let out a mewling nervous laugh, before whispering plaintively, 'I haven't done anything.'

'No, you haven't.'

'I try to be the best Spark I can be.'

'I know that.' He spoke gently, his heart going out to this simple, frightened woman, with dark smudges beneath her eyes and drooping lines of tiredness on her face, who had come, not out of love or defiance, but dependence. Plain and simple. An addict opening up her veins for the next fix. *How did I not see it?* With a pang, he sensed how the story he had written for them did not contain the words of its own undoing. A new vocabulary was needed, a lexicon of untelling that showed them how he had exposed the Lie only to replace it with another.

For a while he continued talking, but they looked at him blankly, despite the shared knowledge that they had turned their backs on family and career and even the basic freedoms of choosing for themselves and, no matter what he said, he couldn't find a way to liberate them. Gradually, the light dimmed then disappeared from their eyes. They avoided his gaze, bowing their heads as if in prayer. Then, one by one, they drifted from the room, until Peter was alone.

Unable to face the shark's-tooth grin of rows and rows of empty seats, he let his head sink down towards his chest. His collar felt too tight and there was a pounding inside his skull. He gripped the sides of the slope until the ivory knots of his knuckles pressed themselves through his flesh, unaware of how long he stood there until a small noise, a soft handclapping, made him slowly raise his head. 'Quite a speech.'

Perdita was leaning against the doorway. When she saw Peter staring up at her, open-mouthed, she stopped clapping and wrapped her arms about her waist. 'I wonder if I might have a word.'

Several seconds passed before Peter realised that he hadn't responded then he blurted, 'I'm sorry. I didn't—'

'Didn't you?'

He gave a small bitter laugh. 'It's been a while.'

She shrugged. 'Why don't we go somewhere we can talk?'

They went back to Perdita's apartments, where she pulled out two glasses and poured herself a generous measure of Lagavulin before remembering Peter. 'Would you like… no, of course not.' She frowned then lifted a jug. 'I can offer you water or…' She lifted a second jug and sniffed it, pulling a face. 'Really water, that's it.'

'Water's fine.'

'Why don't we sit down?'

Perdita sat in the comfortable-looking armchair, legs crossed. Peter perched opposite on a bizarrely mismatched plastic Panton seat, which seemed moulded for a body quite unlike his own.

'Cheers.' Perdita lifted her glass to her lips and took a long sip. Her eyes closed for a moment and she let out a sigh as she opened them again. 'That's better. The Americans are an admirable people, but their whisky tastes like horse piss.' She looked supremely relaxed, studying Peter benignly, as though their meeting had been his suggestion. But Peter's throat had silted with such a log-jam of questions that he was quite speechless. They looked at each other for a long time, then Perdita said, 'Have you heard from Avery?'

The question took him aback. He shook his head and Perdita said. 'Hmmm.' There was another silence then she said, 'Neither have I.'

Surprise loosened his tongue. 'But surely—'

She was staring down into her glass, swirling it slightly and letting the glints catch the light. 'I've been away for a while.'

He leaned forward despite himself. 'I had no idea.' Gears were shifting inside his head. *Was I really that out of the loop?* His fall from grace had been so devastating, so shatteringly absolute that it had not occurred to him that he was not alone in his expulsion. Suddenly he saw himself banished from the garden, forced to leave it by a hissing MacCaa, hand in hand with Perdita as his prickly new Eve. And, struggling against an absurd urge to laugh, he croaked, 'What of MacCaa?'

She frowned slightly. 'Who can say? Probably lying across his mistress' doorway growling poetry.'

'You're saying MacCaa is out of favour?'

'It seems the Prophetess trusts no one.'

He put his glass down angrily. 'You've pushed her too far. Made her do things she wasn't capable of. Cruel things.'

'A mind like Ellisha's has always been capable of cruelty. Most minds are.'

'I don't believe you.'

'Of course you don't.' She lifted her drink to her lips, tilting it until it was drained then rose to her feet. 'Come.'

Irritated, yet unable to think of another course of action, he followed her to a desk where an open laptop lay.

'Take a seat.'

He waited as she woke up the machine and spun it around so that he could see the file she had accessed. 'Well?'

The screen was filled with a still frame of a man sitting with a notepad balanced on his crossed legs. He had a young-old face and the suit he was wearing appeared to be several sizes too big. His facial features hid behind shelter of a prominent nose. Perdita was watching him closely for a reaction. 'Do you remember who this man is?'

He shook his head. *Yet, he is familiar.*

'His name is Hugo Savary.'

Peter went on looking; the name meant nothing.

'Of course it means nothing to you,' Perdita said disconcertingly. 'But he is of great significance.'

Before Peter could ask anything further, she reached out and pressed play. The image shivered into life. Savary changed his position slightly, tapped the notepad with his pen. Then the camera changed angle and showed the back of Ellisha's head.

Peter leaned forwards and something clicked in his brain. 'Was this the first interview? With the reporter from Le Monde.'

'Mediapart,' Perdita corrected. She slid the volume up. Savary was in the middle of saying, 'Thank you for granting me an interview. I believe it is a rare honour.'

'Not at all. I greatly admire French journalism. Mediapart in particular. May I offer you a drink? Tea, coffee? Perhaps something stronger? We have Remy Martin.'

'You know my favourite drink?

'We know many things, Monsieur Savary.'

Perdita turned to look at him. 'Do you remember now?'

'I remember.'

She fast-forwarded to the end. Ellisha had finished speaking and there was silence, the kind of silence that made Peter want to slam his hands against his ears. The ash on Savary's Gauloise crumbled from the tip, but he did not seem to notice. Ellisha rose and placed a hand on his shoulder. 'Drink your brandy, M. Savary. And when you are ready, I will be waiting.'

She left the room. The lights dimmed. But not before Peter had seen a single tear roll down Savary's ravaged cheek.

Peter felt Perdita watching him closely. 'Savary became a Spark?'

'Yes.'

He shook his head. 'I don't— What does any of this prove?'

'He didn't stay one.'

He glanced at her sharply. 'You mean—'

'He was the first apostate.'

Peter's head whipped round to look at Savary again. This man. This shrunken corpse who looked more dead than alive had been the first to turn his back on Ellisha.

'Do you know the statistics on apostasy?'

He didn't. 'Low?'

'Less than one per cent. And why do you think that is? Loyalty? Or because we make it impossible to leave? Most Sparks have nowhere to go. They've burnt their bridges. And those who voice doubts are encouraged to go through the three stages.'

'*Desoulation. Consoulation. Soulace.*'

'Exactly. Well done. Naturally, there is always a tiny minority who leave despite everything.'

'Like Savary.'

'Yes, like Savary. Of course, we have developed ways to deal with them over time. Unfortunately Savary was our first. And he was also a journalist.' She leaned forward and made some adjustments. 'Savary wrote an article shortly after he left.'

Peter ran his eyes over the file. There was no need to read it in detail. Savary's tone ran like sour wine. *There are enough holes in this religion, which is not really a religion at all, to fill the Void they so fear … Are we to believe, in the vast complexity of our universe that God's hand is nowhere to be found?… Ignis Dei has managed to invent a more desolate kind of atheism… Ellisha sweeps up the poor and desperate with the lure of materialism masquerading as enlightenment… The role of prophetess will hardly long contain one who feels herself scintillating with the Divine…*

Peter turned to Perdita. 'What's your point? It's hardly a revelation that some people don't like us.'

'No,' she agreed. 'But what do you think happened next?'

'The story was suppressed.'

'I meant to Savary.' She nudged him aside and opened another file. It was a video of a man in a hospital bed. His head was heavily bandaged and tubes protruded from his body, attaching him to various machines. There was a lurid B-movie quality about it that made Peter unable to accept what he was seeing as real. 'That isn't—' But of course it was.

'Naturally we had removed the article from circulation. But Savary was found twenty-four hours later in a doorway off the Rue de la Glacière. Left for dead.'

'But he didn't die.'

'No. If you can call being in a vegetative state living.'

'You are not suggesting— Ellisha would never sanction something like that.'

Perdita looked at him in surprise. 'Why would she need to? The article made her angry. Once her will was known, she could forget all about it.'

'Ellisha isn't like that.'

'She's exactly like that.'

Peter stiffened. 'You don't know her.'

'Do you? There's a great deal more to Ellisha than either of us expected. On the surface she's innocent, almost child-like. But underneath she's a deeply complex character. There's a kind of double consciousness there.' She smiled suddenly and unnervingly. 'You know, I think we may have underestimated her.'

He felt a chill. 'Are you saying she's been playing us?'

Perdita seemed surprised. 'Good gracious, no. It's much more subliminal than that. Ignis Dei has opened up strange and unmapped places in Ellisha's brain. I doubt even she understands what is happening.'

Something in the way she said it made his skin crawl. 'You think she's mad.'

Perdita was shutting down the laptop. 'Far from it. I think she may be the only sane one amongst us. Wasn't Pandora far smarter after she looked inside the box?'

'Pandora ended up riddled with pain and fear.'

'Show me a great intelligence that isn't.' She straightened and reached for his glass. 'I think you could do with something stronger.'

'I don't want a fucking drink. I don't drink. You know that.' She looked hurt. 'Naturally, I meant tea.'

Naturally. Perdita's relentless calmness was fraying his nerves. He felt unsteady, as though his foundations were washing away from under him. To hide his vertigo, he spoke angrily. 'Where does that leave us now?'

'In a difficult situation. Neither Ellisha nor Mr Avery seem to want to include us in their discussions.'

'But you think they're talking to each other.'

She waved a hand vaguely at the laptop. 'We've been able to pick up certain communications. Avery has been here.'

He sat up straight. 'Here, in the Cathedral?'

'Yes.'

'Without any of us seeing him arrive?'

'Yes. Remarkable when you think about it.'

'What did they discuss?'

'No clue. All we know is that something happened between them. Something quite catastrophic, by all accounts. There are hints that it might have been a kind of falling out. Raised voices were heard and the sound of things smashing against walls. After Avery left, Ellisha stayed in her quarters for three days refusing to speak to anyone.'

'And now?'

'And now the Prophetess is planning something.'

'What?'

'We don't know. I was hoping you might throw some light on the situation.'

He looked at her astonished. 'Me?'

'It did seem a long shot.'

He thought. *It's all*—but could go no further. The tips of his fingers rose almost unconsciously to the bridge of his nose as though in prayer, and he closed his eyes and stared into the blackness. Galaxies spiralled away into infinity and he watched them go with a sense of loss. At last he asked bleakly, 'So what do we do?'

'That depends.'

The crispness of her tone made him look up. 'On what?'

Perdita was watching him with that austere, knowing expression that made her look part mother superior, part gyrfalcon. He said again, 'Depends on what?'

Her brows rose. 'On what's been left behind inside Pandora's box.'

Ellisha was planning something and suddenly the Cathedral was alive with rumour. No official statements were made to Peter's knowledge, yet somehow the message seeped into the consciousness of the Sparks so that one minute no-one knew then suddenly everyone did. He detected Perdita's hand behind the leak and suspected she was trying to force things towards a climax, though she denied involvement, even going so far as to issue an edict forbidding discussion of any hypothetical plans that the Prophetess may or may not choose to share, which naturally drove speculation to fever pitch. Day after day the air tightened, as though a thin, tough membrane were being stretched across the Cathedral, and wherever he wandered, faint, papery sounds, soft murmurs and breathy whisperings came rustling to Peter's ears.

—you know something. I know you know.

—I'm afraid to say.

Emerging from an elevator, he heard,

—energies aligning. Like ley lines in the air.

—Really?

—I have a gift for sensing these things. She's coming. It's really happening. The Goddess is coming. Then, most poignantly, from inside one of the hallowing spaces,

—It's a baby. A holy child to lead us.

—Like an avatar of the Coming Divine?

—That's crazy.

—Crazy enough to be true.

—I meant crazy like awesome.

This last snippet stayed with him and would not be shaken. It couldn't be true. Of course not. But what if… Ellisha's secret, a child? *Ridiculous.* Yet he could not free himself of the image. Some deeply buried nerve inside him had been touched, and now it ached sonorously through all the solid layers of resignation and disappointment that had built up over the years until he had truly believed his longing quite calcified and inert.

But now the thought of becoming a father haunted him. *Ghost baby. Tiny, involuted wisp of flesh. No, don't think it. Don't even think about thinking it. The road to ruin that way, and to pain. Pain heaped upon pain. Still, that rounded curve of her belly...* And suddenly, with a kind of dread awakening, he knew this to be the thing that he had wanted and needed and run from all his life. *Constantly telling myself that the aching emptiness belonged to Ellisha. Her burden, her void to face, when in fact, all along, it was mine.*

Something tight gripped his chest and he was overpowered by a sense of travelling backwards. The sounds of the room, and beyond the room, grew faint as though he were dying, and thick folds of darkness drew him, choking, through a strange, reverse birth canal that brought him all the way back to the beginning. He saw, with a wash of new light that made his skin grow hot, how his struggling, his need to make his mark upon the earth was only distraction and beguilement, and his creation of Ignis Dei, this Frankenstein's monster sewn together from shreds of the world's agony, was nothing but a primal cry against extinction. All that was needed to make the world anew was this being that would be drawn from his being: his child.

He stood there, long after the darkness had receded, feeling the pressure building behind the hot eggs of his eyes until they cracked and burning tears leaked out.

∞

The next day Perdita appeared in his apartment. She stood looking at him with folded arms. 'There's talk of a child.'

'I heard.' On his desk sprawled a mess of papers, and he pretended an interest in rearranging them. He could feel her eyes following him. At last she said, 'If this is Ellisha's secret, it would change everything.'

'Yes.'

'Why do you suppose she's keeping it from you?'

'I don't know.' He glanced up and found Perdita stroking her chin, a thoughtful, faraway look in her eyes.

'I just think it's strange that she wouldn't tell you.' She paused then looked at him shrewdly, and he felt the question she wanted to ask echo inside his head as clearly as though she had given it voice: *Can you possibly be the father?*

As she had not asked the question there was no way to answer it, and he stood staring at her in helpless frustration, the papers in his hands wrinkling under the pressure of his clenching fists, until Perdita wiped her expression clean and exclaimed brightly, 'It's moot anyway. We shall find out soon enough. The Prophetess is about to make an announcement.'

'How do you know?'

'I have my ways.' With a little inward smile, she turned and walked out of the room.

For a moment shock held him fast but then a spasm of pure rage freed him, and he shook off the numbness and followed her. He caught up with her on one of the walkways above the central atrium. 'Wait. What do you mean? How do—'

The chirp of his mobile made him look down reflexively. It had been so long since anyone had sent him a message that the sound was momentarily baffling. But even as he processed it, he was aware of Perdita pulling out her phone, and of hundreds of similar little melodic twangs going off down below in the atrium, like the warm-up of a dissonant modern symphony or the piping of a strange, abbreviated dawn chorus.

Part V

THE DIVINE HAG

READING BETWEEN THE LINES OF Canaanite mythology reveals faint, yet definite traces of our harvest king archetype. The story of Judith and Holofernes seems to deliberately lack historicity, preferring to hang itself on the bones of an ancient mythological source.

In the symbolic role of queen/goddess, Judith beheads Holofernes (dying king) and anoints the one of her choosing, Achior (the rising king).

A curious codicil to this narrative is Judith's refusal to remarry. She is childless, and maintains this state as though there was power in her infertility. She is a creatrix of new orders rather than human flesh…

Iconotropic mythology in the Apocrypha,

Edinburgh University Press, 2019. xii + 260 pp

By McBride Barbara

CHAPTER 37

WITH STIFF, OUTSTRETCHED WINGS, THE plane dropped through the clouds like the body of an expelled angel, and Peter, forehead pressed against the lozenge-shaped window and a lump in his throat, watched the vast slate-coloured expanse of the North Sea rush up to meet him. The plane juddered slightly and he glimpsed familiar islands and estuaries, made alien by the strange perspective, then the land came into view with its cooried castles and small defiant forests, all blurred and dream-like beneath curtains of fine grey rain. And even before he spotted the ugly gash of the airport, he knew by the ache in his bones he was home.

Once they had landed, he stood next to Perdita at the top of the stairs, awaiting permission to disembark. The rain had grown heavier, but he turned his face up and let it pepper his cheeks. It felt good, cleansing. But Perdita, daughter of the south, buttoned her jacket and retreated inside it. 'Edinburgh,' she said with a sniff. 'Seems we've come all the way back to the beginning.'

'Not quite. The first reverence was in February. We're in the middle of summer now.'

Perdita pulled her jacket tighter and shuddered. 'How can you tell?'

He awoke the next day in the Earl of Bothwell's bed. It was a great oaken structure, blackened and carved with something of the catafalque about it, but Peter had become immunized against strangeness, and would have found it stranger to experience strangeness' absence. He lay there allowing memory's map to locate him in Edinburgh, or rather near Edinburgh, high within Borthwick castle's fortified walls.

Across the landing, he knew, Ellisha lay on Mary, Queen of Scots' bed, planning whatever revelation she intended to unveil on Calton Hill, and the thought of her, so near yet so inscrutably unattainable, made a chill of loneliness creep over him so that he pushed the sheets back and hastened out of bed, pulling his clothes on as though donning his familiar pelt would be a kind of amulet against irrelevance.

A high ecstatic light filled the room, and he knew that he was up later than he'd planned. For an instant panic gripped him, then he remembered that nothing was to happen until after dark. Such were Ellisha's instructions, her revelation was to rhyme with the setting sun on the first day of the eighth month, Lughnasadh, Lammas, Gŵyl Awst, August eve.

The air closed about him as he conjured these names—or perhaps he only imagined it did. Suddenly he was afraid of himself, afraid of the thing growing inside himself, which was the need to have his child growing inside Ellisha. He sank down on the edge of the bed and pressed his fingertips into the thin flesh of his forehead. *Let it be true. Please, Ellie. Make this miracle real.*

He stopped, partly appalled, partly amused to find himself praying to his own wife. And all at once he was filled with a wild, improbable hopefulness. He was home; the sun was shining, and he had a great longing to go out and explore the past which was already scintillating in his mind with peculiar half-imagined light, like moments of recollected happiness or memories of childhood summers.

He decided to go into the city, eschewing his usual black for a pale summer jacket he found hanging in the wardrobe. Ellisha's glamour made the practical magics of ordering a car feasible again, and so cheerfully and a little self-consciously he left the bedroom and walked along the gallery nodding to the Sparks he passed on the way. He enquired about Perdita, but her whereabouts were unknown, and he was so eager to taste the Scottish sun again that he was out the main door before he knew it. In the strong light, he stood for a moment blinking, and when his vision cleared he saw a figure in silhouette standing half-way down the great stone staircase that led to ground level.

MacCaa was looking out over the sharp drop of the bailey, watching a bird-of-prey's furious twisting flight. There was something lonely about him, the refugee's oblique shoulders and the absolute stillness of his gaze that arrested Peter's enthusiasm to hurry past. He came to an awkward halt behind MacCaa's sturdy shadow and offered into the silence, 'Kestrel?'

'Merlin.'

Peter looked again. The bird, no more than a little clot of primal darkness, spotted something in the tall grass and plunged faster than vision could follow. The silence returned, but poised as though something had been left unsaid. Self-consciously, Peter studied the lines of the larger man's dejection, and read between them a message addressed directly to him. *MacCaa knows he's not the father.* Instantly a rush of warmth loosened his tongue, if not his brain, and he blurted. 'Strange to find myself sleeping in the Earl of Bothwell's bed last night.'

MacCaa did look round. 'It's no Bothwell's.'

'No?'

'It's a replica o' the wan that James VI slept in when he was crowned.'

'Oh?'

'A right freity man, James.'

'I'm sorry. I don't—'

'Superstitious. Always afraid fate had it in fur him. No' a man tae trust folk. Particularly women.'

'True enough.' Peter had a sudden vivid vision of the haunted king, fleeing as though the hounds of hell were nipping at his heels, from a chained-up woman who had dripped her story into his ear. *A long time since I've thought of that.* The sky the merlin had dropped from was cloudless, but Peter gave a violent shudder as though darkness had fallen across him. And though his recovery was quick, when his focus returned, MacCaa's eyes were on him, waiting to pounce. The man's mouth seemed to open for a long time before any sound came out; he braced himself for verse then realised that MacCaa was looking at his jacket.

'You should put something heavier oan. It's colder oot there than it looks.'

The streets of Edinburgh were solid and unchanged, but the crowds that filled them were so dense it was as though a single febrile creature moved along them, continuously contracting and expanding its gargantuan body in a rippling motion towards some mysterious goal. A significant number were wearing head-dresses and masks, sunbursts and moon disks so that they looked like Russian icons or saints on the stainedglass windows of mediaeval churches. Peter tried to force his way through for a time, but it was impossible, and eventually he stopped struggling, giving up his will to the creature and finding that the sensation was not at all unpleasant, a little like drowning.

He was enveloped in a sea of love, in a sea of people who loved the person that he loved and even the grumbles, erupting from time to time, like a stream of sulphurous bubbles rising to the surface, only seemed to make the love stronger, a note of dung at the heart of an exquisite scent.

—*This is worse than the festival.*

—*It's all tae dae wi those Ignis Dee folk.*

—*I don't get them. They go aboot saying there's nae a God. But they're a religion ur they no?*

—*It's mair like homeopathy. Ah went for ma headaches.*

—*Did it work?*—*Mibbe aye. Mibbe no.*—*Well, which is it?*—*The pain is still there, but I dinna seem tae mind sae much.* Peter wanted to reach out to kiss them, but the voices faded in the swell of the crowd. He glimpsed stalls selling the usual Ignis Dei paraphernalia, tiny temples dedicated more to commerce than impending deity, but today they were beautiful. A group of Soul Searchers went tinkling past, their faces painted like jewels, and the crowd threw coins at them, which they caught in the liquid folds of their robes. A child tugged his arm. She was about seven years old with gossamer hair and large uncompromising eyes.

'Cake?' She took a pastry shape from a basket almost bigger than she was and pushed it into his hands.

'Thank you.' He looked down and saw that the pastry was in the shape of an owl with a man's legs.

'S'god,' the child offered. 'Today's the day you eat the god.'

'Who told you that?'

'Fergus.'

'Who's Fergus?'

'Big brother. He's nine.'

'Well if Fergus says so.' Peter took a bite. 'Delicious.' But already she was off. Little Red Riding Hood disappearing into a forest of legs.

Peter breathed in deeply, his chest opening as though some secret spring had been released and finally freed the mechanism of his breathing. Sunlight glinted off everything and he was struck by how different the light was here in his homeland from the arid suns he'd met abroad. *Some memory of rain still there perhaps? Like tears drying on a newly-smiling face.*

The sentimentality of these thoughts was interrupted by the appearance of a gnome. Bald head, cherry nose sprouting above a cherubic froth of snow-white curls, the man was forcing his way against the crowd, carrying a spray of helium balloons with Ignis Dei slogans written on them and on his back a netting sack filled with Prophetess dolls, some of which carried tiny baby dolls in their arms.

He was plying his wares to anyone who would listen, and was just about to make his pitch to Peter when something arrested his progress. He snapped his mouth shut and put his head to one side, studying first Peter's face then his pale jacket with a look of puzzlement. And Peter, in turn, felt his thin disguise slipping. Other heads were turning, and sensing it was time to go he slid between the crevices made by the crowd, as human bodies will never truly tesselate, and into the nearest open door he spied.

For a second he stood elated but disorientated. He was inside a walled burial ground, and despite the noise outside it was oddly peaceful. Just beyond its high walls he could see the trees covering the spine of Calton Hill. As he looked they gave a restless, almost sensual, shiver in the small wind that had suddenly arisen. No-one joined him, and he wandered beneath an obelisk which threw its shade in a narrow needle, like the gnomon of an enormous sundial, following him as he drifted between stone urns and discreet angels, past a green man grinning out beneath a sailing ship and the doughty tomb of David Hume. He came to rest in front of the grave of Julius Von Yelin, that knightly German scholar, who had come to meet Sir Walter Scott but died before the meeting could take place. And he stood thinking of the ageing Scott, his own sun setting, standing at the funeral whispering, *He dead and I ruined.*

An agreeable kind of melancholy settled over him, and he left the graveyard and wandered the familiar paths that had once been home, a little saddened by their close resemblance to his memories yet somehow with the life gone out of them. He quite lost himself between his old house and the university, dreaming of what name his child might be given. *David? Alexander? Good Scottish names. Names of kings. Classical names too. But, of course, what if it was a daughter?* He racked his brains, trying to think of Scottish queens. But could come up with none save for Gruoch, Macbeth's enigmatic, if inharmoniously appointed, wife.

He was passing the chapel of St Albert the Great when a terrified-looking Spark, flanked by two of MacCaa's men, came running up the lane. The Spark, who had the bespectacled, untidy bird's-nest look of a librarian except for the fevered flush of her cheeks, came to a panting halt before him. 'Reverend Kelso. We've been looking for you everywhere.'

'Well, now you've found me.'

'Please come with us. We have a car waiting.' Her hair was escaping its bun in thin wisps and her glasses were askew. 'Perdita's going crazy. You missed rehearsals.'

He looked at her fondly wondering if she knew she was beautiful. As they walked to the car, he turned, saying conversationally, 'Do you know, there were no rehearsals at all for the first reverence. It was all completely natural.'

She gave him an awed and humouring glance. 'I was only eleven when the first reverence took place.'

Ah, a decade is history to the young, he thought sadly. *And the blink of an eye to the rest of us.* But she redeemed herself by asking in a shy hopeful voice, 'Is it true there's going to be a child?'

Calton Hill had changed in his absence. As they approached—on foot because it was impossible to get through the crowds in a car—Peter was amazed by how dark it had become. The hill was no longer a rippling living thing, as though home to flocks of exotic green-plumed birds, but only a more vivid darkness against the dark of the gathering night. The dying light gave the place a hallucinatory quality that made him feel like a man awakening from a deep enchanted sleep only to find that time had moved differently and centuries had gone by while he slumbered on.

He had donned the black jacket brought by the Spark, remarking his surprise as he did so. 'How did you know where to find me?'

'We didn't.'

'But you brought a jacket.'

'There are dozens of cars searching for you, Reverend Kelso, and they all have jackets.'

With MacCaa's men to either side of him, the crowd opened up and he passed through, looking neither to left nor right but fixedly straight ahead with a sense of solemn purpose, his path the true shot arrow of a king, while behind him he felt the press of bodies, the great hopeful, creaking mass of limbs and heads and torsos interlocked by some collective subconscious instinct that had brought them all here with the turning of the year's clock towards midnight.

He took a roped-off path that led him against the hours, making his way up through the smoky twilight towards the summit. The nearness of the night gave everything a frail, insubstantial quality and wraiths of woodsmoke hung in the air. The smell made him long for the simple good things a man might have without losing himself, and he walked on with renewed vigour. *Ellie, I'm coming.*

There was huge activity up ahead but for the moment he was curiously alone. This was not the Calton Hill of his memory, with the light pouring down and Ellisha trembling in his arms saying, *I can't.* There were huge structures everywhere: fire sculptures of trees with stiff blasted limbs and birds lifting outspread wings which were already engulfed in violent flames. His face scorching, he passed a stag rearing up on its hind legs and a wicker man down on his knees, head bent forwards as though looking for something.

The crowds had begun to chant. *Ell-ish-ah! Ell-ish-aaaah!* And by the time the Doric pillars of the national monument came into sight, the vibration of it was going through him, from head to foot, and he walked with his steps chiming as though he were a perfectly calibrated tuning fork. Onstage, mythos dancers, their chests bare and their heads enclosed in the heads of fantastic creatures, were whipping up the crowd with fantastic contortions to the accompaniment of bodhrans and bagpipes, while drones swept the place in swooping arcs, relaying close-ups of the crowd's reaction onto gigantic screens set about the summit. A continuous scroll of tweets and toots rolled past in endless celebration of the Revelation.

—*Ellisha, we love you.*

—*The child of a godless god IS God!*

—*It's happening. The Beginning of Days is happening.*

In the midst of this din MacCaa appeared out of the shadows, his huge blunt shape so ripely diabolic that Peter laughed.

'Yer late.'

He could barely hear him over the ringing in his ears. 'Where's Perdita?'

'Waiting at the back. She's no happy.'

'I lost track of time. I didn't think—'

'She needs ye roon there now.' The other man's eyes blazed. 'You're the consort tonight.'

Peter needed no second telling. He pushed his way through gaggles of Sparks and Soul Searchers and the rows of security men three deep, aware of his heart hammering ridiculously, like a silly schoolboy sick with first love, and made his way to the rear of the monument. It was just as he remembered it, save for a set of wooden steps erected to allow the Prophetess dignified access to its base and carefully arranged velvet drapes to screen the performers from sight.

Several Sparks were anxiously checking a complicated array of sound equipment and someone was yelling about a problem with feedback, and somebody else was shouting that it was Johnson's fault, and they couldn't fix it because nobody knew where the hell Johnson was, and in the meantime, diviners wandered about sweeping arcs of burning sage through the air and Soul-weavers swayed and hummed and made complicated patterns with their hands.

Perdita was in the middle of it all, mediating a dispute about body paint between two make-up artists. She was immaculate as ever, but between her brows there were small chevrons of anxiety, which disappeared when she spotted Peter. 'Ah, there you are. Good.' She abandoned the make-up artists and joined him. 'You missed rehearsals.' She was shouting to make herself heard.

'I lost track.'

'You should have been here. You're the consort tonight.'

'MacCaa told me.'

A Spark carrying a clipboard ran up. 'Five minutes, Reverend Kelso.' Another Spark was fitting his mic and Bluetooth earpiece.

'So soon?'

'You took longer to find your way out of memory lane than you think. Come now, *hora fugit*. You remember the drill?'

He nodded.

'Good.' Perdita started to walk away.

'Wait!'

She turned, forehead stretched quizzically.

'Did Ellisha say anything? Did she give any clue about—about—'

'No, nothing. Only that she wanted you here tonight and that you were consort.'

CHAPTER 38

WHEN HIS CUE CAME ACROSS the Bluetooth, he stepped through the velvet curtain and the first thing he saw was Venus hanging like a pearl-drop off the ear of the moon. Then his vision tilted and the fire sculptures reared up, throwing showers of candescent confetti far into the night sky, and between them thousands of faces began appearing out of the darkness, reflecting the flames of the fires over and over in glinting bicuspids and the milky moon-like reflections of eyes, until Peter felt he was looking down, not at people, but owls and hares and wolves.

His appearance brought a roar from the crowd, hitting him squarely in the face like a wave of freezing water. He gasped then blinked and even shook his head slightly, throwing up his hands to stem the flow, while on either side Soul Priests bowed and made way for him. He walked forward, his reflection repeated over and over on the giant screens set about the summit, his face, his body walking towards him as though all the ghosts of his past were converging on this one spot, and simultaneously in China and America, in Australia and India, across Europe, in the remotest parts of the Russian steppe and deep in the burning heart of Africa, all across the globe, the world and his wife sat or reclined or crouched or squatted before the man who was consort to the queen of the world.

He lifted his arms above his head, mimicked by the digital colossi, and the crowd quietened, mouths snapping shut like a sea of petals closing in darkness. They were leaning forward now, eager to hear what he had to say, and he looked down at them with great love, knowing in every part of himself that he was here; he was home; he was healed.

'Tonight the Prophetess wants to share something very special.' He spread his hands wider and received the crowd's roar. 'A secret she has known and cherished for some time, waiting for the perfect moment to reveal it. And tonight, here on Calton Hill, she intends to share it with you.' Slowly he lowered his arms and leant forward in bare appeal. 'Tonight you must listen to her as you have never listened to her before. Listen because she is unique among the men and women of this earth. Because she is your eternal guide. Because her heart is good. Because you need her. Because … because—' He paused and the air was perfectly still; the darkness almost complete, save for the sequins and spangles of light sent up by the fires. He smelled the first tang of autumn piquing the chilling air and taking in a long breath like a cool, perfect draught of wine, he looked down at them with the wild joy of a man who knows he is to become a father, and cried, 'Because you love her!'

It was done. His love letter to Ellisha proclaimed. Behind him, there was a swell of music, like an anthem, and flames rushed up the Doric columns. He turned and she was there—Shakti, Psyche, Anima, Isis Sophia, the Holy Spirit—sheathed in a pillar of golden light, an angel set in aspic with upturned face lost in contemplation of the stars.

With the roar of the crowd in his ears, Peter closed the distance between them until there was less than a hand's-breadth between them. 'Ellie?'

Her chin slowly lowered until the green tilt of her eyes was looking directly at him. 'Hullo you.'

He was surprised to see fear in her eyes; he hadn't expected that. There was no sign of the strangeness he had met in the Cathedral, only fear. All the words he had thought and imagined and rehearsed to bring to this moment rose up in the narrow gulley of his throat then washed away. In these few precious seconds they had, their mikes muted, the only thing he could say was, 'It's all right. I understand now.'

'Do you?'

He laughed nervously. 'No. Not really. But it's okay. After tonight everything will be okay.'

She gave him the saddest smile and looked on the verge of tears. Without speaking, she pressed her hand against his chest, and he felt the pressure of those fingers, like frail bars over his imprisoned heart. *Ellie, oh, Ellie.* He wanted to hold her. *To hell with Avery and Perdita and the crowd.* He stretched out his arms, but she reared back and looked up at him with terrible urgency.

'What's wrong? What is it?'

Something gathered behind her eyes and she burst out, 'I want you to know that—' But she couldn't get the words out. 'I need you to know that I always—' The music had started to rise about them. Her head slumped with internal defeat then she looked back at him, eyes flashing. The old Ellie. His Ellie. Spontaneous, laughing, beautiful Ellie whom everyone thought they knew. Her lips parted. 'Asshole.'

'I love you.' He'd meant to mouth, *harpy* or *diva* or even *wee daftie*, but out of his brimming happiness came, *I love you* instead. She gave him a funny look, frowning, head cocked to one side, and he wasn't sure if her reaction was one of surprise or disappointment. He was instantly regretful but it was too late. Her hand was in his and she was already moving forwards towards the crowd. There was now no choice but to follow.

They walked forward, hand-in-hand, until they were at the edge then he lifted their hands aloft and stood for a moment triumphant, facing the crowd. 'Friends.' The word resounded in his head like a familiar old bell, his happiness chiming with it. 'I give you—The Prophetess.' He swept Ellisha's hand to his lips, bowed then backed away until his back touched the solid surface of a pillar which turned out to be MacCaa.

All eyes were on Ellisha, who stared down at her feet without speaking. If the applause had been deafening the silence was ear-splitting. It went on and on and Peter saw anxious looks exchanged between the Soul Priests and felt prickling sensations burrowing out beneath his collar. A couple of the Mythos dancers pawed the ground and glanced over their shoulders, and Peter wondered if they were receiving instructions to improvise. He glanced around at MacCaa, wondering if he was in the know, only to find MacCaa's troubled eyes looking back at his.

Then, just when it seemed Ellisha might stand there forever, a frozen avatar of herself inscribed against the night, she began to speak. 'You are all so small.' She laughed and her laughter rippled out across the crowd. Suddenly she grew wistful. 'Every time I see you, you seem smaller. Or maybe it's me. I move further away.'

The crowd responded uncertainly, flutters of applause, scattered catcalls. Ellisha bent her head for a moment then lifted it resolutely. 'I have something to tell you.' But almost at once she stopped again. 'I don't know how to do this. How do you do this?' She darted a glance from side to side as though seeking an answer. Shaking her head slightly, she started again. 'You can't imagine how many times I've thought of doing this. Of standing here about to tell you something incredible. Something you won't believe.'

At these words Peter's heart gave an aching spasm. *Tell them, Ellie. Tell the world.* Unaware, she continued. 'I've been thinking about it for a long time, what it would be like, how it would feel. I wanted it to be simple and clean. But life—my life—has been… complicated. Things haven't turned out the way I intended.'

Her shoulders rounded slightly as she took in a deep breath. 'You see, I wanted something. I wanted it so badly that I thought dying would be better than going on without it. I think we all have something we think we want more than life. For me it was a baby. I wanted a child more than anything in the world because no-one but a child can give you absolute love, the sort of love which is a kind of hope.

'We crave that kind of love. It's why traditional religion tells us that God demands it, and that the penalties for disobedience are severe. And it seems crazy to us that God would need to ask for love. Why would He need to do that? He can create love, control love, command love. And that's the trouble: if you do any of those things then it's not love. Love has to be free. Love has to be unconditional. Love has to choose. And that kind of love is the holiest of all.'

She drew in another deep shuddering breath, drinking down the night, and watching her struggle Peter experienced the first tingling pinches of doubt. *Something's wrong.* With no thought or plan he took an inching step forward, only to be arrested in his movement by a clod of earth falling upon his shoulder, which was MacCaa's hand. He turned and found, to his amazement, that MacCaa's face had parted to reveal a kind of gentleness. 'Lee her be. She wants tae dae this on her ain.'

But something irrational and imperative had seized Peter, some prescient warning from the angels of his subconscious that made him shake off MacCaa. *Reach her. Speak to her before she says any more.* He spun around intending to break with protocol and damn the consequences but his heart, recognising what his brain was too slow to process, jerked and bucked at the knowledge that it was too late and that Ellisha was already talking.

'We've burned women and hanged women and stoned women for knowing the most mundane secret of all: only mothers can create this most holy enigma, and what we've been looking for all along—the women's mystery—is just that, the ability to create absolute unadulterated love.

'And that's what I came to tell you today. That the secret at the heart of Ignis Dei, at the heart of everything, is no secret at all, but a simple truth. And what we have been trying to bring to life has surrounded us all along.'

Understanding was not immediate. Peter could see ecstatic devotion on many of the upturned faces, but here and there were ripples and eddies of disturbance, moon faces waxing and waning as heads turned and inaudible, unthinkable questions were asked. *What is she saying? A joke? A hoax?* Ellisha saw them too and she went on a little desperately, 'I know this isn't what you came to hear. I didn't want to hear it either. You see, right from the beginning, I knew the secret. I understood the women's mystery, and how women have been left in the shadows because they are the source of the light. And I also knew that I could never share in it. I think maybe I knew from the moment I woke up after the lightning strike.

'But oh, I wanted it so much—you can't know how much—it was all I ever dreamed about… becoming a mother, so I let my husband persuade me that there was a bigger story out there and that I was part of it, perhaps the most important part. And I went along with it because it made me feel better and I knew we were just pretending. But soon everyone was pretending with us and saying they believed and somehow it became real, and for a while I thought… I thought maybe…'

She shook her head violently, shattering her own plea. This was Ellisha, unfaltering in the face of ugly truth. Clearly struggling, she continued, 'Perhaps there is a time when all prophets feel a touch of clay in their footsteps, when they look in a mirror darkly and see only themselves. And what can they do but go on telling and retelling the lie. But I won't do that. Not any more.' Suddenly she threw her arms wide and cried chokingly, despairingly. 'Because I have met with the god of Ignis Dei. And I came here today to tell you she is not who you think!'

There was a sound, which was not a sound because it was a negation of sound, a neonate gasp held in the throats of millions of people across the earth's sphere. For an indeterminable period there was nothing, no reaction, only an immense absorption of shock then across the Bluetooth a voice that was Perdita's, yet did not seem to belong to her, exhaled an exotic double syllable, *Oh fuck!*

Released from his trance, Peter found his hands holding the sides of his head. He felt poisoned, as if his skin were melting. His heart was clanging against his ribcage, driving all coherence from his brain, while words, without shape or meaning, were tolling inside his skull, *whathaveyoudoneOEllieEllieElliewhathaveyoudone?*

Somewhere in the confusion he found himself walking forward, palms raised in jerky puppetry towards the crowd. 'What the Prophetess means—'

But a woman's voice cut across him. She had the look of a skinned hare, paper flesh and bulging eyes, her thin legs balancing on the shoulders of a bearded behemoth, but somehow it was her small voice alone that cut across the eruptions and geysers beginning to pierce the surface of the crowd.

'It's not real? You made it up?'

The drones picked up her distress and echoed it across the screens so that Ellisha's accuser became monolithic and her words legion. *Not real … not real … not real? You made it up?*

'No.' He shook his head, spreading his hands so wide the fingers ached. 'No. You must understand—'

But Ellisha's simple nod was negation to all the intricacies of his argument; that one delicate swan's dive of her neck brought down the house with the aplomb of Samson tearing down Dagon's temple or perhaps more like Eve taking a self-conscious bite of apple.

There was a detonation so thunderous that it did not seem to come from the audience, but rather from some primal chthonic source of nature, a roar like a sequence of rupturing volcanoes, a merciless, incendiary explosion of sound that made his ears ring. 'Ellie!' He was yelling before he understood what was happening. 'Get back. They're coming.' The crowd was on the move.

Men and women, their faces blank with incredulity, were trudging forward as though impelled by the shared intuition that somehow understanding lay in moving closer to the source. Already the security men were going down. There were attenuated shouts followed by dreadful silences, then the sound of women screaming, and still they came. All this happening in a frozen droplet of time, which he stood outside watching, until some savage force pulled him back within himself, and his last coherent thought was, *I'm looking at the end of the world.*

Then all became chaos and misrule. He was running forwards with no memory of beginning the motion. As in a nightmare, heads were appearing and hands were scrabbling to take hold of him, while up ahead, Ellie stood in profile. She had backed away from the menace of the mob until she was standing between two pillars, the flames from the torches lighting her like a woman tied to a stake. 'Ellie!' He screamed the word, while his feet, unable to find the ground, connected with yielding flesh and crunching bone. His brothers and sisters no more, he kicked and tore his way through a universe that had contracted to the pinpoint aperture of a camera obscura.

'Give me your hand!'

She turned, with a look close to shock at finding him there, but did not move.

'Give me your *hand!*'

Focus came into her eyes and she began to reach towards him. At least it seemed she reached, and later in dreams he would always see it that way, Ellisha turning and stretching out her arms towards him. Then, like Lazarus with his fingertips touching heaven, he was brutally dragged backwards, back into the world of jutting stone and agonized flesh. He twisted painfully, trying to free his shoulder from the vice that threatened to wrench it from its socket and found MacCaa's yellow eyes looking into his.

'Let go! Ellie—'

'She doesnae want it. Yer tae stay wi me.'

'No!' He struggled like a man possessed, whipping his head around, crying, 'Tell him—' But there was no-one to do the telling. She was gone. Ellie was gone. His nightmare deepened. He tried to run forward, certain that it was a trick of the night—smoke and mirrors— and she would be there if only he could reach the spot, but MacCaa would not let go.

In desperation he punched. He tore. He screamed and pitted his will against the unyielding grip of this ungentle giant, with his brain hammering out a frenzied Morse code of danger signals, until he finally understood that the mob had closed in and MacCaa's arms, twisted like thickened branches about him, were not there to imprison but to protect.

After that vision reduced to a series of disordered snapshots. Pressure. On his back. In his limbs. Long angry fingers, like the claws of raptors, tearing at his scalp, his clothes. His jacket was gone and his shirt in shreds. And all the time, bands of pain growing tighter and tighter until the breath was driven from his chest.

He hung inside a vacuum in blood-red darkness. There was no air. His lungs swung inside the cage of his ribs, a pair of crushed wings twitching feebly, while shoeless, his feet pawed the ground and his ears filled with the gasping swell of organ music. Blooms and echoes. Flutes and quivers. Deep breathy sounds bringing to life some constructed pulpit buried within his mind where his father's booming voice cried out, *Whom have I in heaven but you?*

Suffused with deep love, he looked up eagerly into his father's face and found, instead, the fiery pits of MacCaa's eyes. A crash of chords. *Organo pleno.* Notes sizzling on the air like sparks. A drone, knocked off course, exploding against a pillar. Blood trickling down his forehead. His own? He thought, disinterestedly, *I'm dying.* Then an overwhelming sense of rapid expansion, of limits breached and sudden shattering release like the popping of a cork.

Air exploded in his lungs; the stars went out.

CHAPTER 39

ASLEEP. THEN NOT. BUT NOT awake either. Everything wobbled a little out of focus, as though his retinas were smeared with Vaseline. He was looking at a matrix of rectangles the colour of bone. A small excrescence of plastic, placed not quite centrally, nudged his memory until he thought, *smoke detector*, and with the thought focus came back to his brain.

'You're awake. Good.' Perdita's face floated above him. 'Can you speak?'

He opened his mouth, but only a faint rasping came out.

'Here.' She held a cup with a straw to his lips and he choked down a few sips of water before he began to cough. 'Good. Can you sit?' She placed a firm hand on his back and helped him up. From this position he could see that he was in a hospital bed beneath a coverlet patterned with blue and yellow stripes. A TV was mounted on the wall opposite. It was tuned to a news channel, but the sound was turned down. A pastiche of scenes from Calton Hill dissolved one into the other, all the more eerie for their silence. Beneath, a rolling banner was saying something about casualties. He slid his eyes away.

Although he hadn't tried to, Perdita said, 'Never mind. Don't try to talk.' She scraped the room's single chair to his bedside and became business-like. He noticed that her eyes were sunk beneath dark shadows and that filaments of hair floated free of their usual regimented ranks. 'We haven't much time. The cat isn't so much in amongst the pigeons as we're standing knee-deep in gore and feathers.'

He was rubbing his side and Perdita caught the movement. 'You've broken two ribs and, naturally, there's extensive bruising.'

He looked down, noticing for the first time how his arms were figured with violet and magenta plumes of discoloured skin.

'You've been lucky. Not everyone walked away.'

The words made him sit upright, ignoring the bolt of pain that made his ribs catch fire. 'MacCaa.' That moment of release. Expelled from the crowd, like a popping cork, while MacCaa went down under the swinging arms and trampling feet, dropping like a corpse. 'Ellie? Where is she?'

The question made Perdita look at him sharply. 'Gone.'

Ellie's hand stretching towards him through the darkness, already unreachable, mist rising over a winter loch, the lady of Shallot in her cold barge floating downstream. 'Gone? Gone where? Back to the Cathedral?'

Perdita shook her head. 'Only she can tell you, I'm afraid.'

'Is MacCaa with her?'

'No.'

'He's— Is he—'

'Dead,' Perdita confirmed. 'A bad business.'

Tears sprang to Peter's eyes. He felt very weak. 'He tried to save me. Ellie made him stay with me. Why did she do that?'

Perdita's lips pursed and she seemed to be drawing on some borrowed resource to give herself the strength to speak. 'Ellisha left instructions to tell you that she wasn't coming back. That it was over. Ignis Dei. Everything.'

He felt a sharp pain in his chest that had nothing to do with his broken ribs. 'Is that all?'

'No. You're also an asshole.'

'She said that?'

'She was very specific about it.'

He cast about. The television was showing a forest fire in Indonesia. Perdita followed his gaze. 'I'm afraid the backlash has started. They're burning her forests.'

It was all too much. He wanted to close his eyes, to sink back into the darkness. A needle of pain in his arm made him open them again. Perdita had pinched him. She was leaning down, scanning his face. 'Peter. Peter? Can you hear me? This is important.'

'Gone.' He said the word aloud because it seemed too big to hold within himself, an ever-expanding immensity that would go on growing until it swallowed the universe, insatiable like the space between stars. A sharp sting on his cheek made his eyes water. Perdita was looking at him with a mixture of concern and disgust. 'I'm not joking. Time is of the essence. Avery wants to meet with you.'

A flicker of hope ignited in the blackness. *Powerful… too much invested to let things fall apart. He'll know what to do. How to find her.* He began pulling himself up the bed. 'Where is he?'

'He said you would know.'

A slump, the pillows cushioning his fall. 'I've no idea.'

'My instructions were to tell you that he would wait all night. But no longer.'

He turned towards the window, but the curtains were impenetrable. 'What time is it?'

'A little before dawn.'

The squeak of the chair-legs against the polished floor made him look round. Perdita was on her feet. 'Well, I must be off.' She lifted a small suitcase that had been placed by the bed.

He nodded vaguely. 'Thank you for coming.'

'You're welcome.' There was an odd expression on her face. At the door she paused and looked back at him over her shoulder. 'Goodbye then.'

'Goodbye.'

The moment he was alone he realised two things. One, she wasn't coming back; her *goodbye* had the permanence of a farewell. And two, he knew exactly where Avery was.

His progress along the shadowed streets was painfully slow. With each jolting step his broken chest would respond with a harrowing scream, and he was forced to stop and rest a great number of times clutching whatever solid object was closest—lampposts, post boxes, and even on one occasion the statue of William Pitt the Younger—until the spasms eventually passed away. But gradually, like an ant crossing a map of the world, he inched forwards towards his destination.

The wood beyond the world was not exactly as he remembered. It was more alive, greener, more secretive than on his first encounter, and despite his urgency, he paused a moment to calm his breathing. It had taken longer, much longer, to reach it than he had anticipated, and now the hallucinatory light of dawn outlined the upmost branches in a corona that made the place tingle as though it were alive, a sentient temple, Gawain's green chapel.

The gate's hinges heralded his arrival with a rusty squeal and he saw that, despite its new furbelows and flounces, the garden was older than when he'd left it, and he went forward with the sense of being in a weird upside-down dream, where his senses, against all logic, were yelling at him to *stay asleep*. But he forged ahead, knowing that, if he was right, Avery would be there waiting for him at the centre.

And she was.

'Hullo, Stone Man.'

Babs McBride. He barely recognised her. She looked like a page from a discarded story, lines crushed across her face and paper thin. She was almost the colour of the bleached stone she sat upon, and it was not clear if there was any distinction between the threads of her hair and a cobweb trailing from a branch behind her head.

'Drink?' She took a dented silver flask from her pocket and proffered it.

'No. Not any more.'

She looked at him sourly. 'Careful, Stone Man, you'll tempt the god of broken promises.' Then she looked at him more carefully and patted the bench. 'Sit down.' When he hesitated, she snapped. 'For God's sake. Before you fall down.'

He realised that it had been a long time since he had heard God invoked in this way. It had gone quite out of fashion. And, simultaneously, he noticed he was clutching his chest and that his shirt had worked its way from his trousers and the tails were trembling against his shaking legs.

As he lowered himself on to the bench, he said, 'Faking your own death. Quite a trick.'

'Not really. After a certain age a woman becomes invisible. I could have stripped naked and ridden the purser through the faculty staffroom and no-one would have batted an eyelid.' She was looking towards a small sundial lost in a tangle of ivy, its hours marked in shade and deeper shade. Without looking around, she said, 'Ask what you like. You've earned that at least.'

'Should I call you Avery?'

She was unscrewing the flask and did not rise to the provocation. 'Can if you want.'

'Is it your real name?'

'What? Good grief, no.' She seemed genuinely surprised. 'It comes from Old French by way of High German. Alberich: the elf king. Look it up in the *chansons de geste*. Changes there to *Auberon*. You'll recognise it as Shakespeare's Oberon, husband of Queen Mab. Or Titania if you prefer. The faerie queen herself. Coincidence, but terribly apt in the circumstance.'

He was so enraged by what he perceived to be the complacent arrogance of this explanation that he snarled, 'MacCaa is dead.'

She nodded, more to the flask than him. Clearly it was not news. 'A pity. He was a rare bird, more myth than man. Not too many of his kind left, a bit like jack-in-the-greens or unicorns.'

She's mad, he thought. *Quite mad.*

As if she had heard, she rolled a baleful eye in his direction. 'He was an old love.'

'Who?' He was startled. 'MacCaa?'

'Avery. He whom you thought to be your saviour. Your champion. The man who plucked you from gaol and brought you to his faerie castle. We met in the eighties, in Palo Alto. I was doing some research into the myths of the Ohlone peoples. Well, you could see what was happening in Silicon Valley even then, if you had an eye for it. All those little companies snuffling at the brink of new technology. Dot com this, dot com that. My historian's antennae twitched, so to speak.' She chuckled to herself. 'Look back at patterns long enough and you develop the ability to see them in the other direction. I gave him some advice. Good advice. He made some very shrewd investments.'

'You made him a billionaire?'

'Not quite. But a wealthy man nonetheless. Fond of buying expensive property in Europe. He owed me. Owed me a good deal.' She took a swig from her flask then brushed strands of hair (or were they cobwebs?) from her forehead. 'Give him his due, he was rather tickled with playing the mysterious billionaire. A little too enthusiastic, if I'm honest. It was all I could do to persuade him against calling his company Wayne Enterprises. Felt sure you'd rumble him.'

In his heart he had known, but hearing her say it altered space: the gaps between the atoms widened and he fell between them. He clutched the bench and closed his eyes, but it made the sensation worse so he opened them almost at once. 'Why?' he asked hoarsely.

She gave him a look, waiting for the penny to drop and eventually he said in a faint voice, 'To control the money.'

'Of course to control the money.'

Some dam gave way in his brain and Avery's words floated up out of the etheric past. *I don't pretend to be able to move a crowd with the power of my voice, and you don't want to think about the money. That's okay. Leave all that to me.* He looked at Babs in anguish. 'We were sitting on the most lucrative deal in history and we handed all the power to him. To you.'

'True. But the real question is, why?'

Suddenly he felt exhausted. Whatever they had given him in the hospital to dull the pain was wearing thin, and sharp-toothed mouths inside his chest were starting to take tentative bites from his tender sides. But Babs was a bad fairy who would force him to follow the proper forms, and so he said wearily, 'For money. For power.'

'You disappoint, Stone Man.'

'What other reason could there be?'

She looked at him for a long time, dark eyes glittering in the fading remnants of her face. Then something in her expression changed, something a little wistful, perhaps even a little greedy, peeped out between the hard brilliants of her stare and she whispered, 'For history.'

Their eyes locked—Apollo and Python; Marduk and Tiamat; George and the Dragon—in a timeless moment that stood for all time just as the wood beyond the world stood for all woods, all worlds. Then Peter found his voice and pushed the words out through the invisible coils that constricted his throat. 'What on earth are you talking about?'

The moment shattered. The pendulum moved. The clock began to tick once more, and wistfulness vanished from Bab's face to be replaced by something hunched and starving. She leaned forward suddenly and caged his hand in her claw-like grip. 'We get tired, you know.'

'What do you mean?' Cobwebs seemed to be growing inside his head. 'Who gets tired?'

He braced for contempt, but she said quite softly, almost to herself. 'Us. Historians. Especially the ones who do not turn their backs on folklore.' Then in the harsh tones of one who has accidentally revealed their intimate selves, she went on, 'It was an experiment, do you see? The ultimate prank played on the god of man. Historians spend their lives as theoreticians, arguing about Caesar's motives in crossing the Rubicon or how much Gregorian chant owes to the Carolingian renaissance.'

She withdrew her hand and stared down morosely into the palm as though the key to some lost innocence might materialize there, then sighed heavily. 'No matter the dynamics of our methods, we are forced to look backwards. The meat we handle has fallen from the bone, decayed under the dust of centuries. But deep down we want to see it live. To shape the clay. To move the chess pieces for ourselves.'

A leaf tipped with bronze fluttered down between them, but neither attempted to catch it. Peter said brokenly, 'So we were nothing but your pawns.'

Her glance was sharp. 'More the queen and her bishop, wouldn't you say? With MacCaa as the knight, of course.' She added the last with a malicious smirk. But, before his anger could be made practical, she said, apropos of nothing, 'You should never have kept her here, you know. I knew it the first time I laid eyes on her. You could feel it.'

'I've no idea what you're talking about.'

Her look said she didn't believe him, but she elaborated. 'An imagination as complex and delicately calibrated as Ellisha's could never stand this sceptred isle with all its dark brooding and its gift for driving poets mad—Taliesin, Ossian, Byron, Plath. Better to have sent her packing, back to a vast hopeful country, like America. A country where she could walk freely.'

He rounded on her, eyes blazing, 'Stop playing games.' He was angry because he knew deep down she was right. 'You used her. You wanted vengeance. On the God of men? On human men? Maybe only on the dons of Edinburgh's Religious History Department. But you used her.'

'Hiding your serpent heart with a flowering face, are we?' His insult had not so much as scratched the surface. Babs took a lazy slug from her flask then wiped her lips on the back of her hand. 'If you would throw "hypocrite" at me, Stone man, look first to the mirror. You were just as willing to hurl aside the gods of men to monetise the God of women. And where was my acknowledgement in the grand scheme of Ignis Dei? You dressed Ellisha up in my grave goods, like Schliemann's wife, without even giving credit to the corpse.'

They were silent for a while then he said with a new kind of humbleness in his voice, 'It wasn't just about money. We came to believe. Ellie believed right from the start. I think from the moment she read about James VI and the witch. But I did too. Eventually. In a place called *Bosquecillo Sagrado*. I was ill, fevered even. But I felt something. A feminine presence in the universe maybe.'

Babs started to cough, a thin dry hack that sounded like the caw of MacCaa's name—*muh ca ahahaha*. Peter looked up in alarm only to find she was laughing. 'Don't be a fool. One only has to think about menstruation, childbirth or menopause to know that God isn't a woman.'

'But you believed. You believed in the Great Goddess.'

'Did I? She paused to wet her lips, perhaps just to whet the sharpness of her tongue then inexplicably asked, 'Do you know what a lachrymatory is?'

The word gave a familiar pulse in his brain, but he shook his head.

'Tear catcher. From the Latin. Goes back to Roman times and carried on until the nineteenth century. Little glass bottles. Often beautifully gilded. Mourners would weep into them, and when the tears evapourated the mourning period was effectively over. Rather beautiful, no?'

He was nodding in bewildered agreement when her smile scythed the shadows. 'Only it isn't true. It's a myth, Stone Man. A story without a shred of archaeological evidence to back it up. Scent bottles, that's what they are. Carelessly classified scent bottles. But it doesn't matter. You see, they've become enshrined in mystery. The historians plead for sanity yet the bottles fly off the shelves into the arms of their ecstatically dolorous owners.'

His head was reeling, but he caught the analogy quickly enough. With his last hope slipping away, he said bleakly, 'So you just made it all up. The whole story.'

The laughter vanished. 'There's no *just* about it. In fact the exact opposite of *just.*'

'Meaning you were unjust?'

'Perhaps.' She looked at him abstractedly; the jibe hadn't taken. 'Great ideas often are. But you of all people, Stone Man, should know that the one thing stories have in common with mortal men is that they are not all created equal. How often do you come across a man or woman simply bursting to tell you about how they're carrying some marvellous tale inside themselves, which ought to be a book? And, if you don't make a quick enough getaway, you are in grave danger of being told all about it.

'But a true story—not the oxymoron it sounds—is not some sentimental boy meets girl *romance d'amour.* It contains some profound and matchless core, some mythopoeic element—perhaps I should say elemental—burning at its heart, making it as wise as it is old. It tells of worlds where *love* will not solve everything. Try to play the hero in such a world and you are more likely to find that girl may well *eat* boy. But it's all the juicier for it.'

Unable to believe what he was hearing, Peter burst out, 'What arrogance, what madness made you think you had the right—'

She looked at him with mild irritation, then mashed out her cigarillo against the bench. Plumes of bitter smoke rose between them and Peter held his breath, afraid that a paroxysm of coughing might make him faint. She took his silence for encouragement and went on. 'The idea for an experiment didn't come at once. No strike of lightning, no Damascene conversion. I believe it evolved on its own in the spaces between words. From the silence that listens to silence.' She glanced sideways to see if he understood, shrugging slightly before continuing. 'It was merely theoretical, a test of the intellect. For me, history is not so much a rigorous science as a way of interpreting the past to justify our futures. Blow a little stardust on to a speck of truth and, *poof*, Cleopatra becomes beautiful, Arthur will rise up from the dead to save us.

'All the great names did it, Thucydides, Herodotus, Livy, Machiavelli. Why not me? I was curious. Mentally stimulated. And this was back in the seventies, mind, when being out of one's head carried significantly more kudos than being in it.

'But could it be done in an age of sophistication? That was the question that troubled me. Fact: James blamed witchcraft for the storm that nearly drowned his Danish bride. Fact: he sought a meeting with one of the accused witches. In the end, a little imagination did the rest, and I penned the details of the interview in ironic mood intending to demonstrate the ease with which fact morphs into mythology.'

She brushed the cigarillo ash away and watched the particles eddy downwards. 'I was castigated, of course. Intellectual irony is rarely the object of appreciation. Ask Canute. Ask Schrodinger. I put it in a drawer. Forgot all about it. Stayed bricked up in my cell like a fallen nun. Then one day my eyes were dazzled by a shaft of light when the door unexpectedly opened, and Ellisha walked in.'

'But why her?' he interrupted. 'Why choose Ellie? Why not do it yourself?'

She shrugged. '*Love likes not the falling fruit, nor the withered tree.* As a species, we may have risen, like angels, to scratch the surface of the moon with our primate toes, but we have not evolved to the point where we will choose the hag over than the maid. Besides, as the writers of the gospels well knew, there is a fascination in seeing the barren tree bear fruit.'

For a second he thought she was referring to herself then his hands clenched into fists, and he spoke in a barely controlled growl. 'You knew. All along you knew Ellie couldn't have children.'

She considered him calmly. 'She had the look.'

'What look? What do you mean?'

'The empty one. They get it, you know. The ones who can't have children and can't reconcile themselves to a future without them.'

He felt as though she had punched him in the stomach. *She's wrong.* 'You don't know anything about Ellie. She was happy. Happy with me.'

'Because she swathed herself in smiles, the way anorexics wrap themselves in oversized clothing to hide the fact they are withering away? You saw her every day, Stone Man, until you couldn't see her at all. But that moment, when she walked into my office, all wreathed in smiles so you wouldn't notice the light dying in her eyes, I knew. Knew I had finally found the missing piece of the puzzle. The key to making it real.'

He made an unintelligible noise in his throat and she scoured him with a look. 'Don't expect you to understand. It's not man's territory. Besides, the question regarding barren women has always been tricksy: are they being divinely punished or celestially ordained for greater things? Even the ancients couldn't make up their minds. Is the hollow womb a mark of Cain or is it a vessel for the birth of miracles? For myself, I tend to the latter school.

'After all, they knew as far back as Babylonia that an empty womb can incubate more than breath and bones. Only think, Stone Man, of how many childless goddesses there are, Artemis, Nephthys, Morrigan. Even the ugly little stone Sheela na gigs spreading their thighs on the sides of Christian chapels are not, as pious male interpreters claim, symbols of human fertility, but a coded message, warning us that universes are brought out of black holes. Creation comes from the Void. A single match strike in the darkness. *Ex nihilo fiat lux.*' She spread her fingers like sunbursts an inch from his face. '*Boom!*'

He grabbed hold of her wrists in blind fury, and for an instant they were joined together, man and woman in a kind of unholy matrimony, until Babs gave an involuntary quiver that seemed less of fear than arousal. Appalled, Peter let go. She held his gaze, drinking the cup of bitterness offered by his rejection, then let her hands fall into her lap. Something bleak passed over her face.

'Babs—' He wanted to say more, to explain what could not be explained, but she lifted her chin with the grace of an old force sensing its dominion waning, and drew her story to an end. 'I don't think I could have done it with anyone else. A woman baptized with lightning. That marvellous synchronicity of features that made everyone think they knew her. For all her sadness, you could see she seemed to have one foot still trailing Eden, as though she was a mythological child created somewhere between the seventh day and all time. I think I knew, even before her lips parted, that I had found something miraculous, a vessel that might carry the World's Soul, the virgin womb in which I might plant a seed.' She gave a chuckle harsh as a fox's bark. 'Not that I'm the first one to come up with that trick.'

He looked down at his unlaced shoes, the gravel path beneath them. Nothing seemed real. 'Did you think it would end like this?'

She lifted the flask to her lips then pulled it back, frowning. Tipping it upside down she shook it in search of drops. Nothing. The angels had taken their share. Disconsolately, she threw it down on the bench beside her. 'Shaw's right. You should never release old forces.'

'Even ones you imagined?'

'Worst of the lot. They demand human sacrifice.'

He caught her meaning. 'You told me once that the goddess always sacrifices her lover.'

'True. True.'

'But Ellie sacrificed MacCaa as well as me.'

'Yes. Yes. She did indeed. Unusual. But there's precedent for it.' She leaned forward, chin resting on her bony knuckles, eyes moving sightlessly. 'Artemis is loved by both Actaeon and Orion yet she has them both torn apart by animals. Guinevere—' She held up a hand as though he had moved to protest. 'Thought by some to be a remnant of the old goddess of sovereignty. She sacrifices Arthur's love and Lancelot's honour.

'Traces of it in Chaucer too. Even Elizabeth I, the Faerie Queene, earthly embodiment of Diana, lets Dudley and the Archduke compete for her affections, then rejects them both.' A smile broke over her face and she caught his sleeve. 'And think, think, think, Stone man. They're all childless.' A pink glow had suffused her face as though some radiant, uncorrupted part was shining through. And suddenly she was laughing, fingers pressed now to her lips. 'Didn't see it. Didn't predict it. But it was right there. In front of my eyes. Don't you see? You can't change history. Not the old archetypes. No indeed. The ancients were wiser than we. They understood that these patterns are woven into the fabric of the universe, written in hieroglyphs amongst the stars. You saw it, Stone man, and I didn't believe you. But it's there—we can't deny it now—the essential holiness of the universe.'

He couldn't share her excitement. The world had ceased to make sense. He said dully, 'But why? Why did she do it?'

The laughter drained from Babs' face. 'There is only ever one reason. She wanted to be free.'

'Even from me?'

'Even from you.'

The spider that had been diligently working at the back of Babs' head had moved to the end of a branch to spin a new web and droplets of dew were collecting along its threads. The light caught them and they shone like prisms on a tiny chandelier. He looked at it in silence for a long while then said, 'Where is she?'

The surprise on Babs' face was genuine. 'I have no idea.'

'But you met with her?'

'Some time ago. Only to step out from behind the curtain, so to speak. To return her humanity. I'd borrowed it long enough.'

'I have to find her.'

'Of course.' She gave her agreement so readily that he looked at her suspiciously.

'You don't think I can?'

'The portents are hard to read. Mythology, I fear, loves tragedy. Think of Orpheus or Oisín.' She caught something in his face that gave her pause then went on more gently, 'But Dante gives us hope. Not everyone who passes through the underworld returns empty-handed.'

'And Ignis Dei is over.'

'Oh, I doubt that, Stone Man. The archetypes of the universe don't die. They merely reform. Did Christianity disappear when its leader died a mortal death? Did Islam, Scientology, the Seventh Day Adventists? Besides, there's something you've overlooked.'

She paused and he was forced to say, 'What?'

'You're the harvest king.'

'I don't—'

'Didn't see it before. MacCaa muddied the waters. But you're both aspects of the same character. He the dying king. You the one to rise.'

He thought of MacCaa's strong arms about him, his body juddering against the buffeting of the mob, remembered his words, *Stay wi
me*, the yellow eyes burning against the night sky. Grief crashed over
him. When it receded not everything was doused; there was a strange
new flicker in his chest. Babs was tidying away the flask. With a soft
moan, she heaved herself from the bench. He looked at her in alarm.
'You're going?'

She was stretching the stiffness from her limbs. 'Overstayed my
welcome.'

'But I'd be happy for you to stay.' He surprised himself by meaning
it.

She stopped stretching and fixed him with a look of amusement. 'I
didn't mean with you. I meant with life.'

Scepticism must have shown on his face because she insisted, 'I
promise you it's real this time. Soon. A few months from now if the
medics are to be believed.' She beamed down at him. 'The moment
has come for me to pass on the grail.' She paused a moment as though
considering something then added defiantly, 'Gladly.'

He was at a loss as to what to say. There were so many questions, so
much that he didn't understand. She was already at the gate, with the
latch lifted, before he called out feebly. 'I'm used to resurrections. I've
reinvented myself before.'

She glanced over her shoulder. 'It'll be harder this time. Many will
see this as divine punishment. Your comeuppance for blasphemy.'

'I know.'

She arched a brow. 'Who's to say they're wrong?'

'No-one.'

She nodded, but more in answer to herself than acknowledgement
of him. 'You'll have to start from the beginning. She's left you with
nothing, naked as only the reborn are.'

'I know.'

She was through the gate now, a shadow, already beyond the golden light filling the garden, which was now the colour of antique wedding bands. To see her he had to shade his eyes with his hand. A step or two and she would melt away like a half-remembered dream.

He felt the flicker again and it propelled him to his feet. With an arm cradling his ribs, he took a stumbling step forwards and called, 'Wait! Please. There must be something more you can tell me. Some fragment. Some clue.'

Her hand was on the gate, but she paused, unsurprised. 'The augurs are silent, the book of life has closed its pages.' She glanced briefly upwards then turned to him, slicing through the shadows with her smile. 'But I'll wager she's still in Scotland.'

His heart filled with hope, but still he asked, 'Why?'

Her laughter came crackling towards him like a dying fire spraying out sparks against the coming night. 'Because, if you're looking for God, it's the best place to find Her.'

Lightning Source UK Ltd.
Milton Keynes UK
UKHW010214161021
392283UK00002B/44/J